Pirates in the Robosphere

PIRATES IN THE ROBOSPHERE

D.S. Rippy

Merrimack Media
Cambridge, Massachusetts

Library of Congress Control Number: 2014939542

ISBN: print: 978-1-939166-45-6
ISBN: ebook: 978-1-939166-46-3

This book was printed in the United States of America

Published by Merrimack Media, Cambridge, Massachusetts
May, 2014

Contents

1

You've Won! An Invitation to Tanglewood

Even in late afternoon, the Texas summer sun still blazed with blistering intensity. Ryan could feel heat radiating off the concrete as he rode his bike down the street. He pedaled up the driveway to his house and into the open garage, parked his bike, and took off his helmet, which felt melted onto the sides of his head. He skipped up the three short steps to the back door, opened it, strode into the kitchen, and poured himself a glass of water.

"Hi, Mom," he said, between gulps.

"Hi, Hon," she replied. "How has your day been? Oh, before I forget, you have a piece of mail."

Mail? For me? Ryan thought to himself. *Since when do I get mail?*

"Who's it from?"

"Robotics Club."

"Uh, okay. Where is it?"

"In your room, on your dresser."

Robotics Club was one of Ryan's favorite activities. He had been in the club for the past three years—since fifth grade. Originally organized by a schoolteacher, the club had grown in size and stature within Ryan's school, Highland Park Middle School in Dallas. Ryan's club now had ten members, and they developed robots that competed in Robot Blasts, events where robots drove around on an arena floor, competing with other robots and doing things like throwing foam balls into the baskets of competing robots. The robots were mechanically designed to launch balls using a variety of different means, such as the catapult, scoop, slingshot, air pump, or conveyor belt, among others.

The field of competition was known as the Robot Zone, and had high, transparent plastic walls around it at each end, like an ice rink. The robot team members stood behind these walls and supported their robots by doing things like throwing balls over them to try to get them to land in the basket of a competing robot in hopes of helping their own robot—and team—win.

Teams also configured their robots to make it difficult for opposing teams to land balls in their buckets by employing mechanical tricks such as elevators, revolving shields, and spinning and tilting features. When balls didn't land in the basket, they would bounce off to the side or high up in the air, like a basketball clanging off the rim of a net. Throws further off target bounded harmlessly across the Zone, often skittering into a corner or getting knocked aside by a moving robot. At the end of the designated time of the match, the team whose robot had the fewest balls in its basket won.

The envelope on Ryan's dresser was emblazoned with the emblem of the Highland Park Middle School in red and gold, the school's colors. Underneath, someone had written the words "Robotics Club" in pen. Ryan opened the envelope. Inside, he unfolded a letter on heavy paper that was folded in thirds. It read:

Congratulations!
You have won this year's HPMS Robotics Fund Raiser!
You are cordially invited to attend
Music and Robotics Camp
at Tanglewood
Lenox, Massachusetts
from August 6t through August 10th
All Expenses Paid. Details Inside.

Ryan had participated in a fundraising campaign to raise money for the Highland Park Robotics Club. He and his fellow club members had walked door-to-door across neighborhoods and sold memberships to civic institutions in the Dallas area to raise money for the club—the science museum, the aquarium, the museum of art, the arboretum, and a few others. He loved all of these places, so it was easy to sell memberships. But, what he loved more than anything else was robots.

Over the past couple of years, Ryan and his friends had been exploring doing other things with robots outside of Robot Blasts. While Robot

Blasts were hugely fun and he loved attending them, Ryan had grown keenly interested in seeing what he could do to make a robot behave like an animal. The lizard was one of the animals with which he was experimenting; specifically a lizard found in Texas called the green anole.

A year ago, Ryan had entered a robotic green anole into an artificial intelligence robotics competition and won. Using a basic robotic starter kit that he ordered online, he added a bunch of features and functionality to the lizard robot mostly on his own. He had found he could fit a few additional computer chips and batteries within the kit's small, lightweight metal frame.

His father had helped him build the lizard's mechanical circuitry which enabled it to move its legs, head, and mouth. Ryan moved the lizard robot with a handheld remote control console that had come with the robot kit. He and his dad made some programming modifications to it to enable the robot to make a broader range of movements with the different parts of its body. Even at the age of thirteen, Ryan was something of a computer programming wiz. His father was an engineer for a semiconductor company, and Ryan spent a lot of time with him tinkering around with robotic concepts, and writing programs to make robots do things—his lizard robot, mainly. His mom was a math whiz, and Ryan often talked with her about physics, range of motion, and using mechanized leverage to do things like make the lizard robot cling to a wall, a major accomplishment.

Ryan also worked hard to make the lizard appear real. He spent hours affixing fine, little plastic shavings with epoxy to the robot's exterior and painted them brownish green to resemble scales. It was a painstaking process, but it was a labor of love. Ryan had fondly named his prize winning green anole Scram. Over the course of time, Ryan was able to make Scram's movements look more like a lizard and less like a mechanical robot. Scram was surprisingly lifelike, and many people who saw him thought Scram was real.

"How did Ryan get this invitation?" his dad asked that evening.

"Fundraiser. Robotics Club," his mom replied. "Nice prize, isn't it?"

"Yes," his dad replied. "It seems pretty fancy."

"It is."

"So how does this music thing combine with robotics?" his dad asked.

"I don't know, now that you mention it," his mom said. "I guess I hadn't thought about it like that."

"Well, I guess it's no different than winning baseball tickets, and it sure beats a video game, or some such nonsense like that," his dad said.

"It covers electronic music and computer programming, I think," said Ryan, having read the brochure that accompanied the invitation. He was hoping his father didn't consider the invitation nonsense.

"Huh," his dad said thoughtfully.

"The brochure says something about incorporating sounds and music into robots, so I guess that's part of the camp," he added.

"Interesting," his dad said. "Perhaps you'd be able to incorporate some of your drumming and music into the program."

Ryan thought Tanglewood sounded pretty cool as he perused the brochure. You could sit in seats under a canopied amphitheater, or you could sit on a grassy lawn and listen to music. The lawn idea seemed fun. You could kick or throw a ball around or just sit and listen. Of course, the camp program did not sound like it involved much sitting around.

Ryan felt a little nervous about the camp, but also excited. The idea of combining robotics, sound effects, and music seemed enticing. He felt he had a pretty good handle on the robotics piece. He might even be one of the best builders there. But, upon reflection, he wondered about the music element.

How did music integrate with a robot? Would the music be classical? What did Ryan know about classical music? Not much, so far as he was aware. Indeed, the music he liked was most likely *not* heard on the lawn at Tanglewood. Bach? Beethoven? Brahms? Mozart? Weren't they old, dead composers his grandparents used to listen to? Ryan liked hip-hop and rock. He played the drums, and the kind of drums he played definitely weren't welcome in a classical symphony.

The brochure said that Tanglewood was the summer home of the Boston Symphony Orchestra, which spent the summer there playing loads of classical music. Ryan suspected they didn't play much hip-hop or rock. Nonetheless, he felt the robotics part of Tanglewood would be fun.

"I'm not sure what to make of the music part of this camp," Ryan said to his mom, "but I'm pretty sure I'll like the robotics part."

"It's a terrific opportunity, dear," his mom said. "It'll get you out of this heat, and it won't interfere with sports or your other robotics events before you start the school year. And it's Tanglewood. You'll get to hear some of the greatest musicians in the world there."

Ryan nodded in acknowledgement. He knew it was a great opportunity. He loved music, even if only certain kinds, and he was pretty good at programming for a thirteen-year-old. He spent the next few weeks surfing the camp's website, wondering what it would be like, and what other sorts of people he would meet there.

Ryan's younger sister, Annie, often observed his near-fanatical obsession about robotics with both interest and skepticism. Inwardly, she was impressed with her brother's abilities. She felt a bit jealous about the adventure he was about to embark upon.

"Don't worry," said Ryan. "I won't be gone that long. And I'll call you."

"Why would I want you to call *me*?" Annie retorted. She could be quite the smart aleck at times.

Over the next few weeks, Ryan and his parents had several calls with staff from the Tanglewood Musical and Robotics Camp to better understand the program and work out the logistics of attending. The people seemed friendly and were thoughtful about planning the whole thing. Ryan knew one or two older kids from the HPMS Robotics Club who had gone in past years and they loved it. Still, Ryan couldn't help feeling nervous about boarding a plane and jetting off into the great unknown. But, it was pretty exciting at the same time, he had to admit.

A few weeks later, at the airport, Ryan got stuck at the security checkpoint because he had brought Scram with him. The security people weren't sure what to make of the metallic object inside Ryan's duffle bag that lit up the metal detector like a neon sign, but which, upon peering inside Ryan's duffle bag, looked like a pet lizard. "Uh, what is this? A pet? With some kind of metal skeleton? No pets allowed on the plane, son," one of the security men told him. "At least, not without a cage that fits under the seat."

"But it's not a pet," Ryan explained. "It's a robot." He eventually took a control chip out of Scram's belly and held it up to the security people, who by now had formed a rather large, curious group.

"Oh, I get it. It's a toy," said one security man to another. "That's why it lit up like a Christmas tree on the scanner."

"But it's not a toy," Ryan protested. "It's a robot. I built it."

"Let me see that thing," said one of the observing security men. He examined Scram, turned him upside down, moved his legs, and opened his mouth. While initially he looked skeptical, he eventually seemed satisfied. "Here's your toy back, kid."

"Robot," Ryan corrected him.

"If you want to get it on your plane, then let's just consider this thing a toy, shall we?" the man said.

"Fine," Ryan said. "It's a toy."

"You and your toy have a nice flight," said the security man, winking at Ryan. "And have fun."

At the airport in Boston, Ryan was met by a tall, friendly-looking older man with wire-rimmed circular glasses who held a placard with his name on it. "Hello, Ryan, I'm Mr. Sandhill," he said with a warm smile and bright flashing eyes. He held out a hand for Ryan to shake. He was a trim man with windswept gray hair. Mr. Sandhill had spoken with Ryan and his parents by telephone several times before Ryan departed on the trip. Ryan took an immediate liking to him.

"I expect you will want to meet your colleagues for the week, yes?" Mr. Sandhill asked, peering at Ryan through round spectacles.

Mr. Sandhill led Ryan to a waiting shuttle bus where there were four kids already aboard. "We have just one more to collect, folks," Mr. Sandhill said. "There will be six of you altogether, but there are five of you flying in. The sixth, a girl from the area around here, is driving out to Tanglewood with her family."

The remaining member of their group arriving by plane, a girl, joined them about twenty minutes later, having just flown in from San Francisco. "Long flight," she said. "Fortunately I was able to listen to tunes." She held up her earphones from a portable music playing device. Her name was Jenny Wong. The bus drove the group to a place called Weatherall University in Cambridge, where they ate dinner together with Mr. Sandhill.

At dinner, Mr. Sandhill encouraged everyone in the group to get to know one another. "You will be spending the next week in each other's company," Mr. Sandhill beamed. "It would seem a good idea to share a little bit about yourselves with each other." He paused for a moment. "I'll start. My name is Thomas Sandhill. I have been involved in music in some form or fashion from about the age of three. I have served in the military, and have coached various sports teams, such as basketball, baseball, and rowing. I have taught mechanical engineering and physics at Weatherall University and Seguin Academy in the Boston area for the past thirty-three years. It's somewhat unusual to have a dual teaching appointment like that, but I do. Seguin Academy is a high school here in the area."

"Holy smokes," gasped a boy to Ryan's right. Thirty-three years seemed like an eternity to Ryan as well.

"I very much like working with young people, and people of all ages, really," Mr. Sandhill continued. "I am a volunteer with the Boston Symphony Orchestra, which is why I am involved in the Tanglewood program. I love cooking, and thus, food, as well as wines. I also like antique furniture and rare art. I'm not overly picky. Catherine of Bologna, the Renaissance masters, including Elizabeth Vigee-LeBrun, and their latter day heirs—Picasso, Renoir, Chagall, Warhol, Johns, Close, O'Keefe, and Rauschenberg will all do. Perhaps we will learn more about them sometime. There's so much to learn, isn't there? So, are there any questions about me or my background?"

A dumbstruck pause lingered over the table. Ryan had heard of a few of those artists, but the others? Forget it. Ryan was dying to ask Mr. Sandhill a thousand questions, but felt hugely intimidated. "Well, there will be more time if you have questions for me," Mr. Sandhill said, smiling. "You've all had a long day and are just off airplane rides, so I imagine you're a bit tired. In any event, before we go around the circle and you introduce yourselves," he continued, "I will share with you a few things you all have in common." Here he paused for a moment.

"You are all excellent students. I know this, because like you, I do my homework. I have it on good authority from talking with your teachers that you are all smart, you work hard, you're motivated, and you're intellectually curious. Coincidentally, you are also all musicians. I'll let each of you share with the group your instruments of choice. You are all pretty good athletes, like I was in my day. But, in my case, it's been a while. And, another common experience you share is that you have all excelled in robotics. Your robotics teachers give you high marks and are impressed with your persistence and intellectual curiosity. And, you have each earned a reputation of being—if I may use the Boston phrase—'wicked awesome' at building robots."

Several kids laughed.

"And, as with various robotics clubs for people of your age around the country, you have each built a robotic animal. Coincidentally, you have each done so with a starter kit that you ordered online from the computer aided design group in my mechanical engineering department at Weatherall University. Once again, I'll leave it to you to explain to your colleagues what robotic animal you have built and why. I'm sure everyone will find it interesting. I know I will. So tell your new friends here what interests you have in a career, if any, and school, sports, or hobbies; share your musical instruments of choice; and describe the basis for your choice of robotic animal."

Jenny Wong spoke first. She was keen on biology. Her parents were doctors. "I will probably be a doctor, too. I like to help people," she told the group. "Um, let's see," she said, trying to think of interesting things to share with her colleagues. "I've studied lots of insects over the past year. Beetles, dragonflies, butterflies, and inchworms."

"Cool," Ryan said. "Some people might think that's strange, but it's no stranger than my studying lizards in Texas," he said, holding up Scram, his lizard robot. Everyone laughed.

"That sounds fun," Jenny said, smiling. Her musical instrument of choice was the violin. She also knew how to play the piano. "Watching the motion of certain insects, like the inch worm, and the flight patterns of the butterfly and dragonfly, help me with my violin playing. The robot I built is actually a dragonfly."

"Awesome," said a boy on Ryan's right, his eyes bulging with enthusiasm.

"In sports, I like to play tennis. It's probably the sport I'm best at."

Carmen Flores spoke next. She was from Phoenix, Arizona. She was interested in multimedia, popular fashion, and soccer, which she played a great deal. In robotics, her animal of choice was the hawk.

"Cool," Jenny mused. "How'd you settle on that?"

"Harris' Hawk is a bird found in the south of Arizona, where I live, and in southern California and Mexico. They are powerful, graceful, predatory birds. They eat mammals, insects, other birds, and lizards."

"Uh oh, I'd better watch out or your robot will eat mine!" Ryan laughed. Everyone else joined him.

"I wouldn't mind being a fashion designer, or a pilot, or a television journalist," Carmen said. "I like too many things to decide right now, though. I love music and the internet. I also like to cook. I'm pretty good at Mexican food."

"As is typical for people your age, you simply have too many interests," said Mr. Sandhill jokingly, and he winked at Carmen. She smiled back at him. "We shall have to see about this Mexican food claim and put it to the test," he said, smacking his lips. "And your musical instrument of choice, Carmen?"

"Oh, yeah. I play the bass cello… And the bass guitar."

"Tanglewood shall most certainly benefit from your service in that department," Mr. Sandhill said.

With the girls having introduced themselves, it was now the boys' turn.

"I'll go next," the boy on Ryan's left said, raising his hand. "I'm James

Ellis. I'm from Atlanta, Georgia. In terms of musical instrument, I play the guitar," James said. "I'm a fan of the blues. I like a lot of rock and jazz, classical, and some hip-hop, although a lot of it doesn't use guitar. Let's see, sports... I like lots of sports. I play football, wide receiver, and I think I like sports medicine, or maybe athletic training. I also like physics and electronics, which is how I got into robotics. But I'd also like to learn to be a pilot. And, what else? Oh yeah, as for the robot... my robotic animal is a snake. The coral snake is fairly common in Georgia and the southeastern United States. They eat other snakes and lizards."

"Another animal that eats lizards!" Ryan lamented.

"Uh oh!" Mr. Sandhill interjected. "Your lizard is really in trouble, Ryan!" Everyone laughed.

"Next I want to make a cobra," James said.

"Cool," said several in the group in unison.

Ryan introduced himself next. He shared that he played the drums. "But they probably wouldn't want me in the drum corps at Tanglewood," he said, smiling.

"You never know, do you?" Mr. Sandhill replied.

Ryan then turned to his personal and sports interests. "I like engineering," he said. "My dad's an engineer, and my mom's good at math. I like designing stuff. I could see being an engineer or computer programmer at some point. I also like a lot of sports, like baseball, soccer, basketball, and lacrosse. But I'm probably best at baseball," he said. "I'm a decent hitter, I play a lot of different positions... I also pitch."

"Goodness," said Mr. Sandhill, impressed. "Is there any baseball position you don't play?"

Ryan thought for a minute. "I haven't played catcher in a while," he smiled. "One of my best friends plays that position."

Mr. Sandhill nodded with mocking approval, as if to suggest it was okay that there was *one* position that Ryan didn't play, given that his best friend played it. Several of the kids giggled.

Ryan continued. "And as for my animal robot, I made a green anole." He held up Scram again. "An anole is a lizard that is found in the American southeast and the south Midwest, including Texas. They eat spiders, flies, crickets, ants, slugs, moths, worms—that kind of stuff."

Jenny laughed and said. "Now it's my dragonfly robot that's in danger of being eaten!" Everyone laughed.

"Well, hopefully no one's robot will be eating anyone else's," Mr. Sandhill said.

The boy on Ryan's right went next. "My name is Sameer Chatterjee. You can call me Sammy," he said. He had a friendly smile. "I'm from Chicago. I like computer design and software. I also like superhero comics, and my favorite sport is hockey, but I also do track, tennis, and swimming."

"Cool," exclaimed a couple of people in unison.

"The robot animal I've worked the most on is the fish," Sammy continued. "I've done a pretty good job with a chinook salmon, which you can find in Lake Michigan. I wouldn't mind trying a killer whale, a dolphin, or a shark."

"Wow!" Ryan mused in awe. His impressed response was echoed by most of the others.

"Quite a group indeed," Mr. Sandhill observed. "Well, now that you've all gotten better acquainted, let's eat, shall we?"

The group was served spaghetti, salad, and rolls. Ryan ate thirds of everything. He was deeply impressed, and more than a bit intimidated, by how smart everybody was and how widely their interests ranged. Hearing all of their stories was good fun and he looked forward to spending the week with his new friends.

That evening the boys and girls grouped together respectively and spent the night in dormitory rooms of Weatherall University. Summer students at the university escorted them to their rooms. Ryan noticed out a window that the sunset was an exquisite blend of orange, blue, pink and purple hues on this warm summer evening. The next day they would board a shuttle bus to take them to Tanglewood. "I think you've had enough travel for one day," Mr. Sandhill observed. Yawning, almost too tired to speak, Jenny Wong agreed with him.

They were awakened early the next morning by two university students at Weatherall University, Brad Lawless and Meagan Rosenkrans, the same people who had shown them their dorm rooms the night before. Brad and Meagan took them to the cafeteria. "We'll be joining you on your week in Tanglewood," Meagan said. "And, since we know you went through a Mr. Sandhill introduction yesterday, we'll do the same for you. We like all kinds of stuff, a lot of it crazy—robotics, music, mechanical design, computing, art, sports, games, you name it. So we'll have lots of fun together." Brad and Meagan knew Mr. Sandhill well, as they had studied with him at Seguin Academy and more recently at Weatherall University. They had been teaching assistants in various courses, including his Physics course at Seguin.

The sun shone brightly as the shuttle bus wound its way through Cambridge and proceeded onto the Massachusetts Turnpike. It headed west towards the Berkshire Mountains and the town of Lenox, the home of Tanglewood.

People were abuzz with excitement as they embarked on their adventure. Jenny and Carmen had put on sunglasses and looked quite cool, not to mention older than their thirteen years. Ryan felt they looked much more stylish than he did, in his frumpy pants and worn tee shirt. However, neither James nor Sammy seemed to care about how they were dressed. The bus driver, an older man named Peter, barked out the names of various sites and bridges as they drove past, which Brad, Meagan, and Mr. Sandhill described in some detail to Ryan and his colleagues.

After about two hours, which felt more like a matter of minutes, they exited the Turnpike and headed north towards Lenox. Pastoral green fields rolled out along their route, bordered by verdant wooded areas with leaves shimmering in the breeze beneath the late morning summer sun.

They pulled into a large farm with several impressively large, red barns, as well as a large house of the same color. A couple of hens scurried out of the way of the bus as it pulled up the gravel driveway. A friendly looking man and his wife, both wearing jeans and work shirts, now strode towards the bus and greeted it with warm smiles.

The shuttle bus door swung open and Mr. Sandhill quickly jumped off the bus and walked out to greet them. "Welcome to the Blaines' farm," he smiled as Ryan and his colleagues stepped off the bus. "This is Mr. and Mrs. Blaine. We will be staying at their farm during the week while attending the program at Tanglewood. I think you'll find it a very nice place."

"I hope you like fresh eggs," Mrs. Blaine said, smiling. "And, if you want, you can milk the cows."

"So, this is the robotics group, is it?" said Mr. Blaine, surveying the group as Ryan, James, Jenny, Sammy, and Carmen all clustered around each other, feeling somewhat shy.

"It is indeed," Mr. Sandhill replied. "They're quite an impressive bunch. Wouldn't you say, Meagan and Brad?

"I would, definitely," said Meagan. "Okay guys, let's get your stuff out of the back of the bus."

Everyone retrieved their luggage and was led into the big red farmhouse by Mrs. Blaine.

They entered through a large, bright yellow kitchen and were led through a large common area with a formidable stone fireplace, then to a foyer and up a staircase. Upstairs, there were many small but warm bedrooms off a long corridor. Each person chose a room for him or herself. They then met in the common area of the farmhouse for an orientation of the week's program, which Mr. Sandhill provided, assisted by Brad and Meagan.

At lunchtime, they were joined by the sixth robotics camper, Ellen Callendar, from a town outside Boston. She had been sailing with her family on Cape Cod the day before. "I'm happy to be off the boat," Ellen exclaimed. "The seas were so choppy."

Ellen played the saxophone. She was a rower, track runner, and did cross country skiing. Ellen's academic interests were chemistry and neural networks.

"Neural networks, cool!" Brad said.

"Wow, somebody who's heard of them for once," Ellen said.

"Neural networks? What are they?" Ryan asked.

"Just, kind of like, circuits of biological neurons in the nervous system, or they could be artificial neurons, too. I like studying how they perform in the brain," Ellen said.

"So, like, in robotics we use computerized neurons—or circuits—to make something like a robot respond or do certain things, don't we?" Sammy asked.

"Yeah, in robotics it's like that," Ellen said.

"So, neural networks could be used to give brain power and response to robots?" asked Carmen.

"Very possibly," Mr. Sandhill mused.

"We should talk. My dragonfly needs some help in that department!" Jenny laughed.

Ellen noted she really liked dogs "because they're really smart," and much of her robotic development had been with dogs, though her latest project had a fox. "They've got this really interesting, slinking, sneaking instinct," she said. "I'd also like to try a cat robot, like a tiger, a bobcat, or a leopard."

After lunch, the group took horseback rides on the Blaines' horses and played soccer in a nearby field, joined by Mr. Sandhill, Brad, Meagan, and the Blaines. A number of musicians from Tanglewood joined them that evening for a barbecue dinner cooked behind the Blaines' house.

While some tended to grills or set tables, others got out their instruments and played music, which lilted breezily and beautifully in the air.

"Mozart," said Jenny at one point. Then, "Brahms" at another. Ryan liked the music, though never in a million years would he have been able to name the composers.

After a while, Brad got his guitar and Meagan got out her violin and they joined the musicians. They were amazingly talented and played with a skill and grace that Ryan had seldom heard before.

"I'll never be that good at an instrument," Ryan sighed, in awe, to James. "They're amazing."

"Sure you can. It just takes practice, Mr. Ferris, practice," whispered Mr. Sandhill with a wink over his shoulder.

James looked from Mr. Sandhill to Ryan and they smiled at each other. They started mimicking playing the violin with their hands together and laughed out loud.

That evening Ryan went to bed feeling happy, excited, and exhausted. He thought about his new friends, robotics, music, and the upcoming week, and wondered for a moment what it all meant. It had been a long day, and he was happy to have a plush, soft pillow under his head.

2

SOUNDS AND SENSATIONS

The next morning the group ate fresh eggs and milk from the farm along with toast and fruit. The eggs tasted better to Ryan than anything he had eaten in his life. Brad, Meagan, and Mr. Sandhill helped serve. The Blaines had merrily done the cooking.

"What a minute, aren't we supposed to serve you?" Sammy asked.

"Yeah," said Carmen.

"All in good time, my friends," Mr. Sandhill replied. "You get to do clean-up. Unless, of course, you can get your robots to do it." He smiled. Ryan and James exchanged furtive glances at this remark. Was he serious?

"I've got a lizard," Ryan shrugged. "How the heck would that work?"

"Don't ask me," James shrugged back. "I've got a snake. No arms or legs there. How would that work?"

"Search me," Ellen said. "I've got a fox. Maybe I can get her to stand on two legs." She smiled.

Mr. Sandhill gave them a coy grin and shrugged. "Well, maybe dish duty isn't in the cards for the robots just yet. Be sure to bring them with you in the van to Tanglewood."

After breakfast and clean up, the group piled into a van that drove them up the road a few miles to a large field edged by a row of tall pine trees. One couldn't really see behind it until the van pulled up a sloping driveway, turned right and drove on a long stretch of drive past a lush green lawn towards a large brown house. Hundreds of yards off in the distance, through some large maple trees, Ryan noticed a large amphitheater—Tanglewood, no doubt—the summer home of the Boston Symphony Orchestra. In the distance, he could hear classical instruments warming up. It was spectacular to look upon.

The van parked in front of the house, and they got out with their robots in hand. Mr. Sandhill led them behind the house, where there was a large ground with sculpted pine trees and hedges planted in straight and curved edges at various intervals. Walking inside it, Ryan discerned that it was a labyrinth of sorts, which, upon navigating to the center, they found a sun dial. The dial cast a shadow indicating the nine o'clock hour. Ryan's sneakers picked up the morning dew on the grass, so they glistened in the bright sunlight as if made of glass.

In a few moments, the group was led to a large, brown building towards the back of the grounds. It looked like a barn, with tall, sliding wooden doors on one side, and a large, but more conventional door to the side on the left. They were led through this door.

It took a little while for one's eyes to get acclimated to the inside lighting, having just stepped out of the bright summer sunshine. Tube lights ran high overhead, punctuated by the dim lamps of spotlights, which pointed at various angles. Most of the inside of the building was elevated in what appeared to be a stage, with a lower observing area at the front. Standing in this lower area, the stage was about four feet off the ground. Staircases at the two sides led up to it.

Two men stood off in the far corner in front of the stage. They spoke to each other in muffled tones. They hovered over some type of board that appeared to have a bunch of dials on it.

"Oh, a mixing board," James observed. "Nice."

"For recording?" Jenny asked.

"It looks like it," observed Carmen.

"Uh oh," Jenny said. "I haven't practiced in, like, forty-eight hours. I can't be recorded this way."

"Seriously?" Ellen said. "Most of us probably haven't practiced in, like, four to eight *weeks*."

Ryan noticed various instruments perched on stands atop the stage—guitars, keyboards, drums, and horns. He immediately grew excited about playing them. "All right!" he exclaimed. "Rock and roll!"

As the kids feasted with their eyes on the musical instruments festooned about the stage, the two men over in the corner became aware they had company. They strode over to the group and shook hands with Mr. Sandhill. The men looked scruffy, but friendly. "Hi, Tommy," one of them said, extending a hand to Mr. Sandhill. Mr. Sandhill gave a warm handshake in return.

"Okay folks, gather around here, if you would," Mr. Sandhill said, calling to everyone. The girls strode over promptly. The boys, awed by the array of musical instruments on the stage, took a bit longer to mosey over.

"I want to introduce you to a couple of people," Mr. Sandhill said.

The taller, flashier-looking of the two men came forward. "I'm Walter Vapiano, but you can just call me Vape," he said. "Everybody else does." He was dressed halfway between an orchestra conductor and a Halloween ghoul. He wore a rumpled tuxedo jacket over a shabby red t-shirt, a Boston Red Sox cap, and a swirl of necklaces dangled around his neck. It was as if on the way to a concert he got caught in a hurricane that made an utter mess of his suit.

The other guy, slightly shorter and plumper, slightly rumpled in appearance, came forward. "And I'm Jerry Rooker. But most people call me Rook. You can too, if you like."

"Rook? As in, the rook on a chess board?" Jenny asked.

"Yep, just like the chess piece," Rook muttered with a wry smile. He had obviously heard this many times before.

"Uh, right," Jenny said awkwardly.

"Rook. Rhymes with 'book,' 'cook,' and 'look,'" Rook said.

"And 'shook,'" Ellen chimed in, trying to make a wise crack.

"And took," Sammy piped up.

"Ssshhh!" Meagan scolded them.

"Okay, so if you comedians are ready to begin today's session, we are going to spend some time on the synthesizer," Rook said.

"Cool!" said Jenny.

"Nice!" exclaimed Ellen.

"To build a realistic robot, you need to consider the sounds and movements that they may make, whether it be a person, animal, vehicle, or what have you," Mr. Sandhill added. "So today we're going to explore electronic music and programming."

"With one of the best," said Vape. "Rook's been making music and doing production for twenty-five years."

"Longer," Rook said, with a wry grin. "But thank you for suggesting that I look younger than I actually am."

"But, before we do some hands-on work of our own, we're going to start with a little movie," Rook said. He went to a switch against the wall and flipped it. To the amazement of everyone, a movie screen descended from the top of the barn and came down to just above the stage. Mr. Sandhill and Vape produced some folding chairs from a caddy off to one side of the stage and placed them at viewing distance from the screen.

They all then watched a film that featured dozens of famous bands, orchestras, and musicians. It showed interviews with musicians who described how they created their music. There was an extensive section on electronic music, in which artists used recordings and created sounds with synthesizers as part of their compositions. Screaming sirens, thundering hooves of animals, streaming water, thunder, faint chirps of grasshoppers, echoing shrieks of chimpanzees, the crashing waves of the ocean, cars in a traffic jam, jet planes screeching through the sky, and various other sounds with varying waves, pitch, and volume were some of the auditory sensations featured in the film. Many of the musicians were famous, and Ryan and the others were amazed to get an inside look at their creative processes. They talked about a feeling they were trying to get with a certain song, or a mood or an emotion. Many of the clips showed musicians creating and working on some of their best-known songs.

"I can't believe it!" exclaimed Carmen at the film's end. "This stuff was filmed before these songs became huge hits. How did you get these film clips?" she demanded. She looked suspiciously at Rook, who shrugged his shoulders, but cast a glance at Mr. Sandhill. Carmen followed Rook's glance, along with everyone else.

"So, how about it?" James asked.

"Why are you looking at me?" Mr. Sandhill said, with feigned innocence.

"Now we know you're hiding something," Sammy said.

"Hiding something? Well, not exactly," said Mr. Sandhill. "But, it's pretty incredible to watch someone in the throes of working intensively, creating something explosively exciting, wouldn't you agree?"

"So can you answer the question?" Ellen said.

"Sure," Mr. Sandhill replied. "Actually, this film is the result of a project done by a graduate student in the Media Lab of Weatherall University some years ago. "Meagan here found it in the archives of the lab. She's now stored it in the university's digital archives, is that correct, Meagan?"

"Yep," Meagan said. "Also in the Library of Congress."

"So you see?" Mr. Sandhill said. "Someone—or rather, some number of people, since the film you just saw was shot by more than one person—went to the trouble of documenting on camera the inventive, imperfect process of creating what you and I might think of as masterful performances, or, dare I say, masterpieces, or 'hits.' Admittedly, no one at the time knew they would become masterpieces, but, the process as you have seen it, has worked in dozens upon dozens of occasions. To be sure, the result is not always a masterpiece, but the process of endeavoring, of doing hard work, with a dose of inspiration can produce remarkable results, wouldn't you say? And, the movie we just saw shows a few examples."

"Sure. But what does this have to do with robotics?" James asked.

"Good question. Well, showing you this film serves a few purposes. One, it is about a subject that you can all relate to—music. Secondly, it is about the manipulation of sound to create moods, feelings, and emotions. Now, I know each of you has created a very impressive robot, but if my memory serves me, your robots at present do not make any sounds, is that correct?"

"Not unless you count the quiet mechanical clicking of my Harris' hawk's wings," Carmen said.

"Or my fox's teeth grinding together once in a while," Ellen chimed in.

"Just so," Mr. Sandhill said. "So, what we will learn here, with the help of Mr. Vapiano—"

"Vape," Walter Vapiano interjected.

"And Mr. Rooker—"

"Rook," Jerry Rooker interjected.

"Right. Mr. Vape and Mr. Rook will help you with creating the vocal expressions, noises, and sounds that your robotic animals make."

"Just like the man said," said Vape.

"So, how will we do that?" asked Ellen.

"With help from us," Rook said. "What, did you think you were going to do it all on your own? You've already done the hard part. You've built these amazing robots. Now, we're going to give them an extra dimension of life."

"Whoa," Ryan said under his breath. It then occurred to him that a green anole didn't exactly make that much noise, but the idea of creating animal sounds was cool.

"Like you said earlier," Vape said, winking at Ryan. "Rock and roll."

Rook pressed a button against a wall that made the movie screen disappear. With the press of another button, a set of doors at the back of the stage slid open to reveal a hidden section of the stage that contained a wide range of computers, synthesizers, and recording gear.

"Wow!" everyone gasped.

"And, once we've created the sounds that your robotic animals need in their repertoire, we'll film each one and try to synchronize the sounds with their movements, and see how we do," Mr. Sandhill explained. "You should leave here with a robotic animal that makes all of the sounds that its real life counterpart would."

"Well, for me I guess this exercise will be pretty basic," Ryan said, "since the green anole makes no sounds."

"The same thing is true for the chinook salmon," said Sammy, staring at his salmon bot.

"Not so fast," Vape said. "We're one step ahead of you. It's true the lizard and the fish don't make many sounds. But, that means you guys get to team up with others whose bot animals do. So Ryan, you will team up with James here on the snake. The two reptile guys will work together. And Sammy, you will team up with Ellen on the fox." Ryan had heard robots referred to as 'bots' before, but he hadn't heard the term used in Tanglewood until now.

"What about the dragonfly?" Jenny asked. "It doesn't make a lot of noise either."

"True," said Rook. "But its wings make a pretty sound as they whirr through the air, don't they? So you can work on that. But, if it proves really easy to nail down—and with you doing it, it probably will—then you can work with Carmen on the hawk bot."

"All right!" said Carmen. She and Jenny smiled at each other.

They spent much of that day and those that followed working with their bots and creating sounds. As Vape had predicted, Jenny's tackling the whirring sounds of dragonfly wings was quite straightforward and she completed it on the first day. Rook showed everyone a myriad array of synthesizers and computers with a dizzying library of sounds and other music and video files stored on them. They contained not just animal sounds, but rock videos and other musical performances, footage of historic events, and thousands of other visual and audio files. Mr. Sandhill filmed each student's bot making hundreds of movements, which they directed via remote control, and he stored these in a digital file for each animal bot. Everyone also created sound files for bots they wanted to build in the future.

They explored many concepts in electronic music and sound, programmed the computers and synthesizers for particular sounds, and played with all sorts of effects pedals that could change the sounds an instrument, or an animal, made with echoes, vibrations, and distortions. The selection of drums was spectacular. Ryan couldn't wait to play them.

Rook, Vape, and Mr. Sandhill at various points endeavored to keep everyone focused on creating and cataloging their animal sounds.

"They keep getting distracted," Rook observed.

"With this equipment and technology around, it was bound to happen," Vape said, not unhappily. "It's better than being a kid in a candy store. Getting distracted happens to the best of us." He winked.

After several days, everyone had catalogued their animal sounds onto files, and they uploaded them electronically along with the bot film footage from Mr. Sandhill into "the cloud."

"It's a place accessed through the Internet where the data is sent electronically and stored," explained Meagan. "So you can access the files from any computer that has access to the Internet."

Once the files were uploaded to the cloud, they were pulled down by some friends of Brad and Meagan at the Media Lab at Weatherall University, who took the animal sounds and, using computers, synchronized some of them with the animal bots' movements and actions. These files were uploaded back to the cloud where Brand, Meagan, Rook, and Vape helped Ryan and his friends download them onto very small, nearly microscopic microchips that they then implanted into each animal bot along with very small amplifiers.

"You know, to project the sound," Vape said. "Like, with a rock band, see those stacks over there?" He pointed with his chin over to large stacks of amplifiers that sat on the stage. "In a rock concert, those things are what make it LOUD!"

"Fortunately for you guys, though," Rook said, "we don't need that much amplification. These amplifiers are super small, but they project sound really well."

While the week hardly qualified as work, it felt to Ryan like the group accomplished a ton. In the late afternoons before dinner, they would take a break, have a jam session with everyone playing an instrument, and then swim in a nearby lake. Often their swim sessions found the boys and girls getting into splash fights. Brad and Meagan, who accompanied them into the water on such occasions, tried to referee these splash fests, only to become splash targets themselves. Mr. Sandhill typically watched quietly from the water's edge, wading into the lake with his pant legs rolled up. Vape and Rook would forego the swimming, but joined them in the evenings.

Each night for dinner, which the Blaines prepared on an outside grill, they were joined by musicians who were playing over at Tanglewood.

One evening, a world famous Korean violinist, Hae Jung Park, joined them at dinner. She was playing at Tanglewood the following weekend. Everyone gave her a demonstration of their animal bot with their new repertoire of sounds. Using their handheld remote control consoles, they had their bots interact with each other.

Scram, Ryan's anole, cautiously walked around James' coral snake, which he had decided to name Slidey. Slidey hissed in a friendly way, if that were possible, but then towards the end, to scare Ryan, James caused Slidey make a threatening hiss that took Ryan completely by surprise. Slidey then slithered towards Scram, looking tense and ready to strike. Ryan quickly maneuvered Scram up onto the chair of Hae Jung Park. Scram then skittered across her lap, causing her to squeal in shock, and then clambered down the other side of the chair, landing on the back of Slidey.

"Now who's got the upper hand?" Ryan said. Everybody laughed.

Next, it was Ellen and Jenny's turn. The dance of the fox and the dragonfly was a thing of beauty and curiosity, as Jenny's dragonfly whizzed up above the head of Ellen's fox. The fox eyed the dragonfly intensely, nipping at the air and yapping, to the amusement of all, while Jenny maneuvered the dragonfly adroitly out of the fox's reach. At one point, the fox leapt up for a moment on two legs, its tail wagging playfully behind it. Jenny sent the dragonfly flying in circles just above the fox's head, and the fox started spinning around in circles in pursuit. The group erupted in laughter. The dragonfly flew higher, and the fox sat on its hind legs, gazing skyward. Eventually, the dragonfly flew lower, landed on the fox's nose, and the fox stuck its tongue out, as if to say 'hello.'

"Bravo! Bravo!" exclaimed Mr. Sandhill, clapping.

Next up were Sammy and Carmen. Mr. Blaine produced a children's wading pool and filled it with water using a hose from the barn. Then Sammy placed his chinook salmon in the pool. Its scales shimmered in the waning sun and it powered itself around the pool with its stalwart tail, which wriggled back and forth. Carmen's hawk soared up in the sky, and everyone craned their necks to follow it in the bluish hue of the approaching night. Its wings fluttered majestically high above. The hawk gradually glided downward in narrowing circles, until it departed from its circular path and dive bombed the swimming pool, grabbing the chinook in its talons. It lifted the chinook a few feet in the air with some effort, and then let go, allowing Sammy the opportunity to show the chinook arching its back in the air and opening its mouth in greeting.

"All of the bots... they're so lifelike," Hae Jung Park said.

"I love the dances they make," Vape said, swaying from side to side.

After dinner, Hae Jung Park produced a violin. Each member of the robotics group took turns maneuvering their animal bots around while Hea Jung played violin music that mimicked each creature. For the chinook, she played long, alternating high and low pitched fluttering passages to mimic swimming, whereas for the snake she played lower pitch notes punctuated by some high staccato jabs when it coiled to strike. For the dragonfly she played colorful flourishes that echoed its gliding and meandering flight patterns. For the fox, hawk, and anole, she likewise played progressions that synchronized with their movements and actions. At one point, Mr. Blaine started dancing with Ellen's fox, and Rook picked up James' snake, Slidey, and started dancing around with it in his hands.

"A snake charmer, eh Rook?" Vape called out.

Everyone went to bed that night amused... and exhausted.

The next day was the last one in camp before everyone was to depart. In the morning the group recorded a few songs together at the "Tanglewood shack," as they had taken to calling it. Vape and Rook did the recording. Mr. Sandhill filmed it. Vape and Rook seemed to know their way around a recording studio the way a bee navigates a flowerbed. Vape helped sing several of the songs, and he was so talented—he sang and danced with such memorable style—that everyone wondered if they hadn't seen him or heard his music somewhere before.

"Well, I do sing for a rock band every now and then," Vape said, smiling. He seemed mildly amused.

Mr. Sandhill filmed a rollicking jam session towards the end of the recording. Ryan was playing the drums. James and Jenny played guitar. Carmen played bass guitar, Sammy the piano, and Ellen the saxophone. Brad and Meagan alternated among a bunch of instruments—percussion, synthesizers, and guitar. Meanwhile, Vape was dancing and bounding around the stage, singing into a microphone and cajoling with everyone. His long coat—he had worn a different one every day of the week—had tails that streamed behind him as he whirled around, twisted, and turned. He foisted the microphone into everyone's face periodically. It was an unusual way to request that people sing along, but eventually they got the message. All the while, Rook sat behind the mixing board, recording the raucous music, nodding his head up and down in time with the beat.

"Showoffs," Carmen said to Meagan and Brad after the jam session.

"What do you mean?" Meagan asked.

"Playing fifteen different instruments during the jam session," Ellen retorted.

"Hey, we just like to experiment," Brad shrugged.

"Vape can belt out a tune, wouldn't you say?" James said to Ryan. "I was completely surprised."

"Yeah. You are awesome on the guitar," Ryan observed. "That was cool."

"You rocked on the drums," James said.

"Yeah, you almost kept up with my bass playing, drum stick man," Carmen said to Ryan. Everyone laughed.

They spent the afternoon hiking in nearby Mount Washington State Forest, followed by a cool, relieving swim in a place called Bash Bish Falls State Park. They brought their sound enhanced bots with them to experiment in the forest as they walked along. From several ridge tops at Mount Washington they could see across lush valleys and trace the lines of deep, dropping ravines.

"The falls whisper their own name to you, don't they?" said Vape. "Bashbish, bashbish, bashbish…" Vape had left his trademark long tailed coat behind for this excursion.

They started the hike back to the trail head with dinner on their minds, joking and laughing, occasionally watching each other's animals bound or fly around the trail. Vape, whose energy seemed boundless, was hopping from person to person, coercing them to play with their animal bot or trying to get a reaction out of them. All were in jovial spirits when they walked around a bend with a steep pitch and found themselves staring straight into the face of the unanticipated.

A bobcat sat hunched, low to the ground, tensely perched on its feet, staring right at them. Roughly the size of a large fox, its taut, tense, appearance was menacing. It did not seem happy to have encountered the group, and indicated as much by making an ominous snarl, baring its fierce jaws, and growling so fiercely that it sent icy shivers down their spines. It looked tense enough to explode at any second. Everyone froze instantly.

"Uh, comedy hour's over," Brad said quietly.

"What do we do?" whispered Ellen, shooting frenetic glances to the others. She and Jenny were bordering on hysterics.

"Nobody move," whispered Vape. He was rattled, but trying not to let on.

"Pssst, James," whispered Brad. "Your snake."

James gave the most subtle of nods in his direction.

Slowly, tentatively, James produced Slidey, his coral snake bot, from the rucksack he had brought him in. With measured deliberation, he inserted a hand, withdrew his console and flipped a switch on it, and with the other, lowered the sack containing the snake to the ground, facing the bobcat. James and the snake were about five meters away. With a timid, but fluid movement, James glided his hands out in front of him, pulled open the sack gingerly, and the snake slithered out slowly. Its sidewinding movement was mesmerizing, with its black, red, and yellow stripes gliding in waves over the ground. It looked completely alive. James delicately used his compact remote controller to guide the snake's movements. With everyone else motionless, the bobcat's eyes fixed intently on the snake as it moved slowly in its direction.

The snake hissed softly as it approached the bobcat. The cat looked ready to pounce. Its front paws sat low to the ground near its face, its body compressed in a taut coil. The snake stopped about a meter from the bobcat and raised its head up.

In a flash, the cat pounced on the snake. It caught the snake in its mouth somewhat down on its body, so that its head was free. The two rolled over in a tumble that concluded with the cat standing upright, holding the snake its mouth. At that moment, the snake bit the cat in the neck with its fangs, causing it to jump back. The cat immediately dropped the snake, turned, and ran. Its forceful, grappling paws sent brush, wisps of dirt, and leaves shooting out behind it as it ran off like a lightning bolt. As quickly as the cat had appeared, it was gone.

For a few long seconds, time stood still. Everyone was stunned. Then, they gradually regained their composure. "Wow," said Rook, letting go a huge sigh. "That was scary."

"How's your snake?" asked Ellen, looking at James.

"Let me check," James said. He looked off in the direction the bobcat had run, as if to make sure it was not returning. He approached Slidey, who sat on the ground, looking lifeless, as James had stopped controlling him. James picked it up in two hands and looked at the area where the bobcat had bitten the snake and held it in its mouth. "A couple of scratches, but otherwise okay," James said. "The scales and shell are made of super strong titanium, so I'm guessing the cat was pretty surprised when he took a bite out of Slidey and he didn't taste like snake burger."

That evening the Tanglewood group held a last barbecue at the

Blaines' house. Mr. Sandhill presented everyone with certificates acknowledging their week's accomplishments in music and robotics. All felt sad that the session had come to an end so soon. "Let's stay in touch," Vape said.

Lying in bed that evening, Ryan listened to the wind rustle gently through the leaves of nearby tree branches outside his open window. It rolled through them as waves cascading on a shore, making them dance with a gentle rushing sound. Ryan reflected on how much fun he had had in the past week. It had been a time to remember.

The next morning, the shuttle bus arrived to pick up the group after breakfast, which consisted of a last farm-fresh meal, courtesy of the Blaines. Everyone took a final, wistful look around at the Blaines' farm, the trees, nearby rolling hills, and cloudless blue sky of a mid-summer day. They said their goodbyes to the Blaines, Vape, and Rook and climbed into the van.

"I'd swear Vape is in a rock band," James said.

"Yeah, the way he dances, I mean, most girls can't do anything *close* to that, let alone guys," Jenny noted.

"All right, all right. I'll let you in on little secret," Mr. Sandhill said, a smile peeling across his face. "I'm a little surprised none of you guessed at it, but maybe Mr. Vapiano is a bit ahead of your time. Walter Vapiano—or Vape, as he is called—is in fact the lead singer of the rock band Voltaic. Perhaps you've heard of them?"

"Voltaic? No way!" Carmen exclaimed. "He definitely looked familiar."

"Darn!" Sammy said. "We didn't get his autograph!"

"I knew it!" Ellen said.

"You knew it? Then why didn't you say anything?" Jenny chided.

"Well, I thought I knew it," Ellen said. "I mean, I think my parents used to listen to Voltaic."

"I knew it," Meagan said.

"Then why didn't you say anything?" Jenny asked.

"Because she figured you guys wouldn't get any work done if you knew," Brad said.

"True," Meagan agreed.

As the van approached the airport in Boston, everyone swapped email addresses and agreed to stay in touch as they went their separate ways. They all felt they shared a new, special bond. For Ryan it felt unlike anything he had known before. He sensed he had a new club of comrades that would come to his aid at any moment.

As they were disembarking from the van at the airport in Boston, a toddler and her family were unloading from a parked car some distance away. Momentarily ignored by her parents, the little girl wandered aimlessly off the curb and out into the street. In the distance, fast moving traffic approached. In a flash, Jenny withdrew her dragonfly bot—she had it named Skye this past week—and released her into the air. Skye shot off with a buzz of her wings and came to a hovering position right above the little girl. Jenny maneuvered Skye so that she circled in and out of the girl's field of vision. Curious, the little girl gazed up at Skye, followed her, and tried to catch her with her hands. Skye remained just out of reach. Jenny piloted Skye back over the sidewalk, and the girl walked after her, up onto the safety of the sidewalk and out of the street. Seconds later, a taxi cab sped past.

"Rebecca!" called out the girl's mother. "Oh, there you are, sweetie. Come, hold my hand."

The girl turned away to look at her mother and then strode towards her. Jenny quickly piloted Skye back to herself. Skye fluttered gently down onto the palm of Jenny's outstretched hand. The others looked on in amazement.

Mr. Sandhill looked at Jenny and winked. "Well done," he said.

3

HALLOWEEN DANCE: LIZARDS NOT INVITED

As late summer gave way to early fall, the Tanglewood group members all began writing each other via email. Ryan noticed as soon as camp had ended, that Carmen began sending emails to him specifically, in addition to those she sent to the entire group. In turn, he engaged in direct dialogue with her as well as the broader group conversation. Ryan was flattered to have a new personal email pen pal in Carmen, though a bit perplexed. Had he done something special that stood out to her? He hadn't really done anything remarkable during the week at Tanglewood he could think of, yet they had struck up something of a kinship. Ryan couldn't completely figure it out, but having a secret friend was kind of cool.

A few weeks after Tanglewood, Carmen sent an email to Ryan. "Our soccer team is doing great," she wrote. "We might make the state championships. And when school ends, we're traveling to Holland to play some teams there. I can't wait to go there, since I will get to escape the Arizona heat. How do you think your sports teams will do this year?"

Living in Dallas, Ryan could relate to wanting to escape hot weather. Holland sounded fascinating. Ryan's soccer team was okay, but not great. His school baseball team was pretty good, and he wondered if the team might go anywhere half as interesting as Holland in the spring time. He doubted it.

The Highland Park Middle School Robotics Club kicked off in the fall. It had now expanded to fourteen members, and was starting to become a legitimate club at school, as opposed to something people thought of as a secret group of nerds. "Hey, it's got more members than the coin or stamp collecting clubs," Ryan wrote to his Tanglewood mates.

"We're in danger of becoming real." The club held its own mini Robot Blasts, which was great, because it showed Ryan and his colleagues where they needed to improve their bots and their robotic gaming skills. Each year the Robot Blasts changed a little bit. The object of the game became something different, so there was always a new challenge to tackle.

Ryan also continued to work with Scram, playing with his movements and feet, enabling him to cling for increasingly longer periods of time in strange positions, such as on the sides of walls or upside down underneath his desk. Ryan had been playing with some very tiny lightweight sections of Scram's toes and tail, which, when configured and moved appropriately, enabled him to perform these seemingly gravity-defying feats. Ryan had researched the anole and learned—largely by trial and error—what he needed to do with Scram to mimic the anole's bodily movements. This work could be hugely time consuming, but for Ryan the reward of seeing Scram clinging upside down and walking around on the ceiling or underneath a table was worth it. In fact, the notion of Scram *not* being able to do such things seemed absurd to Ryan. The Tanglewood members found it fun to share among the group the different things everyone was doing with his or her bot, and the new ones they were creating.

"I've been working on a design for a killer whale," Sammy wrote to his friends. "It's almost done." It was a hugely ambitious project.

"I'm ordering a design for a leopard from Mr. Sandhill's computer-aided design group at Weatherall University," Ellen wrote. "At some point I'd also like to try a Doberman pinscher."

"I'm working on a bee. At some point I'd like to try a house fly, and maybe a hornet," Jenny wrote.

"I'm working on a sidewinder," James wrote. "I'd also like to try a turtle."

"I wouldn't mind trying a seagull, or a heron," Carmen wrote. "I like the idea of having a bird land on the water, and then swim below the surface."

Ryan wrote that he might like to try a spider at some point, and an alligator. "They're two totally different things," he said. "And they would have different challenges."

The summer heat of east Texas abated some in late summer so that by mid-October temperatures grew cooler. Halloween was rapidly approaching. As an event, Halloween was losing its appeal to Ryan, and dressing up in a costume was becoming increasingly uncool. "I don't know what to do for Halloween," Ryan told his Tanglewood friends in an email. "It seems dumb to dress up for it at my age. I mean, maybe I'll dress up to go trick or treating with my younger sister because my parents will make me, but otherwise, I don't see the point."

"What do you mean? Candy is the point!" Sammy wrote back. Clearly he still had no mixed feelings about the excitement of Halloween—or at least its candy reaping potential.

"I'm sure your sister would like it if you went out with her," Carmen wrote. "I still like dressing up for Halloween, even if we are getting too old for it. Maybe I'll go as a soccer player."

"That's not much of a stretch," James replied. "You *are* a soccer player."

"Or maybe I'll dress as a rodeo cowgirl," Carmen posited. She seemed to want to be something, though she hadn't quite sorted out what just yet.

"I was thinking of being a doctor," Jenny wrote. "But I've been a doctor for the past four years. So I'm going to dress up as a dragonfly this year. I will be Madame Libellule. That's 'Madame Dragonfly' in French," she noted. She was enjoying her French class this year. "I have designed a cool, blue-metallic dress with mesh wings that really does look the part. I also thought about bringing my violin, and playing a musical piece to mimic Skye like Hae Jung Park did."

"That sounds really cool," Carmen wrote.

"I am going to be the Wicked Witch of the West," Ellen wrote. "Our school has a costume party, and there are prizes for the best costumes. Maybe I'll bring Trixie along with me," she wrote. Trixie was the name she had given her robotic fox.

Ellen's comment about bringing Trixie got Ryan thinking. *I could do something with Scram for Halloween,* he told himself. *I could dress up... as a camouflaged dude or a burglar or something... and bring Scram with me, and make him walk around and freak people out.* Now *that* was an idea. Halloween was beginning to feel exciting again. He told Annie he thought he had an idea of what to be for Halloween.

"What is it?" she asked, her curiosity piqued.

"You'll see," Ryan said. Annie followed his eyes as they settled on Scram. Ryan occasionally let Annie play with Scram, but only when he was around. Experience had taught him that if he left Annie alone with something of his, the item frequently got returned in a decidedly different, more used condition.

Annie often wanted to tag along with Ryan and his friends. She had friends of her own, but she frequently became intrigued by what her older brother and his friends were doing. While not opposed to things that appealed to many girls her age, such as dolls, finger and toe nail paints, and the color pink, Annie also liked to explore scientific things—things that were decidedly un-pink. Her mom and dad fostered this interest within her, as they had with Ryan.

"I'm going to be an astronaut for Halloween," eleven year-old Annie proudly told her brother.

Over time, as he was able to do more and more with Scram, Ryan came to realize the wisdom of having multiple copies of the lizard bot. Experimenting with Scram was hugely engaging and fun, but, as Ryan learned, one had to be prepared for the occasional accident. Once, Annie borrowed Scram from Ryan and absent-mindedly left him out in the street, where he got run over by a truck. There wasn't much Ryan could do to resuscitate that version of Scram, and he landed on the scrap heap. Another time, a dog picked up Scram and started chewing him like a toy. Given Scram's composition of light weight, but very durable metal, he emerged from that episode mostly unscathed, expect for a couple of teeth marks that Ryan was able to make vanish with a few touches of paint. Scram also smelled like dog breath for the next week, but the smell eventually wore off.

Having multiple copies of Scram meant if one got damaged or destroyed, Ryan still had others to work with. Like an auto mechanic, he could also use salvageable parts from a beat up one on a new version. And, whenever a Scram bot got mangled or destroyed, with each next version Ryan was always working on refinements and improvements.

Highland Park Middle School held an annual Halloween dance. *The dance will be the perfect place for me to take Scram*, Ryan thought to himself. "What if I took Scram to the Halloween dance and made some people completely flip out?" he asked his friends in robotics club.

"Well, why would you do that?" one friend asked.

"Why not?" said another.

"Exactly, why not?" said Ryan. "It'll be hilarious."

In the end, they loved the idea. Of course, they didn't think he was serious. Robotics club was a setting in which people often asked off the wall 'what if' questions. What if this robot could climb stairs? What if that robot could perform surgery on a person? Thus, Ryan's original question about taking Scram to the dance was not at all out of the ordinary. Sometimes people in robotics club were serious about following through on these crazy questions. Sometimes they weren't.

On the night of the dance, Ryan felt gleeful in anticipation of his prank. The weather was pleasant, a warm temperature with a gentle breeze. There would be lots of people at the dance. Ryan looked ridiculous as a cat burglar, wearing military camouflage with a black eye mask across his face and his cheeks smeared with dark grease.

"You're a what?" Ryan's dad asked as he headed towards the front door with Annie. Scram was safely tucked out of sight in his trick-or-treat bag.

"A cat burglar," Ryan said.

"Out of all the things in the world you could be, you chose to be a *cat burglar?*" his dad asked.

"I couldn't think of anything else," Ryan shrugged. His dad gave him a look that said he was unimpressed and gazed back at the newspaper he was reading.

His mom wasn't much more receptive. "I like Annie's astronaut costume, and yours is... interesting," she said to Ryan.

Ryan walked with Annie to the middle school. Annie had just started at the middle school this fall, and was feeling very grown up to be accompanying her big brother to a school dance. A large throng of costume-wearing kids stood at the entrance, slowly winding their way into the building.

Ryan recognized a couple of his friends. "Hey, Ryan... Is that you?" one of them asked. It was hard to tell in the darkness and Ryan wearing smeared grease on his face.

"Yeah," Ryan said.

"What are you supposed to be?"

"Cat burglar," Ryan said.

"Huh. Cool astronaut costume, Annie," the friend said.

Annie, who was a bit more recognizable in her costume in the evening darkness, soon found some of her friends and wandered off with them. Ryan was grateful, as it enabled him to pursue his scare plan with Scram without distraction. He found a couple of his robotics club mates, and told them he had brought Scram, gesturing to his bag.

"What? You're serious?" one of his friends asked. "Don't you think something will happen to him? Like, maybe he'll get stomped on?"

"Unlikely," Ryan said. "He's pretty fast. Not to mention, it would take more than a stomp to break him."

"Well, he sure does look real. Acts totally real, too. I'm sure he'll freak some people out," said the friend. "Before he gets trampled," he added.

About an hour into the dance, many kids had crowded into the gymnasium. Colorful lights were splashing all around from fixtures placed in various spots around the gym. Loud music punctuated by crunching drum beats pulsed through the hall. If you didn't know the song that was playing by heart, it would be indecipherable due to the muddy reverberations of the speakers that sounded like thunder in the cavernous gym, and overwhelmed the eardrums. A disc jockey wore sun glasses and a snazzy, reflective metallic looking jacket and matching pants. He stood at one end of the gym where large stacks of speakers and light racks stood, playing music, looking not unlike a mad sorcerer run amok in a discotheque. A crowd of kids was gathered at that end of the gym, basking in the sea of light and sound blaring from the speakers. The DJ seemed pretty sure they were all worshipping him.

The time felt right to Ryan. With two of his bot club mates, he slinked off down a hallway towards the school cafeteria to get ready to unleash Scram. His initial plan was to withdraw Scram from the gunny sack he had brought for tricks and treats and let him loose in the middle of the gymnasium. But, with all the music blaring and people dancing and moseying all about, he grew concerned that Scram wouldn't get noticed. But then, glancing down the hallway, he noticed a line of girls waiting to get inside the girls' bathroom. It was a smaller crowd of people, but Ryan figured Scram would sure as heck get noticed by the crowd of jittery girls waiting to use a toilet.

Ryan gestured to his friends. They ambled down the hallway, pretending to look at some posters on the walls. They waited until the line of girls had grown short enough that there were none waiting in the hallway. They could hear muted girlish chatter and giggling from behind the bathroom door. Ryan crossed the hall, withdrew Scram from his sack, and smoothly set him on the floor just outside the girls' bathroom. Then, he pulled out Scram's remote controller, turned it on, and guided Scram under the door. Fortunately, he was thin enough to make it. It didn't take long for shrieks to start emanating out of the bathroom. Ryan and his robotics club mates stood to one side in the hallway and watched the bathroom door suddenly swing open, whereupon a flood of costumed, hysterically screaming girls came pouring out. Once it became clear the room was empty, Ryan directed Scram to exit the bathroom with his remote controller, scooped him up, and tucked him back in his sack.

"Hurry up!" one of his friends shrieked. "People will be coming!"

"It's a challenge because I can't see where he's going if I'm not in the same room," Ryan told his friends. "So, I just had him walk around in a circle. Evidently that was sufficient."

It probably would have turned out okay if the prank had ended there, but it didn't. Like a greedy kid seeking another Halloween fistful of candy, Ryan was eager to do more. The frightened girls who had fled the bathroom found one of the teacher chaperones at the dance and screeched about having seen a lizard there. The teacher, who wasn't quite sure she heard the girls correctly above the raucous din of the music, heard that there was some type of lizard in the bathroom and felt there was little point to her going into the women's bathroom alone. Nor did she want to, without any means to capture the critter. So she, in turn, informed the head janitor on duty. The janitor immediately barked for the assistance of two of his colleagues and they strode off in the direction of the bathroom.

Meantime, Ryan brought Scram out onto the gymnasium floor—unnoticed beside a stack of speakers—and made him start climbing the back of a boy standing near the DJ. A girl spotted the lizard climbing on the boy's shoulder and immediately started to scream. The boy, alarmed, then noticed the lizard and immediately shook and brushed himself violently to get it off him, which looked terribly funny since he was dressed as a football player for Halloween. This spectacle succeeded in garnering the attention of a lot of people on the dance floor, as well as the DJ.

"And jock boy over here is giving new meaning to the term 'shakin' all over!'" the DJ squawked over the loudspeakers.

Ryan quickly made Scram dart off into a crowd of people, who had started to scamper out of his way. This was unfortunate for Ryan, since he was trying to hide Scram just then.

The janitors, who had been summoned earlier by the teacher, were passing through the gym on their way to the girls' bathroom with tools in hand when they observed the commotion. With a large net, a plant container, and a rake, they weren't exactly ideally prepared to capture the fleet-footed Scram. The janitors chased him around the gym, and for some time, he eluded them.

Kids were stampeding out of the way at every turn. Ultimately, Ryan made Scram climb to the top of one of the music speakers. While it afforded a temporary escape, Scram was now trapped. The janitors, with their odd assortment of implements, were in no position to grab Scram, who sat at a height well above their heads. However, one of the janitors stood watch while the other two ran off to gather more supplies.

At this point, kids were in hysterics, screaming and laughing, and looking and pointing up at the top of the speaker where Scram was perched, sitting low and clinging to the speaker as if his life depended on it.

The DJ was trying to flash a light up on top of the speaker without success, since he was standing well below it. However, he fed the frenzy by shouting loudly, "Folks, there's some sort of creature in here! How's that for a Halloween trick!?!" The music still blared at near ear splitting volume. "Let's see if we can feature that creature!" he called out, pointing a light from his table top up at the speaker. He was clearly very proud of his rhyming skills.

Ryan was stuck. If he brought Scram down and picked him up, everyone would know Ryan had something to do with him and all the chaos he was causing. Regrettably, the janitors were more resourceful than Ryan hoped they would be. The two came running back over to their colleague with a ladder and a large sheet. This forced Ryan's hand. He had Scram climb up, then jump down from the speaker, and tried to veer him off in the direction of a group of kids, but they scattered. This left an opening for the janitors to swoop in with the sheet. They held it at about knee height in the air and stretched it out over the area where Scram was sitting. They dropped it quickly, before Scram could bolt out from underneath it. With the sheet thrown over him and the janitors placing their feet and hands on the edges of the sheet to make it taut, they knew exactly where Scram was underneath it, and now he couldn't move anywhere nearly as easily or as fast. The head janitor briefly ran off, but materialized within seconds, pushing a large, heavy lawn roller. While it couldn't possibly have been good for the hard wood floor of the gym, the janitor approached the sheet on the floor with the roller and promptly rolled it—right over Scram.

"And... Presto! No more lizard! Or whatever it is!" announced one of the janitors proudly, looking at the throng of people around him. He even made eye contact with Ryan, presumably expecting Ryan to look happy, just like everyone else. Ryan thought he had heard the faint crunching of metal as the roller went over Scram.

And that was how Ryan lost another copy of Scram. His heart sank.

He thought of the hundreds of hours he had spent programming Scram and building the intricate wiring and mechanics into his feet, legs, and body that enabled him to move and climb. He could, of course, do it again, and he had multiple copies of Scram at varying stages of completion, but it would take a while. Maybe a long while.

"Oooh!" a bunch of kids screamed in unison, assuming there was now a lizard pancake on the underside of the sheet. They were not far from wrong.

The janitors, like Ryan, also thought they heard a metallic *crunch!* in their attempt to exterminate the lizard, though it was hard to be sure with the loud music blaring about. When they pulled the sheet back, they saw a series of small chips, wiring, and electronic components sticking out from the body of the flattened anole.

"Well, I'll be darned," said one of the janitors. "It looks like a mechanic animal, or a doll, or a machine of some sort. Is it, like, is it a... robot?"

"Well, I'll be..." the other said.

"It's my brother's!" squealed an over-zealous Annie, pointing at Ryan. He didn't know where she had materialized from, but he suddenly wished she hadn't.

"Thanks," Ryan said, feeling the stares of dozens of onlookers fixate on him. He was beginning to feel his cat burglar costume did not disguise him nearly enough.

4

ANOTHER UNEXPECTED INVITATION

The teacher chaperone, who earlier had been besieged by young girls fleeing the girls' bathroom at the sight of the lizard, approached Ryan, walking briskly. She looked angry. "What's your name, young man?" she demanded of Ryan, pointing her finger at him. Ryan told her his name.

"And is this... *thing*... yours?" She pointed to the flattened, tangled remnants of Scram. "Does it belong to you?"

"Uh, kind of. Yes," Ryan said with a sigh.

"Well, I think we'll just plan a little audience for you and Mr. Willoughby on Monday morning," the teacher said. Mr. Willoughby was the Principal of Highland Park Middle School. Ryan thought he detected pride in the way she said it. She promptly ushered Ryan out of the dance, which had been hugely disrupted. After all the drama, the exclamations of the DJ trying to get a crowd back on the dance floor sounded almost ridiculous to everyone as Ryan was walked off the school grounds.

The following Monday morning, as promised, Ryan found himself summoned to the office of Mr. Willoughby. Ryan would have preferred to be in his biology class.

"So, Mr. Ferris," Mr. Willoughby began, as Ryan sat uncomfortably in a chair in front of his desk. "I understand there was some mischief at the dance this past Friday."

"Mischief?" Ryan said.

"Yeah. Mischief," Mr. Willoughby repeated. "I heard from Ms. Ketter about a... lizard? A robotic lizard? That she claims belongs to you?" He held up a cardboard box that contained the flattened, mangled metallic body of Scram, an array of wires and chips poking out from various places. Other small smashed pieces lay in a small pile in the box.

"Oh, that," Ryan said.

"Yeah, that," said Mr. Willoughby. "So you know what I'm talking about?"

"Kind of."

"I'll take that as a 'yes,'" Mr. Willoughby replied.

Ryan shrugged and nodded his head up and down ever so slightly.

Mr. Willoughby looked at the small box with the remnants of the flattened Scram "So, I take it the work that went into this is yours, then. It looks like a whole lot of work," he said.

"Yes, um, sir. It is a lot of work. And it is... mine," Ryan said.

"Well, here it is. You'll probably want it back, for spare parts or something," Mr. Willoughby said. Ryan was stunned that Mr. Willoughby could know such a thing.

"Uh, thanks," Ryan said, nervously sliding the box onto his lap.

"Now. I must say," Mr. Willoughby continued. "Everybody, the teachers, parents, janitors, and kids, were positive that lizard was *real*. The way it moved, the way it climbed, it sounds pretty incredible. So whatever you're doing, keep doing it, because it's darned impressive. But, the school is not a zoo, Ryan. You can't go sending lizards or some such things skittering into the girls' bathroom, or dances, or other places in this school that are going to land you in my office. And you can't really let this type of thing loose in a school, or any other public place full of unsuspecting people, for that matter. With your talent, you should be landing yourself on the evening news for piloting a space mission or something, but not on my doorstep. You got that?"

"Yeah," Ryan said. *Unsuspecting people,* that phrase stuck in his mind.

"Now, I can't... and won't... let you off the hook free and clear, especially after all the disruption you caused," said Mr. Willoughby. "So I'm giving you two weeks of detentions. You can probably use the time to work on formulating your team's design plan for next spring's Grand International Robotics Blast in St. Louis. If it's not complete by the end of next week, you keep going until it is. Do we understand each other?"

"Yes," Ryan said. "I'll definitely have it done by then."

All in all, Mr. Willoughby was a pretty decent guy, Ryan thought to himself as he walked down the hall back to class. Ryan knew Mr. Willoughby had to punish him to satisfy Ms. Ketter, the other teachers, the janitors, and basically anybody who was disturbed by Scram at the dance, which included just about everyone. And, word of his punishment would travel fast. But, Ryan had to admit, Mr. Willoughby had found a pretty innovative way of doing it. Detention was a huge drag, but he would not be bored working on the Robotics Club's plans for the Grand International Robotics Blast. He had been looking forward to it for months. He knew he would use the detention time wisely.

Now Ryan had to do something he was dreading almost even more—explain the detentions to his parents. He was pretty sure they weren't going to be as understanding as Mr. Willoughby had been. He was right.

"You took Scram to the dance and set him loose on your unsuspecting schoolmates?" his dad said with amazement. "How smart was that?" There was that word again... *Unsuspecting.*

"Not very?" Ryan asked, in a meek attempt to find the answer his dad might be seeking.

"You are now grounded from visiting with friends for the next two weeks."

Ryan hung his shoulders low and wandered off to his bedroom. *At least I have my Tanglewood friends*, he thought.

Ryan sent them an email about the school dance incident with Scram. Perhaps unsurprisingly, he got a range of opinions from the Tanglewood-ians. Some of the girls were nonplussed.

"You sent Scram into the girls' bathroom?" Jenny asked, incredulously. She could make you feel small with minimal effort.

"Nice move," Ellen wrote. "Scaring a bunch of girls? I thought you were bigger and better than that."

"I didn't do it because they were *girls*," Ryan wrote, feeling compelled to defend himself. "There were a bunch of people all in one place... who just happened to be girls."

"Pretty funny," James said. Ryan could almost hear him laughing. "I got busted recently at school for having my snake in my locker. Kids totally freaked out. I can't bring it to school anymore."

"I can't bring Scram, either," Ryan wrote. It didn't mean he would rule out doing it again, however. But, probably not at *this* school.

"Pretty ridiculous," Carmen wrote. "It sounds like the punishment from your principal was pretty light."

"Well, from my parents it wasn't," Ryan wrote back. He felt a bit stung by Carmen's remark.

"Lucky you have us for friends, aren't you?" Carmen wrote. "We can all visit each other without being in the same place."

"It's so cool that people thought Scram was real. I should try doing something like that at a community pool with my fish," Sammy wrote. "I bet I'd empty it out in three seconds."

"Well, I thought Scram could weave through a crowd no problem," Ryan wrote, "but he got trapped. He's super-fast, but it was a challenge steering him through a crowd when I couldn't see him."

"As a teacher I cannot officially endorse such behavior," Mr. Sandhill wrote to Ryan of his ill-fated prank. "However, as your friend, I find it downright funny."

Ryan was impressed with Mr. Sandhill's message, and found it not unkind.

"By the way, here at Weatherall University, they have an expression for those types of stunts—the 'broink.' And I daresay you have just completed your first one. However, the main goal, the highest priority above all else—at least at Weatherall—is generally not to be seen or to get caught doing it."

"Well, I obviously failed to achieve that goal," Ryan wrote. "So, what types of things do people consider a broink?"

"They're silly acts, most typically harmless stunts, but usually very clever. For example, one year some students at Weatherall placed an entire car on the top of the Weatherall Dome," Mr. Sandhill wrote in reply. "That was one of the more famous broinks. Though there have been hundreds of them through the years."

"So, where does the word 'broink' come from?" Ellen wrote.

Mr. Sandhill wrote back: "The theories about its origins vary. It has been posited that its basis lies in the combination of the words 'brain' and 'boink,' or 'doink.' But, other words are often cited as its possible origin as well, such as 'boing,' 'oink,' and doubtless others."

Vape and Rook weighed in on Ryan's recent dance hall mishap as well. "Greetings from L.A. Voltaic show here is tomorrow. Well done, trouble maker," Vape wrote. "You must be taking after me."

Rook chimed in. "I've spent many years trying to keep Vape out of trouble, with only limited success. Are you following in these footsteps? Despite my lackluster attempts to reign in Vape, we did manage to sell more than a hundred million records, so I guess that's something," Rook wrote. "Scram is a great lizard. Keep it up."

While the Scram prank at Halloween was mostly memorable to Ryan for positive reasons, despite getting two weeks' worth of detentions and grounding, there was one rather unpleasant consequence of it. The boy who had been dressed up as a football player at the dance, the one whom Scram had climbed prior to total chaos erupting, actually *was* a football player. Chip McCollum was a big, hulking defensive lineman who generally detested anyone making fun of him. And, in the aftermath of the lizard wreaking havoc at the Halloween dance, Chip came away looking like a buffoon as the person who was prancing and shaking all over the place, trying to free himself from what everyone in school now knew was a tiny, harmless lizard robot that was no larger than a toy.

Chip McCollum was known mainly behind his back as "Cheater" McCollum because of his tendency to play dirty in sports. For all Ryan knew, maybe he cheated in school, too. Ryan didn't really know Chip and hadn't anticipated any fallout from him relative to the Halloween fiasco. But he was wrong.

One day, after a detention had ended, Ryan was walking home from school and he was jumped from behind. Chip McCollum and two thuggish friends from the football team tackled him. Before he knew what was going on, Ryan had been punched in the nose and about the head, and was pinned down on each side by a boy who was easily larger and stronger than he.

"You may not know what this is for, robot-head," said Chip McCollum. "But nobody makes me look like an idiot without paying for it."

"What? Uh, sorry," said Ryan in a daze, as a stream of what he learned was blood flowed from his nose to his mouth.

Chip grabbed handfuls of grass from the ground and stuffed them down Ryan's shirt, and took a big pile and rubbed it around in his hair.

"You will be even more sorry if anything like this happens again," Chip said with a sneer. He and his friends walked off hurriedly.

Ryan felt tears and dust rolling off his face as he slowly rose to his feet. He began collecting his books, some of which had fallen half out of his backpack in the assault. He felt alarmed and shocked. But, despite feeling some pain about his face, the thing that hurt most was his pride.

Moments later, an ambulance from a fire department drove by. No lights were flashing or sirens blaring. The ambulance happened to be driving past just as the melee occurred, and the driver, an emergency responder, had seen it all.

"What was that all about?" the driver asked Ryan. He had produced a first aid kit from his ambulance and was starting to clean Ryan up.

"It was payback for a prank, I think," Ryan said.

"Must have been some prank," the man exclaimed.

"I guess," said Ryan.

"Well, it's not going to be very funny when the school and parents of those kids hear about what happened to you," the man said. "And what happens to them probably won't seem like a prank."

Chip McCollum's punishment was swift and severe. He and his friends were suspended from school for three days, given one month's worth of detentions, and were barred from football practice or games for the entire month they were on detention. They each came to Ryan's house with their parents and personally apologized to him for the incident. Even the football coach came to Ryan's house to personally apologize.

"How does all of this make you feel?" his dad asked the evening after the coach had come over to express his apologies.

"Embarrassed, mostly," Ryan said. "It's a waste of time. I wish it hadn't happened. I wish I hadn't been beat up, and I wish Cheater—Chip—and his friends hadn't lost out on playing in those games. Our school will suffer because of that." Indeed, the Highland Park Middle School football team would go on to fail to make the regional playoffs that year.

"Well, none of it would have happened if you hadn't brought the lizard robot to the school dance in the first place," his dad said. Ryan had to agree there was some truth to that.

Even Mr. Willoughby, the Highland Park Middle School principal, visited with Ryan in his office the day after the incident. "Ryan, I am deeply disappointed with what happened. I'm shocked and ashamed and I have made it clear to Chip and the others that we will absolutely not tolerate this type of behavior. Unfortunately, you find in this world that not everybody wants to be your friend. But, you cannot and should not let that stop you from being the person you are and want to be."

"Thanks, Mr. Willoughby," Ryan muttered. He wasn't sure what else to say.

Ryan did take care to make sure that wherever he was in school for the next several months, he was nowhere near Chip McCollum. It wasn't difficult. Chip was in none of the same classes as Ryan.

In the spring, the matter of another school dance came up. Ryan decided, quite wisely, that he would not bring Scram to this dance. He had spent the past several months re-building new Scram models. His correspondence with Carmen had kept up over the months, as it had with the other Tanglewoodians. Ryan told her of the upcoming dance, but neglected to mention that a girl had invited him—to go as her date. Somehow he thought Carmen wouldn't want to know that.

"Sounds fun," she wrote. "We have a dance coming up too. No one really goes as anybody's date. We just go. The girls basically dance with each other and most of the boys stand against the wall." That sounded pretty much like what Ryan would be doing at the dance, if it were up to him—standing against the wall and making fun of the girls. Somehow he didn't think his date would see it that way, though.

The HPMS Robotics Club team attended the Grand International Robotics Blast that following April in St. Louis, Missouri. During the year, they had to raise money through fundraising activities to pay for the travel. The robotics club worked through the spring to raise the funds. Ryan's dad had gotten his company to match the first thousand dollars the group raised for the trip, a great first step. Now the question was: how would they raise the funds that could be matched?

Ryan and his fellow club members decided to approach the school athletics department to see if they could sell tickets to sports games and collect an extra fee of two dollars per ticket, to be contributed to the Robotics Blast fundraising effort. "I'd love to help you guys," said the middle school athletic head, who was also a math teacher, "but here's my problem. If I help you, then every other club in school is going to come to me to ask if they can do the same thing for their club. By the time I give every club the same opportunity, a ticket to a basketball game will cost three hundred dollars."

"But no one else has come to you with this idea," Ryan said.

"True. But once they hear about it, they will," the man replied.

Ryan walked away, feeling dejected.

"That's so bogus," Ryan said to his friends. "He could have helped us if he wanted to. So what do we do now?"

They decided upon a car wash event in early March. One of the club members' neighbors owned a hamburger restaurant and agreed to let the club use part of his parking lot for the event over the course of a weekend. Ryan and his club mates advertised the car wash throughout the school and in neighborhoods all over town by going door to door, or in the case of the school, locker to locker, distributing flyers. The event was so successful the club did it again a few weeks later, and by the end of March, had raised four thousand dollars, enough for all club members to attend the Grand International Robotics Blast in St. Louis. Ryan's entire family drove with him to the event. And, as the name indicated, the event was a blast.

Later in the spring, baseball kicked into high gear. One late, hot May afternoon Ryan came home from a baseball game. He had seen a lot of action. He got three hits and scored twice—once on a sliding play at home plate. He had also been busy at shortstop, turning a double play and making a series of defensive dives. His uniform was dirty from head to toe and fine dust coated his hands, arms, and face, such that a bead of sweat etched a small, clear runnel down his cheek through the grime.

"Ryan, honey, you have a piece of mail," his mom said as he strode through the kitchen. "It's on your dresser in your bedroom. You may want to wash off before opening it. You're covered in dirt."

"Thanks, Mom," Ryan said. Sometimes she had a way of stating the obvious that Ryan didn't think it required, but he knew she meant well.

He washed off, went into his bedroom, and found the letter sitting on his dresser. While it vaguely reminded him of the letter he had received with the invitation to Tanglewood the previous summer, this letter had different colors from the red and gold of the Highland Park Middle School. Instead, its colors were green and grey.

The letter was from the Seguin Academy in Milton, Massachusetts. It informed Ryan that he was cordially invited to attend the school—on a full scholarship starting in the fall.

"What the—" Ryan said to himself softly as he read the letter.

The last sentence removed some of the mystery for Ryan. It said: "We have it on good authority from Mr. Thomas Sandhill, one of our teachers here at Seguin, that you will make an excellent student." The letter was signed by a Mrs. Catherine Bergeron, head of school at Seguin Academy.

Usually when Ryan's father arrived home during the week, he was accustomed to receiving one-word replies from Ryan to his questions. Indeed, the word *"fine"* seemed the standard response that sufficed for a great number of questions.

"How was your day, Ryan?"

"Fine."

"How was school?"

"Fine."

"How are your friends?"

"Fine."

"How was the baseball game?"

"Fine."

But, today the conversation was a bit different.

"Hi, Ryan, how was your day?"

"Good, Dad. I had a great baseball game."

"Excellent. I'd love to hear more about it."

"Um, Dad?"

"Yes, son?"

"I think there's something we need to talk about."

5

HITTING THE HIGHWAY

The news was something of a shock. Mr. Sandhill emailed Ryan to inform him that he would be visiting Dallas-Fort Worth on some business for Seguin Academy and Weatherall University within the next few weeks. He wanted to invite Ryan and his family to dinner to answer any questions they had about Seguin Academy and Ryan's potentially attending. Ryan had traveled some, though not a lot, and he hadn't considered attending school anywhere other than his hometown. If he were to go to school in—where was it? Milton, Massachusetts—*that* was a whole different ball game. He liked most of the kids at Highland Park Middle School and cherished his friends in the Robotics Club. How could he say goodbye to them and go off to the unknown?

Ryan emailed his fellow Tanglewoodians to share the news of the invitation to attend Seguin Academy in the fall. To his amazement, everyone else had received the same invitation. It seemed that Mr. Sandhill had more than a few tricks up his sleeve.

"This will be so much fun!" Ellen wrote. For her, the decision to attend Seguin Academy was easy. She lived in the area and could live at home if she wanted to. "But I will probably want to live on campus," she said. "Otherwise, I'll miss out on half the fun you guys will be having."

"It's pretty incredible," James wrote. "My parents probably couldn't afford something like this. They told me I'd be a fool not to do it. They'll be pretty bummed out not have me around, but my younger brother is already making plans to take over my bedroom."

"Seguin is a long way from home," Carmen said, "but I'm in the same boat. My parents told me this is the opportunity of a lifetime. And I've never seen snow before."

"I'm going," Jenny said. "I was worried about staying in touch with my family too. But, then I went to the academy's website and it says that you are required to visit with your family online at least once a week with VideoLink. They encourage you to do it more, but that's the minimum. And, you can do the same thing with friends."

"My parents are pretty concerned about my going to a boarding school and the distance as well," Sammy wrote. "I hope they let me do it if I want to. I have an uncle who told them Seguin Academy is one of the best schools on the planet. And the winter weather there can't be any worse than Chicago's."

Ryan's parents, like him, were stunned at the news of the invitation to Seguin Academy. But, they were also incredibly proud, and hard-pressed to find reasons for him not to go. Ryan's mother had a cousin who lived in the Boston area, which gave his parents some comfort as she contemplated sending her son off to a new place to go to school.

"Why do you think they invited me to that school?" Ryan asked his parents.

"Because they want you," his mom said. "They think you're hardworking and capable. They're right, aren't they?"

"They want you because they think you're talented and that you have a lot of potential," his dad said with a shrug, as if such things happened every day. Ryan could tell, though, that his father was more impressed than he let on.

"Talented? Ryan?" said Annie, who was more than a little jealous of Ryan just then. "Seriously?"

"Thanks," Ryan said sarcastically. Annie laughed. She was frequently impressed by her own jokes.

Mr. Sandhill visited the Ferrises the following week. He took them out to a Mexican restaurant for dinner. The Ferrises asked a lot of questions. What were the classes like? How heavy was the homework? What sports did people play? How much time off did people get between terms? What did they do for fun? Did the school have a good robotics program?

At this last question, Mr. Sandhill laughed. "Yes, oh yes," he said. "I can quite assure you of that."

Mr. Sandhill made quite the impression on Ryan's parents. It was easy to see why. He was an approachable, friendly person who just made you want to spend time with him. He knew so much, yet was so mild-mannered, humble, and unassuming. Nothing seemed to bother him or bend him out of shape.

"Mom, I can't believe you asked Mr. Sandhill if Seguin had a good robotics program!" Ryan huffed later. "It's only, like, the best place in the universe for it!"

Ryan's dad told him that Mr. Sandhill had invented a great number of things, robotic and otherwise. His father had done a search on Mr. Thomas Sandhill through the U.S. patent office website, and was amazed to find more than five hundred patents on which Mr. Sandhill was a listed inventor. On many, he was *the only* inventor. According to Ryan's father, his inventions spanned a number of fields, such as computer chips, circuit systems, switches, electronics, robotics, and software.

At dinner, when his dad asked about it, Mr. Sandhill casually replied, "Yes, I have invented a few things."

"I'll say you've invented a few things," Ryan's father said. "More than five hundred things."

"Really? Is it that many?" Mr. Sandhill said. "One works on odds and ends as time permits," he said, smiling and chuckling.

"That's a lot of odds and ends," Annie observed. She was more than capable of keeping up with the conversation, and was listening and watching Mr. Sandhill intently.

"If you say so, Annie," Mr. Sandhill said, smiling and giving her an affectionate wink. "I bet you could improve upon most of them."

"Maybe," she said. "But I don't even know what they *are*... yet."

"Ah, but it sounds like you're going to find out," Mr. Sandhill said.

Ryan and his family flew to Boston in the summertime to visit Seguin Academy and drove to the campus in the nearby town of Milton. All of the Tanglewoodians were there as well with members of their families, a source of great comfort to them all. While Mr. Sandhill was a key member of the Seguin faculty hosting the visit, the person who led much of the discussion was the head of school, Catherine Bergeron, who had signed their invitation letters. She had an elegant French accent that Ryan enjoyed listening to.

Inside a stately red brick building with white Greek pillars and colonial windows, Mrs. Bergeron welcomed the group to Seguin. She was tall, had dark blond hair, and was impeccably dressed in a dark maroon suit. Her hair, with a few wisps of grey, was pulled back in a bun and she wore a colorful scarf. Her regal air was somewhat intimidating to Ryan, and she seemed to him alternately cool and warm at times, but overall her demeanor was friendly. Her welcoming remarks were cordial enough, but one of her chillier moments came when she described how hard students worked at Seguin. "Zee students here at Seguin work quite hard," she said. At this, Ryan could almost feel the weight of fifteen heavy books bearing down on his back. Her 'h' in the word 'hard' was so soft as to be silent. "But, zey apply zemselves with great enthusiasm, as you children have done." Ryan didn't like being called a child, but if it would help lighten the workload, maybe he could stomach it.

"She's a marine biologist," Jenny whispered to several of the group as they started the tour. "She's, like, world famous. Have you seen her on the Worldscapes Channel?"

Ryan thought about it for a moment. "Uh, not sure," he whispered. Come to think of it, he had seen a couple of episodes of a program called *Sea Adventures,* which featured a woman with a French accent. *That* woman was Catherine Bergeron? Wow. "Now that you mention it, yeah, I have seen her on television before!" he whispered back. Jenny nodded.

The Seguin campus was truly impressive. The grounds, full of lush, green trees and lawns, were superbly maintained. The buildings were all elegant, with historic looking exteriors, but very modern inside. The gymnasiums were pristine—and enormous. Ryan couldn't wait to play basketball on the courts. At one point, they passed by a building with a nameplate on it that said "Sandhill Science Building." Ryan, along with many in the crowd, shot a glance at Mr. Sandhill. *Had he donated the building?*

Mr. Sandhill, sensing the curiosity of the others, looked at the placard on the building as if for the first time, simply shrugged, and said "Don't look at me. Never heard of him." He winked at Ellen and Ryan when he said it. It was becoming increasingly evident there was a lot more to Mr. Sandhill than met the eye.

The group visited various classrooms, the libraries, student center, cafeteria, computer and science labs, which were in the Sandhill Building, and the theater. Ryan felt deliciously overwhelmed, in the way you feel when you've eaten too much wonderfully tasting food. All that day and those that followed, he imagined attending school at Seguin. It was easy to do, knowing, as he already did, a number of his potential classmates. It seemed to Ryan that the student body was an amazing mix of people and interests. And indeed, the Tanglewoodians themselves were a pretty diverse bunch. He wondered how he would fit in with the broader student population. His mind gyrated with anticipation as he thought about embarking on a new adventure that was at once nerve-wracking and thrilling.

He remembered some of the parting words of Mrs. Bergeron, or Dr. Bergeron, as he heard some of the others call her. "We will push you to work hard to achieve, but really we will challenge you to push yourselves, to see what you are capable of. For real learning takes place when you are working with your colleagues, striving to solve problems, addressing challenges together. That is where the real fun happens. We very much hope we will be seeing you in the middle of August."

That brought Ryan to a critical decision point. Would he choose to attend Seguin Academy? If so, it felt as though it would put his life on a different, incredible path. If not, high school at home would be fine. He would know lots of people. It would be much more familiar, much less mysterious. But if he chose not to attend Seguin, he felt he just might regret it for the rest of his life.

"So, you're going, right?" Carmen wrote him one night.

"I think so… It's kind of scary but… Yes," Ryan wrote back. "Are you?"

"No… Duh… YES, of course, I'm going! It is a little scary, but mostly it's just exciting! See you there."

"Cool! Yeah, see you there!" Ryan wrote in reply.

August arrived in a hurry. Back home in Texas, Ryan had spent weeks slowly packing up his belongings for the trip to Boston. It had been tough telling his friends he was going to school in a faraway place and that he would not see them anywhere nearly as often as he had before. Then again, hopefully he would avoid being beaten up by hulking characters like Chip "Cheater" McCollum just because he liked robots. He and his bot buddies at Highland Park Middle School pledged to stay in touch over email and VideoLink.

Once at Seguin Academy, he could fly home during a long October weekend if he wanted to. There was also an event in October called the Head of the Charles Regatta, which was some kind of boat race involving row boats and crews, his mom told him. Apparently it was a big deal. Even though that was less than eight weeks away, to Ryan it felt like an eternity.

Ryan's dad flew with him to Boston in mid-August to help him get settled at Seguin. On the Seguin campus, they located Sellinger Hall, the dormitory where Ryan would spend the next year. Sellinger was a boys' dormitory, located across a small courtyard from Donnington, a girls' dormitory. Carmen, Ellen, and Jenny would all be living there, Ryan learned. James and Sammy would be living in Sellinger with Ryan. They would all share a suite that had a common area, a small kitchenette, and three bedrooms. The tantalizing possibilities of staying up late—without parents around telling anyone to go to bed—started to dawn on Ryan.

The campus was not yet that busy with students, as only the first year students had arrived. School would start in little more than two weeks, but first years had been asked to arrive early to get an orientation to Seguin. During his first afternoon on campus, Ryan said 'hello' and got a little acquainted with various other boys in his dormitory. All of the students around had a parent or two with them, it seemed, though as they began to get comfortable with being at Seguin, and the excitement of making new friends and the upcoming school year grew, they seemed fairly keen to have their parents depart.

Ryan's father spent the evening at a guest house nearby, and he and Ryan said goodbye the next morning after breakfast. Ryan returned to his room, finished unpacking his bags, and organized most of his things in a dresser and closet in the bedroom. There was also a desk, and he put Scram on top of it. He put a box with extra Scram models and a toolbox in his bedroom closet. At present, the cream white walls of the room looked bare and empty, though not gloomy. Ryan already felt he was missing his mom's sense of decoration, and the room felt very much like a blank page. Outside of a couple of family photographs which he put on his dresser and desk, Ryan pondered how to decorate the otherwise naked room. Scram helped, with his small black eyes peering out of his round, ultra-green eye sockets. Ryan picked up Scram's remote controller and made him climb up on the wall. He parked Scram there for a moment. Scram looked quite amusing situated there against a white background. Yes, the presence of Scram, despite his small size, could fill a fairly large space, Ryan thought.

"As in life, there are some things that will be unpredictable here at Seguin," Mr. Sandhill had said. This morning one such instance of unpredictability was about to be sprung upon Ryan and his Tanglewood friends. After breakfast, students were assembled into groups. Ryan found himself grouped with his friends from Tanglewood. They were asked to return to their dormitories, and then go to the student center with backpacks and necessities for a week's trip, as well as their bots and robotic tool kits.

"What the heck is this all about?" Sammy asked Ryan and James. After all, most everybody had just gotten off an airplane the day before. "Where are we going?"

"Search me," James shrugged.

"I don't know," Ryan said. "But I hope it's fun."

Mr. Sandhill stood expectantly at the student center as everyone arrived with their bags. "Hello friends. I'm sure you're all wondering at this point what we're up to today," Mr. Sandhill said. "As you may have guessed, for your first activity, we're taking a trip."

"Where to?" Jenny asked.

"A number of places," Mr. Sandhill replied. "Dr. Bergeron and I will be your chaperones."

"Call me Catherine, please, Thomas," said Mrs. Bergeron. "And students, you can call me Catherine or Mrs. Bergeron," she said.

Just then, touring buses pulled up in front of the student center. At almost the same time, Brad Lawless and Meagan Rosenkrans strode up to the Tanglewood group with backpacks, dropped them by the side luggage compartment of one of the buses, and approached the group.

"Brad! Meagan! Are you coming with us?" Ellen asked.

"Yeah," Meagan said as they approached the door.

"Awesome!" shouted Carmen, amid other cheers and whistles from the other kids.

"So, is it just us going on this trip?" James asked.

"On this particular trip, yes. But all new students are going on trips, to different places with different faculty members," Mr. Sandhill said. "You will be something of a cohort, if you like, here at Seguin. Your interests, abilities, talents, make you well suited to working as a team on certain projects, as we've already seen, and I expect we'll see a great deal more."

"Huh," Ryan said. He appreciated their shared experience at Tanglewood and interest in animal bots, but wasn't sure he understood what Mr. Sandhill meant by 'certain projects.'

The bus was impressively modern. It had a refrigerator, a microwave oven, and movie screens. Neither Ryan nor his friends had seen anything like it before.

"This is sick," said James. "Do they have soda and chips in here?"

"Healthy foods, dude," said the driver, an older, friendly-looking man named Larry. "Have some fruit or vegetables if you like. I think there may also be some nut bars and rice cakes."

"Oh," James said.

"No, really, you'll enjoy the food," said Larry. "And it's much better for you than so much of the junk that's out there."

"So, on this trip we will have an adventure, or a series of adventures, if you will," Mr. Sandhill said. "Our next stop is… Ohio! We'll make a brief stop at the Rock and Roll Hall of Fame. From there we visit the Wright-Patterson Air Force Base!"

Enthusiastic shouts went up from everyone. Ryan assumed the cheers were for the Rock and Roll Hall of Fame. In terms of fun, the air base was less of a sure thing.

"Um, Mr. Sandhill. What are we going to do at an air force base?" Ellen asked when the noise had quieted down. Evidently Ryan wasn't the only one curious about the air base as a destination.

"Just a guess, but I'd say we're going to fly some things, is that right?" Carmen said, holding up her Harris' hawk bot, which she had named, fittingly enough, Harris.

"Quite likely," Mr. Sandhill replied.

"And so what's with the Rock and Roll Hall of Fame?" Sammy asked.

"You have a certain friend or two who may be there," Mr. Sandhill replied.

"Vape!" screamed Ellen.

"And Rook?" Sammy asked.

"Maybe," said Mr. Sandhill.

"Thomas, you aren't giving it all away at the beginning, are you? Where's the fun in that?" Mrs. Bergeron asked.

They all piled onto the bus and set off. As they drove down the road, Mrs. Bergeron was full of advice about what *not* to do. "Don't stand up without holding onto something… Don't spill food… Don't lean against the window."

At one point, James had turned on music, which, on closer examination, was found to be coming out of the mouth of Slidey, his snake bot. "Don't play that music too loudly," Mrs. Bergeron warned.

"Is there anything we can do?" James asked in exasperation.

"Yes. Do have fun!" exhorted Mrs. Bergeron.

"How the heck are we supposed to do that if we can't do anything?" James retorted.

Then James got an idea. He withdrew towards the back of the bus with Slidey. He summoned the others back with him. You could hear whispers from the front of the bus, but Mrs. Bergeron paid no attention. She was talking with Mr. Sandhill, Brad, and Meagan, and was deep in conversation. A short while later, while Mrs. Bergeron remained absorbed in discussion with Mr. Sandhill, Brad and Meagan observed Slidey slithering over her shoulder. Mrs. Bergeron, however, was so caught up in the conversation she could not be interrupted.

"Uh, Mrs. Bergeron?" Meagan said.

"Not now, Meagan," Mrs. Bergeron said. "So, as I was saying..." she turned again to Mr. Sandhill to finish her important thought.

"Mrs. Bergeron..."

"In a minute, Meagan..."

Brad then intervened. "Mrs. Bergeron, you have a *snake* on your shoulder!"

"Ahhh!" Mrs. Bergeron screamed, jumping up. Why didn't you tell me?" She shook herself and the snake went flying up in the air, landing in the aisle.

"You didn't want to be interrupted," Meagan shrugged. "Don't worry. It's not real, it's a bot."

James and everyone else erupted in laughter. Mrs. Bergeron looked back at the group and said, "I'm glad *someone* on this bus is having fun!"

"We're doing what you told us to do," James laughed.

Shortly thereafter, everyone sent their bot down the aisle of the bus to harass Mrs. Bergeron. Skye, Jenny's dragonfly bot, came next. It buzzed up above Mrs. Bergeron's head, zooming around, finally landing on her hair bun. Mrs. Bergeron flailed about as Skye airlifted off her head and Jenny sent her flying up around the roof of the bus. Next up, Ryan and Ellen sent Scram and Trixie down the aisle.

"All right, all right, enough with the menagerie!" Larry barked from behind the steering wheel. "This is not a zoo. Please store the animals... er, uh, robots... in the overhead compartments or underneath the seats in front of you." He was mimicking the luggage stowage announcement typical of airlines.

Strangely, not long afterwards, Mrs. Bergeron said to James: "Can I play with your robot?"

"Don't do anything dangerous with the robot!" James stammered in jest, wagging his finger at Mrs. Bergeron. Her unchanged blank facial expression told him she did not consider his joke funny. "Uh, just kidding," James muttered. "Here." He handed Slidey to Mrs. Bergeron.

At that point, James and Mr. Sandhill proceeded to show Mrs. Bergeron various aspects of the snake bot, how it worked, how to control it, and so forth. Before long, Mrs. Bergeron was guiding the snake up the aisle of the bus, to the amusement of everyone. Claps and shouts rang out.

"Not bad for a marine biologist, eh?" said Mrs. Bergeron.

"So, uh, Mrs. Bergeron," Larry the driver said, glancing into the rearview mirror. "You're not going to create any problems with that snake, are you?"

"Well it depends on what you mean by problems," Mrs. Bergeron laughed.

The drive to Ohio, while long and monotonous at times, gave the group plenty of time to get to know each other better—and each other's robots.

Sammy showed his bot to Mrs. Bergeron. He had named it Chinny, and even out of water he was able to demonstrate Chinny's swiveling, swimming body and the use of his fins. Mrs. Bergeron was most intrigued. "Very impressive, Sammy. Do you think you could make other, different types of fish and sea creatures? These could come in very handy in my research. All of them could."

"Probably," Sammy shrugged. "What would you like?"

"Let me think," said Mrs. Bergeron. Her eyes widened as she imagined the possibilities of a collection of sea creatures at her disposal. "What wouldn't I like? There are so many great possibilities."

"Uh, building all of them could take a while," Sammy said.

At one point, Mr. Sandhill showed a movie composed of footage from their prior summer at Tanglewood. Everyone cheered and hooted in applause throughout. It brought back fond memories of the work they had done building out the sound repertoires of their bots, the music they created, and the adventures with Vape and Rook. The Blaines and many of the musicians who had visited them at Tanglewood, including Hae Jung Park, were featured as well. While everyone watched and discussed the movie, time flew past.

6

ROCK, TALK... AND SHOCK

The bus pulled into a hotel in Cleveland after dinner that evening. The next morning, they drove to the Rock and Roll Hall of Fame and were given a tour.

Ryan and his friends knew a few of the groups and artists, but did not know many others featured at the museum, or had only a vague sense about them. However, they all became electrified when they came to the exhibit featuring the rock group Voltaic.

The exhibit had a life-sized cutout of the members of the band performing in concert. There Vape stood in the center in a top hat—his signature stage look—and an outrageous bright green, colonial, military-looking tail coat, his outstretched hand holding a microphone stand with a long scarf streaming off it. During the previous summer at Tanglewood everyone had become acquainted with Vape's outlandish attire and by now was quite familiar with it. Around Vape were the other Voltaic band members, including Chet Harmon, Voltaic's lead guitar player, who, with Vape, constituted the heart and soul of the band. Chet's cutout captured him right in the middle of a screaming guitar solo. He had a grimacing face that suggested he was trying to squeeze every ounce of sound from the guitar.

While Ryan and everyone were crowing over the Voltaic exhibit, the members of the actual band strode into the exhibit area. Everyone erupted in boisterous chatter. Ryan observed Meagan blushing when she gave Vape a hug. Brad seemed to notice it as well. Rook was with the band, and he held outstretched arms to the Seguin group.

Voltaic was in town to perform a concert, which they had done the prior evening. They had stuck around to visit the Rock and Roll Hall of Fame to give input into the exhibit everyone was now standing in. "And to see you guys, of course," Vape chortled.

"Hey, do you guys have your bots?" Vape asked.

The group then moved out to the bus and everyone proceeded to give a demonstration of their bots to the Voltaic band members, who were mesmerized by them.

"We have to use these in a video," said Vape.

"Or the stage show," Rook said. "We could film them."

Before too long, Mr. Sandhill sadly informed everyone that the bus had to depart. "We have to move on to our next appointment, which, like this one, you won't want to miss," Mr. Sandhill said. "And the Voltaic tour bus needs to be on its way as well."

Everyone exchanged goodbyes with Voltaic, who promised Mr. Sandhill they would visit Seguin Academy when they were back in Boston, which was where they were from. The Seguin group then departed in the bus for the three hour ride to the air base outside Dayton. The trip went quickly, principally because Voltaic had given them a bunch of the band's music, which they played on the bus stereo at loud volume. They were also brainstorming what they could do with their bots as part of a Voltaic video.

"Even I know some of Voltaic's songs," said Mrs. Bergeron.

"As do I," Mr. Sandhill added. "Can you believe it?"

Later in the bus ride, Mr. Sandhill surprised the group with a stunning revelation. "You might be interested to know," he said, arousing curiosity, "that Walter Vapiano, or 'Vape' as he is often called, is a graduate of Seguin Academy."

"No way!" everyone gaped.

"Yes, and this afternoon we're meeting another successful Seguin graduate. This person was a schoolmate of Walter Vapiano, although he was perhaps one or two years behind him."

"Who's that?" everyone wanted to know.

"Patience. You'll meet him soon enough," Mr. Sandhill said. He winked at Brad and Meagan.

"All right, who is it? What do you guys know about this person?" Ellen said looking pointedly at Brad and Meagan. "You must know. You went so Seguin Academy, too."

"Huh?" said Meagan, with feigned innocence.

"What person?" Brad said, attempting to keep a straight face.

"Never mind," Ellen said, slumping back in her chair.

Everyone knew they were close to Wright-Patterson Air Force

Base—really close—when a huge jet plane flew over the bus so low they could see the faces of the pilots.

"Oh my god!" shouted Jenny as the jet screamed past the bus.

The jet's wheels were down. It had two engines under each wing which extended from the top of the plan's midsection. Each had a fin at its end. The bus reverberated noticeably from the wake of the plane passing overhead. The thunderous noise from the plane was incredible and those who had been sitting quietly were jolted to attention by it.

"That plane was enormous!" Ryan exclaimed.

"*Ginormous!*" Carmen squealed.

"That's a cargo plane," Brad said. "They're designed to carry heavy equipment all over the world."

Within minutes the bus entered the gates of the air force base and proceeded to a terminal area, where it parked. Everyone got off the bus and went into the terminal. There, a tall, energetic man named Jasper Townley greeted them.

"Ask him about his jump shot in basketball," Mr. Sandhill said.

"What? You got a good jumper?" Sammy asked.

"Well, I did hit a three in a college game to win a division final one year," Townley said. "Somebody gave me the nickname 'Jumpshot,' and it stuck. I had to go into the Air Force to get rid of it." While speaking, he was looking over at Mr. Sandhill.

"You gave him the nickname?" James asked.

"Uh, well, uh, no, er, uh, by accident, maybe...?" Mr. Sandhill said sheepishly.

They ate lunch in a base cafeteria. Over lunch, Townley explained that he had been a forward on the Weatherall University basketball team. He told the story of how the team went to its divisional final game, and was losing by two points with three seconds left in the game, when he took an inbound pass and put up a three-point shot that went in at the buzzer to give Weatherall the victory.

"Did you think about going pro?" Ryan asked.

"Eh, a little bit," Townley said. "But Weatherall's not exactly known for turning out pro athletes. There have been a couple here and there. I probably wouldn't have had a long career, and would have sat on the bench a lot of the time. I do love basketball, and I play on a team here at the base. But for my career, well, once I got behind the wheel of an airplane, there was nothin' else I wanted to from that point on. Still don't. I love to fly, and I've been all around the world doing it."

Mr. Sandhill explained that he had been introduced to Townley by a former student who had become a professor in Los Angeles. "So one day I'm visiting my friend in the aeronautical engineering department at UCLA, and there's this kid at the door, holding a basketball," Mr. Sandhill recalled. "And after realizing he wasn't there looking for players for a pickup game, we—or I should say, he—started talking about the science of flight. Well, it wasn't long before I figured out that this young man needed to come to Seguin Academy."

"And life has never been the same since," Townley said, smiling at Mr. Sandhill.

After lunch, Townley escorted them into an amphitheater. "You may be wondering what we're doing here today," he said. "In addition to talking a little bit about flight, and things that fly, which is my line of work, we're going to talk about some of the stuff you guys are working on—robotics, automated machines, animal bots—which I understand from Mr. S and Mrs. B is your gig, or at least, one of them. To start off, we're going to watch a brief movie about one of my favorite topics—flight."

As the lights dimmed, curtains across the stage at the front of the amphitheater pulled away to reveal a huge movie screen. The movie covered a brief history of early flight, starting with kite flying in China more than two thousand years ago. It then described the fifteenth century flying machine designs of Leonardo da Vinci; the hot air balloons of the seventeenth and eighteenth centuries; and the aviation work of the Wright brothers and their famous flights at Kitty Hawk, North Carolina in 1903. It showed vignettes of other historic figures in the history of flight before moving to modern day flight. There were segments on fighter jets, small aircraft, helicopters, seaplanes, commercial planes, and jumbo aircraft. The film then turned to space travel, rockets, manned travels to the moon, and the space shuttle.

The film revealed Captain Jasper "Jumpshot" Townley to be hotshot as a pilot. He was shown in the movie flying several different aircraft. In one clip, from an airshow, a jet he was flying rolled over completely in one direction, and then rolled over in the opposite direction. In another clip—"That's him again!" several people shouted—his plane appeared to literally be falling out of the sky and then it shot out of its fall, rolling over several times and pitching skyward once again.

Incredibly, the last segments of the film showed Carmen's hawk bot, Harris, and Jenny's dragonfly bot, Skye, both in their respective forms of flight. Everyone buzzed with excitement at the realization of what they were now watching. The film segments had been taken at Tanglewood the previous summer. Harris soared majestically high up in the air, his wings spread wide, with the Berkshire mountain forest trees swaying in the breeze below him. Skye flew above a pond and momentarily landed on a lily pad, with her veined pairs of wings shimmering in the sun. Then she took off again in the air, with another dragonfly, perhaps a suitor, following her.

The narrator of the film ended with a parting comment: "We've learned so much about flight. Yet, there is still so much to learn. Where will flight take you in the future?"

After the movie, the group went outside and conversed with Townley. Everyone gave him a demonstration of their bot. Despite his professed love of flying, he was appreciative of every bot, whether it flew or not. Other people from the base started to gather around to watch what appeared to be trained animals doing stunts and tricks for an audience.

When it came time for Sammy to show Chinny, his salmon bot, to Townley, they walked to a pond across the road from the air base. Sammy demonstrated Chinny's moves, showing how he could jump out of the water, dive, and swim in a straight line while flipping his tail side to side. Jumpshot looked up from the pond and said, "Very impressive. Do you think you could launch this thing out of the water and into the air? Do you think we can make it fly?"

"I don't know, Sammy said. "I mean, salmon don't fly, really. I never really thought about it, though."

"You think salmon don't fly? Are you sure?" Townley asked. "Think about it. Towards the end of their lives they have to climb the waterfalls, traveling back up the freshwater streams they came from when they were born, where they go to fertilize their eggs after living in the ocean. They literally fly up those waterfalls, don't they? That's when all the bears are standing around for them, in the waterfalls, trying to grab 'em with their jaws out of the air, isn't it?"

"Uh, yeah, sure," Sammy acknowledged.

"I bet you'd do some fancy flyin', too, if somebody were trying to take a big bite out of your backside," Townley laughed.

"See? And you thought salmon didn't fly," said Mrs. Bergeron, laughing with Sammy.

Townley pulled Sammy aside to talk with him, evidently about some ideas for making a fish fly. Meanwhile, the people from the air base who had gathered to see Ryan and his friends demonstrate their bots had all kinds of questions: Could a bot clamp onto a fast moving object, like a car or an airplane? Could a bot tunnel into the ground? Could it interact with, or command other animals? Could it transmit light waves and radio waves? Could you attach hidden wheels to a bot so that it could speed over land if it needed to? Ryan was amazed by all of their questions, many of which he had never thought about before.

That night they slept in barracks at the air base. While others talked in their beds that night, Sammy spent time sitting on the floor with his tool box, tinkering intently with a model of Chinny.

"What are you doing?" James asked him.

"You'll see," Sammy replied.

In the morning, after breakfast, the group drove in the bus to a remote part of the airbase that was no longer used for plane take-offs and landings. It bordered a forest off in the distance. Sammy presented Townley with the modified edition of Chinny The Chinny bot didn't look much different to Ryan, and he wondered what Sammy had done to him. "I think we've got the right hooks attached to it now like we talked about, so you can attach a payload to it," Sammy said.

"Payload?" Ellen asked.

"Charge," Sammy said.

"What, like an electric charge?" Ellen said.

"No. As in, an explosive charge," Townley said.

"Seriously?" Jenny asked.

"Yeah. See that makeshift barn down there?" Townley pointed way off in the distance to a small shack-like building, perhaps a couple of miles away.

"Yes," Ellen said.

"I set it up for the drill we're gonna do. Keep your eye on it."

Townley went into a nearby building and soon came out carrying a small, greyish-white, tube-shaped object. It was mostly covered by his hand. It looked like a pellet to Ryan. Or, perhaps like a tube that might be used to hold a roll of paper. Townley took Chinny and pulled out a series of small hooks that Sammy had installed into Chinny the night before. To these he attached the pellet. Looking at Chinny from above, one could not see the pellet underneath him.

Then, at Townley's request, Sammy placed Chinny into a small pond—it was more like a large puddle—that sat to one side of the tarmac where they stood. Sammy started working the control console for

Chinny and handed it to Townley. They could see Chinny swimming around in the clear water of the pond, his body wriggling side-to-side, just like a typical salmon. Then, in a split second, as Townley worked a control stick, Chinny flew straight out of the water and rocketed over it at low altitude, with a thin, fine trail of smoke streaming behind. Chinny then rose slightly, tracing the gently sloping terrain of the ground.

"His butt's on fire," Jenny said. She was observing the flame blazing from the underside of Chinny that was propelling him through the air at spectacular speed.

"Just watch," Townley said.

In a moment, now at a distance of about two miles, Chinny flew straight into the fake barn Townley had set up as a target, which resulted in a terrifically huge explosion. Splintered boards and wood panels went flying in all directions. The barn was obliterated, and there was merely a rising cloud of smoke where it had stood.

"Anybody want some plank roasted salmon?" Townley asked, looking pleased with himself. "Or how about some salmon chopped salad?"

He looked over at Mrs. Bergeron. "Catherine, how's that for some marine biology?" he asked.

"Like nothing I've ever seen before," Mrs. Bergeron said. She looked shocked, though Ryan did think her facial expression belied the slightest hint of pride.

"Wow! That was awesome!" Ryan blurted out, as if talking only to himself. Shouts and remarks arose from his friends as well. They were stunned by what they had just witnessed.

"What happened to Chinny?" Ellen asked.

"It's one of my older models," Sammy said, allaying her concern that a recent model had just been vaporized. "At least, it used to be."

Looking at Mr. Sandhill and Mrs. Bergeron, Townley said, "Admit it. You're impressed."

"You always were one of our better students," Mr. Sandhill said.

"Thankfully, with only a few pyrotechnical urges to control at times," Mrs. Bergeron added.

"Fortunately, they never let me outta this place, at least not often," Townley said, laughing, referring to the air base. "So nobody gets hurt."

He then turned to Ryan and his friends. "But seriously, safety is one of my biggest concerns," he added. "And when it comes to navigating and piloting planes and things like that, even bots, let's just say I'm pretty good."

They all stood and stared at Townley. No one doubted him.

Next, they took a ride in the cargo jet they had seen landing as they approached the air base the day before. Prior to taking a brief flight, they had a tour of the aircraft. It was cavernous. Most of it was empty space. "It's for carrying large vehicles and other types of equipment," Townley said. "This plane can carry helicopters, land rovers, bridges, you name it."

The flight was amazing. Ryan could feel the enormous thrust of the engines as the plane lifted off. "Wow, there's a lot of power in this thing," he said.

"You bet there is," Townley said. "Heck, with this thing empty, it practically leaps off the runway. I almost can't control the thing right now. It's so light! Just kidding! They're usually loaded with tons of stuff when I fly 'em."

After their short flight, they flew back to the base and had lunch. During the afternoon, they worked on mounting small rockets to bot frames, courtesy of Mr. Sandhill's robotics lab at Weatherall University. And then, they did some more target practice, with results similarly explosive to what they had seen earlier. It occurred to Ryan that working on bots with a guy like Townley was a good reason to have lots of extra bot kits around.

"I don't know," Ellen said, after they had finished blowing up several more mock building structures. "I realize our bots have the ability to go into an area and be perceived as just an animal. But, here we're arming them with a seriously explosive weapon, and that isn't exactly what I had in mind for Trixie," she said of her fox bot.

"I hear you, loud and clear, Ellen," Townley replied. "And there will be many, many uses for bots like these. There will be needs for them to help with space travel, medicine, transporting stuff, protecting us, geological exploration, manufacturing and assembly, search and rescue, research, security, learning about animal species. There will be a million uses for your bots."

"You left out marine biology," Catherine Bergeron interjected.

"It was inferred in several of the things I just mentioned," Townley smiled, "but okay, marine biology." Catherine Bergeron returned the smile.

"And I think you guys are going to explore a bunch of different uses for your bots while you're on this trip, isn't that right, Thomas?"

Mr. Sandhill nodded.

"But let's also understand something. There is evil in this world. Not everybody wants to be our friend. Some people feel they have no hope;

some want to bend the world to their will; and some just want to tear others down. So, they become committed to doing bad things to others—and to us. That becomes their motivating force. And, as much as we'd like to ignore it, it is there. At some point, you have to deal with it."

Ryan had listened, transfixed to Jumpshot's comments. There were those words again: *Not everybody wants to be your friend.* Ryan immediately recalled what Mr. Willoughby, his middle school principal, had said to him about Cheater McCollum, the boy who had bullied him in Texas. *And at some point, you have to deal with it...*

7

LEARNING TO FLY

The bus departed early the next morning for Chicago. It wound out of the air force base onto an interstate highway, across central Indiana towards Indianapolis. From there, it headed northwest towards the "Windy City," as Sammy called it—his hometown.

"So, where are we going in Chicago?" James asked Mr. Sandhill.

"You'll find out. In good time," Mr. Sandhill said.

"I should know not to ask Mr. Sandhill straight forward questions," James sighed, sitting back in his seat.

"Hopefully, we'll get some deep dish pizza out of the deal," Ellen said hopefully.

Ryan, Carmen, and Ellen fell to talking about flight and how Carmen had learned to make Harris, her hawk bot, fly. She showed them the controller she used to navigate Harris. She pointed out which buttons and switches she used to make him soar, then descend back down to the ground, flap his wings rapidly, and also glide on the wind.

Ryan noticed there was a button called "Dive-Bomb" on the control stick. "So, the 'Dive-Bomb' button is obviously for dive bombing, huh? Cool."

"Yeah," said Carmen. "But it's a bit tough for him to catch anything in a dive-bomb, because right now it's entirely based on my visual read of where the target is."

"But you'd be able to dive-bomb Chinny, wouldn't you? If he were close to the surface of the water?" Ellen asked, pointing with her eyes over at Sammy's salmon bot.

"Probably, if he were close to the surface of the water," Carmen said. "The deeper something is, the harder it would be, because I have to eyeball it to move Harris' talons. They're pretty strong and they grip well. But I could be more accurate if I had a honing mechanism built into him."

"Something tells me Mr. Sandhill might be able to help with that," Ryan said.

"Yeah, Brad and Meagan probably can help too," Ellen suggested.

Meagan, who had overheard the conversation, looked over at Ellen and winked.

Everyone's excitement grew as the rolling farmlands and prairies of northern Indiana gave way to increasingly suburban terrain and ultimately, the city of Chicago. Shortly after lunchtime, the bus arrived at its next destination, the Shedd Aquarium. The aquarium sat at the edge of Lake Michigan. As they approached, Ryan could see a blue expanse of the lake that went on for miles and disappeared on the horizon. At the Shedd, everyone hopped off the bus and took a few minutes to stretch their arms and legs. Sammy's parents had come to meet the group and welcome everyone to their hometown. They hugged Sammy, who was clearly embarrassed, smiled from ear to ear, and enthusiastically shook hands with everyone. A few minutes later the group was led into a spacious auditorium. They were asked to bring their bots with them. Several staff members from the Shedd came into the auditorium and joined the group.

Mrs. Bergeron strode to the front of the auditorium in an elegant, slightly intimidating manner that Ryan had come to associate with her. "So, people," she said, as if she were actually *not* one of the people, "this afternoon, we are going to have a tour… and a very exciting one at that… of the Shedd Aquarium, led by someone with expertise in marine biology."

"Cool! Who's that?" Ryan barked out.

"Why, me, of course! Who did you think?" Mrs. Bergeron said, looking at him in feigned surprise. Everyone laughed. Mrs. Bergeron winked at him.

"I don't know, maybe one of the two hundred staff people milling around here?" Ryan quipped. But he immediately thought better of his remark. "Uh, sorry, dumb question," he said, slouching down in his chair.

"And who do you suppose has helped teach them about marine life?" Mrs. Bergeron asked.

"Uh, you?" Ryan said.

"He's quick," Mrs. Bergeron said, looking at Mr. Sandhill. Ryan could hear muted laughter of the people around him.

"Sometimes a little *too* quick," Mr. Sandhill smiled.

"But, before our tour, we will see a movie that I hope you'll enjoy," Mrs. Bergeron said to the audience.

The movie showed many different scenes of marine life and how people were developing new tools, robotic and otherwise, to explore oceans, lakes, and rivers. Human piloted vehicles were featured exploring deep underwater areas of the ocean as well as shipwrecks and undersea caves. Other parts of the film showed a robot based on marine creatures. Various scenes showed bots based on a lobster, a lamprey eel, an octopus, a sea turtle, a dolphin, and a water spider. These bots—all in various stages of experimental testing—were doing things like cleaning the ocean floor, helping to map and explore deep, dark undersea areas, picking things up, and interacting with other sea creatures.

The water spider elicited a lot of "oohs" and "aahs" from the group because it was so small. Everyone was deeply impressed that all of the circuitry and components that made it move and navigate could be made so small as to fit inside its tiny body.

"I could do that," Jenny whispered to Meagan and Ryan, who were sitting next to her.

"You're not competitive or anything, are you?" Meagan teased.

"She could," Ryan whispered. "I probably could, too."

"Well, you guys *have* worked on smaller bots," Meagan acknowledged.

A few moments later, Ryan felt fingers crawling on his back, mimicking the water spider on the screen. He immediately looked over at Jenny. "What are you doing to me?" he asked.

"What are you doing to *me?*" she shot back.

They then both looked at Meagan, whose feigned naïve look belied a guilty smirk. "Aha! You're the water spider!" Jenny whispered.

Another scene from the movie showed algae being grown at Wright-Patterson Air Force base that researchers were trying to convert into jet fuel. Jasper Townley was actually in one of the scenes. "Townley!" everybody yelled out upon seeing him.

After the movie, men and women of the staff of the Shedd assembled at the front of the auditorium behind Mrs. Bergeron. "Now the tour begins," Mrs. Bergeron said. "My friends are here to answer any questions you may have. I want you to pay particular attention to the different ways in which the animals move—how they propel themselves through the water. Mr. Sandhill and I would like to hear what you learned after our tour."

For the next several hours, they watched hundreds of different aquatic creatures in a dizzying number of aquariums. They observed a trio of Pacific white-sided dolphins in an enormous tank, jumping high up out of the water, somersaulting in midair, and then diving back into the water with a punctuating splash. Once they hit the water, they plunged deep down in the tank where they generated tremendous momentum by whipping their tails up and down, propelling themselves back up to the surface and up and out of the water again in powerful, surging jumps. The tank had a winding walkway around it, such that you could observe the dolphins both above and below the water.

They wandered through an Amazon River exhibit, where they saw piranhas, anacondas, rays, and crocodiles. There were displays of churning river channels, still lakes, and flooded treetops. They saw tetras, river turtles, and tambaqui—fruit eating fish. Exhibits showed how the region's animals, plants and people adapt to the Amazon River's dramatic annual rise and fall. There was a caiman sitting in the water, which looked like a small alligator. It was the closest to anything they'd seen so far that looked like Scram, a notion not lost on Carmen.

"Hey, Ryan, that caiman looks a little like Scram, except it's like, eight times bigger," Carmen observed, moving her eyes from Scram to the caiman.

"Yeah," Ryan agreed. "But I bet Scram can outrun the caiman." He started moving Scram's legs with his hands as if to simulate running.

"Sure. He has to be quick," Carmen concurred. "Like you've said, Scram has all kinds of fast-moving predators trying to make him lunch." One of the Shedd guides, a young woman who had been walking with Ryan and Carmen through the Amazon exhibit, laughed.

A while later they passed through exhibits featuring the earth's Polar regions, a Pacific Northwest coastal ecosystem, and the waters of the world, consisting of rivers, lakes, streams, tide pools, estuaries. In the South Polar Region gallery, they all tried on a person-sized penguin suit to feel what it would be like to be a penguin.

"Quite wobbly, for me," Sammy said.

"I had it down," Jenny said. "I'd make a perfect penguin."

"Well, we can't all be perfect," said Ellen. Jenny gave her a glaring stare.

"Easy, girls," Meagan said.

The group then proceeded to a Caribbean reef exhibit. They eyed multitudes of tropical fish weaving in and on out of spindly coral branches—and each other. Sea turtles glided effortlessly through the water on the propulsion of their flippers. Rays and sharks similarly sailed through the water with seemingly little exertion. The head of a yellow moray eel peered out from a junction of rock and coral. It then swam out of its hiding place, undulating like a yellow ribbon blowing in the wind and cruised to another place in the reef. It disappeared as quickly as it had emerged.

Sammy, like everyone else, found his head dizzy from the sensory overload of all the different animals they watched and discussed intensely throughout the tour. He was feeling stir crazy, so he decided to have some fun.

Standing at the top of the giant aquarium, while no one was looking, he slipped Chinny into the water. He then secretly withdrew his controller and started navigating Chinny around the reef. He quickly found it was much easier to steer him from the side of the aquarium where he could actually see Chinny as opposed to the top, so he darted down the steps to where he had a good view of the him, as well as the reef, and all of the aquarium's other inhabitants.

There were several black tip reef sharks milling around the aquarium. They seemed to take little notice of Chinny, as if he were just another fish. A bonnethead shark, a smaller version of the hammerhead shark, swam past Chinny as well, its mallet-like head sidling from side to side as part of its strange swimming motion. Sammy was feeling rather pleased with himself. Chinny, swimming along with powerful, fluid strokes of his tail, had become the newest adopted member of the Caribbean Reef club at the Shedd. Sammy's euphoria, however, was to prove short-lived.

"Hey, wait a second. What the—" exclaimed one of the Shedd guides as he observed a Chinook salmon swimming around in the aquarium. There aren't any *salmon* in a coral reef! What the heck is *that thing* doing in there?"

"Hey, what's that?" James shouted, now seeing Chinny and pointing at him inside the tank. "It's Chinny!" he blurted out.

"That thing belongs to you?" the guide asked James.

"No, not me. Chinny belongs to Sammy, er, uh, whoops—" James said. He realized, too late, that he had just given Sammy away.

"That thing's *yours?*" the guide said, gazing at Sammy. He didn't seem to know exactly what was going on, but by now he had certainly taken notice of Sammy working a remote control unit and staring at the unusual fish inside the aquarium.

"Uh, sort of," Sammy said nervously, aware that he was now the object of attention.

By now Ryan and his classmates from Seguin Academy were all pressed up against the glass of the aquarium, fixated on Chinny, chattering away, wondering if he would be viewed as an imposter. It would have been one thing for Chinny to be swimming in the Lake Michigan or Pacific Northwest galleries, where one would expect to see a Chinook salmon, but for him to be here in the Caribbean reef setting was a different matter entirely.

Sammy was looking on, admiring his handiwork, unsure of how to deal with the youthful Shedd guide who had strode over towards him. He soon felt the presence of someone else standing close behind him. He pulled his hand off the controller for a moment and gazed back slowly to find the intimidating gaze of Mrs. Bergeron bearing down on him like a ton of bricks.

"So, Mr. Chatterjee, it's rather unusual to find a salmon swimming in the Caribbean Sea, wouldn't you say?"

"Uh, yes, yes it is, Mrs. Bergeron."

"Well, since it is highly unusual, and since I don't think that the salmon we see in the tank got in there by himself, perhaps you could help out the staff here and *get him out of the tank?*" she remarked. Mrs. Bergeron had conjured up a disapproving scowl on her face. However, Sammy and the others couldn't help but notice she seemed modestly impressed at the same time.

Sammy's mother and father, drawn like everyone else by the commotion around one side of the tank, looked on disapprovingly at Sammy.

"You're grounded," Sammy's father said.

"Okay, whatever that means," Sammy said. "I'm living fifteen hundred miles away from you now, remember?"

"Uh, right," his father said. "Well, you're still grounded. You can make sure he is grounded, right?" Sammy's dad said to Mr. Sandhill.

"Oh, we have our ways of keeping tabs on people," Mr. Sandhill said.

"Sameer, we will address this situation upon our return to Boston," Mrs. Bergeron said sternly to him with a hawkish stare. Sammy looked around sheepishly and shrugged.

"Sometimes you just have to take a leap," he said. He was pretty sure he wasn't going to like what Mrs. Bergeron had in mind for him, but he appreciated her not making a complete spectacle of him in front of his parents and new schoolmates.

"True. But you should be mindful and demonstrate good manners when you are the guest of someone else in their place," Mrs. Bergeron retorted.

Sammy's parents were looking at him as if their eyes were daggers.

For dinner, the group dined at an Italian restaurant where most people gorged themselves on deep-dish pizza. Ryan could not believe how wonderful it tasted. A hot blend of flavors of cheeses, tangy tomato sauce, pepperoni, and vegetables all exploded in his mouth.

"Have you ever had pizza this good before?" he asked to the group rhetorically.

"With the possible exception of Italy, no, I have not," Mr. Sandhill replied.

"I am partial to French pizza, but this is delightful," Mrs. Bergeron remarked.

"French pizza?" Jenny asked. Nobody else said anything. Mrs. Bergeron gave Jenny a mock stern look.

"I can confirm that French pizza, like Italian pizza, is quite delicious," Mr. Sandhill said.

The following day, the group visited the Sears Tower. It was a clear day, so from the top, one could see for miles. In the afternoon, after gorging themselves on more deep dish pizza at the insistence of James, Ellen, and Carmen, they drove in the bus to the nearby town of Oak Park. Here they toured some homes and buildings designed by the famous architect Frank Lloyd Wright. They talked about architectural design and the flow of the buildings they visited.

"Obviously these are entirely different structures from the design of robots," Mr. Sandhill noted. "But, they mesh with their environments, and their forms very much align with the function of the place. Just as your bots must function in certain ways while looking like the animals you envisioned them to be."

The next day, the group departed Chicago, and headed west. Their next destination was Yellowstone National Park.

"As in, Wyoming?" Ellen asked.

"Uh, yes, Wyoming," Mr. Sandhill nodded.

"This is going to take forever," Jenny sighed.

"Where are my ear phones?" James mused. He assumed he would have hours to listen to music.

But, Mrs. Bergeron had other ideas. A young man—a graduate of Seguin Academy and now a graduate student at Weatherall University—joined them in Chicago. "I'll be riding to Wyoming and Nevada with you," the youngish man said, smiling.

"Nevada?" Ryan gasped.

"Where aren't we going on this trip?" Carmen asked.

"We should have loaded up on more deep dish pizza in Chicago," Sammy mused. He was only half joking.

They learned that the Weatherall graduate student joining them on this leg of the journey was named Carey Kaiser. He told them he was doing research work in global positioning systems, remote mounted cameras, and targeting at Weatherall University. Mr. Sandhill was one of his graduate advisors.

"I help figure out how to move objects and for those objects to 'see' where they are, and for us to see those objects as well, even if we're not with them," Carey explained.

"So, even if the object is flying?" Carmen asked.

"*Especially* if the object is flying," Carey said. "Speaking of which, I think we're going to have some fun with your hawk on this trip. Harris, right? That's the hawk's name, isn't it?"

"Yeah," said Carmen. She began eyeing Carey suspiciously. "But Harris is most familiar with my piloting him. Most people probably couldn't figure it out that easily."

"Of course," said Carey. "That's why you're his pilot. But, I can probably help you get Harris to do some things you'd like to see him do."

"Like what?"

"Oh, fly across the country. Fly in and out of tunnels. Fly while you're piloting him from the other side of the world."

"What?" Carmen said. She looked skeptically at Carey.

"Yeah, you know, fly places he was meant to go."

"Seriously?" Carmen said. She felt Carey was teasing her.

"Is the sky blue? With a couple of light weight boosters, we could probably make him fly at a couple of hundred miles per hour. That would obviously be for unique situations."

Carmen thought for a moment. "I'd never thought of that before," she said.

"Why would you?" Carey shrugged. "He's a hawk. But he could be more than a hawk, if you wanted him to be…"

The bus rolled out of the city towards the western Illinois prairie and on to Iowa. Ryan had never seen so many corn fields in all his life. The corn harvest was approaching, but had not yet begun in earnest, so endlessly sprawling corn rows stood tall as if worshipping the sun, their leafy stalks and green enveloping ears tinged with gold. And, while the prospect of driving for hours through cornfields was about the dullest thing Ryan and his friends could imagine doing, they would spend precious little time staring out the windows.

Carey told everyone their bots were about to get some major upgrades. "By the time we get off this bus in Wyoming, your bots will have a built in global positioning system, a small camera mounted inside them, and a targeting system built in. You'll each build a new console with which to control your bots with these new features, courtesy of the GPS and Media Labs at Weatherall University. Heck, we might even figure out how to mount small engines on them for superfast flight, but that's a bonus if we get to it."

"How are you going to do all of this?" Sammy asked.

"I'm not going to do all of this. You are!" Carey exclaimed.

"This seems like a ton of work," Jenny sighed.

"Which is why we need to get started," Carey said. "Come on. Brad and Meagan will help us."

And, they proceeded to work all that day and most of the next, and the miles sped by quickly. In fact, what might have seemed rather boring—views of miles upon miles of flat farmland—became a peaceful, welcome break from the intense work of building new instruments and capabilities into their bots.

From racks at the back of the bus, Carey produced trays and small toolboxes that he handed out to the Seguin students. Screwdrivers, soldering irons, small pliers, computer chips and wires were the tools of choice in performing the painstaking work. Along with Carey, Brad and Meagan seemed to know a lot about the devices and how to install them, and while they gave lots of guidance, they let everyone do the actual work on their own bot.

For Jenny, the work was particularly painstaking. Carey had produced a special microscope for her to use to work on Skye. Given that Skye could fit neatly into the palm of your hand, the pieces she would be adding to Skye had to be especially small and lightweight. She was using tweezers to manipulate various pieces and parts. "We had to invent new technology to make the parts that small," Carey declared proudly. "We even filed patents on it."

The overnight hotel stay somewhere in Nebraska was a needed reprieve from the intense work of installing, testing, tweaking, and testing again the compact pieces of equipment they were building into their bots.

On the afternoon of the second day, Ryan noticed the prairies becoming mountainous, followed by a long stretch of prairie interspersed with rolling hills. In the mid-afternoon, they followed the highway around a big right hand turn and proceeded north to Jackson, the small western town nestled among the Wyoming, Teton, and Wind River Ranges of the Rocky Mountains. By this time, night was descending, and the orange halo of the sun was partially beyond the Wyoming Mountain range. The sun's gorgeous orange and pink glow gave the silhouette of the mountains a rich, purple-blue hue.

Having been cramped up in the bus for most of the day, and using their brains, but not so much their bodies, everyone stretched out when they climbed off the bus in the parking lot of their hotel. Mr. Sandhill and Mrs. Bergeron went to check the group in at the hotel's front desk. Everyone else remained outside. Off in the distance, aided by nearby hotel lights amid the evening darkness, Ellen spotted a raccoon climbing out of a dumpster and decided to have some fun. She took Trixie over to the dumpster and moved the bot into the proximity of the raccoon. Trixie, now live, gave a grunt in the direction of the raccoon.

This immediately caught the attention of the raccoon, and as it clambered down from the dumpster, it hissed and bore its teeth at Trixie, who stood some yards away. Trixie took another playful step in the direction of the raccoon.

"Uh oh, bad move," Jenny said.

The raccoon hissed even more angrily at Trixie, turned quickly, and scampered off into some brush at the edge of the parking lot.

"What is going on over here?" Mrs. Bergeron asked, as she strode over from the hotel.

"I was just trying to see if Trixie could make friends with a raccoon," Ellen said in jest.

"Really? Foxes eat raccoons," Mrs. Bergeron said tersely, but not unkindly. She hadn't picked up on Ellen's humor.

Not everybody wants to be your friend, Ryan thought to himself.

"I know," Ellen said giggling. "I was just seeing how they would interact."

Everyone meandered across the parking lot towards the hotel with their bags and bots in hand. "It's pretty cool that the raccoon thought Trixie was a fox," Ellen said to Jenny and Carmen as they headed off to bed. She was proud of her ability to maneuver Trixie and make her behave convincingly.

"She totally looks and acts like a fox. What did you think the raccoon would make her out to be—an elephant?" Jenny said. She was trying to make a compliment, even though she sometimes had a backhanded way of giving them.

They arose the next morning and proceeded to drive north, through the Teton National Park to Yellowstone National Park. As they drove, they stared in awe at the Teton Mountains that jutted up out of the ground off the left hand side of the bus, their snow-white peaks glistening gold in the sunlight.

"Teton Mountain Range, nine o'clock," Larry, the bus driver announced. "It doesn't get much better than that."

They entered Yellowstone National Park and proceeded to the north side of Yellowstone Lake. Here, they would stay for two days in cabins, studying the wildlife of the park. Having taken in the scenery on the drive, everyone was wide awake and eager to have an adventure.

While carrying her bag to the cabin, Carmen observed a large, round brownish clump of dirt and grass sitting in the path. "What the heck is that?" she asked.

"Beats me," James said. "Looks like a cow patty."

"A what?" said Jenny.

"That, my friends, is a buffalo turd," Carey announced.

"Is that a technical term?" Mr. Sandhill asked Carey in jest.

"Eeooohh," Ellen exclaimed.

"What's the matter? You have a dog. Haven't you ever seen dog poop before?" James said.

"It's not that big," Ellen said. "And dog poop usually gets picked up, at least by responsible dog owners."

"Well, they don't pick up buffalo turds because if they did, it would take all day," Carey said. "They're everywhere."

"They are?" Jenny asked.

"Sure. The buffalo run this place," Brad said.

For the next two days, they explored different parts of Yellowstone, rising early to view much of the wildlife that was out in the waning hours of darkness. For their part, the buffalo were still asleep in the early morning. But foxes, wolves, bears, moose, elk, and deer, among other creatures, were not.

"They just lie down wherever," Meagan observed of the buffalo, after she had tiptoed safely around a sleeping buffalo that lay in the path from the cabin to the parking lot. They all gave the sleeping buffalo a wide girth as they crept by. It seemed obvious that one did not want to suddenly arouse a sleeping buffalo from its slumber.

They drove to various hot springs, with their acrid, sulfuric odor, and explored them. It was remarkable to watch the buffalo standing right among the springs in some places. "What's up with that?" Carmen asked.

"Buffalo spa," Mrs. Bergeron remarked.

The springs were not the only places the buffalo communed. They could be seen in herds dotting rolling hills and mountainsides, meandering down to the water's edge for a drink, or a swim. Occasionally, a few of the graceful beasts could be seen rolling around in the dirt with each other, in their own version of rough-housing.

One of the more memorable stops on their tour of Yellowstone came at the Lower Falls of the Yellowstone River. The group hiked from the road down a winding trail with dozens of switchbacks to the river's edge, where speech was barely audible above the thunderous, rumbling churn of a huge set of waterfalls, plunging several hundred feet—seemingly into air. A rising layer of mist obscured the bottom, so that by the time one could see the river down below, it emerged miles downstream.

At the bottom of the hiking trail, as they stood on a platform beside the falls, Mr. Sandhill surprised everyone, but Carmen most, when he looked at her and said. "Carmen, what do you think? Should we let Harris fly?"

"What?"

"Shall we throw him out over the waterfall down there and see what he can do?"

"Are you crazy?" Carmen stammered. "I'll lose him. I... I won't be able to see him. He'll land in the water and plunge to the bottom of the falls."

"You think so?" Mr. Sandhill asked.

"I know so!" Carmen retorted. She had raised her voice to be heard over the loud rushing sound of tons of water hurtling over the falls.

"You don't think he'll soar?" Carey asked.

"You think he will?" Carmen asked.

"I know he will," Carey said. "Or rather, I know he can. But what's most important is that *you* believe he can do it. Like you said, you're his pilot. So if you don't believe it, then I don't believe it either." Carey paused for a moment, and his comment hung in the air.

Carmen's shoulders had tensed during the conversation. Her taut lips covered clenched teeth. She thought hard about what Carey was saying as she looked at him and then scanned across her friends to Mr. Sandhill and Mrs. Bergeron. She thought about how it would look if she didn't want to let Harris fly. She would be letting everyone down. She took a long deep breath, relaxed her shoulders, and said to Carey, "Harris can do this. But, if anything happens to him, you are going to build me five more, propeller-head."

Carey thought for a moment, and then said, "Deal."

The next few seconds felt like an eternity to Ryan. Carmen held Harris up at the edge of the stone precipice and listened to the water thundering past down below. She placed Harris on the wire fence that corralled them above the river. Harris looked about, turning his head vigilantly as a hawk would. Carmen then pushed a button on the remote controller she held in her hands. Harris flapped his wings and soared up, out, and over the river. He caught an updraft just before hitting a downdraft, which made him dive out over the falls, disappearing into the mist. One might have assumed he had done just as Carmen had predicted—fallen into the water and plunged with it to the rocks down below. But, the way Carmen stared intently at the screen on the remote controller, still maneuvering it, they knew this was not the case. On the remote video screen, Ryan could see water and land far below, the image transmitted by the camera now implanted behind Harris' eye. Carmen guided Harris into a series of wide, arcing circles down the canyon, settling into a glide above the river, which lay some three hundred feet below them.

"It's like flying a kite, except a thousand times cooler," Ryan muttered under his breath.

8

CREATURE COMFORTS

"It's like flying a plane by remote," Ellen observed. Watching a hawk soaring above the river off in the distance was hardly an unusual scene in Yellowstone, but the realization that this one was being piloted by one of their own was remarkable to the kids from Seguin.

Before they departed Yellowstone, all of the Seguin students accomplished something improbable with their animal bot. On their first afternoon in Wyoming, the group took a rafting trip down the Yellowstone River. At a big stretch of thundering, dancing whitewater, Sammy piloted Chinny and made him swim, and jump, upstream, ultimately hurdling his way past the onslaught of white water. From there, Chinny continued to swim up river. They could see trout swimming about in the river as Chinny swam, the images transmitted to his control console from Chinny's new camera.

"Hey, slow it down, man!" Carey barked at Sammy from the pilot seat on the raft. He was rowing, along with Brad and Meagan. They were all trying to keep pace with the streaking Chinny, which was proving impossible.

"Yeah!" Meagan and Brad shouted in unison between gulping breaths.

From a distance, Jenny landed Skye on the back of a prong tail elk that was sleeping in the grass. "You can really appreciate the light weight of Skye," Mr. Sandhill noted. "Those prong tail elk spring awake at the slightest touch or movement, and that one is still sleeping, which means it doesn't feel Skye at all, or just thinks she's another insect." Later Jenny flew Skye among a herd of buffalo that was playfully running down a steep hill towards some mud flats near a river. She was able to fly Skye from hundreds of yards away and still see all the action because of the tiny camera now implanted in the dragon fly bot. At one point, she saw a large buffalo deliberately rambling in the direction of another as they both ran, and saw that Skye was directly in its path. She quickly piloted Skye upwards, timing the ascent perfectly so that Skye narrowly avoided getting smashed between the two frolicking beasts. Ryan could hear the grunts and huffs of the charging herd captured by the camera and transmitted back to Jenny's controller.

"Watching the camera view while bouncing around in the air makes me nauseous," Jenny observed.

"Yeah, it kind of makes you seasick, doesn't it?" Sammy said.

On a hike, James piloted Slidey—also with a newly installed camera—down a trail. He managed to catch a mouse in Slidey's jaws. The entire event took place hundreds of yards ahead on the trail, completely out of sight of the group. They all watched the action on James' remote control console, as if it were a video game. "It takes a little to get used to the timing when you pull the trigger, because it's sensitive, and superfast," James said, referring to when he hit the 'strike' button that activated Slidey's jaws, "but that was incredible!"

James was also learning to lift Slidey's head up every now and then to get a better view of where he was going. "It's kind of hard to get a good perspective of where you are if your head's sitting on the ground all the time," James said of Slidey.

For his part, Ryan had Scram climb a tall, dead pine tree that had been scorched by forest fire. Since the charred tree's branches were bare, it was easier to see Scram from below. At Mrs. Bergeron's behest, Ryan made Scram jump from one tree to another, about thirty feet above the ground. The trees stood about eight feet apart. Ryan had no idea whether Scram could make the leap, but he did, and he managed to hold on after the jump. The camera on his control console gave Ryan the new ability to see as if he were Scram, and to move Scram's limbs and adjust his movements accordingly. It took some getting used to, and Scram fell several times before Ryan grew more familiar with maneuvering him, based on the camera views. At times, it felt like Scram was on a roller coaster ride. To his delight, Ryan even managed to hit a fly with Scram's tongue while Scram was on the tree. "Bull's eye!" he shouted.

Ellen piloted Trixie through a large, rolling meadow and succeeded in chasing down a small rabbit. Remarkably, a hawk—not Harris—circling above swooped down to try to claim Trixie's prize. Trixie dropped the rabbit, turned, and looked up at the hawk and bared her teeth. Ellen made her hiss, bark, and then run in the direction of the hawk.

"Wow!" Meagan said. "Ellen's going right after the hawk! I mean, Trixie!"

"That hawk's trying to eat my supper!" Ellen said. "I mean, Trixie's supper!"

The hawk circled low in the proximity of the rabbit, but Trixie followed it, frequently jumping up on two legs in attempt to get closer and snap at the hawk. After a few swoops and circles, the hawk realized it would not get past the fox easily and flew off.

"Get your food elsewhere, lazy!" Ellen barked. She thought for a moment. "Of course, since Trixie is not actually going to eat the rabbit, I guess it will get claimed by some other animal."

"Yep," Brad agreed. "But you made darn sure that hawk was getting its dinner somewhere else."

After a few days in Yellowstone, the group piled onto the bus one morning and headed towards the south end of the park. "Uh, so where are we going now?" Ellen asked.

"We're heading south," Mr. Sandhill said.

"I figured out that much," Ellen said. "We're going back the same way we came in."

"Thomas, don't tease!" Mrs. Bergeron admonished. "What he means to say, Ellen, is that we're going to go south, through Utah," she said.

"Utah," Ellen said.

"Ever been there?" Brad asked.

"No, but I think I've flown over it a few times," Ellen said.

"It's a spectacularly interesting place," Mr. Sandhill said.

"I've visited there before," Jenny said. "My family has spent some time in the parks there."

"Me too," said Sammy. "There are lots of dinosaur fossils there."

"True indeed," Mrs. Bergeron said. "Unfortunately on this trip we probably won't have time to see too many of them."

The bus wound its way through southwestern Wyoming, past rolling hills dotted with alder leaf mountain mahogany shrubs and intermittent evergreen trees of twisted, gnarled wood. One could see cattle here and there, which reminded Ryan of Jenny's near mid-air collision involving Skye and a couple of rambunctious buffalo. But again, there was little time to stare out the windows, as the group continued its robotic work sessions.

"So, what did you learn about your bots at Yellowstone?" Meagan asked the group.

"They have sharp teeth," Sammy mused. Neither he nor the others had expected they could take down animal prey with their bots.

"Well, it's one reason why some of you spent hours sharpening their teeth and reinforcing their jaws on the drive out here," Meagan said. "The bots are more credible as animals if they can behave like real animals, aren't they?"

"No question," James said.

"What else did you learn?" Meagan asked.

"I learned that our bots can do things I didn't think they could do," Jenny said.

"I like that," Mrs. Bergeron said. "And I think you're exactly right, Jenny. I think we all learned that."

"No doubt about it," Mr. Sandhill said. "My eyes have definitely been opened up to the broad possibilities of what these marvelous creatures can do." That Mrs. Bergeron and Mr. Sandhill had gained greater appreciation for the bots gave the Seguin students a deep sense of pride.

Crossing into Utah, the bus passed the outskirts of Salt Lake City, and headed south to Provo, around Utah Lake, where it rolled down an interstate highway that paralleled the Wasatch Mountain Range to the east. They took a few hours' break in the late afternoon and visited Zion National Park without their bots. Some of the sheer rock faces in Zion were spectacular.

"It would be so cool to fly Harris from the top of Angel's Landing," Carmen gushed.

"All in good time," Mrs. Bergeron said.

They stopped for the night in a small town called Cedar City. It was a pleasant looking place, with a friendly main street and inviting shops, but there was no time to explore. They simply piled off the bus and into the hotel for the evening.

"This must be what it's like when the guys from Voltaic go on tour," Sammy mused. "You go to a lot of cool places, but you probably don't get to see too much."

"I guess most of the sightseeing has to wait until the tour's over," Ryan said.

The next morning they hopped on the bus and drove for a few hours to their next destination, Creech Air Force Base in Nevada. On the latter part of this journey, Mr. Sandhill explained that they were traveling along the Desert Wildlife National Refuge, which lay to the north, out their right hand side windows. As they approached the base, Ryan could see mountains with scrub brush growth rising in various directions around them. The base lay at the edge of some desert flats that ran for what appeared to be many miles. Tall, barbed wire fence ran along its perimeters. With little delay at a gateway check point, they were given admittance to Creech Air Force Base.

"So, it seems like there's pretty good security here," Carmen said as she observed the concrete blocks that abutted the checkpoint of the base.

"It does indeed," Mr. Sandhill said.

"So is it difficult to get admission to the air base?" James asked.

"Not if you're Mr. Sandhill," Meagan responded.

The bus drove down a long, fairly straight road that ended at the air base complex. Off in the distance, they could see a couple of fighter jets landing. Various aircraft parked inside and next to hangars. The bus pulled up at an administrative looking building that was a couple of floors high. Once off the bus, the group was escorted into the building and led to a meeting room. It was an amphitheater with rows of seats surrounding an open area. The seats were padded and comfortable, and could have been ritzy movie theater seats, positioned in front of a series of screens. Recessed lights traced the circular edge of the amphitheater and gave it a warm feeling.

"Okay. Welcome, take a seat, everyone," said the man who had escorted them off the bus. Everyone took a seat and a pregnant pause of anticipation hung in the air. "Let's see, I think our emcee should be here any minute—"

At just that moment, in long, hurried steps, in strode Jasper Townley wearing what looked to Ryan like some kind of pilot suit. Cheers and shouts of excitement went up from the Seguin crowd. People were pumping their fists.

"It's good to see you again as well," Townley said. "What's it been? Seven or eight days? It sure is different from Ohio out here, isn't it? We need to export some of this sunlight back to there. Anyway, Mr. Sandhill and Mrs. Bergeron tell me you had terrific visits in Chicago and then Yellowstone. And you did a bunch of work on your bots along the way. Fantastic. Well, welcome to Creech Air Force Base. This is where we fly a lot of our drones from."

"You mean, those flying planes that don't have any pilot?" Carmen asked.

"Exactly. The drones are great because they are unmanned aircraft, so they are a lot less expensive to fly than those jets you just saw landing a few minutes ago. I was piloting one of them, by the way. Drones can stay in the air for a really long time. And, there's no pilot fatigue or tiredness, because they are being piloted remotely. The person flying the thing can actually hand off the controls to somebody else. And we can fly them anywhere from here, even on the other side of the world."

Several people issued hushed exclamations of amazement.

"Huh... So what are we going to do here?" Ryan asked.

"We are going to run some tests, piloting and navigating your bots," Townley said. "You see, one of the amazing things about your bots is they offer the potential to send an animal, a robotic avatar, if you like, into a place where we don't want to be conspicuous."

"You mean like a war zone?" Sammy asked.

"Yes, very possibly. But it could also be a place where perhaps we are trying to gather intelligence about someone or something."

"You mean, like, like spying?" Ellen asked.

"I like to think of it as intelligence gathering," Jumpshot said. "But, let's be clear. In some instances, yes, it could be spying."

"But isn't that wrong? It feels kind of sinister," Ellen said ponderously.

"Ellen, I don't want to pop your bubble about the world. But, let's understand something. Most people and nations in this world are good. They are law abiding people who want to do the right thing. Most of them love and embrace freedom. But, remember our conversation in Ohio. *Not everybody wants to be our friend.* Sadly, there are some people in this world who, in some cases are trying to control or assert their will over others, and who don't always treat fellow people humanely. Maybe they even treat them very *inhumanely*. These are people who do not want others to live in freedom. Maybe they're plotting to do bad things, really bad things, to us or people in their own country, or people in a country nearby. In some cases, they even have designs on trying to subvert, dominate, or kill others, or tear down law-abiding governments. If we can document that these sorts of things are happening without getting our butts shot off, then we can shine a light on these types of atrocities, work to contain and eliminate them, and hopefully prevent them from happening in the future."

"That sounds pretty secretive... Having the bots... It's like having an unfair advantage," Ellen pondered.

"It *is* secretive," Jumpshot said. "And it *is* like having an unfair advantage. And we are trying give ourselves every unfair advantage we can. But, let's consider why. By sending in a machine, we avoid sending in a real person, so we avoid putting a life at risk. And, if we can send in something that won't be detected, there is a greater likelihood that it will come back in one piece. So, by using machines in place of humans, bots, in this case, we are actually making this type of work safer. Not to mention, the people who are plotting bad things, say, the murder of others, aren't the least bit interested in playing fair. So when it comes to dealing with them, why should we?"

"Huh. I see your point," Ellen said.

"Just to make one more," Jumpshot continued. "It's not like we're looking for reasons to use bot technology for spying as if we have nothing better to do. There are a lot of problems and challenges around the world. And bots have the potential to help us solve all kinds of problems." Townley paused to let the group reflect. "And as you know, not all of these problems are in the domain of military security and spying and secrecy. In fact, most of them aren't. For example, we could use James' snake bot, or something like it, to help us fix cables or wires deep underground or under the sea, or find people trapped in a building collapsed by an earthquake."

"Or a fish bot to do deep sea exploration," Sammy said.

"Or a dragonfly bot to explore caves, or even other planets," Jenny mused.

"Exactly, Jenny. Speaking of the dragonfly, Mr. Sandhill was pretty impressed watching Skye avoid getting taken down by a couple of buffalo," Townley said to Jenny.

"Yup," Jenny said. "Skye got out of there in a hurry."

"Yes, she did. I saw the footage. Nice bit of flying, by the way. There's no way a person could have kept up with those running buffalo or avoided being crushed if they charged," Townley said. "So that brings us to another advantage of the bots," he continued. "Let's say you can't access a place you need to be able to get into, like, getting underneath a locked door. Some of your bots can get underneath that door."

Ryan immediately thought of Scram skittering underneath the door of the girls' bathroom during the dance back at Highland Park Middle School. "I did something like that once," he said. "I got into some trouble over it." *That was putting it mildly*, he thought.

"But, you could also get *out* of trouble with it, couldn't you?" Jumpshot said. "What if you were being held someplace against your will?"

"Like a prison cell," Carmen suggested.

"Right, or a collapsed building," posited Townley.

"You just might be able to give yourself a chance to get out of there, you know?" Townley asked. "Like, by sending the bot out to tell your friends where you are being held, or telling them what kind of place you are being held in. Or, helping you to find an escape route."

"Yeah!" Sammy exclaimed. Like the others, he had grown excited hearing Townley's talk.

"But enough of my banter," Townley said, looking at his watch. At that moment, a couple of people appeared at the doorway at the side of the room. "Let's get some lunch, and I want to introduce you to some of the folks here at Creech."

A couple of young men and women strode in to the room wearing military uniforms. They saluted Townley and introduced themselves. The group from Seguin Academy reciprocated. Townley then led them down the hall to a cafeteria. There they got some food and talked over lunch. The Seguin students learned that these young men and women were drone pilots.

"So, *you* actually *fly* drones," Carmen said.

"Yep. That's what we do," one of the women said.

"Here at Creech, and actually, all over the world," Townley said.

"All from here?" Ryan asked.

"All from here," one of the young men answered.

"So, how does that work?" Carmen asked.

"Well, it's a bit like flying an airplane on a jet flight simulator," one of the men said. "You start on a runway or a launch pad, and guide the craft through take-off, flight, and landing."

"Even if it's dark?" Sammy asked.

"Sure," another young man said. "Day, night, anytime."

"It's a lot like playing a video game," another woman chimed in.

"Would you believe that this is a field where playing video games actually helps you?" Mr. Sandhill said. "It took me a while to convince Mrs. Bergeron of it," he smiled.

"I must say, I was a bit skeptical at first," Mrs. Bergeron said, returning the smile. "But then, after getting some exposure to bots, I realized the potential of what they could do for us. And, in so many different areas."

Ryan figured none of the people from the Creech group were much older than Brad and Meagan, and definitely not older than Carey, who had a few years on them. Brad and Meagan had apparently met the

Creech members previously, as Ryan had overheard them saying, "Nice to see you again," to each other.

After lunch, the group returned to a dark, cool room near the amphitheater that did not have any windows. Jumpshot gave a few introductory remarks and then turned the floor over to the Creech team.

"Are you ready to fly a drone today?" a young woman named Brenda Gibbs asked.

"Yeah!" said Ryan and several others. Other affirmative shouts went up from the Seguin group.

"Good!" Brenda said. "We're gonna have some fun. The drones are just a warm up act. Because, after you've had a little fun with the drones, we're going to see you in action with your bots."

Each of the Creech team made a few remarks about flying drones. They then watched a brief movie about Creech Air Force Base and the aircraft housed there—drones, fighter jets, and other aircraft. After the movie, the back wall of the room slid apart in two halves and revealed a series of stations. It was not dissimilar to the one Ryan had seen in the old barn in Tanglewood, although instead of there being rows upon rows of musical instruments, amplifiers, and recording technology, there were work stations with computers, keyboards, control panels, joysticks, and video screens—lots of them. Ryan also noticed foam panels, for sound insulation, all around the room.

"Okay. The students from Seguin Academy should now each pair off with a person from Creech," said Brenda.

Ryan found himself paired up with a woman named Debbie Tan. For the next day and a half, they went over drone piloting steps and maneuvers. With the exception of take-offs and landings, Ryan found it to be easier than he would have expected. And with Debbie guiding him, he really couldn't mess up. What a huge relief. While there was a constant chattering in the background of other discussions between the Creech and Seguin people, it was minimally distracting thanks to the room's sound insulation.

On the second day, the Seguin students sat in the pilot seat and their Creech counterparts sat beside them. On the screens in front of him, Ryan could see a film view, which was through a camera mounted on the drone, as well as a video topographical view, which was more like a video game. Debbie explained that this view was best for night flying and in cloudy skies. There was also a ground-mounted camera so people could watch their bots taking off and landing. Each bot had been fitted with a high-powered, acutely sensitive receiver that could field and execute instructions from the command center at Creech. It was much more powerful than the ones they had used in their bots until now.

"This receiver is what will make it possible for you to pilot your bot on the other side of the planet," one of the Creech guys, Jack Timlin, said. Since Harris and Skye were the only two bots that flew, the Seguin students each took turns flying them. The views from the cameras mounted on the bots were incredible. With Harris and Skye they flew up thousands of feet over desert mountains, and swooped down just a few feet off the ground. At one point, Sammy navigated Skye through the hole in a low standing tree.

"Show off," Jenny said. Not to be outdone, she then landed Skye on the back of a mountain goat.

They then took turns maneuvering Slidey and Scram over desert terrain.

"I wish Scram could fly," Ryan said wistfully.

"Oh, we can make anything fly," Townley said. "You just have to hook it up to the right thing. Sammy knows that better than anyone, right Sammy? Remember how we flew Chinny about four miles in about half a second in Ohio?"

"How could I forget?" Sammy said. "The results were explosive."

"Yeah, we had a bit of fun, didn't we?" Townley said, giggling.

"So, the thing is, it's important for everyone to try out each bot because they can each do different, but all important things," Mr. Sandhill said. "With Scram, we're going to practice climbing on the sides of cliff walls, crawling under rocks, and underneath closed doors. None of the other bots can do all these things. Each bot is remarkable because of their different capabilities, you see?"

"Yeah, I think so," Ryan said. But he remained jealous about the bots that could fly. He told Carmen as much later.

"Are you kidding?" Carmen said. "Like Townley said, hook an engine up to Scram, or any bot, and it can fly. Sure, with flying the views are great. But, I love the idea that Scram can fit into some really small places. And he can climb walls. There's no way Harris could do that."

Later in the day they took turns navigating Scram, Slidey, and Trixie in different situations. To practice with Scram, Harris carried Scram in his claws and flew to the top of a mountain several thousand feet high. Each member of the Seguin group then navigated Scram up and down the vertical rock face. Ryan was proud of the fact that Scram stuck to the wall and was able to maneuver in some pretty tight places. The view down the rock face from the dizzying height, taken with the camera mounted inside Scram, was extraordinary.

Carmen had teased Ryan about using Harris to transport Scram. "Hitching a ride on my bot, huh? That'll cost you, mister." Ryan could feel his face turning red.

For Slidey and Trixie, the Creech group had laid out obstacle courses at one side of the base. For Slidey, there were holes, tunnels, a couple of boards sandwiched together with a tight crack between them, and some fake animals were being moved along wires for Slidey to strike with his fangs. The Creech team was impressed with Slidey's striking abilities.

"Heck, Slidey already took down a real animal—that mouse back at Yellowstone. So, I expected he'd be able to get his teeth into some stuffed animals, even if they are moving," James laughed.

At a nearby creek, an obstacle course had been set up for Chinny. Each member of the group took turns navigating the obstacle course. There were hoops to jump through, poles to jump over, and a slalom course of poles to swim in and out of. They timed each other. Sammy, with the unfair advantage of being Chinny's inventor, won the event. But, the competition was close.

That evening the group dined at a nearby restaurant with their Creech hosts. The next morning, they had breakfast at their motel with Townley before taking the bus to Las Vegas where they would board a plane for home.

"I realize some of this is pretty heavy stuff for people your age," Townley said. "But, you wouldn't be here if you weren't super smart, super motivated, and super capable. Seguin Academy will push you to do some pretty incredible things, maybe things you didn't think were possible. Helping you to see that which is possible—despite its seeming to be impossible—is why you are on this trip. Because if there isn't a real world application for something, you might say, 'Why do it?' Well, as you are seeing, there are very definitely some real world applications for what you all are doing."

Everybody posed for photos with Townley before they got on the bus. It had been a whirlwind trip, and Ryan felt somewhat drained by it all. He had learned so much, but had also worked really hard. He felt tremendous satisfaction as he considered the new functionalities Scram had picked up. a new camera so he could see exactly what was around; a global positioning system to navigate digitally; and a far more powerful communications chip to operate virtually anywhere in the world, despite being hundreds or thousands of miles away. He started to think of the possibilities.

"Just so we're clear," Mrs. Bergeron said. "The new functionality you have in your bots is only to be used under strict teacher supervision."

"Aw, c'mon," several in the group moaned.

"Thank God we're flying home instead of driving," Jenny said.

"Why are we flying instead of driving?" Carmen asked Mrs. Bergeron.

"Because you have school, of course!" Mrs. Bergeron replied.

Larry, the bus driver, would be returning to Seguin with a bus full of parts, components, and control boards for the newly enhanced bots.

"That's a lot of stuff," Ellen observed.

"It is, especially when you multiply it by six, or eight," Larry said.

On the way home, Sammy was hopeful that Mrs. Bergeron and Mr. Sandhill had forgotten about his being "grounded" for his prank at the Shedd Aquarium in Chicago. To his dismay, they did remember the incident, and perhaps more importantly, fulfilled on the commitment to Sammy's parents that Sammy be punished for it. Mr. Sandhill told Sammy he would spend the next two weeks in early-morning detentions in the Seguin Robotics Lab. While he missed the opportunity to eat breakfast with his friends, Sammy told himself he wouldn't let the time go to waste. He resolved to continue to work on his plans for a killer whale bot.

9

LAWLESSNESS AND ORDER

Back in Milton, it suddenly felt to Ryan as if the trip hadn't happened. He was, of course, reminded daily by James and Sammy that it had indeed happened. But upon their return, Ryan felt they weren't seeing as much of the girls, or Brad, Meagan, Mrs. Bergeron, and Mr. Sandhill, for that matter, as they had on the trip. It felt like a chapter ended. They simply didn't spend as much time with each other upon their return, even though Sellinger, the boys' dormitory, sat just across a courtyard from the girls' Donnington dormitory. It occurred to Ryan that you probably would never spend as much time with someone as being cooped up with them on a bus all day long for days at a time.

Brad and Meagan had their studies at Weatherall University, so they didn't make it over to Seguin Academy all that often, though as teaching assistants at Seguin they were around occasionally. Mr. Sandhill and Mrs. Bergeron had their teaching and administrative responsibilities. Happily, Ryan learned that he and his classmates would be taking classes from both of them so they would, of course, be seeing them routinely.

It wasn't that fellow students didn't cross paths frequently at Seguin, they did, pretty much every day. But, it became evident to Ryan and his friends upon their return to school that there would be a lot of competing priorities for their time. The bots were a critically important element of their education, but Mrs. Bergeron and Mr. Sandhill had made it pretty clear they were one of many. And, based on the way Brad and Meagan talked about what to expect from student life at Seguin, Ryan sensed the workload would soon be overwhelming. He was no stranger to homework, but he had a foreboding sense that Seguin Academy would take its meaning to a whole different level.

"It sounds like there's a lot... a ton, actually... to stay on top of at Seguin," Ryan said to Brad on the plane flight to Boston.

"Yeah, in some ways, there is," Brad said, "but it's not impossible. It will require you to manage your time really well. Your friends at home may have a spare window of time here or there to play a video game, a pickup sports game, or watch a movie. You won't have time for those luxuries, except maybe on weekends. You'll have fun at Seguin, more fun than you've ever had in your life. There's no doubt about it, but you will be challenged like never before." For Ryan, home was starting to sound pretty good, and feeling really far away. He would next go home at Thanksgiving time.

The school convocation that took place the Monday after their return reinforced Ryan's premonitions about the intensity of his academic future. Mrs. Bergeron, Mr. Sandhill, and various other teachers stood in front of the school, about sixteen hundred students in all, and welcomed them back to Seguin. For Ryan's class, the ninth graders, often referred to as the first years, they were being welcomed to the academy for the first time.

Mrs. Bergeron, as headmistress of the school, started off with some welcoming remarks. These were followed by a brief series of introductions of new teachers, administrative items, and so on. Certain changes to the usual school routine were reviewed. But, for Ryan and his friends, the whole routine was new, so whatever had changed was of little consequence to them.

Towards the end of her remarks, Mrs. Bergeron said something that surprised everyone, the first years perhaps the most. "Also, I want to make you aware of a few temporary changes taking place around the school later on in the year. For the second half of the fall and the full spring semester, I will be taking a sabbatical, to do research. Mr. Sandhill will be filling in for me as acting headmaster of the school. And, for those Biology students who have me as teacher, the schedule is that I will teach you up through your mid-terms during fall semester," Mrs. Bergeron said. "For the remainder of the fall semester and the full spring semester, Mr. Guzman here will be teaching you." She gestured to a friendly looking man off to her side.

"A suh-what-ical?" Carmen asked. She hadn't meant to blurt it out, but many people in the room heard her remark, including Mrs. Bergeron. Several people in the room giggled in hushed voices.

"A sabbatical—thank you, Carmen—which is a temporary leave of absence, in this case to do research work. I will be sailing around the world and doing documentary filming of a variety of ocean ecosystems and environments. You'll all get to see it at some point."

"More work for the Worldscapes channel, no doubt," Sammy whispered to Ryan and James.

"However, I will never be far from Seguin Academy. You will be able to track my boat and its position, and there will be a daily posting online as well as on the big board in the student center." The big board was a jumbo sized digital screen that ran announcements, video, and other media pertaining to the school and its activities. "And, I still expect to communicate with my Biology classes through VideoLink," she added. "So, in this way, I won't really be leaving, you see?" But, she had just said, of course, that she would be leaving, if only temporarily.

For Ryan and his classmates, to whom Mrs. Bergeron was a very big fixture of Seguin Academy, this announcement came across as something of a bombshell. However, little time was afforded to come to grips with Mrs. Bergeron's announcement, as it proved to be just one of many Ryan heard throughout the day, which went by in a dizzying whirl. After the convocation, Ryan found himself walking, quickly, to his first class, which was English. How hard could that be? Here, Ryan learned the emphasis would be on reading, writing, listening, and speaking skills.

"Did you hear that? This class will also emphasize *listening* skills," Ellen whispered to Jenny.

In response, Jenny stuck her tongue out at Ellen.

Ryan couldn't tell if the sometimes testy relationship between Jenny and Ellen was in fun or if it were actually competitive, maybe even adversarial at times. Maybe it was a bit of both. Carmen had also told him at times she felt stuck in the middle. But, for the most part, all three girls got along fine.

Works by William Shakespeare, Mark Twain, Jack London, Emily Dickinson, some dude who went by the moniker "e.e. cummings," and some other dude known as Nikolai Gogol were on the syllabus. Story structure, topical research, poetry structure and format, and a biographical paper were also on the agenda, among other things. The teacher of the class was a woman named Mrs. Reilly, who, in addition to teaching at Seguin, wrote about the history of science and technology.

Math was next. The teacher, Michael Stansfield, was "a Brit, as you can discern from my accent," he said. "Yorkshire," he added. He reviewed the syllabus for the fall semester, which consisted of short, but concentrated units in geometry, pre-algebra, algebra, pre-calculus, and calculus.

"Isn't this, like, three years' worth of math?" Ellen asked.

"For you—Ellen, isn't it? Right—this should be a breeze," Mr. Stansfield said.

"We're dead," Sammy sighed.

"Now, I've had it on good authority from Mr. Sandhill and Mrs. Bergeron that you are all very bright, capable students," Mr. Stansfield said. "The students in this room were in four different orientation sessions, and you all accomplished very promising things. You each traveled about the country in cohorts, working together, learning, and tackling new challenges together—challenges that involved your ability to do math, and a lot of it, among other things. Your cohort, Ellen, with its bots—that is, robots; Angie's group here with its laser projects; Shawn's group with its energy creating technologies; and Kim Soo's group focused on miniaturized computing devices. It's pretty clear that you all have some competence in math." Suddenly, Ryan's bot work felt almost boring compared to the work he was hearing about in these other fields. He was struck by Mr. Stansfield's rundown of people's names and orientation projects, which he recited without any notes.

"To be able to do the project work you are currently doing, you already pretty much know at least half of this semester's work without lifting a finger," Mr. Stansfield continued. Ryan hoped he was right. Good or bad, Ryan also learned that Mr. Stansfield was one of the boys' soccer coaches. For a guy who was going to push the class through the academic equivalent of a four-minute mile, he seemed fairly calm. Of course, he wouldn't be doing any of the work. He was merely assigning it.

A recognizable face and personality came next, in Physics, taught by Mr. Sandhill. Here Ryan felt like he had landed at a port of acquaintance in a sea of otherwise unknown islands. The pleasantly familiar aspects of Mr. Sandhill, his passion and encouragement of asking questions, exploring, and experimenting, did not appear to lighten the burden as far as workload was concerned, however. Ryan knew as much when Mr. Sandhill produced the textbook the class would be using. It looked like it weighted thirty pounds.

"When will they make *that* thing an electronic book?" Sammy whispered under his breath. "Sure would weigh less."

"How the heck am I supposed to carry that thing around?" Jenny whispered.

As if anticipating students' concerns, Mr. Sandhill said, "Several copies of the textbook are in the stacks at the Seguin library, so you don't need to haul a copy of it all over campus. Though doing so does help build muscle strength." He chuckled at this bit of humor, but no one else was laughing. Knowing Mr. Sandhill as the bots group did from their orientation, Ryan figured that, at least in Physics, they would not get annihilated without seeing it coming first. So far, he couldn't say that about his other classes. Mr. Sandhill also mentioned that Brad Lawless and Meagan Rosenkrans would be attending class occasionally and assisting with some of the outside projects, a welcome piece of news.

Computer Science came next. Everyone in Ryan's grade had been given a notebook computer over the weekend that would be their own for the coming years at school. Ryan figured the notebook would come in handy in computer science class above all others, and he was not wrong to think so. The teacher was a thin, wiry man named Charlie Lin. He spoke in a quiet, but clear voice. It occurred to everyone in the class that, in order to hear what he was saying, they would have to keep quiet. One thing that everyone picked up on immediately was that Mr. Lin despised the use of paper. His goal was to do everything electronically. Homework assignments, readings, and basically any work associated with the class were to be done and submitted using a computer.

"Well, at least that will partially offset the weight of the Physics book," Ryan whispered.

"Some of you are already highly advanced in your use of computers," Mr. Lin said in his calm, quiet voice to the class. "So it will be important for you to help your classmates who may be less so."

Ryan figured Computer Science was one class where he might not feel like he was drowning, at least not in the first week. Thanks to his parents and schooling up to this point, he was a bit of a programming whiz. Perhaps not so much compared to Brad, Meagan, and Carey, but they were students at Weatherall University, and at least several years of ahead of him.

Lunch came next, a forty-five minute interval that flew past. Ryan joined his colleagues at the Seguin cafeteria. Everyone was chattering about their classes and teachers. Ryan ate hurriedly. Carmen, Ellen, Jenny, Sammy, and James all weighed in with some kind of prediction along the lines that their collective rear ends were about to meet with a large, heavy boot. "What do you think about all this, Ryan?" Carmen asked, as if hoping he might have something different to say.

"We're toast," Ryan said conclusively, biting into a sandwich.

"Profound," Jenny said.

"You said the same thing," Ryan shrugged. "Oh, my mistake, I stand corrected. You said 'road kill.' World of difference."

Despite feelings of imminent doom, everyone seemed intrigued by their classes and teachers so far. Ryan figured that even if the captivation was temporary, as with the calm before a storm, it was pleasant in its own fleeting way. It was also nerve-wracking in ways neither he nor his schoolmates had experienced before.

History came next. Ms. Sheets, an athletic-looking woman, would be teaching this class. Ms. Sheets had played hockey in college, and was a coach of the Seguin girls' hockey team.

"In other words, don't mess with her," Jenny whispered.

Historic tools and practices; emerging civilizations around the world; monarchies and empires; revolution and nationalism; global wars; patterns of social order; technologies and changing global connections; and patterns of history would all be units for the class.

"Why don't we throw in the dinosaurs while we're at it?" Carmen joked.

Ryan had a VideoLink call with his parents that night. "I think school is going to be brutal," he told them. "You wouldn't believe how much work is involved."

"Now Ryan, I'm sure it's not that bad," his dad said. He always took a pragmatic point of view, even when confronted with things that seemed impossible.

"What do your friends say?" his mom asked. She was always trying more than his father to calm him down when he had frayed nerves.

"They think we're going to get crushed."

"Now, it can't be *that* difficult," his mother said.

"No, it *is* that difficult," Ryan responded.

"Yay! Ryan's going to get *crushed!*" Annie squealed on the phone. She had been hiding below the screen and popped into view at just that moment. She had a real knack for contributing to chaos where Ryan was concerned.

"Thanks, Annie," Ryan muttered. Her provocation aside, Ryan was glad to see her.

Despite feeling he was about to be run over by a freight train, Ryan realized the surface of something had only been scratched that first day at Seguin Academy. In large measure, this was because on Tuesday, he had his first Robotics class. It was different in many ways, for many reasons, even compared to other classes at Seguin.

The Robotics class was much smaller. Only Ryan and his bot mates from the trip were taking this class. Another difference from other Seguin classes, Ryan learned, was that the group would go to Weatherall University every other Tuesday to hold their Robotics class. There, they would interact with students and faculty from Weatherall, including Brad Lawless and Meagan Rosenkrans, and contribute to various robotics projects. Now *that* was exciting.

Another difference with Robotics was that two teachers would be teaching it, Arthur Freekenhorst and Leonard Zachary. Ryan had learned that at Seguin it was not unusual to take a class from teachers who also served on the faculty at nearby Weatherall University. Mr. Sandhill and Mrs. Bergeron were proof enough of that with their academic appointments there. It turned out that Mr. Freekenhorst and Mr. Zachary were also on the faculty at Weatherall.

One of the more remarkable revelations from Mr. Freekenhorst and Mr. Zachary was their preference for how they wished to be addressed by students. "In general, and in case you haven't already heard, the student body here at Seguin, along with people at Weatherall University, in the robotics field, and elsewhere, refer to us as… *Freak and Zeek*," Mr. Freekenhorst said. Everyone laughed.

"Freak and Zeek?" Ellen said, her mouth scrunched up as if she had just tasted something bitter.

"Freak and Zeek," Mr. Zachary repeated. The way he pronounced it made it sound like '*Freakenzeek*.'

"So, that is generally how you should refer to us. Everybody else does," Mr. Freekenhorst continued. "People are always asking if they should call one or the other of us 'doctor,' or 'professor,' or—"

"Or a lot of other names that we can't repeat here," Mr. Zachary—Zeek—said, giggling. "It may sound offensive to some, but we find it's shorter to pronounce."

"And, thus, way more efficient—like robotics," chimed in the man now known as Freak.

The whole class spent the next half hour in disbelief that they were taking a robotics class from teachers nicknamed Freak and Zeek. Remarkably, despite going through the fall syllabus and the class schedule, the texts, the exam dates, and so forth, Freak and Zeek had this remarkable ability to make you feel like you weren't actually going to be doing real work. At least, it didn't feel like it would be work. It felt like it was going to be fun.

Towards the end of class, Jenny rubbed her eyes as if she were tired.

"Is something the matter?" Freak asked. "Not enough sleep, perhaps?"

"No. Nothing's the matter. Except for the two hundred pages of reading I had to do last night. This all sounds great... except we're going to get our you-know-whats- kicked," Jenny lamented.

"What do you mean?" asked Zeek.

"This school. They pile on the work and bury you," she said.

"Here? Nah, not really," Freak said.

"It's not so much of a pile as it is a head-on collision," Zeek added. "And it really doesn't hurt that bad."

"And here's a little secret... A lot of it actually isn't even work at all," Freak said, in a loud whisper. "And you *will* get through it. We have lots of incentive to make sure you do."

"Here's the Freak and Zeek guarantee to you," Zeek said. "If, at the end of this year, you feel like this class was actually *work*, then we have failed in our duties as teachers."

"So what's the guarantee?" asked James.

"Uh, right. So... the guarantee is that we will do everything we can to make you feel like this class is not work," Freak said.

"Yeah, that's it," Zeek said.

"How can you guarantee something like that?" Ellen asked.

"Uh, we can't. But I don't think in the twelve years of teaching this class we've had anyone who felt like it was actually doing real work," Freak said.

"Really?" Jenny asked, skeptically.

"Well, let's see," Zeek pondered. "Okay, maybe there was *one* student, about eleven years ago. I think *he* felt like it was work."

"Just one?" said Ryan.

"Yeah. And I think we learned... by the time final exams rolled around, that he had been placed in Robotics by mistake," Freak added.

"Yeah, that's right," Zeek said. "So it really wasn't our fault. He was supposed to have been assigned to the Biological Engines group. And, even so, he finished the Robotics course, aced the final exam... and later enrolled at Weatherall University, in the Robotics department with us. So he couldn't have hated it that much."

"Yeah, I mean, how bad could he have hated the class if we actually *converted* him to Robotics?" Freak said.

"So, in twelve years you've basically had no one tell you this class felt like work?" Ellen said.

"Yeah, pretty much, that's right," said Zeek.

"What's your secret?" she asked. "Why does everyone universally love you?"

"I don't know that they all love us, do you, Zeek?" Freak said.

"Yeah, I don't know if they would all say that," Zeek paused. "But they generally seem to *like* the class. Do you know why?"

"No," everyone said.

"We encourage people to ask the crazy question," Freak said.

"Ask the crazy question?" Ryan muttered along with those around him.

"Yeah. When most people are asking 'why' about something, we are always posing the question, 'why not?'" Zeek said.

"I mean, I assume that's why most of you are here," Freak said. "You don't typically get into the field of robotics if you're always asking 'why?' Robotics people tend to more of the 'why not?' variety. Otherwise, why would you bother to spend time building bots?"

Ryan thought about his desire to build Scram in the first place, then of his desire to cause a ruckus with Scram at the middle school dance. Even though the dance episode had some unintended consequences, he had thought it would be fun to try to cause some mayhem. He even remembered asking his robotics club friends, "Why not?"

Though Ryan wasn't quite sure what to make of Freak and Zeek, he had to admit, they had a disarming way of making you feel like what loomed ahead at Seguin wasn't as impossible as you first imagined. Their optimism even made you feel you had some control, even if only a little bit, like a surfer trying to stay balanced while riding a massive wave.

Ryan hoped his first Seguin soccer practice that afternoon would be a welcome change to the meat grinder he had gone through in the past two days. The crisp, fresh fall air felt good as he left the locker room and headed out onto the field. He and the other members of the soccer team made their way onto a large, beautiful field that lay near the center of a sprawling series of green, well-manicured fields. Under the leadership of two guys who seemed to be the team captains, people started doing some stretching exercises. After about fifteen minutes, Mr. Stansfield appeared, accompanied by another faculty member of Seguin Academy. Mr. Stansfield shouted out a few introductory remarks, then announced to the group, "Okay, time for our two laps around Seguin Field. For those of you who are new, this is how we start our practices."

A few groans went up from members of the team. "What's Seguin Field?" Ryan asked a boy next to him.

"It's that whole thing," the boy said, pointing outward with both hands and then spreading them to each side, extending to the entire expanse of fields that lay before them.

"So, around everything?" Ryan said.

"Yeah. It's about two and half miles around the whole thing," the boy replied.

In response to the groans, primarily from the first years, who had not yet experienced a Seguin Academy soccer practice, Mr. Stansfield said, "Oh, this is nothing. We're *only* going to do *two* laps around it." Ryan looked in near disbelief at the massive field. The notion that practice would *begin* after a run that looked like a marathon was almost laughable to Ryan, except that Mr. Stansfield was serious.

Despite feeling like he was going to die, not to mention throw up, several times along the way, running in the cool fall air had a calming effect. Even though he broke a sweat, the cool air kept him downright comfortable. Surprisingly, starting soccer practice after the longest run he had probably ever done, Ryan found the drills and the strategy of different soccer plays and situations were actually interesting and exciting. Sure, there was still physical toil involved, but compared to the drudgery of a five-mile run, it was almost nothing.

"How was your soccer practice?" Carmen asked at dinner.

"Got our butts kicked," Ryan said. "How about yours?"

"Same."

Meagan had stopped by the Seguin student cafeteria on Tuesday evening after a meeting with Mr. Sandhill to say hello to the bots cohort. "So how's it going?" she asked.

Everyone weighed in. They all felt deluged with work. Meagan gave a knowing smile. "Yes, it definitely seems overwhelming at first," she said. "But you'll manage. You'll see. Think about our trip. Think about the incredible things you guys did, and with such focus. You can do this. You *will* do this."

The talk turned to their teachers. "And you've got Freak and Zeek for

Robotics?" Meagan exclaimed. "I would have killed to have them at your age! They're the best! I love the work we do with them at Weatherall!"

At the end of day, Ryan, James, and Sammy commiserated while taking a brief study break, sitting in the living room of their dormitory suite. "I spoke to my parents a little while ago," Sammy said. "They didn't believe I'm taking Robotics from two guys called 'Freak' and 'Zeek.' They thought I was joking."

"I guess there are some things you just have to see to believe," James shrugged.

"They also didn't like that idea of 'Ask the crazy question,'" Sammy added.

"Really? I thought that made Freak and Zeek seem cool," Ryan said.

"Me, too," agreed James.

"Well, I'm in the same boat." Sammy said. "But I don't think my parents want me to rock the boat... you know, like I did in Chicago."

"Putting Chinny in the salt water tank? It wasn't even that big a deal," James said. "It was funny, though."

"Yeah, but if it were my parents, they'd have kicked my butt, too," Ryan said.

"Yeah. I guess parents are always worried about their kids sticking out, doing something weird, huh?" James said.

"Rebelling," said Sammy.

Remarkably, because his body was aching so much from the afternoon's soccer practice, Ryan found doing school work actually pleasant by comparison. It involved movement of nothing other than his eyes and fingers. His ankles, shins, knees, legs, back, and shoulders felt banged up and strained, so not moving them meant avoiding pain. Tiredness eventually overtook Ryan, and he fell asleep with his face on his book. He awoke at a wee hour of the morning, turned off his desk light, and threw himself into bed.

A few weeks later, on a Friday evening, Brad invited the bots group over to his dormitory at Weatherall University in Cambridge. Ryan and his friends took a shuttle van that ran from Seguin Academy into Boston and Cambridge. Several people had brought their bots with them, possibly to play around with. They had taken to carrying their animal bots around in duffel bags, backpacks, or the occasional carrying case, so they could avoid attracting attention and freaking people out with them. Ellen had brought the prototype of the new bot she had been developing, a leopard, to show to Brad and Meagan. Carmen and Jenny gushed to her about its surprisingly realistic appearance.

Next door to Brad's building on the Weatherall campus there was a fraternity house. As the Seguin students arrived, they could hear the loud, raucous noise of a party booming from it. "You know, I like a good time as much as the next person," Brad said, opening the door for everyone. "But, I have to get through four hundred pages of reading this weekend, as well as a robotics lab write-up, and there's basically no way I'm going to get any sleep tonight with all that noise next door. Not to mention, those guys will probably be partying all weekend long."

They had not eaten dinner yet, and the group from Seguin was looking forward to some non-cafeteria food for a change. "Tell you what," Brad said, "Since I promised Ellen I'd take a look at her new leopard bot for a few minutes, why don't some of you go pick up a couple of pizzas at the pizza place at the campus center and bring them back here? My treat. We can call in the order from here and it will be ready when you get there. We'll eat when you get back."

Brad called in the order. Meagan, Carmen, Sammy, and James said they'd go pick up the pizza. Ryan, Jenny, and Ellen stayed behind with Brad. Ellen could sometimes be a bit secretive with her robotic work, and Ryan was keen to see what the new leopard bot was capable of. Maybe there were ideas he could glean from Ellen and build them into Scram.

Ellen unzipped a large roller board on wheels that she had brought with her and gently withdrew a large, compact, folded up, fuzzy object. It had dark brown spots amid smooth, white, yellow, and orange swashes of color in its fur. On closer examination, Ryan recognized it as a leopard. Ellen gradually unfolded its legs, extended its neck, and stretched out its body. A replica of an adult leopard, it stood almost three feet high at the shoulders on soft looking padded feet, and had eerily piercing eyes. Ryan grew nervous looking at it. He would have been scared if he hadn't just seen it unpacked from a bag.

Ellen powered up the leopard, which took a few minutes. With her remote control console, she started walking the leopard around the room. "His name's Leo," she said. Leo strode back and forth in the room in a very catlike way. For Ryan, it was very convincing. Leo gave a low growl.

"Wow, this thing seems real!" Brad exclaimed. "It could totally freak people out."

Ellen stopped Leo, and using her hands on Leo's legs, she showed

Brad how she was having some difficulty mimicking the movements of a leopard when trying to make Leo run fast.

"Well, that's understandable, given that a leopard can run at something like thirty-six miles per hour," Brad said. "So you've got to synchronize the upper and lower legs. Here, let's take a look at how you have it set up. Brad sat down at a computer and pulled up some code that Ellen had sent to him via email. He then pulled up some video clips of a leopard sprinting. "Ultimately we'll need to put him on a track or a treadmill or something to see him running at full tilt," Brad said. "Obviously, space won't allow us to do that in here." He gestured with his eyes at the dormitory room they were standing in. While generous by university standards, it was clearly too small for testing the running gait of something as large—and as fast—as a leopard.

"Yeah, so the head and the legs need to be a bit more synchronized, like what I've been able to do with Trixie," Ellen said, referring to her fox bot. She was staring at the computer screen with Brad.

"Since a fox doesn't run as fast as a leopard, the way you have the mechanics working for Trixie are fine," Brad said. Ryan could see a fox shape in silhouette on the computer screen. The parts of the fox bot were outlined in light lines so you could see the different parts that made up its body. Brad was simulating the running movements of a fox using the design parts that had been made by the team in Mr. Sandhill's CAD lab at Weatherall University.

Okay, so the head and limb mobility need a little work—no big deal," Brad said, staring admiringly at Leo. "This is awesome."

At that moment, the group that had gone to get pizza arrived. A warm, delicious aroma immediately filled the room.

"So, how'd you do it?" Carmen asked Ellen, referring to the building of Leo. Everybody was diving into pizza boxes in a hungry, disorganized manner.

"I was able to use a lot of the same componentry that I use in Trixie," Ellen said. "And Brad and Meagan's friends in the CAD—computer aided design—lab were able to help me in designing and printing the body parts using the three dimensional printer."

"Yeah, they can do a lot with those 3-D printers, can't they?" Brad said. "It's awesome how they can create these lightweight, super strong plastic pieces, isn't it?"

Meagan was equally impressed. "Did you find a lot of leopard sounds to download from the web and build them into the bot?" she asked. In answer, Ellen pushed a button on a control console that made Leo give a ferocious growl. "Wow!" Meagan said. "I guess that's a yes." Ellen giggled. Jenny looked on, somewhat jealously.

"Thanks to the tricks that Vape, Rooker, and you guys showed us in Tanglewood, yes," Ellen said. "I got a lot of great sound clips from videos that came from zoos and wild animal explorers."

They ate all four boxes of pizza. Then Ellen started doing a few tricks with Leo. She also made him growl some more. People were laughing and reveling in Leo's sounds, which prompted Ellen to turn up the volume of the growls.

"You better keep the volume down on that thing," Meagan warned, "or it'll freak out the entire building."

"Yeah," Ryan said. Leo, played loud, was starting to unnerve him a little.

"Although probably no one will hear it because of the noise from the party next door," Jenny said.

There was a momentary pause. Then Brad's eyebrows perked up. "Wait a second. I've got an idea…"

"Uh oh," said Meagan. "I'm not sure I'm going to like this."

In a few minutes, the group was outside Brad's dormitory, standing in the darkness beside the fraternity house. Brad was playing around with Leo's control console, trying different movements and motions with Leo. He had muted the sound to practice, and was able to make Leo produce snarling, biting, and growling gestures. Partygoers were trickling in to the fraternity house every now and then, but they paid no attention to the small group of people lingering in the shadows.

"Are you going to do what I think you're going to do?" Ellen asked. She was trying to keep her voice down, but with all the noise emanating from the fraternity house, she actually had to speak up to be heard.

"Yeah. This should work," Brad said. He crouched down and slid to the front edge of the fraternity house. For the next few minutes, he watched the front area, and waited until there were no would-be partiers nearby. Then, he lifted up the control console to go to work.

"Really?" Ellen asked.

"It'll be fine," Brad said. With Leo striding alongside him, he crept up the steps to the front door of the fraternity house and rang the doorbell.

Within the fraternity house, the sound of the doorbell ringing was barely audible above the din of music and loud voices that pervaded the house. One of the fraternity brothers who heard it wondered to himself why someone would be so polite to bother ringing the doorbell when it was so obvious that a huge party was raging inside. He stumbled past a few people to the door, opened it, and immediately froze.

What people inside heard next was a low-pitched, rasping growl with a tinny edge that silenced and stunned everyone in the front rooms of the house. Instantly, peoples' chattering noise and laughter ceased. The music, which had seemed loud in comparison, faded to background noise in the wake of the sharp growls that now permeated the place.

The second growl convinced everyone that the large, ominous-looking cat they had heard and were staring at was real, and that it meant business. That was all they needed to begin a stampede. Dozens of people trampled over and past each other as they ran for the back of the house. The rush to escape out the back created an enormous traffic jam of people clamoring to get out. A few of the savvier ones figured out they could push open a partially opened window and jump out that way, which a few did, soon followed by many more. The people at the back of the house when the doorbell rang were initially bewildered by their suddenly crazed colleagues who had come barreling at them from the front of the house. Just what exactly was happening? They wondered.

Those who had seen Leo were not all exactly sure which species of feline animal had stood menacingly before them in their crazed madness to flee and they weren't stopping to take mental notes. But they were unanimous in saying they had seen a wild cat that you most certainly did not see in houses, or at the parties of said houses. Even when the house in question was a frat house.

"There's a wild jaguar on the loose at the front door!" somebody shrieked.

"Cougar!" shouted another.

"Leopard! Mountain lion! Bobcat! Tiger!" still others shouted.

The exact variety of cat was unimportant. Getting out of the house was. Leo took a few steps towards the fleeing masses of people. Glasses, windows, and dishes broke. People were screaming in terror. Incredibly, Brad was maneuvering Leo from just outside one of the windows of the fraternity house, peering inside to view the action. If anyone fleeing out a window had stopped for half a second to look at him, they might have wondered why he was just standing there, perfectly calm, with some boxy looking device in his hands. But no one did.

10

CATHERINE BERGERON SETS SAIL

After the berserk masses of people had flown from the front rooms of the frat house, Leo gave one more bone-rattling growl. People were pouring out of the back doorway of the frat house, shouting and screaming, falling over each other, and sprinting off to other buildings on campus. Brad steered Leo back out the front door of the frat house, around the front corner to the Seguin group, whereupon Leo sat obediently on his hind legs.

"We better get out of here," Meagan said. That was the understatement of the week. "Let's go!" Ryan considered the consequences if the houseful of people, whose frat party had just been brought to a crashing halt, discovered that the ferocious cat scare was a prank. He figured the battering he'd taken from Chip McCollum for his bot shenanigans the previous fall would look like child's play by comparison.

Faster than taking a bite of pizza, Ellen collapsed the major parts of Leo's body, folded him up, and put him back in the wheeled suitcase in which she had brought him. Ryan thought it was incredibly lucky that Ellen had remembered to bring it with her. Without it, they could have been discovered, and possibly throttled by an angry mob. Quickly and quietly, the group beat a path back to Brad's dormitory building. As they walked, they kept to the shadows. Upon entering, they hopped on the elevator and piled into Brad's room as fast as they could.

A few brief minutes ticked by. Everyone was out of breath, from fear more than anything else. They all collapsed on the sofas in Brad's living room. Brad was wearing a cunning, self-assured smile, but the mood of everyone else was far from jovial. Shortly, one siren, then another, and then another rang out. They grew louder with each passing second. From

Brad's window, Ryan could soon see police lights glaring outside down below, and he heard occasional shouts and screams of people who had been at the frat house party.

"Uh, quick, I think we need to hide this thing!" Brad said, pointing to Ellen's roller board that contained Leo.

"What are you talking about?" Meagan asked, bewildered.

"They'll probably stop by—they'll go door-to-door—to alert us of some wild animal roaming around here," Brad said. "That seems to be what they usually do in cases like this, not that there have been that many." Ryan was impressed by Brad's knowledge of such matters, and wondered how he had come by it. Brad took the roller board and shoved it, with difficulty, into a crowded closet at one side of the room. "It's already hidden in the suitcase, but it's best not to leave it out."

Tense minutes oozed past. People sat glued on the sofas around a coffee table, pretending to socialize, wishing they could leave, but feeling paralyzed to do so, given the mayhem now ensuing outside. Brad turned on a stereo on for some background music. Occasionally, they glanced out the window. Down below, people were still shrieking in hysterics, and police were trying to get a sense for what had happened and maintain some sense of order. Sure enough, as Brad had predicted, a while later his doorbell rang. Brad opened the door. Two campus policemen stood in the doorway.

"Uh, hi folks. Sorry to interrupt. There have been reports tonight of a wild animal, a wild cat of some kind, like a mountain lion or a leopard loose here in the area this evening," one of the officers said. "Have you heard or seen anything like that?"

"Uh, no, officer," Brad said, trying in earnest to keep a serious looking face. "We've just been hanging out here. It was quite noisy for a while, from the party, I suppose, then it got quite loud, and then the noise died down. I guess that must have been from the—"

"Disturbance," the officer said.

"Right," Brad agreed.

The officer took a quick glance around the room at everyone. It seemed that he and his colleague were pressed for time. That made sense to Ryan if they were alerting everyone in the entire building—all ten floors of it—to be on the lookout for a wild animal. "Well, please stay safe," the officer continued. "We prefer that everyone stay inside right now, but if anyone must leave the building, we recommend you go in groups and have a flash light with you. Make noise as you walk. We are also trying to get escorts and make them available. We will have officers stationed down below for the next few hours. Don't hesitate to talk to one of us if you need assistance." Then the officers were gone as quickly as they had come.

"So how do we get Leo out of here?" Ellen asked Brad accusatively. "They'll have cops stationed down there for hours."

"No big deal," Brad said. "Leo's in the roller board. You are simply passing through with a suitcase. That happens all the time on a college campus. Why would they think that was weird?"

"Why would I be leaving the campus in the vicinity of a college frat party with a suitcase on a Friday night?" Ellen said.

"Uh... good point. You can leave Leo here and get him later if you want," Brad said.

Ellen didn't like it, but she felt it was the better option. If anything happened to Leo, she would be furious. She had put so much work into building him and would hate to have to start all over. So, she agreed to leave Leo with Brad until the following week, when Brad would bring him back to her at Seguin. Ryan, Ellen, and the others from Seguin lingered at Brad's dorm until a few minutes before ten o'clock, in part to calm frayed nerves and in part to allow most of the commotion to die down. They had to leave then because ten o'clock was the time of the last departing shuttle bus from Weatherall to Seguin.

Ryan felt tired on the shuttle bus ride. It had been a nerve-wracking Friday night. The rest of the weekend was filled with reading, soccer games, tinkering with Scram, more reading, and other schoolwork, but he kept recalling the stunt they pulled at Weatherall with Leo the leopard bot. It was amazing to consider the reaction one could get from an animal bot.

The following Tuesday in Robotics, Freak and Zeek were not impressed. Brad and Meagan were in attendance with the Seguin students, a surprise in and of itself. Ryan wondered what they were doing there. Freak and Zeek paused until everyone had come into the classroom and was seated. There was a momentary pause and a heavy sigh from Zeek.

"I get it," Freak said. He was looking directly at Brad. "You wanted to have a little fun at the expense of a fraternity at Weatherall this weekend by unleashing a leopard bot into their festivities."

"What do you mean?" Brad asked. "What are you talking about?"

"Come on, Brad. We know you better than that," Zeek said.

"Well, it was a loud, unruly party," Brad said. "It needed to be quieted down a little."

"Calling the campus police didn't occur to you as a possible option?"

"That's what I should have done," Brad said. A quiver of his lips told Ryan he was lying.

"Scaring the wits out of unsuspecting college kids through possible criminal activity is not the way to make the evening news, Brad," Zeek said.

"We... Uh, the story, uh, made the evening news?" Brad said.

"Yep. And it was a bit difficult for me to have to call the campus *and* city police to explain to them that no, I was pretty sure a leopard did not escape from the city zoo, and well, how did I know that, and that, well, I knew some students, probably not *my* students mind you, but some students had been doing some work on robots. And these robots occasionally take on the resemblance of, say, animals you might find in the wild. Since I was at home, and nowhere near campus, thankfully, I could not point out anyone nearby who might have been involved, since I didn't know for certain if this was indeed the cause of the wild cat sighting. But, as was later confirmed by the area zoos, none of their wild cats were missing, and I'm not aware of anyone raising a wild leopard in the Cambridge area. So, in a word, let's see, how to say this? I kind of saved your bacon. And so, with all of that said, do you have anything to say for yourselves?"

"Uh, we're sorry... for what happened?" Brad said. "And, uh, thanks?"

"That's a good start," Zeek said.

"It was Brad's idea," Ellen blurted out.

"Thanks, Ellen," Brad said icily.

"Well, it was. And it could have cost me weeks of work if anything had happened," Ellen shot back.

"Brad, and you, Meagan, I'm a bit disappointed in you," Zeek said.

"Me?" said Meagan defensively. "You know once Brad gets an idea in his head there's no stopping him."

"Wow, thanks to you, too, Meagan," Brad said. "What is this? Beat on Brad day?"

"Well, you did cause a small gathering of... oh... about three hundred students to fear for their lives," Zeek said.

"Fortunately, there was truly never any danger," Brad said.

"Well, I'm pretty sure they'd see it differently if you were to try to explain it to them," Freak said. "Not to mention, people could have been seriously hurt in the stampede to get out of the house and escape from the cat... bot... er, leopard."

"You're right," Brad sighed with resignation.

"Well, we'll deal with this matter with you, Brad, and Meagan separately, and privately, since everyone else here was involved, but not in the same way," Zeek said. "They were, in a way, passengers on your runaway train adventure."

"Fair enough," Brad said.

With the typically upbeat, happy mood of Robotics class effectively killed for the day, Freak and Zeek ended the class a few minutes early. They asked Brad and Megan to stay behind. Afterwards, Ryan and the group caught up with them.

"You got a bit of a tongue lashing in there," Meagan said to Brad.

"Could have been worse," Brad said. "Besides, these guys have to learn about broinks some time." He gestured with his eyes to the Seguin students. Ryan suddenly remembered Mr. Sandhill's mention of 'broinks' from two summers ago, pranks that students would play in order to confound faculty, students, and occasionally law enforcement at Weatherall University.

"I will say, I don't really see you as the type of guy who would call the campus police to make a party quiet down," James said.

"If it's not a life and death situation, calling the campus police is basically useless," Brad said. "Of course, the cops came flying when it was *perceived* to be a life and death situation with a wild animal on the loose."

"Sorry—not entirely, but a little bit—that I gave you up in there," Ellen said. She had most certainly been unhappy with Brad's decision to launch the frat party stunt with Leo, but she considered Brad a friend.

"Well, it was probably not the right thing to do, and it was a bit reckless," Brad acknowledged. "And, I'm sorry you thought something was going to happen to Leo. I was sure that nothing would happen, but you didn't know that. And, fortunately, despite being scared out of their minds, no one got seriously hurt. And, guess what, there was one more upside to the whole thing..."

"What's that?" Ryan asked.

"I got to read in peace and quiet for the next two nights," he smiled.

For Ryan, going to school in a place near the seacoast gave him more exposure to boating than he ever had before. Sure, there were lakes in

Texas. His family had friends who sailed and he had been out on their boats a few times. But, the whole of his boating experience felt small compared to the sailing, rowing, and boating he saw around him in the Seguin community. For starters, Seguin had a rowing team. Ryan had never heard of such a thing. In fact, neither had most of his Seguin friends. Ellen, who was from Massachusetts, was the only one really familiar with it, because she had grown up around it. Her family sailed routinely and she was on the girls' rowing team at Seguin. Then, of course, there was the proximity of Seguin Academy to the coast, and various classes and excursions to Boston and other shore points that exposed students to boats and ships, large and small.

Ryan and his friends from the bot group were talking about rowing one day at lunch. It was a happier topic than discussing more miserable ones, such as the latest two hundred pages of Physics or History or next week's Math quiz.

"So how's the rowing team doing?" Sammy asked of Ellen.

"It's going okay," Ellen said. "Except there's this one girl who isn't quite pulling her weight in the quad and the eight. Those are my events."

"Woe to that girl," Jenny said. She was trying to make a joke, but Ellen did not appreciate it.

"Unlike in *singles tennis*," Ellen said, referring to Jenny's sport, "when you have a number of people on the team and one of them isn't pulling their weight, it makes it harder for everyone else, and it basically makes it impossible for the team to win."

"I get it," Jenny said. "I was just trying to make a joke."

"Uh, okay," Ellen said awkwardly. "Anyway, we're trying to get ready for a big rowing competition that happens in the fall each year, called the Head of the Charles Regatta."

"Head of the Charles? Is that like Day of the Dead?" asked Carmen, also trying be humorous.

"Uh, not really, no. Though Day of the Dead is a cool holiday, and if you've rowed in the Head of the Charles you *feel* like you're dead afterwards! Every year, in Cambridge, rowing teams come from all over the place, from all over the world, I guess, for this big rowing competition. You row in different age groups and in different boat types. But, I am sort of freaking out about it because as I said, we've got a loose link in the chain, so to speak."

"Well, can you talk to her? Ask her if something's wrong?" James asked.

"Yeah, I suppose. It's a little delicate, you know? You don't really want to come across as if you're saying 'Hey, I see you're really screwing it up on rowing, what can I do to help?' You know what I mean?"

"Sure," James said. "But doing nothing about it will get you nowhere just as fast."

"True," Ellen said.

"Let us know how it goes," James said. Diplomacy had not proven to be Ellen's strong suit, but she meant well. Ryan figured she was probably the brightest member of the bot cohort at Seguin.

Inspired by Mrs. Bergeron and her affinity for marine biology, Sammy continued to work diligently on his killer whale bot project. He was frequently on the phone with Brad, Meagan, Mr. Sandhill, or someone else over at Weatherall University trying to work out the designs for the bots.

"Awesome. I'll have all the parts for the orca bots next week," Sammy said blissfully after getting off the phone one evening with the Weatherall CAD lab.

"Bots, as in, plural? So, how many are you planning to build?" Ryan asked.

"Two," Sammy replied.

"Aren't the killer whale bots going to be fairly huge?" Ryan asked.

"Yeah. Life sized," Sammy replied.

"So where will you keep them?" James asked.

"Not sure, yet," Sammy said. "But, I can't move them too far from Weatherall, where the parts are coming from, since they will be so huge. I think I can keep them in one of the Weatherall boathouses, for just a little while."

"So what will you call them?" James asked.

"Chomp and Tux," Sammy said.

"Chompentucks?" James repeated.

"Chomp, as in, teeth," Sammy said, making a biting motion with his mouth. "And Tux, as in, tuxedo. You know, the black and white formal suit that hopefully I'll never have to wear."

By the following week, as promised, Sammy had received all the parts of his killer whale bots. While he did much of the assembly of the smaller internal parts and components of the bots in his dorm room at Seguin, he had to do the assembly of the bodies outside at Weatherall. He took the main body parts to a dock near one of the Weatherall boathouses to assemble them. Despite some large panels that were made of a special, super strong, flexible plastic, there were a huge number of pieces. Sammy spent most of the next few weekends down at the Weatherall docks by the Charles River in Cambridge assembling Chomp and Tux. "It goes a lot faster once you figure out how to put one of them together," he said on a Sunday morning in early October as he headed off to Cambridge on the shuttle bus to continue his work on the bots. They were nearing completion. He had covered the bots on a dock—which they barely fit onto—with some old boat covers from the marina. Happily for Sammy, the tarp-covered orcas appeared to be boats sitting on stilts out of water and no one gave them a second thought.

Sammy knew he could not keep the orca bots sitting on the Weatherall docks for much longer, since the famed Head of the Charles Regatta, with its throngs of crowds, would be happening in a few days. Rowers were already starting to arrive in large numbers and doing practice runs on the river. He decided it would be best to move the orcas inside the Weatherall boathouse. So along with Brad, Meagan, and the Seguin bot cohort, Sammy devised a makeshift crane from miscellaneous wood beams, poles, and some rope from the boathouse. They managed to persuade the Seguin shuttle van driver to help them move Chomp and Tux into the Weatherall boathouse by mounting the crane on top of the shuttle van. With effort, they lifted Chomp, then Tux onto boat trailer frames on wheels in order to roll them off the docks up to the boathouse loading area. Then, with ropes secured under Chomp and Tux, at the entry to the boathouse, using the crane mounted atop the shuttle van, they were able to hoist the hulking bots and gingerly drive them into the boathouse. There they secured each of them with rope to the rafters high above, so that they were somewhat, but not quite completely, out of the way.

No sooner had they completed this sweat–inducing chore when the Weatherall boathouse manager arrived. Nobody said anything as he strode into the boathouse. However, it took only a millisecond for him to notice the killer whale bots hanging mere inches above eye level.

"What the—" said the boathouse manager. With the Head of the Charles happening in a few days' time, he was busy with a million different tasks. "Are these things real?"

"No. They're... robots. Can I store these in here, for just a few days? Please?" Sammy pleaded.

"Dude, no way. You can't keep killer whales or robots or whatever they are in the boat house," the boathouse manager said. "Especially with all the pre-race activity starting tomorrow. People will kill me."

"I get it," Sammy said, disheartened.

The manager immediately began wheeling a trailer hookup into the boathouse for the express purpose of lowering the orcas onto it and moving them out of the boathouse.

"So what the heck do we do now?" James asked.

"I don't know, but let me think about it," Sammy said. They pondered their predicament with Brad and Meagan.

"We could take 'em out for a spin," Sammy said.

"You think they're ready?" Ryan asked.

"Yeah. Besides, we gotta test 'em out sometime," Sammy replied.

"All right, well, this is a job for a grownup," Brad said. "So I should be one of the test pilots." He was only joking with the grownup bit, but he definitely looked intrigued by the prospect of taking an orca bot out for a ride. Each orca bot had a piloting compartment so it could be piloted manually like a submarine as well as remotely.

"I don't know if that's a good idea," Meagan said. "With all of the boaters out on the river and everything..."

"It'll be fine," Brad said.

Ryan was pretty sure Meagan was right, but her advice was not to be heeded by Brad and Sammy.

"We'll just take the orcas out for a quick test drive. Then we'll park them down the river a bit in the Brownings Club boat house," Brad said. "I've used it a few times. There's plenty of space. One of the Weatherall professors belongs there and we'll just leave the orcas there, in the water, for a few days until we figure out where to put them longer term."

"Sounds good to me," Sammy said.

Minutes later, the boathouse manager, Sammy and the others, with the help of the makeshift crane, hoisted the orcas from their places in the boathouse and hauled them out onto the docks. Eager to avoid drawing attention to the orcas, Sammy quickly helped the boathouse manager lower them into the water. They now sat submerged, like submarines, just below the surface of the water, with only a portion of their backs and ominous dorsal fins visible, sticking up a good three feet above the waterline.

Ryan, Meagan, and the others looked on with trepidation as Sammy and Brad raised lids, small doors, actually, on the backs of Chomp and Tux. They climbed inside the piloting capsules in the bodies of the bots.

"They can also be piloted with a remote console from the outside," Sammy noted. "But, piloting them manually probably gives us a little more precision while we're still in learning mode."

It was a bit unnerving watching Sammy and Brad shimmy into the cockpits of the orca bots and close the hatches. Within minutes, the orcas swam off from the boathouse and began to dive down into the dark waters of the river, their powerful tales undulating up and down, propelling them forcefully through the water.

"I can't believe I'm watching this," Ryan said.

"Well, you are," James said. "It's real."

"That's the problem," Meagan sighed. "It's real, and those enormous things are going to cause some real trouble with all the boaters out at the Charles River today. Look at them, they're everywhere."

And indeed they were. Brad and Sammy hadn't necessarily chosen to pilot the orcas in the direction of rowers, but with so many of them out on the river, it was virtually impossible to do otherwise. As the orcas intersected with a series of crew skulls rowing past, Brad and Sammy evidently decided to have some fun.

"Uh oh, I don't like this," Meagan remarked.

"Me either." Ellen echoed.

From the boathouse dock, Meagan and the rest of the group were motionless. They watched the relatively calm waters of the Charles River, and followed with their eyes along the water the twin paths they imagined the massive robotic orcas to be swimming.

"You know, if any rowers see the orcas, they are going to completely freak out," Jenny said. The same thought was just now occurring to everyone else as well.

"No kidding," Ellen agreed.

"Uh oh," Jenny blurted out suddenly.

Everyone's eyes turned to a pair of crew boats coming down the river. Each boat had two rowers aboard, rowing hard with intense concentration. It seemed that little could distract their focus. That is, until they saw the dorsal fins of the killer whales. The fins appeared some thirty yards away from the rowers, rising up out of the water and holding steady as they carved through the river, gaining rapidly on the boats. Suddenly, the rowers, sitting backwards in their shells and facing the orcas, started to scream at the tops of their lungs. There was little for them to do. They weren't about to jump overboard and there was no shore nearby. However, the lead boat was somewhat close to a bridge, and it appeared that the panicking rower closest to it was trying to make a grab for the brick-work of one of its arches in an effort to climb up and out.

The other rowers pulled their oars from the water and were brandishing them as spears they could use to hurl or try to stave off the oncoming orcas. Such effort, however, was fruitless. Onlookers were stunned by what happened next. The dorsal fins disappeared underwater. Then, some seconds later, two huge killer whales breeched up out of the water in a magnificent surge. You could see them unmistakably, their massive, black backs, white undersides, and white spots on the sides of their heads, with their powerful tails propelling them skyward. You could see their gleaming white teeth rimming their large, grinning jaws. As they hauled up out of the water, each lifted a rowing shell up out of the water with it, causing the rowers in each boat to go airborne, so that boats, oars, and rowers were all lofted up high into the air, landing along with the killer whales in a terrific splash in the Charles River. The incident completely upended an otherwise peaceful and glorious colorful fall visage in Cambridge.

People were now shrieking and yelling. The water-logged rowers, shocked and stunned, began swimming for their lives towards the shore-line. Other rowers, initially hesitant to row into the area where they had just seen two killer whales soar out of the water, soon overcame their fears and rowed over to pick up the hapless upended rowers. Crowds cheered upon realizing the rowers were otherwise unharmed, despite being soaking wet. Once the rowers were brought in to shore, people could be seen attending to them. The rowers were doubtlessly more terrified than anything else at the moment.

Within minutes, news teams from all over the country, many who were already in attendance to cover the Head of the Charles Regatta, were pouring down to the place of the incident at the edge of the Charles River. The scene erupted into chaos. Photographers were taking pictures of the section of river around the bridge where the boats had been upended. People were now crowding around the spot. Reporters in search of an interview chased after just about anyone who moved, followed by dutiful camera teams wielding photography and lighting equipment. Students at nearby Weatherall University and others, curious about the commotion, wandered down to the riverside to see what was going on. This led, in turn, to more people being accosted by reporters for an interview; though a good many of them hadn't been present at the scene when the "orca incident" occurred. Police cars, a fire truck, and ambulances ultimately arrived on the scene.

The attention of most everyone had immediately turned to the hapless rowers, who had found themselves tossed up into the air and into the water like rag dolls by the bulldozing orcas. So, Brad and Sammy were able to dive deep down in the river with the orcas and swim away as quickly as they had materialized. They guided the orcas to the upstream boathouse which Brad had mentioned earlier. That boathouse sat around a bend in the river, so Brad and Sammy were able to moor the orcas quietly behind it without being noticed by the throng of people now gathering downstream.

It felt to Ryan and the others that now was an excellent time to leave, so they did. It was a painfully long wait for the shuttle bus to take them back to Seguin, but it eventually came. The blocking off of streets for the racing festivities had temporarily changed its route. Later, they met up with Sammy at the Seguin Student Center. While they were sitting there, a newscast came on the big board, the center's large television screen.

"And, an exciting, harrowing development at the Head of the Charles Regatta activities today… something you don't usually see on the Charles River—killer whales. Yes, you heard me, killer whales. And, not just one, but two."

"And I thought killer whales lived in the ocean," guffawed the co-anchorwoman.

"Me, too," chortled her co-anchorman. "But, watch this video that was shot by a bystander of some rowers in their boats, doing a practice run at about two forty-five this afternoon. Right from the sidewalk on Memorial Drive, just watch what happens. Keep your eye on the crew shells at the left of your picture."

As the video played, Ryan, James, and Sammy re-watched the catastrophe that had unfolded earlier in the day.

"Man, I hate watching repeats," James said. "You always know what's going to happen. And, in this case, it's pretty ugly."

"If I didn't think we were in serious trouble, I would say that's just about the funniest thing I've ever seen in my life," Ryan said, trying unsuccessfully to stifle a laugh.

"That is one for those silly home video television shows, isn't it?" Jenny said, laughing.

The next day, Sammy, Ryan, and the others found themselves summoned by Mrs. Bergeron to her office. Exchanging pleasantries was not on the agenda. Mr. Sandhill was present as well, as were Brad and Meagan.

"So perhaps you can tell me about the incident involving killer whale bots and a few boaters down at the Charles River yesterday?"

"What makes you think we had anything to do with it?" Sammy asked.

"Oh, you mean aside from the fact that you took delivery on parts for two robotic killer whale robots from the CAD lab at Weatherall University a few weeks ago? You know, you're right. I mean, why would you be under suspicion?" Mrs. Bergeron said sarcastically.

"And you, Brad, I'm surprised at you. Encouraging this sort of behavior? Where does this inspiration come from?"

"We were just thinking it would be... you know, fun," Brad said quietly.

"It was my idea, not Brad's," Sammy said. Ryan was impressed that Sammy was sticking up for his friend.

"Not true," Brad said. "I told Sammy we should do it."

"Well, regardless of whose idea it was... You know, normally I'm in favor of generating publicity on behalf of Seguin Academy," Mrs. Bergeron continued. "But right now my phone is ringing off the hook with reporters wanting to know the story behind the killer whales that made an appearance in the Charles River yesterday. What exactly would you like me to say to them?"

The conversation went on like this for about an hour. Strangely, Mrs. Bergeron did not hand down a specific punishment.

"Maybe she's trying to think of one that will be severe enough," Carmen muttered.

She did openly consider whether to cancel the participation of the Seguin rowing team in the Head of the Charles events, which caused Ellen to shoot a look of contempt at Sammy and Brad. If she'd been holding daggers just then, she'd have thrown them.

Later, Mrs. Bergeron dismissed the Seguin students, but asked Brad and Meagan to stay behind.

Brad stopped by Sellinger dormitory to talk with Sammy, James, and Ryan. "Catherine wasn't too hard on us. It could've been worse," Brad said. "I said 'Look, if you're going to punish anyone, it should be me, or me and Sammy. But, nobody else had anything to do with it,'" Brad recounted. "So Sammy and I will pay the price. For me and Sammy, there will be a month of no social activities, which, at least for me won't be too bad, since I already basically have no social life," he continued.

"But, the worst part is, Catherine is taking away the controls to everyone's bots for a month," Brad said. Sammy looked crestfallen.

"Everyone? As in, all of us?" James asked.

"Everyone," Brad replied. "All the master controls, chips, anything you could use to control them. I'm here to pick them up."

That was heartbreaking to everyone.

"*Seguin May Be Linked to Scandal That Rocked the Head of the Charles Event*," read the headline of the Seguin Weekly newspaper the following week. Reporters appeared at the perimeter of the Seguin Academy campus trying to get a scoop on the killer whales and the Head of the Charles Regatta incident. Mrs. Bergeron would not permit them on campus, so they accosted people coming and going to and from the campus, with little success. There was a suspected linkage between Seguin and Weatherall University since the two schools were known for collaborations in various facets of the sciences, including robotics.

Ryan thought it was incredible that no names of people were disclosed in the Seguin Weekly. But, the students had their suspicions, and they knew full well who the members of the bot cohort were. Ryan and his friends layed low, or at least they tried to. Their task was made easier by not having any hands-on controls to use with their robots. Thus, there were no sights of robotic animals skittering or flying across the campus to draw attention.

The hullaballoo over the killer whales gradually subsided over the next few weeks. The killer whales were widely suspected to be robots, since the creatures were never actually found. This only added to the public's curiosity, and their mystique. Many in the press pointed out repeatedly that orcas are salt water animals and that, *really*, what animal could actually survive in the Charles River? Brad's recommended mooring location for the orcas of the distant boathouse proved to be a surprisingly good hiding place.

With more free time on their hands, Ryan and his Seguin friends soon began turning their attention to a different sort of boat—the *Shakti*—the boat that would soon bear Catherine Bergeron, her husband, Francois, and a camera crew on a trip around the world to do research. Despite their occasional run-ins with Catherine, which, if truth be told, were largely of their own doing, everyone had found her to be a highly motivating and encouraging head of school, and they really began to feel they would miss her when she took her leave of absence. Mrs. Bergeron and Mr. Sandhill were both their teachers and the bot cohort academic advisors to Ryan and his friends. So, Catherine went to great lengths to familiarize Ryan and the bot cohort students about her upcoming voyage. And, in the weeks leading up to her departure, she took the bot cohort frequently to Woods Hole, on the south coast of Massachusetts, so they could be a part of the preparations for the journey. The first trip there was memorable for all.

The *Shakti* ran about thirty-six feet long. It was a fine, polished white color, which accentuated its sleek, smooth lines against the dark, glassy water in which it sat in the marina. The mainsail was neatly rolled up in a sleeve sitting on the boom, low and perpendicular to the main mast, and parallel to the hull. For all of the *Shakti's* design, though, Ryan had been expecting more. He wasn't sure why. Perhaps because he wouldn't want to be caught in the towering waves of a storm on the open seas in a boat that looked like it could get tossed around like a rubber duck in a bathtub. Evidently, he was not the only one.

"You're going to cross the ocean in *that?*" Jenny asked. She was the most uninhibited of the group when it came to asking blunt, direct questions. At times, her manner could be brusque, but in this case, she asked what was on everyone's mind.

"Yes, this is the boat," Mrs. Bergeron responded, without a hint of hesitation.

"It looks smaller than you were expecting, perhaps?" said Mr. Bergeron. He laughed. "Not all boats that cross the ocean are tankers or ocean liners. In fact, most are not."

"Do you ever get seasick on the *Shakti* on the open seas?" Ellen asked.

"Oh, you get used to it," Mrs. Bergeron said. Watching the boat bobbing up and down gently, Ryan wondered how many barf bags it would take for him to 'get used to it' on the open ocean, or if it were even possible.

"How many of you are going on the trip?" asked Sammy.

"Five," said Mr. Bergeron. "Catherine, and three film crewmembers, and me. Since the boat sleeps six, we should be okay."

Shortly the film crewmembers, two men and a woman, arrived at the dock. They made several trips down to the dock, bringing what appeared to be several bags and cases of film equipment as well as some travel bags. They seemed excited to be heading off on a big adventure.

Mrs. Bergeron introduced the students to the film crew. "My students can't believe we don't get completely seasick from being on a small sail boat on the open seas," she laughed.

"That's nothing compared to staring into the jaws of a great white shark through a camera lens," one of the men from the film crew laughed.

On their last trip to Woods Hole before Mrs. Bergeron's departure, Ryan and his friends helped the *Shakti* team haul a bunch of stuff onto the boat. While they loaded boxes of food and supplies onto the boat, they didn't know where it all got stored once aboard. So there came a point when they generally just tried to stay out of the way and watched from the docks. Catherine and Francois Bergeron were in their element on the *Shakti*. They knew where everything belonged, and you got the sense they had sailed on boat trips like this one many, many times before.

As the Bergerons and the crew were making their final preparations for launch, Meagan produced a laptop computer. "I'll show you guys the remote tracking tool," she said. "I'll send you guys the link, and we'll all be able to track the *Shakti* online as she goes on her trip.

Everyone said goodbye. For Ryan, it was a somber moment. Mrs. Bergeron was a very familiar fixture in his life at Seguin, and he was losing that now. "Keep doing what you're doing," Mrs. Bergeron said as the *Shakti* pulled away. "We will be connected most of the time, so whether you like it or not, I will never actually be all that far away!"

The *Shakti* motored briefly at slow speed out of the marina. The Seguin students, Mr. Sandhill, Brad, and Meagan waved from the dock. Catherine and Francois Bergeron and the film crew waved back. Once out of the marina and in the harbor, the *Shakti* cut its engine and began to sail. Aided by a brisk wind, the *Shakti* sailed smoothly out of the harbor, and out to sea. The group watched for about twenty minutes, by which time the *Shakti* was a small, faint object on the horizon.

"So, is the tracker working?" Brad asked Meagan.

"Yeah," Meagan said. "You can see where they are, right here." Everyone drew close to Meagan and looked on her laptop computer. On the screen was a nautical map of the area of south Cape Cod and Nantucket Sound. The islands of Martha's Vineyard and Nantucket and various others were visible. Meagan pointed to a dot on the screen, just outside Woods Hole in Nantucket Sound. She then zoomed out so everyone could see the broad mass of ocean that awaited the *Shakti*.

"Wow, there sure is a lot of blank space on that screen," Ryan said.

"Well, there sure is a lot of blank space out there," Meagan said, pointing with her eyes to the vast expanse of the ocean.

11

DR. SPEAKEASY

Soon thereafter, fall gave way to winter. Ryan felt its full force after returning to Seguin from a visit home during the mid-year holiday break. The winter cold had a nasty bite, and it kept Ryan and his friends inside much of the time. Fortunately, they did not lack for things to do. Amid their usual deluge of schoolwork, they intently followed the *Shakti's* journey online as it crossed the Atlantic Ocean and headed south around the tip of Africa, frequently reading the posts that Catherine and Francois Bergeron would put on the ship's travel web site, and sending comments in reply. And, while staying indoors did sometimes feel limiting in terms of what one could do with one's bot, Ryan and company found themselves playing with variations on the theme of the animal bot they had started with, trying to build related, but different animal bot concepts. Thus, Ryan was making a lot of progress on a spider bot, Jenny was rapidly having success with the intricacies of a house fly bot, James with a turtle bot, Ellen continued work with Leo the leopard bot, and Carmen with a heron bot. All of the skeletal components had been developed courtesy of the Sandhill Lab at Weatherall University. Brad and Meagan had helped them design the parts. As Sammy had pushed the design envelope quite a bit with his building of the orca bots, people often came to him with questions.

"How was the CAD group at Weatherall able to accommodate the size of something like a killer whale?" Ryan asked, amazed that such a thing was possible.

"I thought it might be a bit tricky at first, but Brad and Meagan told me they've developed frames for some pretty large objects before," Sammy said. "They've borrowed some design and molding technology from the Weatherall Aeronautics Department in the past. Actually, that's where they sent me first, to the Aeronautics group. They design all kinds of large things there, wings and tails for aircraft, panel designs for satellites, that sort of thing."

"What did they say to you when you said you were trying to build a killer whale?" James asked.

"Nothing. To them it was no more unusual than a lot of the things they're asked to design—rocket parts, submarines, parts for space stations. I could just as easily have been asking them to design the wing on one of Townley's cargo planes."

"Wow. It seems like no idea's too crazy for them," Ryan said.

"Well, when you tell them Mr. Sandhill is a sponsor of one of your projects, it seems like you get more attention, or maybe a higher priority than you might otherwise get," Sammy said. "Dropping the names of Brad, Meagan, and Carey doesn't hurt either."

"Huh," Ryan and James mused.

One bright spot in the gloomy depths of January was the visit they made every two weeks to the Media Lab at Weatherall University. Every other Wednesday afternoon they piled into a Weatherall van that picked them up and drove them from Seguin Academy to the Weatherall Media Lab in Cambridge where they would attend class led by Freak and Zeek. The Media Lab itself actually consisted of a couple of large buildings dedicated to media and technology of all kinds: information, cameras, imaging, robotics, mechanical devices, biological systems, neurological systems, computer systems and surfaces, and novel materials, to name a few.

Ryan found the trips to the Media Lab a welcome interruption from the humdrum routine of school at Seguin. The brightly lit, white interiors of the main building afforded a cheery escape from the otherwise grey weather outside, and there was so much to see at the Media Lab that one couldn't help but become absorbed in the place upon entering. During the Media Lab working sessions, the Seguin students would refine their bots, add new features and functionality, and exchange ideas with each other. It also afforded an opportunity for the Seguin students to wander around, talk to Weatherall students about their research projects, and get advice on their own bot projects. Sometimes the conversation would result in a student roaming across campus to another lab or department, as in the case of Sammy seeking to refine his killer whale bots, which necessitated occasional visits to the Aeronautics Department.

The Seguin Weatherall Media Lab sessions were a different way of spending time in school. While people worked on their bots, Freak and

Zeek would roam around the room, pointing things out to people, asking questions, inviting discussion, and, of course, poking fun at people. It was fun for everyone to take the occasional break from fine-tuning their bots and wander over to the side of the room where Freak and Zeek's creations, often works in process, sat on a long bank of lab tables.

The Freak and Zeek Lab, housed within the Weatherall Media Lab, was twice as large as most labs, basically because it had two laboratory heads, namely, Freak and Zeek. The two were known for teaching courses and collaborating on a great many projects together, so it was unsurprising that they had one lab between the two of them. But, it hadn't always been that way.

"For years, Freak and I each had our own lab and they were right next to each other," Zeek explained. "We were running back and forth down the hall between the two labs all the time and so were our students. But, one day, the bot that one of our students made accidentally launched a projectile into the wall between our labs, and it created a hole."

"We figured out that the wall, made of cheap plasterboard, wasn't very thick, and people started talking and handing things through the hole in the wall, and so it got bigger," Freak continued.

"So that a few years ago you could actually *walk through* the hole in the wall," Carey said.

"And it just kept getting bigger and bigger. And, eventually, some students just said, 'The heck with it.' And they basically removed the rest of the wall," Freak said.

"There really wasn't that much wall left to remove," Carey interjected.

"And, in our digitally obsessed world, even though people can text each other or send emails or whatever, sometimes you just have to be in the same place talking face to face," Zeek noted.

"Particularly when you're trying to work together to solve problems," Carey Kaiser said.

Ryan quickly came to understand that the Freak and Zeek Lab was a place that invited exploratory weirdness and surprises. The Seguin students were sitting in a robotics work session at the Media Lab one grey, chilly Wednesday afternoon when Meagan strode in.

"You guys should come check this out," Meagan said.

"What is it?" asked Ellen.

"Something you've never seen before."

"That would probably describe a lot of things to this group, Meagan,"

Freak said in his fairly usual wisecrack tone. "Can you whet people's appetites a bit more?"

"Or, at least give them a better idea as to what you're talking about?" Zeek chimed in.

"Just come here," Meagan said gesturing to the students, with a roll of her eyes. She summoned them out of the room.

They exited and walked down the hall to another room behind a set of double doors. It was a room that Ryan had not visited before, though he often wondered what happened there. The wall on the inside of the building had only a few small windows, so one could see little of the room beyond it. However, upon setting foot in the room, one could see that the entire far wall was composed of windows, and there was a beautiful view out onto a treed courtyard of the Weatherall University campus. After taking in the view, one observed a series of long workbenches placed in long rows running down the room. A wide range of tools, devices, wires, and components sat on top of the workbenches.

In a far corner, sitting upright in a chair was a human-shaped figure. It might have been a person, except that it was a silver, metallic color. The person seemed to be staring at a wall, which would be a strange thing to do.

"He's off right now," Meagan commented, as if anticipating the question as to why the person-object sat there motionless. She strode to the back of the robot and flipped a small switch. It took a couple of minutes for anything to happen. Initially, Ryan wasn't sure anything would. But it did.

After the silent pause, the robot lifted its head, sat up in the chair, wheeled it around and faced the group. Ryan saw that the person-robot's face changed from a dull metallic color to a flesh-toned color, akin to that of human skin.

"Hello, I'm Dr. Speakeasy," the robot said in a plain, friendly tone. "How are you today? I like your red shirt."

"Is this a joke?" Sammy asked.

"What do you mean?" asked James.

"Who's making this guy talk? How does he know my shirt is red?" Sammy said in disbelief.

"It looks like he just does," Jenny said, matter-of-factly. "Here, how many fingers am I holding up?" she held up three fingers in front of Speakeasy.

"Three," said Speakeasy.

"Wow!" Ellen said, barely louder than a whisper.

"Oh, yeah… that," Zeek said. He and Freak had just arrived. They had walked down the hall in contrast to everyone else, who had practically run. "Dr. Speakeasy's a project we've been working on for a while. Doing some pretty cool things with him. Not sure if he's ready for prime time or not, but he's pretty talented."

"Pretty talented?" Carmen said.

"I'm sorry, I didn't get your name," Speakeasy said to Carmen.

"Uh, Carmen," she replied, dumbfounded.

"Carmen. That's a very nice name," replied Speakeasy. "Pleased to meet you Carmen," he said.

"Pleased to meet you, Dr. Speakeasy," Carmen said. She was so stunned that she simply mimicked his speech pattern.

"Dr. Speakeasy," said Freak in an effort to get his attention.

"Oh! Hi, Arthur, I didn't see you there for a minute. How are you today?" Speakeasy responded.

"Dr. S, you don't need to call me Arthur," Freak said. "Only my mother calls me Arthur."

"Oh. Okay, Arthur. What would you like me to call you?"

"Freak!" yelled Jenny.

"Okay. Freak. That's a funny name, isn't it?" Speakeasy said. Everyone burst out laughing, including Freak and Zeek.

"Have you performed any surgeries lately, Dr. Speakeasy?" Freak asked.

"I repaired a heart valve of a pig the other day," Speakeasy said.

"You didn't!" Ellen shrieked.

"I did," said Speakeasy.

"I'm so jealous!" Ellen remarked.

"Don't be," said Speakeasy. There's no need to be jealous of a creature that has a tear in its heart valve."

People laughed. Freak, Zeek, Brad, Meagan, and Carey were laughing the hardest.

"No, no, I'm not jealous of the pig!" Ellen said. "I'm jealous of you! I want to be a surgeon some day!"

"Me too!" said Jenny. "And I want to do cardio, so valve repair is right up my alley. Ellen, you want to do neuro—"

"Hey, surgery's surgery!" Ellen countered.

"I'd like that, too," Sammy said.

"Not me," said James.

"Me either," said Ryan.

"I think I'll pass," Carmen said.

"Can I scrub in with you the next time you do a surgery?" Jenny asked.

"And me, too?" Ellen said.

"Uh, ladies, Dr. Speakeasy's surgeries are just research at this stage," Zeek said.

At first, Ryan thought Jenny and Ellen might have been joking, but then he realized they could not have been more serious.

It was all Freak and Zeek could do to extract the Seguin audience from the work room and herd them back to their lab. Everyone was abuzz about Dr. Speakeasy.

"His movements, of his face in particular, were so human," Sammy said. "How did you do that?"

"It took a lot of work," Freak said.

"Over a period of years," Zeek added.

"Getting even a few muscles to move in the face was a huge challenge," Zeek said. "He doesn't have a full set of human musculature, but he can definitely fool people."

"He sure can," Ryan said.

Freak and Zeek explained that Speakeasy's face was covered in a pixilated, gel laminate that enabled him to change his facial expressions and that even the color of his "skin" could be changed. "We can make his skin any color you want: pink, orange, black, white, olive, red, green, blue, polka-dot, whatever," said Zeek.

"But, the rest of his body is not yet coated in the same laminate and, as you saw, the rest of his body is that silver metallic color," said Freak.

"For the time being," said Zeek.

"So Dr. Speakeasy is being developed by your lab?" Ellen asked Freak and Zeek.

"Uh, well, kind of..." Freak responded.

"In a matter of speaking," Zeek added.

"Well, if not your lab, then whose lab is it?" James asked.

"Well, you might think of it as—the No Name Lab," Zeek said.

"That's a good one," Carey chuckled. "The No Name Lab. I like that."

The Seguin students discovered another capability of Speakeasy on a subsequent visit to the Freak and Zeek Lab at Weatherall University.

"Say something," Meagan beckoned to Sammy while they were sitting in the No Name Lab one Wednesday afternoon.

"Something," said Sammy.

Meagan was not amused. "Say a few words," she said tersely.

"A few words, a few words, a few words... Meagan asked me to say a few words," Sammy said. He was trying to wise off to impress his classmates.

"Did you get enough, Dr. S?" Meagan asked.

"Just a moment," Speakeasy said. He was processing the information from Sammy's speech. "Yes... Yes, I did get enough information."

"So what's happening?" Ellen demanded.

"Just wait a second. Have some patience," Meagan said.

Momentarily, Speakeasy started talking. "My name is Sammy. I am from Chicago. I love the Chicago Bulls and deep dish pizza," Speakeasy said, in a voice that could not have been more like Sammy's.

"Get out! He didn't just do that!" Sammy said.

"He did!" Meagan exclaimed.

"He didn't!" Carmen said.

"You were talking!" Jenny said, pointing a finger accusatively at Sammy.

"I wasn't," Sammy protested. "I don't know where it came from, if not him."

"Let's see if Dr. S can replicate that performance," Jenny said skeptically. "Dr. Speakeasy, can you imitate me?" Jenny said in a confident, doubting tone.

"Can you say a few more words, please?" Speakeasy asked.

"Sure. My name is Jenny Wong. I am from San Francisco, California. I like to play the violin. I go to Seguin academy. I have a dragonfly bot named Skye..."

Speakeasy paused for a few moments, and then repeated back to Jenny verbatim exactly what she had just said.

"That's no big deal," Jenny said in a righteous tone. "You just recorded what I said and played it back. That's not difficult. A tape recorder could do that."

But then, Speakeasy started talking again in Jenny's voice. "I hope to be a surgeon someday. I'm a wiz at biology, but I'm not as good as I'd like to be at sports. I think I'm the smartest person here, although I'm not sure..."

"Hey!" Jenny shouted. She turned bright red from embarrassment. She was aghast at Speakeasy's ability to imitate her speech patterns, but even more so that he had shared thoughts of hers that as far as she was concerned, were private. She had shared those sentiments with no one.

Although she now considered that perhaps the way she talked conveyed them.

The others stood looking on, amazed, and then amused. They laughed. Jenny felt her face burning with anger. "How can he say things like that?" Jenny demanded of Meagan.

"It sounds like he's been listening to you guys talk when you're around him. He's picked up things about you from the way you talk," Brad said. "His hearing system has been in the Freak and Zeek Lab when you guys have visited before, so he has stored things you've said. So not only did he nail your accents and speech patterns, but he has gleaned things about your personality from listening to you over the past few weeks." Jenny was humbled. She suddenly felt highly insecure and exposed. The realization began to dawn on her that she perhaps needed to be a bit more careful about the way she spoke.

"Don't be embarrassed, Jenny," Brad said. "If you didn't have a feisty demeanor, you might not be here today," he teased. Jenny chased him across the room in mock anger and began hitting him, though in a not unfriendly way. "You see?" Brad giggled. "You *are* motivated!"

Everyone took turns speaking and having Speakeasy imitate their speech. It had become quite clear that Speakeasy, given enough exposure to one's speech, could indeed imitate them in a spectacularly realistic way. If that weren't enough, they also came to learn that Speakeasy could then mimic that person's speech and accent in speaking a foreign language.

One day, in Mrs. Westervelt's Spanish class at Seguin Academy, Ryan and his friends were talking about Speakeasy. They were bragging about his ability to speak various languages and the ability to change his accent to mimic that of a person whose speech he had heard. Mrs. Westervelt thought they were playing a joke on her.

"People, you may think I'm getting old to the point of being senile, but really, a robot that can imitate your own voice? And your own accent? And personality? That seems pretty farfetched," Mrs. Westervelt said. She had taught enough students at Seguin over the years to know they were prone to playing pranks and making practical jokes.

"No, really," they implored. "He can really do it."

"I don't believe it," Mrs. Westervelt chuckled.

So they asked Freak and Zeek if they could bring Dr. Speakeasy to a language class one day. Freak and Zeek, looking to have some fun, accompanied Speakeasy to Mrs. Westervelt's class. "You know, we have to make sure he behaves," Freak said.

"Right," Meagan said skeptically.

Mrs. Westervelt had the expected skeptical reaction when Dr. Speakeasy strode into the classroom, escorted by Freak and Zeek.

"Hi Mrs. Westervelt, pleased to meet you," Speakeasy said to her as he entered the class and passed by her.

Given Freak and Zeek's well-established reputations for doing wacky and zany things, Mrs. Westervelt seemed more convinced than ever she was the potential object of a practical joke. "Is this a broink you are playing for Weatherall University?" she asked.

"No, Mrs. Westervelt, honest," Freak said.

Mrs. Westervelt started conversing with Speakeasy in English, then French, then Spanish, and then German. She was telling him things about herself, where she was from, how many children she had, that sort of thing. Speakeasy adopted Mrs. Westervelt's accent, was equally comfortable conversing in each language, and had no difficulty switching from one to the other. Jenny then spoke some Chinese to Speakeasy, and once again, he started speaking to her in Chinese, with her accent.

"Well, I must say, I'm rather impressed," Mrs. Westervelt said.

"I'm always so impressed by people from Europe," Speakeasy said. "You all seem to speak at least several different languages. How many languages do you speak?"

"Oh, let's see... I'd say about six, give or take," said Mrs. W. "Dutch, Flemish, French, Spanish, German, and English. But, it might be more if you include Swedish and Italian, though I'm not fluent in those. How many do you speak?"

"Oh, let's see... about six thousand, give or take," said Dr. Speakeasy.

The class looked on in stunned amazement.

"There are still a few languages on earth that I don't know. They're dialects mainly, of languages that I do know," Speakeasy continued.

Completely amazed by the linguistic and speaking capabilities of Dr. Speakeasy, Mrs. Westervelt asked to join Ryan and his classmates for a Freak and Zeek robotics session at Weatherall University one Wednesday. Just like everybody else who had met Speakeasy, she wanted to interact with him more.

"This Dr. Speakeasy is incredible," she gushed. "Absolutely amazing. Is there anything he can't do?"

"Sure. There are lots of things he can't do," Freak said.

"He can't read people's emotions—" Zeek said.

"Not very well," said Freak. "Not yet, anyway."

"He can *project* people's emotions or sentiments in imitating their speech, but it's done based on what he hears them say. So, for example, if someone walked into a room and slammed a door in anger, he wouldn't necessarily know the person was angry... Well, maybe he would... And, he can't do a ton of abstract thinking," Zeek added. "Well, maybe just a bit."

"Abstract what?" Carmen asked.

"Abstract thinking," Zeek said. "You know, like recognizing patterns of things—like, people's behavior, or connecting a couple of ideas together."

"Again, he can do some, but not a ton," Freak said.

"And he can't run very fast," Zeek said. "He won't be trying out for the track team any time soon."

"He does, however, have an unbelievable grip," Freak said. "So if you needed him to grip onto, say, a bar for some reason, he could hang on to it—"

"Basically forever," Zeek interrupted.

"Since he has to have absolutely precise surgical technique, we had to enable him to hold and manipulate a surgical instrument perfectly," Freak said.

"That's because when you're doing surgery, you have, like, no margin for error," Zeek said. "So he needs to be able to hold the instrument perfectly still, in exactly the right place, and can't move it at all, unless the surgery calls for it. So, he has a strong, precise grip. You wouldn't want to get into an arm wrestling contest with him."

"I guess not. So what was the inspiration for giving him the ability to speak so many languages?" Mrs. Westervelt asked.

"Well, we figured if he's potentially going to get sent into the bush, or remote mountains, or desolate places wherever in the world," Freak said, "then he'd need to be able to speak and understand the language of the people wherever he was."

"Of course. Remarkable," Mrs. Westervelt remarked.

Everyone was amazed to learn that Carey had built a small data tracking system into Speakeasy as well, which could pull a variety of data, including weather patterns, from all over the world.

"And, if we're going to send Dr. S to these far flung places," Freak explained, "he needs to be able to access data. For example, he needs to be prepared for some exotic—and potentially dangerous at times—weather patterns. Wouldn't you say, Carey?"

Carey, who was present at the session with Freak and Zeek, looked up from the computer tablet he was reading. "Right," he said.

"So he can access the data center of the Weatherall University Weather Lab," Zeek said.

"Really? All right, let's test it out," Jenny said. She was skeptical of yet another extraordinary claim of Speakeasy's capabilities. "Dr. Speakeasy," Jenny said. "What's the weather going to be like for Mrs. Bergeron and her ship, the *Shakti*, over the next few days? From my online tracker, I see they should be running alongside Madagascar, off Africa, right about now."

"Uh, okay, let's see, give me a moment here," said Speakeasy. "Madagascar... East Africa..." He sat pondering, as though perhaps there were wheels turning in his head, which Ryan figured, there probably were.

"So, Dr. S, you can download from the beacon aboard the *Shakti*," Carey said.

"Right, thanks Carey," said Speakeasy. He just sat there, looking like a man deep in his thoughts, not looking at anyone, staring straight ahead, as if listening to some inaudible code.

A minute passed. Then another.

"So what's happening?" Jenny asked. "Why is it taking so long? The others were also beginning to get anxious.

"Relax, give it a moment," said Freak. "The *Shakti* is basically on the other side of the planet. It takes a little while for Speakeasy to download the information. It has to travel through some communications satellites."

"Shouldn't that be fairly instant?" Ellen asked.

"Not if the weather's bad," Carey said.

Just then, Speakeasy seemed to come to life. "Uh, um... I see... I see...," he muttered. "Oh, not good, not good."

"What is it?" Sammy asked.

"There's a tropical storm in the southwest Indian Ocean that is heading for Madagascar," Speakeasy said.

"Uh oh," James said. "That sounds like bad news."

"Well, it isn't good news," Carey said, getting up from a desk at the back of the room. While he had only been paying half attention to the discussion to this point, he was now fully engaged. "Dr. S, can you project against that wall over there?"

Speakeasy turned his head to face a blank wall at one side of Mrs. Westervelt's classroom. To the amazement of Ryan and all of his classmates, one of Speakeasy's eyes withdrew back into his head and in its place, a projecting lens appeared. Momentarily, a light went on, and an image was projected against the wall a few yards away. The image that appeared was a weather map just like the one you would see watching the news on television. A map of the world appeared at first. Then the view zoomed in on the southwest Indian Ocean and the eastern coast of Africa. Everyone could see the island of Madagascar and some nearby islands. There was a red diamond on the map to the east of Madagascar. The *Shakti*, Ryan guessed.

"That's the *Shakti*," Carey said, pointing to the red diamond, confirming Ryan's suspicion.

Juxtaposed onto the map in the ocean some miles away—it was hard to tell how many—was a dark green spiral-shaped swirl spinning in slow, animated circles, which was the storm, no doubt. From the edges of the swirl on the map, various trails of dotted lines began to move out from it, heading in slightly different directions, but all heading in the general direction of Madagascar.

"Those dotted lines mark the possible paths that the storm might take," Carey explained. "Wow, the storm has changed directions in the past twenty-four hours. I don't know how often Catherine is getting weather downloads, but she may not be aware of the change in the storm path. I'm going to ping her right now to make sure she's aware of the change." He immediately glanced back at his computer tablet and started punching letter keys.

"Of course, if the weather's bad your message might not get through," Freak noted.

"True. But I have to try," Carey said.

A hushed silence hung in the room like a soggy towel. No one was saying anything, but they all now had a foreboding sense that Catherine and Francois Bergeron were in danger. At that moment, Speakeasy turned off the projector, which withdrew back into his head, and the eyeball reappeared in its place.

"Yeah, but weather patterns can change, right?" Ellen said, trying to sound optimistic.

"Sure, a storm's exact path is always based on models, which aren't always accurate," Carey said, momentarily looking up from his cell phone keypad. "Dr. S has run the probabilities of the storm paths based on a bunch of indicators and variables, thanks to several hundred years' worth of weather, atmospheric and climate pattern data from the Weather Lab here at the university. So, we have a general sense of where this storm's going to go, as you saw from the dotted lines on the weather map, and the *Shakti* is either going to get totally hammered or merely slammed."

"So Dr. S, where do you think the storm is going to pass?" Freak asked.

"Straight answer?" Speakeasy queried.

"Straight answer," Zeek replied.

"I think the storm is going to run right into the *Shakti*," Speakeasy said.

12

PIRATES!

The storm had made little news in Boston, or anywhere else in the western hemisphere, for that matter. It was on the other side of the world, so scant attention was paid to it. But at Seguin Academy and Weatherall University, a certain few students began to focus on it like a laser beam. As the hours crept on, the *Shakti* seemed to blow more and more off course when the tracking software was able to pick up its signal, which was becoming increasingly difficult given the bad weather. Ryan and his friends watched it on their computers in their rooms at Seguin. It wasn't exactly clear how far the *Shakti* was being taken off course, but it was definitely moving in the wrong direction, to the east, away from Africa. On the computer screen, the ship appeared as an oversized dot plotted against a vast expanse of oceanic no man's land, where the Indian Ocean and the Arabian Sea met, north of Madagascar. Ryan had an ominous, foreboding feeling about the storm.

Everyone was shooting texts and emails back and forth with Carey Kaiser, Brad, and Meagan at Weatherall University, as they had invaded the university's Weather Lab that evening to learn what they could about the storm.

"I'm pretty sure they don't really appreciate us being here," Meagan wrote of the students working in the lab, upon whom she, Brad, and Carey had imposed their presence. "But, knowing that one of Weatherall's star faculty members, Mrs. Bergeron, is involved, seems to carry some weight with these people."

Ryan had picked up from Brad and Meagan that students, like teachers, could be territorial when it came to their own classes and laboratories. If you were from someone else's lab, you were basically unwelcome at a different lab until you had a reason to be there. Since collaborations between labs and students happened all the time at Weatherall, you weren't unwelcome if you had a purpose in visiting, but it could be a delicate line. Brad, Meagan, and Carey did not exactly have an academic purpose in visiting the Weather Lab, but Mrs. Bergeron's being in danger seemed to have the desired effect of allowing them to impose.

There was good reason for the imposition. Weatherall University had one of the most sophisticated meteorological weather stations in the world in its Weather Lab. It was loaded with tracking computers containing countless models of weather patterns, and it could provide highly accurate readouts on weather patterns almost anywhere in the world.

In his dorm room, Ryan found himself checking his computer, compulsively, almost frantically, every couple of minutes as the night wore on. He was checking for texts from Meagan as well as monitoring the course of the *Shakti* online. Following the ship was too important, and homework, at least at that moment, seemed too unimportant. Ryan was pretty sure his teachers wouldn't see it that way, though, except maybe Mr. Sandhill. Ryan could practically hear the admonitions of his teachers if he told them his incomplete homework assignments were the result of being distracted by following a fuzzy blip on a computer screen halfway around the world. Mrs. Bergeron was an experienced sailor and world famous marine biologist. Hadn't she been in storms before? Surely she would be fine. And there was nothing Ryan could do about it anyway, so why get distracted by it? Indeed, Ryan felt hugely preoccupied, diverted as if by magnetic force, and yet powerless to ignore the *Shakti's* plight. And if that weren't enough, his inability to do anything about it was in large part *why* he was so distracted. It was maddening.

As the night drew on, to Ryan's relief, it seemed that the storm had stopped blowing the *Shakti* further off course. He couldn't be completely sure, but it appeared that the *Shakti* had at least stopped moving in the wrong direction, even if it wasn't moving in the right one. Ryan checked his computer screen one last time before drifting into a restless sleep. Thankfully, yes, the *Shakti* seemed now indeed to be making its way back, slowly, of course, towards the plotted path of its route. It was still quite off course, by perhaps as much as three hundred miles, by the estimates at the Weatherall Media Lab. But, looking at the massive ocean on his computer screen to where the storm could have sent the boat, it was clear to Ryan it could have been worse.

Over the next few days, his studies commanded the bulk of Ryan's attention. Thankfully, the *Shakti* appeared to be more or less back to its planned course. Ryan and his friends were relieved to see an email from Mrs. Bergeron that said, "Nasty, storm! Blown miles off course! But made it through. Everyone ok." It had been sent a couple of days earlier, so presumably it was delayed due to the bad weather. But, just as Ryan and his friends were feeling confident that Mrs. Bergeron and her crew were safe, they soon discovered otherwise.

The February night was biting cold outside with a breeze that whipped through the dormitory courtyards. Listening to it howl made you feel glad to be inside. Ryan slept fitfully and had a dream. He was taking a test in Mr. Sandhill's Physics class. He was struggling with it, and was running out of time. Everyone else in the class was scrawling furiously in their notebooks to answer the questions on the test. They, too, seemed pressed for time. A bell was ringing, telling everyone that time was up. The bell kept ringing on and off, almost as if it were an alarm warning of a threat. Ryan was in a panic, because he hadn't finished answering all of the questions, and yet the bell signaled the end of the test. A huge sense of failure rushed over him, and he felt himself falling from his desk, as if exhausted from exertion. In a moment, he slouched off his desk chair and hit the floor. His body suddenly jerked in his bed with a start.

"Psst! Ryan! Wake up!" Ryan felt himself being shaken.

"Psst! Ryan, wake up!" Again, he was shaken.

"Huh?" Ryan mumbled in a barely conscious stupor. He felt pressure on his shoulder, but his head stayed firmly on his pillow. Having hit the floor in his dream, he could fall no further, and the floor felt comfortable to a weary soul.

"Ryan. You have to get up! We have to go!" James pleaded with him. Sammy stood behind him, wearing only pants but holding a long sleeved tee shirt he was about put on. "I just got off the phone with Mr. Sandhill!" James exclaimed.

"What are you talking about?" Ryan murmured. His eyes were now barely slit open. He was aware of lights on in his room. He held his hands over his eyes to shield them. He was exhausted. "What time is it?"

"It's three thirty in the morning," Sammy said, as if it were a perfectly normal time to be shaken out of one's sleep by one's roommates issuing a demand to get out bed.

"What's going on?" Ryan asked, now slightly more awake than he had been two seconds prior, but not much.

"Uh, Mrs. Bergeron's in trouble," James said.

"What do you mean?" Ryan asked. He was now only slightly more certain he was awake than dreaming.

"She's been kidnapped! By pirates!" Sammy blurted out.

"What? Pirates?" Ryan asked. "What do you mean?" He wondered for a second in his sleepy haze if he was the butt of a joke.

"She and Mr. Bergeron and the film crew! They got kidnapped last night... I mean, earlier today! They're eight hours ahead of us," Sammy said.

Ryan rubbed his eyes. The light was blinding. A dream—even one in which he was getting roughed up on a test—would have been far more preferable. "Seriously?" he posited.

"Like cancer," James said. He now began tapping Ryan's bedpost loudly, with a shoe to wake him up. It was incredibly annoying.

Waving off James, Ryan sheepishly dragged himself out of bed, meandered down the hall to the bathroom, and splashed some water on his face and hair. It was cold, but it did jolt him to alertness. He threw on some clothes. The news of Mrs. Bergeron's kidnapping was definitely sinking in and beginning to feel real. He was now fairly awake, despite the ridiculously early hour. Having donned heavy winter coats, the three boys strode outside and down the exterior stone steps of Sellinger Hall and into the dark, chilly air of the early morning. A coat of icy snow lay across rooftops and grass spaces.

Mr. Sandhill was parked in a Seguin van, waiting next to Donnington, the girls' dormitory. "So, the girls are coming as well?" Sammy asked.

Mr. Sandhill nodded.

"So, how do you like that?" James asked. "We're waiting on the girls. We had to walk across the freezing cold courtyard to get here, and they'll have to walk about ten feet, and yet, we're still here before they are."

"Why do you think I parked the van over here?" Mr. Sandhill replied.

"So what exactly is going on?" Sammy said.

"I'll wait for the girls to get here so I don't have to repeat everything," Mr. Sandhill said. Ryan was amazed at his ability to maintain an utterly calm demeanor in the face of anything, including the news of Mrs. Bergeron and the *Shakti* crew being kidnapped.

In a few moments, Ellen, Carmen, and Jenny arrived at the van looking tired and bewildered. They opened the van door and climbed in. Mr. Sandhill started to drive. It was still dark outside at that hour, and the streets were empty.

"You are, no doubt, wondering why you've been abruptly awakened at this most unusual hour," Mr. Sandhill said. "I've spoken with a couple of you, those who answered the phone this morning, so you may have some idea of what is happening. Mrs. Bergeron, Francois, and the film crew were kidnapped this morning, or late last night our time, by a rogue band of pirates."

This elicited an immediate clamoring chorus of voices in the van. How? Where? What happened? How could this be?

"I don't know many of the details yet. It's not as if I got the news from Catherine herself. The U.S. Embassy in Addis Ababa, Ethiopia and the Consul General in the Seychelle Islands received word this morning that a group of pirates, likely from Somalia, has kidnapped the crewmembers of the *Shakti* along with several other boats, including a Dutch oil tanker. All were sailing as a convoy to try to get past that part of the Arabian Sea, which is notorious for pirates—pirates who are known to hijack ships and take hostages. All of the ships in the convoy had been disrupted by the recent storm in that part of the Indian Ocean."

"So how did you first hear about it?" Ellen asked.

"I was called by the State Department and the U.S. Armed Forces," Mr. Sandhill said. "Specifically, by one, Jasper Townley."

"No way! How did Townley know about it?" Ellen asked.

"He's a surprisingly well connected guy, inside and outside the military," Mr. Sandhill said. "And, like you, he's been following her trip online."

"Wow," several people muttered.

"And, like you, Townley took Biology from Mrs. Bergeron, so he's pretty hopped up about it," Mr. Sandhill continued.

"Is he getting involved? What can he do?" Carmen asked.

"Well, yes, as it turns out, he *is* getting involved and, as you may have observed, he's capable of quite a lot. I have a feeling he's about to give a whole new meaning to the basketball phrase 'hitting from downtown.'"

"So, where are we going now?" Carmen asked.

"Hanscom Air Force Base, to pick him up," Mr. Sandhill replied. "He's landing there in about half an hour."

"What? Wow! He doesn't fool around, does he?" Ellen remarked.

"Not so much," Mr. Sandhill replied.

"Why are we meeting him?" Sammy asked.

"He seems to want something... from you," Mr. Sandhill replied.

"What could he possibly want from us?" Ryan said. But the answer became perfectly clear the moment he said it. *"He wants our bots,"* he continued, answering his own question.

"I would guess that, yes, the bots are what might motivate him to stop here on his trip half way around the world," Mr. Sandhill said. "That and a decent cup of coffee."

The van drove to Hanscom Air Force Base. The ride took about forty-five minutes in the early morning with little traffic. Townley had landed his plane when they arrived and was standing just inside a terminal building waiting for them. He was still in his flight fatigues.

"Where to?" Mr. Sandhill said, mimicking a cab driver, as he pulled up next to an anxiously waiting Townley at a curb.

"Seguin," Townley said. "But first, let's get some coffee. Puh! The coffee in that place stinks."

They made a brief stop and Townley bought himself a coffee, and everyone else hot chocolate and doughnuts at a nearby coffee shop. They ate and drank in the van on their way back to the academy.

"So, uh, you may be wondering what prompted me to stop here," Townley said. "I need your bots." He paused. "Let me rephrase that. I'd like to *borrow* your bots."

"What for?" Jenny asked.

"Yeah, what do you want to do with the bots?" Ryan asked.

"No specific plans. Not sure I'll even need them," Townley replied. "But, I like to take things along to be prepared. You know. Be prepared. Like they say in scouts?"

"You know, you didn't exactly *borrow* Chinny in Ohio, did you?" Carmen said. "It's sort of hard to consider something borrowed if it's been blown up."

"True," Townley said, a smile unfolding across his lips. "But, that's why you have multiple copies. And, if I blow anything up, I, and the U.S. armed services, will personally pay you back for it, or see that you get new replacement models built."

"I mean, they haven't been completely tested yet," Ellen said, referring to the bots.

"Also true. And you know, Ellen, if we were going to send a man up to the moon in them, I'd say you're absolutely right, that we should not be putting totally untested equipment into use," Townley said. "And, to your point, since they haven't been fully tested, I'd have to be really cautious about a situation in which I would think of using them. At the moment,

I don't really know exactly what I'd use them for. But I'll promise you this—I won't use them unless I absolutely have to. And, remember, we have seen them tested *some*. It's not like they haven't been tested at all," Townley added. "In fact, they've had some fairly rigorous testing done on them at this point, if I recall. Scaling mountainsides, taking out prey, and flying through valleys? You guys have built some pretty solid bots."

"Well, obviously if you need the bots, you've got them," Sammy said. Everyone nodded in agreement.

"Great. So when we get to your dorms, I need you to go and get them for me. Oh, and bring me the ones you've been working on recently as well, like Leo," Townley said to Ellen, referring to her leopard bot. Here he laughed for a moment. "Mr. Sandhill told me a pretty funny story about Leo. And I want Chomp and Tux as well," he said to Sammy. "And that housefly bot you've been working on Jenny? That, too. And the hornet bot."

The hornet bot had been something of a group project within the bot cohort that really hadn't been through much testing, but, in Ryan's opinion, it held great promise as a bot.

"Uh, okay," people muttered. It wasn't like they were about to refuse a guy who had flown through the wee hours of the morning, just landed his own plane, and started barking orders in every direction. Not to mention that he had just bought them hot chocolate and doughnuts on a freezing cold morning. Ryan and the others had observed that Townley could come on like a hurricane. He had a ton of energy and he could be unstoppable when he wanted to be.

"How do you know about all the other bots?" James asked, referring to the bot concepts they had developed since their orientation trip when they first met Townley.

Everyone's eyes immediately turned to Mr. Sandhill. "Er, I like to keep alumni informed of the work that is being done here," he said.

"Well, I'd say you've kept Townley pretty well informed," Jenny observed.

"It's my job to be well informed," Townley said, winking at her.

Townley shared a few more details with the group about the events involving the *Shakti*. "We believe the pirates involved are from Somalia, though they seem to operate out of some of the remote Seychelle Islands," he said. "We are told there is a total of six ships that have been taken. Five sailing yachts, pretty much like the *Shakti*, and an oil tanker from the

Netherlands. As far as we are aware right now, the crews of the hijacked ships are still on their vessels, but that could change. We have to do what we can to try to get the hostages out of there."

"How the heck are you going to do that?" James asked.

"Not sure, yet," Townley replied. "But we'll figure it out, though. We always do." Ryan was becoming more certain by the minute that you didn't want to mess with Jasper Townley.

Everyone, including Mr. Sandhill, continued to pepper Townley with questions. After much conversing back and forth, there was a brief pause.

"Well, is there anything else you need from us at this point, Jasper?" Mr. Sandhill asked.

"Uh, let's see... uh, no, I don't think so," Townley said. "Oh wait, maybe there is one more thing, Thomas..."

"Yes?"

"Can we get Speakeasy?" Townley asked.

"No promises. I'll see what I can do," Mr. Sandhill said. "I'll call F and Z right now."

"Wow, he wants Speakeasy," Carmen whispered. "Freak and Zeek are going to... uh, freak."

"Okay great," said Townley to Mr. Sandhill. "And Thomas?"

"Yes, Jasper?"

"Drive faster!"

"Okay, Jasper, but I'll try to keep within the speed limit."

"And Thomas?"

"Yes?"

"One more thing."

"What's that?"

"Don't call me Jasper! My *mother* calls me Jasper!"

Upon their arrival at Seguin Academy everyone quickly ran to the dormitories to get their various bots and control units. With the exception of the orcas, the bots would fit in the van since the Seguin students would not be riding back to Hanscom Air Force Base with Townley and Mr. Sandhill. However, one disappointment for Townley was that Freak and Zeek adamantly refused his request to take Speakeasy.

"We simply don't have another copy, and there's too much wiring and computational input that hasn't been adequately documented or backed up yet," Freak said to Townley. Mr. Sandhill had conferenced in both Freak and Zeek for a phone call, which he put on speaker. They seemed none too happy to be summoned to a conference call at about six-thirty in the morning, but you got the impression it had happened to them a few times before.

"Besides, the single greatest benefit Speakeasy could offer you right now, aside from limited surgery in the battlefield, would be his ability to copy and transmit voices," Zeek said. "And he can do that remotely. So if you have the other bots in the theater and can record a voice that you want to copy, we can copy it, transmit it to Speakeasy, perform language mimicking, and transmit it back to the bot, or some other communications device, from here. Otherwise, I don't think Speakeasy will do you much good. He sure as heck isn't going to fool anyone into thinking he's a real human physical specimen. Not in the same way the Seguin bots can convince people they are real animals."

"Okay, I get it," Townley sighed.

After the call with Freak and Zeek ended, Sammy spoke up. "Uh, Townley?"

"Yeah, Sammy, what's up?"

"How the heck are we going to move Chomp and Tux?" Sammy asked.

"You'll see," Townley said. "Excellent question. I'm one step ahead of you, my man."

As soon as they had loaded the bots into the van at Seguin, Mr. Sandhill departed to drive them to Hanscom Air Force Base. Townley stayed behind and asked a few people to assist him with his next task, getting Chomp and Tux from the boathouse along the Charles River. Everyone insisted on helping. Ryan could hardly believe what happened next. A large truck pulled up next to the Seguin dormitories. On closer inspection, it was a produce truck, bearing a sign that said, "*Produce Fresh from Our Fields to Your Homes and Hearts*," on the sides. Large, colorful images of vegetables accompanied the sign.

"We'll move them in this truck," Townley said.

"That's hilarious, a produce truck," Sammy said. "And orcas aren't even vegetarians."

"I get the impression that Townley didn't want to make a scene by pulling up in a heavily armored military truck, you know what I mean?" Ryan said.

"But really, a *produce truck*?" Jenny spat.

"Well, who cares what's *on* the truck," James said. "It's plenty big enough to hold Chomp and Tux." Everyone clambered aboard the truck and they drove to the Weatherall University boathouse. Several men, dressed as produce workers, but who Ryan suspected were probably military people in disguise, sat on the back of the truck and talked in a very friendly way with the group from Seguin. Once they arrived at the boathouse, Townley opened the back door of the truck and everyone climbed out. Ice had formed in sheets at intervals along the Charles River, but fortunately it had not yet frozen completely, as it would have greatly complicated the task of extracting Chomp and Tux from the water, if not made it impossible.

Minutes later, a crane extended out from the back of the truck. It was remarkably similar to the makeshift one that Sammy and the group had used to move Chomp and Tux off the docks not more than three months ago. Sammy showed Townley where Chomp and Tux were located under the water, just to one side of the boathouse. The produce worker guys started maneuvering the truck beside the area near the boathouse where Chomp and Tux were submerged. In almost no time they affixed thick ropes around one of the submerged bots and attached them to the crane. They then lifted the bots up out of the water and let the water drain that helped keep them submerged, and with the crane, hoisted them up and into the truck. The entire process couldn't have taken more than thirty minutes, which, at the hour of seven o'clock in the morning on a cold winter day, went virtually unnoticed. Even at a slightly later hour, the site of two killer whales being lifted out of the Charles River, along a busy thoroughfare amid droves of cars and people, would have created pandemonium.

"So, what else did you need from us?" Ryan asked. He and his friends really hadn't helped Townley as much as watch him and his team load the killer whale bots onto the truck.

"Not much," Townley said. "I just needed someone to show me where the orcas were," he smiled.

"Oh," Ryan said. He felt a bit disappointed.

"But it was pretty cool to watch, wasn't it?" Townley said.

"Yeah," Ryan muttered.

"And if there had been any trouble moving Chomp and Tux, I would definitely have needed you guys, so I'm glad you came along. Besides, I may not see you for a little while, so it's good to get this time together."

Everyone wished Townley luck as he headed off to Hanscom Air Force Base in the produce truck. He was still dressed improbably in his flight fatigues. The site of a fighter pilot climbing into a produce truck was amusing.

"Thanks all. Will talk to you real soon," Townley said. "By VideoLink, texting, or something like that, from the other side of the world." And as quickly as they had arrived, Townley and his fellow working crewmembers departed in the non-descript produce truck.

"From the other side of the world," Carmen said, in a contemplative tone.

Ryan and company waited out of the cold in the lobby of Meagan's dormitory at Weatherall University for a shuttle bus back to Milton and Seguin Academy a short while later. Despite feeling tired, they went to the Seguin cafeteria for breakfast. It was not even mid-morning, yet it felt like it had already been a long day. As they strode back from the dining hall towards the dorms, they noticed that numerous trucks had pulled up and parked on the Seguin campus. On closer examination, they turned out to be news trucks. Reporters and journalists were bustling around. People were setting up cameras and lights. Television antennae were being raised up in the air above the news trucks. Droves of Seguin students passing by were stopping and staring at the curious spectacle.

"What the heck is all this?" Ryan asked as they crossed a roadway that ran through the middle of the Seguin campus.

His question was soon answered. A woman carrying a microphone being trailed by a man wielding a camera approached them. She saw Ryan, made straight for him, and foisted the microphone in his face. Suddenly, a bright light went on, seemingly appearing out of nowhere, and Ryan found himself squinting. The woman spoke. "Hi, I'm Peg Sizemore from Channel Five News. I wanted to ask you a few questions about the kidnapping of Dr. Catherine Bergeron, head of school at Seguin Academy. Are you aware that earlier today Dr. Bergeron was kidnapped by pirates while sailing in the Indian Ocean, somewhere north of Madagascar?"

"Uh, yes," Ryan said.

Peg's eyes lit up as if she had just hit the jackpot. "Are you all students at Seguin Academy?" she asked, pointing with the microphone at Ryan's friends. Another man, holding a bright light, directed it at them, hitting them in the eyes so that they were nearly blinded.

"Yes," Ryan replied. "Does that clarify the picture?" he added sarcastically.

Peg ignored the sarcasm. "What was Dr. Bergeron doing sailing in that part of the world?" she asked.

"She's conducting research," Ryan said. "She's a marine biologist."

The next moment, the man holding a camera trained on Peg Sizemore pointed his finger at her as if to say, 'You're on the air.' Peg now struck an authoritative, television-like tone that suggested the narrative she was now speaking would be a part of a news broadcast. "Hi, Peg Sizemore here, Channel Five News. I'm here at Seguin Academy with a group of students from the school to get reactions to the kidnapping of the world famous marine biologist, Dr. Catherine Bergeron, head of school at Seguin Academy, and frequently featured scientist on the Worldscapes Channel and its *Sea Adventures* program. Dr. Bergeron has been kidnapped while sailing in the Indian Ocean off the coast of Africa, near the island of Madagascar and the Seychelle Islands."

Turning to Ryan, she said, "And, sir, you're a student here at Seguin Academy. What is your name?"

Ryan gave his name.

"So, Ryan, what is your reaction to the kidnapping of Catherine Bergeron?"

"We're very concerned about it. And angry as well. But, mainly we are concerned for the safety of Catherine Bergeron, her husband, Francois, and the crew that is traveling with her, as well as the other hostages," Ryan said.

"Pirates, like those believed to have kidnapped Dr. Bergeron and her crew, have been a big problem in that part of the world. What do you believe the United States should do to respond?" Peg asked Ryan.

"I think we should—"

"Here, I'll handle that," Mr. Sandhill interjected, having just arrived on the scene. He quickly maneuvered his way through the growing crowd that had gathered around Peg Sizemore. He extended a hand as if suggesting a path for Ryan to take off to the side, a gesture for which Ryan was grateful.

"And who, sir, are you?" Peg asked, thrusting the microphone into Mr. Sandhill's face.

"Thomas Sandhill, a teacher and administrator here at Seguin Academy," Mr. Sandhill replied. "As Ryan says, the school is obviously very concerned for all aboard the ship carrying Catherine Bergeron, as well as the other ships that have been hijacked. We really can't comment further at this time, other than to say we have been in touch with government officials who are keeping us abreast of the situation."

"Right. Yes, we understand there are potentially several other ships involved, and that they had been traveling as a convoy," Peg said, realizing she had forgotten to mention the other ships. "And, what do you think the plan will be to liberate Catherine Bergeron and her colleagues from this perilous situation, as well as the crews from the other ships involved?" she demanded.

"I don't know," Mr. Sandhill replied. "But, as I say, we are in contact with government authorities and they are monitoring developments."

"Are you aware that pirates in these situations typically demand significant sums of ransom money in return for the safe release of their hostages?" Peg pointedly asked.

"Yes," Mr. Sandhill sighed. "I believe so."

"And yet, the position of certain countries, including that of the United States, has been to not negotiate with hostage takers such as terrorists or pirates. So where do you think that leaves the situation with Dr. Bergeron?"

"I don't know," a beleaguered Mr. Sandhill shrugged. "But, as I say, I believe our government, as well as those of the other passengers and ships affected, will do everything in their power to secure the safe release of the people being held with as little incident as possible."

The discussion between Peg Sizemore and Mr. Sandhill continued in this way for another painful minute or so and then, mercifully, came to an end. Peg and her crew thanked Mr. Sandhill, Ryan, and the others, and headed off, presumably to their truck to escape the bitter cold, or perhaps to find another unsuspecting interview target.

"Wow, this is crazy!" Jenny exclaimed, once Peg Sizemore and her cameraman were out of earshot.

"This isn't good," Mr. Sandhill muttered.

"What do you mean?" Ellen said.

"Well, the news is making a big splash about Catherine," Mr. Sandhill sighed.

"What's wrong with people knowing Catherine's been kidnapped?" Ellen asked.

"Well, now the pirates will know she's famous," Mr. Sandhill replied.

"Okay, yeah, so...?"

"So that means they will ask for an even greater amount of ransom money to get her back."

Everyone stared silently with comprehending looks, as the impact of what Mr. Sandhill had just said began to sink in.

"Like, how much?" Ryan asked.

"I don't know," Mr. Sandhill sighed, "but you can be sure it will be more than it would have been otherwise."

"So, it'll be okay, won't it?" Carmen asked. "I mean, Catherine, Francois and the crew… They'll be okay, right?"

"I don't know," Mr. Sandhill murmured. "These situations sometimes turn out okay, and sometimes they have turned out… badly."

"How badly?" James asked.

Mr. Sandhill looked off in the distance mournfully, considering something he deeply wished not to contemplate. "People haven't come home," he sighed in a low voice. A resounding silence followed, disturbed only by the distant chatter of news reporters and students.

Strangely, while back in his room and trying to focus on his studies, Ryan received an email on his notepad computer from Brad saying that he and Meagan wouldn't be showing up in Mr. Sandhill's Physics class for a while.

"Where are you guys going?" Ryan wrote.

"Away," Brad replied.

"Gee, thanks for the illuminating response," Ryan wrote back. "You're doing something to help Townley and Mrs. Bergeron. Is that it?"

"Good guess. Definitely a possibility," Brad wrote back.

"Isn't that something for military or clandestine services or something?" Ryan replied.

"What makes you think we're not one of those things?" Brad replied. "Gotta run. Speak with you again soon."

I guess because I thought you were college students, Ryan mused to himself.

Ryan reflected on Brad and Meagan's departure. Were they on the plane with Townley? Yes. He was almost sure of it. They were involved in something mysterious, something they had never shared with Ryan or any of his friends at Seguin Academy. Ryan thought it strange that he considered them close friends, yet it seemed they held a deep, dark secret, one they had kept from everyone. It hurt in a way, but surely they knew they weren't fooling anyone as to where they were going. Or rather, why.

From his computer, Ryan tracked Townley's jet over the Atlantic Ocean. Everyone's bots were aboard the jet, and Ryan had set up and programmed a bot tracking system to monitor all of them, so the tracking beacons made the plane light up like laser points on the computer screen. Even while reading and doing homework, Ryan kept checking the status of the plane every hour or so. And with each passing hour, the plane had traveled a significant distance, even on the computer screen. By the time Ryan awoke, Townley would be somewhere in the general vicinity of the Seychelle Islands, north of Madagascar. Where exactly was he going to land? Ryan wondered. Upon reflection, Ryan considered how amazing Townley was at executing a plan, any plan, whether it was flying a jet, assembling and launching a bot rocket, or simply preparing a meal.

After all that had happened, Ryan now felt the absence of something else. His very best unit of Scram was now gone. It seemed like yet another companion had left him. Sure, he had several other Scram units that were in late stages of completion, but he had gotten a solid feel for the one that now sat in the dark bowels of a military jet, streaking across the ocean.

Jenny emailed everyone to say she knew for a fact that Brad and Meagan were on the plane with Townley.

"How do you know?" Ryan wrote.

"I put a tracking bug on Meagan, and am following it with the tracking software," Jenny wrote back. "She's Hornet A." Ryan looked at the bottom corner of his screen where there was a color code for the different tracking beacons of all the different bots. Sure enough, below the beacons named for Scram, Trixie, Harris, Leo, and the other animal bots, there was one called "Hornet A" that he now understood referred to the hornet bot that Jenny had planted on Meagan.

"Wow. That was sneaky," Ryan wrote.

"That's just the beginning," Jenny wrote back.

13

TRIBULATION STATION

Early that morning, before heading to classes, Ryan looked on his computer at the tracking program to see where Townley had flown. Following Townley had turned out to be remarkably easy. There, on the screen, as soon as Ryan's computer awoke, was the splotchy mass of illuminated dots. The tracking beacons on the bots all sitting atop one another lit up in east Africa. On closer examination, zooming in on the screen, Ryan saw that Townley's jet had landed in the country of Djibouti, on the east African coast. Zooming in further, Ryan saw that it had landed in Djibouti City, the country's capital. Zooming out on the map, Ryan observed that the country of Djibouti was fairly small, shaped like an elongated letter "C," or a letter "U" tipped on its side, nestled snugly among the eastern African countries of Eritrea, Ethiopia, and Somalia. A news article told him that the northern part of Somalia, called Somaliland, was peaceful, but that its sister region to the south was full of hostile, warring factions of people, and there was essentially no rule of law there. The dozens of newscasts and articles he had seen in the past few days pointed strongly to this place as the region from which the suspected pirate kidnappers operated.

Ryan found the computerized tracking map to be surprisingly detailed. From it, he saw that Djibouti was located on a body of water called the Gulf of Tdjoura. This gulf was an inlet of the Gulf of Aden, at the junction where the Indian Ocean met up with the Red Sea. It was south of the Arabian Peninsula, at a passage called Bab-el-Mandeb, or the Mandeb Strait. It was not encouraging to see that its name, translated from Arabic, meant "the Gate of Grief." Ryan also noted that Djibouti was a pretty fair distance from the Seychelle Islands and Madagascar, over fourteen hundred miles, according to the map. How was Townley's being in Djibouti going to help Catherine Bergeron and the others who had been kidnapped if they were so far away?

"Uh oh," Ryan muttered to himself. "I don't like this."

Zooming in still further on the map of Djibouti City, Ryan traced the bot tracking beacons to a region in the south of the city, to a place called Camp Lemonnier. Clicking on this location on the map opened a webpage that told Ryan Camp Lemonnier was a U.S. naval and military base. Okay, that made some sense. It occurred to Ryan that Townley probably couldn't just land a military jet wherever he wanted to, at least not without arousing the awareness and, most likely, the ire of local authorities. Not to mention, Townley would want to keep his mission secret. It would be disastrous if Scram and the other animal bots fell into the wrong hands, like those of a hostile government, or pirates. Townley's whereabouts was beginning to make more sense to Ryan, despite being such a long distance from the hijacked vessels. He thought again of Catherine Bergeron and all of the other hostages.

That morning in their Robotics class Ryan and the bot cohort got Townley on a VideoLink connection on a notebook computer. He had sent an email telling them to try him at the start of class, which corresponded to six o'clock in the evening in Djibouti.

"Greetings from eastern Africa," Townley said with a wide grin and sporting a pair of large sunglasses. The sun was setting off to one side of him. He was wearing a t-shirt, a decidedly different look from the pilot fatigues in which they'd seen him a day earlier in Massachusetts, with its biting cold weather. If Ryan hadn't known better, he might have thought Townley was on a vacation.

"Well, aren't you looking peppy?" Ellen said.

"It's amazing what a few hours of sleep, some jet lag, and a little sunshine will do for you," Townley replied.

"Say 'hi' to Brad and Meagan for us," Ellen said, trying to sound witty.

"Huh?" Townley said. He tried to feign a perplexed look.

"Oh, come on, whaddya think? We were born yesterday?" Ellen admonished. "We put a tracker on Meagan before you left. The tracker signal says she's sitting right next to you."

"Well, I, uh…" Townley stuttered. For the first time since Ryan had known him, Townley actually seemed stymied. "You know, you can be a bit of a know-it-all, Ellen," Townley said. "But don't get me wrong, I like it," he chuckled. "It's good to be in the know."

"One of these days you'll thank me for it," Ellen quipped.

"Hi guys," Meagan said. Just then she and Brad appeared on the screen on each side of Townley. Having overheard the conversation thus far, she seemed uninterested in perpetuating the guessing game as to where she was.

"You guys didn't seriously think we wouldn't know where you were going, did you?" Ryan said.

"Nah, we knew you'd figure it out," Meagan replied. "And, we would have told you anyway. But we couldn't tell you until we had left."

"How come?" Carmen said, looking puzzled.

"Because word would get out to people, people who might try to prevent us from going," Brad said.

"Like who?" demanded James.

"Like me," said Mr. Sandhill. No one had seen him enter the room. He stood at the doorway, and had been listening for a minute or so. He strode over to the computer screen. "Brad and Meagan, and Jasper, I'm disappointed in you."

"I needed them, Thomas," Townley said.

"I assume you are not planning to put them in harm's way, are you?" Mr. Sandhill asked.

"Correct," Townley replied. "And I have every reason to believe they will not be. Having said that, this is a serious operation, and, well, obviously, people's lives are at stake."

Heavy tension hung in the room upon hearing Townley's words. For Ryan, it wasn't so much caused by what he was saying. Rather, it was what he *wasn't* saying that raised concern. It was hard for Ryan to envision Brad and Meagan being put in harm's way, but it was easy to see how heading in the direction of a band of pirates—*armed* pirates who had taken hostages—could put you there in a hurry.

At that moment, Mr. Sandhill seemed to be pondering the same line of thought as Ryan. "What are you hoping they can help accomplish?" he asked Townley, referring to Brad and Meagan.

"Well, they know more about the *Shakti* than anyone else, except maybe the Bergerons themselves," Townley said. "They've been on it with the Bergerons dozens of times, and their knowledge of it, and yachts, will matter as we think about how to rescue Catherine, Francois, and the others."

"Certainly true," Mr. Sandhill said.

"And they can help with any of the bots if we do any reconnaissance activity," Townley added.

"Yes," Mr. Sandhill agreed. "Of course, I'm sincerely hoping that won't be necessary."

"Agreed. And, Carey's here to help if we need any special ops," Townley continued.

"Huh? Carey?" several of the group grunted.

"Carey Kaiser, yes, your other colleague from Weatherall University and from your fall orientation field trip," Townley said matter-of-factly. It suddenly felt to Ryan like one secret after another was marching out of a closet like a parade of skeletons.

"Hi guys," Carey said, peeping into view from beside Jumpshot. He was also wearing sunglasses. "Good to see you."

"If the situation weren't so serious, I would say this was a bad joke," Mr. Sandhill muttered.

"Well, we are bad, but it's no joke," Townley retorted with a laugh. He was trying to make light of an otherwise humorless situation.

They discussed Camp Lemonnier, and what sort of plan Townley envisioned preparing to attempt to rescue the hostages. Townley spoke in oblique terms so no one really understood him, presumably because he didn't want people to discern anything revealing about his plans. The storm had blown the *Shakti* eastward towards the Seychelle Islands, and a pirate vessel had launched from Somalia not long after the storm abated. Townley called it a "mother ship." The pirate mother ship, accompanied by a fleet of small, fast motorboats called skiffs, intercepted the *Shakti* and the other ships in the convoy a few days later. Heavily armed pirates had launched the skiffs from the mother ship and taken control of the boats in the convoy.

"And so we'll need you, the bots team back at Seguin, to be prepared to help us if we need anything," Townley said. "You'll be able to track the movement of the bots, which will largely mirror our movements. And we may need your help with them at some point."

"Unbelievable!" Sammy exclaimed after they wrapped up the VideoLink call. "Half of Weatherall University is in Djibouti with Townley, about to chase down a bunch of pirates! I hope they'll be okay."

"So do I," Mr. Sandhill echoed. "So do I."

It became virtually impossible for Ryan and his Seguin friends to concentrate on their studies for the next several days. There was a constant desire to check an electronic notebook, a computer, or an internet phone, whatever one had nearby that had a web connection, to see what movements Townley and the team were making or if there were any communications from him or the others. There was little. Sammy and James argued, fantasized, really, that they should find a way to go to Africa to help free Catherine Bergeron and the other hostages. How could they do it? Where would they go? Their services would not be welcome by Townley and they would most likely only be in the way, even if they were successful in catching up with him. The frustration of knowing friends were in danger and feeling totally helpless to do anything about it was unbearable.

Taking Ryan's mind off the kidnapping, if only fleetingly, were the Seguin junior varsity boys basketball team and an upcoming Valentine's Day dance. The hoops team was doing well in its league and was poised to make the playoffs toward the end of the season in March. Basketball also helped distract Ryan from the mind-boggling amount of homework that generally awaited him when he was finished. If nothing else, basketball made him so exhausted that he couldn't muster the energy to protest the workload. He just had to press on and find a way to try to get through it. Remarkably, he mused to himself, he was actually learning some things.

The Valentine's Day dance posed a different sort of challenge for Ryan, and for this reason, he was trying to ignore it. There were one or two girls he might have asked to the dance, but didn't know them that well, and he thought they might laugh him off, or worse, consider him a robotics geek. So, ultimately he did not plan to invite anyone, and half thought about quietly knocking off some reading the night of the dance instead of going to it. One afternoon, Carmen asked him if he was planning to go.

"I don't know," Ryan said. "I hadn't given it much thought. I mean, are other people going?"

Carmen shrugged. "I don't know. Maybe we can go as a group."

"Yeah," Ryan agreed hurriedly. "A group sounds like a good idea." Going as a group took any pressure off the need to feel that he had to find a date.

As it turned out, however, the tension around the dance was still not completely over for Ryan. Ellen brought matters to a head when she surprised Ryan two days later in the cafeteria. Everyone had been eating lunch and was headed off to History. Ryan found himself walking with Ellen at the back of the pack. They were just out of earshot of the others.

"So, do you have a date for the Valentine's Day dance?" Ellen asked. She could just as easily have been asking Ryan if he had finished the latest Biology assignment.

"Uh, no, I hadn't thought about it much," Ryan fibbed. He was surprised to hear Ellen mention a topic other than an academic subject, or herself.

"Want to go as my date?" Ellen asked.

"Um, uh, sure," Ryan said.

It was only later that it sank in that he had agreed to go the dance, with a girl. Moreover, he was going to the dance as… gulp… *Ellen's date.* Had she really used the word "date?" Maybe she had said "friend." Nope, she hadn't.

Date. It was a word Ryan felt he did not comprehend, as if it had never been applied to him. Which, come to think of it, until now, it hadn't.

News of his acceptance of Ellen's invitation, however, traveled like lightning, thanks largely to Ellen herself, who proudly announced to their History class the next day that she and Ryan were going to the dance "together."

"You are?" Carmen asked. She looked crestfallen.

"Yes, he is," Ellen answered on Ryan's behalf.

"Uh, well, yeah. Ellen and I are going, and hopefully you guys are all going with us," Ryan said awkwardly. "You know, as a group… like, as friends."

"What's *that* supposed to mean?" Ellen retorted.

"You know, I think if you said less—actually, if you said nothing—right now, you'd stop putting your foot in it," James whispered to Ryan.

"Thanks," Ryan huffed back.

Ryan had never put his hands on a live electric wire before, but the matter of the dance made him suddenly feel as if he had.

A lot happened over the next few days. Ryan felt like he got crushed on Biology and Computer Science exams, the basketball team got knocked out of the playoffs, and the dance happened, without much fanfare, fortunately. Ryan, Ellen, and their friends *did* go largely as a group, and Ellen didn't get defensive about whether Ryan was dancing with her or others, since most of the time they were dancing in a large group, if they were dancing at all. And though it involved more dancing than he had done in his whole life, Ryan still didn't dance all that much.

A few short days later Ryan and his friends were in Mr. Sandhill's office, presumably to talk about Physics, but the discussion immediately turned to a different topic. "Well, we now know what the ask is," Mr. Sandhill sighed.

"The ask?" James repeated.

"Yes. The ask. The ransom from the kidnappers. The amount of money the pirates are asking for in exchange for the safe return for the members of the hijacked convoy of ships in the Indian Ocean, the *Shakti* and the others."

"So, how much is the ask... uh, the ransom?" Carmen asked.

"If you must know," Mr. Sandhill sighed, "it's fifteen million dollars for all of the hostages and the oil on the tanker."

"Ouch," Sammy yelped.

"Not exactly pocket change if you're joy-riding around in the Indian Ocean," Mr. Sandhill said wryly.

All humor aside, Ryan came to learn that Townley had meant business when talking about an action plan. The next day Ryan and his friends saw from their trackers that Townley, Brad, Meagan, and Carey had flown from Djibouti to the Seychelle Islands in the Indian Ocean. Despite everyone's jokes that Townley and company were vacationing in the exotic island archipelago, they knew the stop in the Seychelles was not for recreation. Townley's new location was confirmed by a reluctant Mr. Sandhill.

"I'd rather you didn't know where he was," Mr. Sandhill told the bot cohort, "but since you're tracking him with those beacons, there's no concealing it." Mr. Sandhill also shared a few more details under sworn secrecy from Ryan and his friends.

Townley had managed to obtain the use of a defender class response boat and its crew from the Seychelles Coast Guard—very significant assets. It was a relatively small boat, but it occurred to Ryan that that probably suited Townley's needs. He had no intention of broadcasting his presence to the pirates if he could avoid it. No doubt, that meant approaching the kidnapped convoy under the cover of night. Stealth and secrecy would be of highest priority for his purposes.

Helping Townley's cause was the fact that the hijacked boats and hostages were from several different countries. Thus, the matter of discussing ransom payments would become accordingly complex, which would most definitely lengthen the time frame for discussions and negotiations among the various governments whose citizens were involved. Time, at least for now, was on Townley's side, Mr. Sandhill explained.

Not to mention, the story of the kidnappings had become an international sensation, so numerous government diplomats and military officials would have to ensure they were playing it right, given the public's attention to the story around the world. Every move they made or word they spoke would be picked up by major news media around the globe.

"So what does all this diplomatic activity mean?" Carmen asked.

"Well, coordinating among various world governments is a bit like trying to get something through the U.S. Congress, only worse," Mr. Sandhill quipped.

"Huh?" James asked.

"Never mind," Mr. Sandhill replied. "Trust me, though. It's good news in terms of the amount of time everything will take. That gives Townley more time to formulate and lay out his plan. I just hope the pirates don't get overly impatient."

It took more than two precious days, but more good luck came when Townley learned from the Seychelles Coast Guard that a German container ship, headed for the Suez Canal from China and guarded by an armed security team, would be passing within the vicinity of the hijacked convoy in the next few days. Townley had little difficulty convincing the German ship's captain to permit the Seychelles Coast Guard defender to shadow his ship in order to avoid detection, especially since the defender's mission was to free kidnapped hostages. The German captain, a veteran of the high seas, knew firsthand the problems pirates caused for ships in that part of the world, and was only too happy to oblige.

After a little more negotiating with the German ship's captain, Townley was able to get extra fuel aboard the container ship so the defender could fill its tank and leave with some additional fuel reserves once it was in close proximity to the kidnapped convoy. "We may need the full tank to outrun the kidnappers if they spot us," Townley noted. Meagan later said she hoped he had been joking. He wasn't.

Brad, Meagan, and Carey soon learned that "vicinity" was relative when it came to the vastness of the earth's oceans. Shadowing the German container ship on the Indian Ocean to reach the general area of the convoy proved painstaking. The trip lasted nearly fourteen hours. Meagan later told everyone that Ryan and Carey had turned green from the ship tossing about on the waves. In turn, they said Meagan's skin took on a similar color. Fortunately, the air was warm so they could spread out somewhat on the defender, and not have to huddle for warmth inside the boat's tightly cramped cabin. The timetable of the container ship served their purposes well, as the ship would pass near the hijacked convoy at night.

"The cover of night gives us the best chance of getting to the boats and rescuing people," Townley explained.

Ryan was stunned to learn that Brad, Meagan, and Carey Kaiser were all aboard the coast guard defender with Townley. It seemed they were headed into the jaws of a dragon. Mr. Sandhill's look and body language told him he was equally surprised, and dismayed.

Having re-filled its fuel tank and taken on reserve fuel, the defender and the container ship parted ways at about eleven o'clock that night. It was a time when the pirate kidnappers would let their guard down or be asleep, or so Townley hoped. He was also banking on the same being true for any radar or tracking capability the pirates might possess, either aboard their mother ship or possibly somewhere in Somalia.

All lights on the defender had been dim for some time, but the few that had not been covered or turned off now were. Its engine thrumming quietly, the defender approached the convoy without incident. The loudest audible sound was the peaceful, sloshing roll of the waves, darker than the night itself, rising and falling in the distance. With the aid of night vision binoculars, Townley directed Pascal, the defender's captain, to halt and anchor the boat several thousand yards away from the hijacked convoy in hopes of avoiding being seen. The coast guard crew then produced a black inflatable raft that had been equipped with a super small, quiet motor. In the cabin, Carey now changed into a black camouflage uniform as dark as the ocean, as did Townley. Respecting the up and down rhythms of the swaying ocean, they clambered into the raft from the defender and piloted it off through the dark night air atop the even darker ocean.

Townley piloted the raft and Carey rode in the middle. Brad and Meagan remained on the coast guard defender with the Seychelles Coast Guard patrol and watched using night vision binoculars. Townley maneuvered the raft up to the side of the last hijacked boat in the convoy, a yacht. Watching through her binoculars, Meagan couldn't see the rope that tethered the yacht to the next ship in the convoy about thirty yards away, but she knew it was there, because the distance between the two ships remained constant. It was a clear night, with a waxing moon, but even so, the night vision binoculars were necessary to see very far. Far off in the distance, she knew the tanker loomed, and somewhere beyond that in the darkness, the pirate mother ship.

Minutes oozed by. There were no signs of people on the decks of the convoy ships as far as Meagan could tell. She shifted her binoculars back to the raft, which was now a small blotch in her view. It was now quite close to the last kidnapped boat in the convoy. It occurred to Meagan that watching the raft's course felt as long as the day's journey they had made shadowing the German container ship. Finally, Carey tethered the raft alongside the last yacht in the convoy, loosely, since they might need a fast escape. He and Townley then deftly clambered off the raft onto the back of the yacht, hoisting themselves up onto it by gripping its metal railings.

Carey crept alongside the walkway of the boat's port side. Strangely, there appeared to be no guards on the deck of the boat. Carey hoped perhaps the pirates were more disorganized than he expected, which would make freeing the hostages easier. In stealth, he and Townley crept around the deck of the yacht, staying low to the floor. On the upper deck, slouched in a captain's seat, they found a dozing pirate, an automatic weapon slung at his side. In utter silence, they quickly rendered him unconscious with a needle stick of a powerful sedative drug, bound him, and seized his weapon. They then slowly disappeared down the steps below deck. They were unsure of what they would find, so they were cautious in their approach. They could find more armed kidnappers, hostages, or quite possibly both.

After a few minutes, Meagan saw them emerge from down below the deck, escorting a dazed man and a woman. Meagan saw Carey extend an arm brandishing what appeared to be a knife. He made a slashing motion at the yacht's edge, and Meagan assumed Carey was cutting the rope that tethered the yacht to the rest of the convoy. Her suspicions were confirmed a minute later, as she thought she observed a widening distance between the yacht and the next to last boat in the convoy, another yacht. It was difficult to tell initially, since she had been awake for nearly twenty hours, and a yearning desire for sleep had crept over her.

Having started slowly, the yacht began to drift away with gradually increasing speed. Watching the boat drift listlessly felt to Meagan like watching paint dry. Presently she sensed a low vibration reverberating on the defender as its engine quietly came to life. The captain of the defender, Pascal, was at the wheel. He started to pilot the defender slowly towards the drifting yacht. He had waited for the yacht to drift some distance before approaching it to avoid being seen by possible captors on the other ships in the convoy.

The untethered yacht was now several hundred yards away from the rest of the convoy. The defender pulled up alongside her on the side facing away from the convoy once again to remain stealthy. Townley and Carey helped a very confused man and woman, former hostages now liberated, who had no doubt undergone a tremendous ordeal, clamber awkwardly aboard the defender. Amid murmurs and quick, hushed movements, the defender's crew greeted the man and woman with blankets and water.

"Gotta go get more," Townley said as he and Carey climbed back aboard the drifting yacht. Their raft was still tethered to it. Meagan's muscles ached, her eyes were sore, and her brain felt it was working at half speed. Carey and Townley proceeded to untie the raft from the yacht and headed off in the direction of the next kidnapped yacht in the convoy. Various members of the defender crew tended to the rescued man and woman.

"I can't believe this is just the first boat," Meagan said to Brad. "How much more do you think they'll try to do tonight?"

"I don't know," Brad said.

Meagan watched through night vision binoculars as the raft neared and then docked at what was now the last yacht in the convoy. Once again, she saw Townley and Carey tether and cautiously clamber aboard. As they had done with the first yacht, they scoured the yacht's deck, then disappeared below. This time, they cut the tether holding the yacht to the convoy before they did so. Now a second yacht had been severed from the convoy.

All had gone as expected up to that point. However, events were about to take an unwelcome turn. Earlier in the night, as the defender had approached the convoy, Townley had used radar to identify and plot the locations of the six hijacked vessels, the pirate mother ship, and three pirate skiffs operating in the area. Moments earlier, Meagan had watched one of the pirate skiffs head off in the direction of the first yacht in the convoy, the one which had been first severed by Carey and now drifted nearly a mile from the rest of the convoy. She was not gravely concerned about it, since all that would be found on the yacht at this point would be a couple of unconscious pirates, and it would take precious time for the pirates on the skiff to fully investigate.

Of greater concern was that Townley's radar scan had missed a fourth skiff, one moored directly next to the mother pirate ship. This skiff now launched and set off in the direction of the yacht that had just been sent adrift, the one now occupied by Townley and Carey. Presumably, the mother ship had tried to contact the pirate guards on this yacht and failed to get a response. Furthermore, it would soon become evident to anyone watching that this yacht was also untethered and now drifting away from the convoy.

Watching the pirate skiff draw closer, Brad and Meagan now expected a clash at the drifting yacht. The pirates on the skiff would likely soon discover Townley and Carey's raft moored alongside her. Evidently, Pascal read the situation the same way, because from the control deck on the defender he began urgently barking into a mouthpiece, which transmitted to earpieces that Townley and Carey were wearing.

"Tangos approaching! Repeat! Tangos approaching!" he stammered. He waited for a moment. No reply came. Meagan knew "Tangos" referred to the pirates.

"Get out of there! Repeat, get out of there!" demanded Pascal.

There was still silence from Townley and Carey on the boat, most likely because they were in close proximity to pirates, and speaking would give them away or endanger them. Or, so Meagan assumed.

A few seconds later Pascal barked his message again. This time, his message was soon answered, not by words, but by gunfire. Aboard the defender, they heard gunshots strafing the night air, coming from the yacht. Through binoculars, Brad could barely make out Townley standing on the deck of the yacht, brandishing an automatic weapon, firing in the direction of the closest skiff. In response to the gunshots, the other pirate skiff, which had been approaching the first untethered yacht, now turned and veered back towards the yacht that Townley was aboard. Evidently, Townley's marksmanship served him well. Through his binoculars, Brad could make out three pirates in the first skiff, furiously bailing water while trying to lie low. Townley had shot holes in the wood hull of the skiff and she was taking on water.

"It looks like Townley hit the skiff!" Brad announced. "I think she's sinking!"

"Unfortunately those in the second skiff will not be so foolish," Pascal replied. "They will shoot first and ask questions later."

"Can't Townley hold the yacht?" Brad asked.

"For a while," Pascal replied. "But he has to get off. The pirates will send more skiffs with more guns, and he cannot outrun skiffs in that yacht," he added grimly.

As if he could hear Pascal, Townley was waving to two other people, a man and a woman, on the deck of the yacht. He was guiding them towards the stern near where the getaway raft was moored. Like the couple who had been rescued from the first yacht, this couple also seemed disoriented and confused, not to mention terrified. Their emotions intensified when the second skiff approached and started spraying gunfire as it neared the yacht. Brad now spied Carey up on the yacht's deck, trying to guide the couple.

Townley had jumped down into the raft, and was trying to urge the couple towards him so they could leap into it. However, a furious spray of gunfire was now pummeling the deck of the yacht, splintering pieces of wood and fiberglass and sending sparks shooting off metal railings, splaying into the night. The ferocity of the gunfire forced Carey and the couple to hit the deck of the yacht. Meanwhile, Townley had untethered the raft from the yacht, hoping the others would be joining him. Just then, a large ocean swell roiled through the area and sent the yacht and the raft rolling up and then steeply down. The subsequent upswell caught Townley's raft on the other side of it from the yacht, so that the raft and yacht were now separated by a dozen yards.

Meagan could now see that Townley was in a difficult position because he was trying to maneuver the raft, hold onto a weapon, and see what was happening up on the deck of the yacht all at the same time, and all while positioned on the other side of the yacht from the approaching skiff. Just as Townley had shot holes in the pirate skiff earlier, causing it to slowly sink, he was now at perilous risk of the same fate in an inflatable raft.

Waiting as long as he could for some sign of Carey and the hostages, but seeing no movement, Townley turned the raft and started to head towards the defender. The torrent of gunfire pelting the yacht soon subsided, and Meagan could see the heads of a couple of pirates peering up on the yacht deck, having approached it from the side opposite Townley and the defender. They had clambered aboard. It was a horrific scene. What had happened to Carey and the hostages? Were the hostages Catherine and Francois Bergeron? Were they alive? Were they dead?

The minute or so it took Townley to reach the defender was jarring to Meagan.

"Should we go after the yacht?" Brad urged of Pascal.

"I don't think so," he conceded. "There are now several skiffs swarming with armed pirates around her, with potentially more firepower than we have. It is dark, and the likelihood of hitting one of our own or a hostage is too high. And, the element of stealth, or surprise, for that matter, is gone now." He sighed heavily.

Moments later, Townley reached the defender in the inflatable raft. The crew quickly helped him up out of the raft and hauled it in. Townley was beside himself. "Blast it!" he yelled. He was visibly distraught and upset with himself over what had just happened. Meagan shared his distress, as did Brad. They had gotten one couple off a hijacked yacht, but they had failed to do the same on the second yacht. As for the hostages they freed, they paid a steep price for it, since the pirates now had Carey, and they didn't know whether he was dead or alive.

14

PROJECT BLACKJACK

Back at Seguin Academy, Ryan had a note taped to his locker after basketball practice that afternoon. The name on the front was written in an unfamiliar pen, but upon opening it he recognized Mr. Sandhill's handwriting.

Ryan, can you meet me in my office at 6:30 pm after dinner? Thomas.

Most of Ryan's interactions with Mr. Sandhill at Seguin took place in a classroom, the student center, the library, the cafeteria, the gym, or some other fairly public place. In short, they happened just about anywhere except Mr. Sandhill's office, so Ryan knew something was up. He soon learned that his friends had received similar invitations.

"Do you think it has to do with Townley and the kidnappings?" Sammy asked.

"What do you think?" Ellen asked, in her now familiar brusque tone.

"That means 'yes,'" Jenny interjected.

Everyone walked purposefully across the Seguin campus to Mr. Sandhill's office after dinner.

"So, you might be wondering why I've asked you to the office," Mr. Sandhill said.

"Not really," Carmen replied.

"Yeah, I mean, we assume we're here to talk about Townley and the hostages, right?" Sammy said.

"Yes," Mr. Sandhill replied.

"So, is there bad news?" Jenny asked.

"Some," Mr. Sandhill said. "Though it could be worse... Far worse."

"Well, that's encouraging... I guess," Ryan said.

"The pirates have captured Carey Kaiser," Mr. Sandhill continued.

"What?" Everyone exclaimed, dumbfounded.

"How did it happen?" James gasped.

Mr. Sandhill proceeded to tell the group about Townley and Carey's hostage rescue attempts, both successful and unsuccessful. The couple that had been rescued was from Brazil. Townley and the defender crew had needed to beat a hasty retreat back to a base on the Seychelles after being nearly overwhelmed by pirates.

"Do we know whether Carey's alive? If so, how?" Ryan asked.

"He has a transmitting beacon, somewhat like those affixed to your bots. He uses it manually to signal if he is alive, in danger, whether he's injured or not, and a few other things," Mr. Sandhill replied. "The transmitter is attached to one of his finger nails, so he can send messages with it even if his hands are bound."

"Wow, that's pretty smart," Carmen observed.

"One tries," Mr. Sandhill said.

"So, as you were saying, we know Carey's alive because he's been transmitting messages?" Ellen asked, as if still in need of confirmation.

"Yes," Mr. Sandhill said. "He is alive, his hands are bound, and at the moment he is being held aboard the same yacht he and Townley were trying to free last night when they got caught by the pirates. The hostages on that boat are also alive. One of them, a man, is being kept in the same room as Carey, while another, the wife of the man, is being kept elsewhere."

"That's a lot of intelligence for a finger nail," Jenny mused.

"Yes, it is," Mr. Sandhill said. "Now, to get to the point of why I asked you here... I think Townley is planning to use the bots to help do reconnaissance, intelligence gathering, and maybe more, as part of the plan to rescue the hostages, which now include Carey."

"Wow, that's great," Ellen said. "What can we do to help?"

"Yeah, I mean... *are* there things we can do to help?" Carmen asked. There was uncertainty in her voice. It wasn't entirely obvious to her that they could help, being half a world away.

"It appears that you may very well indeed be able to help," Mr. Sandhill replied. "There is additional urgency in the matter. While the governments of the hostages' home countries are working furiously to try to negotiate their release, or at least stall for time, the pirates have taken action of their own. They have started moving the convoy towards Somalia. If they make it to land, they could sequester the hostages away where they might never be found. Any delay in negotiations for the lives of the hostages becomes dramatically more dangerous at that point. It is much more desirable that we stop them while they're on the ocean."

"So that's where you think we can help?" James queried.

"Yes, logistically there are a few challenges," Mr. Sandhill continued, "but they're largely mine to sort out. Mine and Townley's."

"What do you mean?" Sammy asked.

"Well, I think you may be going on the road, on assignment, as it were, for a few days."

"Really? Where are we going?" Jenny asked.

"I'll give you a hint. It's a place that you've been to before, not too long ago, where you learned to do something new," Mr. Sandhill said.

Ryan's mind began to race to find the answer to the riddle. The school dance? The Seguin library? The science building? Weatherall University? Where else had they been recently?

"Uh, Yellowstone?" Carmen guessed after a brief pause.

"Excellent guess," Mr. Sandhill replied. Ryan kicked himself for thinking only of places he had visited in the past two weeks. "But, it's not the correct answer, in this case, though it could be. Directionally you are very much on the mark, Carmen."

"Um... Okay let's see... Creech!" Carmen blurted out.

"Yes!" Mr. Sandhill exclaimed.

Creech Air Force Base. It all made sense. The place where they had taken quantum steps forward in their abilities to move and manipulate their bots in difficult situations. And from which they could pilot their bots on the other side of the world.

"So we're going to Creech?" Sammy asked expectantly.

"It would appear... yes," Mr. Sandhill replied. "Subject to my ability to manage your absences, and your willingness to go."

"Do we have a choice?" James asked.

"Of course. There is always a choice," Mr. Sandhill replied. "I will say, in this case, it would be greatly appreciated by Mrs. Bergeron, Francois, the crew, all of the other hostages, Townley and the rest of the armed services. Not to mention me, if you elected to go."

"Well, when you put it like that, it's pretty much a no brainer," James said. "Not to mention, we'll get to miss some classes." His eyes lit up.

"Yeah, what about our classes? We will obviously miss some, won't we?" Jenny noted, a hopeful tone in her question.

"Yes, I should say you will," Mr. Sandhill replied.

"So we will get to skip some of our assignments?" Ellen asked in a hopeful tone.

"I didn't say that now, did I?" Mr. Sandhill said. "No, your assignments will, of course, be due. We'll just have to make some special arrangements. Some of your assignments might be a little late, shall we say."

"So, what will we tell our teachers and classmates to explain our absence?" Ryan asked.

They all looked each other for a moment. "Field trip!" They all chorused in unison.

"Something like that, yes," Mr. Sandhill acknowledged. "Although it will need to sound less fun. To be sure, this excursion will be many things, but fun is probably not one of them. As you are aware, the work you will be doing could not be more serious. Lives of many innocent people are at stake, including people we know. Maybe we'll call it an emergency field exercise, specific to the Robotics class. If we call it a field trip, everyone at Seguin Academy will be requesting one," he smiled. "And then, I'll have a bunch of angry parents on my hands wondering why their children were denied one."

There was a brief pause. Then Ellen spoke. "Um, so Creech was an amazing experience and everything, but I'm trying to figure it out. What specifically did we learn at Creech that was new?" she asked in a polite tone.

Mr. Sandhill considered for a moment. "Fair point, Ellen," he said. "So, what specifically did you learn at Creech? Well, the way I see it, you learned to be pioneers."

Ryan reflected on their visit to Creech the previous August, when they had used the bots to climb vertical walls, dive bomb from lofty heights, carry other bots, maneuver in highly challenging terrain, enter and navigate within buildings, and shoot at targets. It was an unforgettable experience. He then thought about how real the bots seemed as he remembered the fraternity house party incident that fall with Brad and Ellen's leopard bot, Leo, who caused the frat house to empty out as if it were a five alarm fire.

He also reflected on the stunt Sammy and Brad pulled at the Head of the Charles with Chomp and Tux, who completely freaked out an entire river's worth of rowers, having convinced them and thousands of onlookers that there were real killer whales swimming in the Charles River. Their high-flying breaches out of the water, sending crew skulls flying up in the air, with stunned rowers arcing in space and swimming for dear life upon hitting the water, had made national news. Ryan even thought back on his antics with Scram at the Highland Park Middle School dance, when he had convinced a gymnasium full of people that a green lizard was in their midst, and that it could climb walls and people to boot. Yes, the bots really could do some pretty amazing things, especially if you controlled them correctly.

The group departed early the next morning for Las Vegas. The travel was long, but uneventful. It seemed strange to Ryan that they were flying west to try to help friends located some thousands of miles to the east of them, with the distance of separation expanding by the second. Mr. Sandhill reminded everyone that Creech was one of the most sophisticated remote piloting facilities in the world, where they had seen and used various piloting, tracking, monitoring, and video technologies with their bots. Using an animal bot with all of the space age technology and communications technology at Creech made playing routine computer games seem like watching grass grow by comparison.

Ryan spent much of the flight wondering what Townley would devise in the way of a plan. He had no idea how it would work or what it would look like, but he assumed Townley had some specifics in mind. He usually did.

In Las Vegas, the group caught a shuttle bus that drove them to Creech Air Force Base. The Air Force team members that Ryan and his bot mates had met the previous August were all there: Brenda Gibbs, Amanda Harte, Rick Hutchins, Carlos Silva, Debbie Tan, and Jack Timlin. There was a reunion of sorts as people exchanged greetings, handshakes, and high fives. Everyone enjoyed the brief celebratory interlude before being soberly reminded of the serious purpose of their visit.

They ate a fairly quick lunch at the cantina on the base, talking as they ate. "So, first things first, we're going to need to do some bot practice drills," Carlos said to the group. "And, fortunately we have copies of your bots to do that."

"So, how'd you get copies of our bots?" Ellen asked.

"Um, we had them made," Brenda replied.

"Without our knowing about it? That's pretty sneaky," Jenny observed.

"Well, the parts and supplies that you bought for your bots were made available through a government grant. When you purchased your bot kits, there was some fine print saying that you agreed to let the government use the resulting creations, in extreme or urgent circumstances, if the need arose. I'd say we have a pressing need right now, wouldn't you?" Brenda posited.

"Uh, yeah," Ryan admitted.

"Is this true?" Carmen asked of Mr. Sandhill.

"Why, yes it is, wouldn't you say?" Mr. Sandhill replied. "We very definitely have a pressing need," he said.

"No, I meant, can these creations really be copied?"

Mr. Sandhill paused for a moment. "Yes," he said.

"Only under extreme or urgent circumstances," Brenda added. "Don't you think saving the lives of your friends qualifies?"

"Sure, of course it does," Sammy agreed.

"No one ever really reads fine print, do they?" Brenda said. Everyone stared blankly at each other. "I blame the lawyers," she remarked.

"We had them built for you guys," Amanda noted, referring to the bot copies. "We also made a few refinements to the bots which we can talk about." Everyone from Seguin cast curious glances at each other in response.

Ryan found himself wondering what else about Scram others might know. Brenda readily acknowledged that no one besides him knew how to operate Scram, and she was probably not mistaken in thinking so. But, in time, surely others could learn to build and operate a bot like Scram. Operating him was highly complex and challenging, but it wasn't impossible. Wouldn't it be a good thing if others started to work with Scram and push his performance limits? Ryan felt it likely was, so long as the bot was put to positive use.

After lunch, they went into the same auditorium they had sat in the previous August, where a huge image of Townley was projected on a screen via VideoLink. It was evening in the Seychelle Islands. Everyone exchanged greetings with him.

"My friends, it's time to turn to our unfair advantages," Townley said, getting down to business. "Our friends at Creech are going to help you and us, me, Brad, Meagan, and the Seychelles Coast Guard team, prepare for a mission to complete the rescue of the hostages. Now, you might be wondering why we would want to use bots to help in this process instead of major military assets like a battle ship, a submarine, or fighter jets. Unfortunately, we can't use those things for a couple of reasons. One, the pirates already know we're onto them and they are on the lookout for such things, so we've lost that element of surprise. And, they could pick up any of those large objects on radar. The bots for the most part are much smaller and are much less likely to get picked up. Two, the reason the pirates have kept the hostages spread out on the convoy is so that we cannot make one strike and free everybody at once. There are hostages on multiple boats, so there will have to be multiple rescue missions. Three, we need to be able to get eyes and ears on the boats so we can figure out how many kidnappers and hostages there are on each and take out the kidnappers, but not the hostages. So it's pretty tricky, you know what I mean?"

Ryan and several others found themselves nodding and muttering in agreement. It often felt to Ryan as if Townley's mind were racing at supersonic speed, which, given the speeds of the aircraft he flew, wasn't surprising. But, Ryan was impressed with Townley's ability to juggle a dizzying array of different variables relating to, say, the current hostage situation. With lives hanging in the balance, you really had to devise a workable plan, even when you didn't have all the facts, like not knowing how many kidnappers were on each ship, or how many pirates there were, or what kinds of weapons they had. It seemed that Townley's intuition was right. The pirates no doubt felt that freeing the convoy one ship at a time posed a far greater challenge to any would-be rescuers than if all the hostages were aboard one vessel.

The pirates had pulled the two yachts that had been severed from the convoy back to it, tethered them again, and let them continue to float individually in sequence. Given the occasional roughness of the seas, that was logical. Two boats floating in close proximity amid violent waves could easily damage each other.

"So what's next?" Sammy asked.

"We'll, we've got the design plans on the boats involved," Brenda said. "So we're going to study those and figure out how to gain access to them, and the best way to do that, so we can disable captors and free the hostages."

"We do? We will?" James asked.

"We do," Debbie replied.

"We will," Mr. Sandhill added. "To the best of our ability."

"So, uh, where are we going to do all this?" Carmen asked.

"We'll, the boat plans are here," Jack Timlin replied. "All six of them, including the Dutch tanker." He produced a large tube from which he withdrew a large sheaf of papers.

"The bots and copies of the boats are in the Seychelles islands. So you'll be operating them from here, but the action will all be happening over there," Amanda said.

"It sounds almost like a video game," Sammy observed.

"Yes, it's a lot like a video game," Jack said. "But, in contrast to a video game, it's way more real than any video game. The movements of everything, the bots, boats, and people are all real. And, as you are aware, the lives of the people being held hostage are real and at stake."

"Yup, that's pretty different from a video game," Ellen agreed.

A solemn moment of silence hung heavily in the air.

"Uh, well, let's get started," Carmen said, trying to change the mood. "What do we need to do first?"

"Practice," muttered Rick Hutchins.

"That's right," Townley echoed. "Right now, you're going to practice some maneuvers at Creech, and then tomorrow we're going to do some simulated work with the boats here in the Seychelles. And we're going to practice a lot. We've got a lot of work to do to get ready."

Ryan was stunned and amazed to think that soon Scram could be doing something on the other side of the world, something that could help save lives. He reflected on Townley's comments. It might be work, but it sure didn't feel like it.

That afternoon they practiced a number of maneuvers with their bots among several ponds that lay to one far edge of the air base. While the ponds were generally shallow and never held a great deal of water, they were deliberately filled with more water to facilitate the practice sessions that ensued. A couple of motorized boats were placed in the ponds. They were neither the size nor the scale of the hijacked boats in the Indian Ocean, but as they moved about, they definitely gave one some sense of what it would be like to land a bot on a boat, by flying, swimming, or climbing. Everyone took turns with all of the different bots so they got a feel for how each would operate. They landed them on boats, moved them around, used their video cameras, and shot darts at targets with them.

Ryan felt he could maneuver Scram in nearly any situation, and his self-confidence was growing rapidly. "I'm ready to go," he told James and Sammy. "I can do anything I want with Scram."

"Easy there, cowboy," Brenda Gibbs chimed in. "Wait 'til you get a taste of the open ocean. It's a whole different thing."

About midway through the afternoon, Ellen started focusing more on her leopard bot, Leo. "Leo's more native to Africa," she explained. "Plus, he's more likely to scare the bejesus out of pirates."

"No doubt about it," Rick Hutchins agreed.

The location of Townley and the others in the Indian Ocean was eight hours ahead of Creech. That would give certain advantages to the group, as many of its activities would be at nighttime in the Indian Ocean, but would happen in the daytime at Creech. The Seychelles Coast Guard had borrowed a few yachts from locals to stage and rehearse operations with the animal bots.

The next morning at Creech, the Seguin team was taken to a room they had not seen before at the base. It was down several flights of stairs from the ground level, and thus had no windows to the outside. It was a dark, very spacious room with very high ceilings. They learned it was a central control room, where remote controlled flying craft and robots could be operated pretty much anywhere in the world. There were over a dozen computer workstations situated about the room, and each had a half dozen large screens positioned at different heights so they didn't block each other.

"Welcome to the war room," Debbie Tan from the Creech team announced to the group.

Ryan and his Seguin schoolmates were each guided by a member of the Creech team to a workstation. One of their screens showed a live VideoLink image of Townley and the Seychelles group: Brad, Meagan, Carey, Townley, Pascal, and the Seychelles Coast Guard team. They were all standing on a dock at a marina in the beautiful, lush, tropical environment of the Seychelles and everyone's greetings would have been joyous if the circumstances were not so dire.

"Going forward, for our practice drills and for the real operation, we're going to be using a real-time, secure communications hookup," Townley said. "That way, we can all be talking to each other in real time. As much as I like the VideoLink service, at this stage we need something a little more proprietary that can't be hacked."

"Wow," mused Ryan and several others. The whole enterprise was becoming more high tech by the minute.

"So, what haven't you thought of?" Ellen asked of the Creech team and Townley.

"Plenty," replied Rick Hutchins from the Creech team. "That's why we're going to practice some more."

In the distance on the screen, behind Townley and the others they could see several yachts moored in a marina. These were the yachts borrowed by the Seychelles Coast Guard that they would use for their practice drills. While the entire situation still seemed a bit abstract to Ryan, it was becoming more real by the minute. Everyone was instructed to put on a headset that had earphones and a mouthpiece.

They discussed the zone of engagement, the "theater of operations," as Amanda described it.

"'Theater' is more of a term that is used for large scale warfare, and obviously this situation is a much smaller scale, but it is no less dangerous," she cautioned. "But if you have a different name for it that would be easier to remember, we could use it."

"How about... the robosphere?" Ellen said.

"The robosphere," Amanda said, thinking for a moment. "'Sphere for short... Huh... Yeah, you know... I kinda like it."

"So, how will we get all of the bots to the theater... um, I mean, the robosphere?" Ryan asked. "Will the defender transport them?"

"Yes, we'll use the defender to get us to the convoy, like before," Townley replied. "But, once we're there, in the 'sphere, black and white power take over."

"Huh?" Ellen said.

"I think I get it!" Sammy interjected. "Black and white power... You mean Chomp and Tux!"

"Bingo!" Towney replied. "Chomp and Tux will be tethered to the defender. We will haul them underwater so they can't be seen. Once we are in the 'sphere, or at least within a few thousand yards of it, we launch the orcas. Brad and Meagan will be inside and will pilot them. With additional assistance from Creech, of course. They can be piloted solely from Creech, so if Brad or Meagan has to disembark, we will move the piloting function of the killer whales to Creech."

They reviewed the plans of each of the yachts and the sequence in which they planned to engage the yachts and free the hostages. Then they prepared to run through an extensive series of drills. Brand and Meagan each climbed into the cockpit of the orca bots.

"So are there any differences between Chomp and Tux?" Meagan asked.

"Not really," said Sammy. "Well, other than Chomp will weigh slightly less with you on board instead of Brad."

"Since, as we all know, you weigh five hundred pounds more than me," Meagan said to Brad.

"Hey!" Brad said. Everyone laughed.

Townley would be stationed on the Seychelles Coast Guard defender with Pascal and his crew. He would command operations while Pascal and his team would continuously monitor the zone of operations for pirates on the skiffs and protect the defender. The orcas would launch various bots at the yachts to go aboard the hijacked boats, determine where the hostages were, and take out the pirates with tranquilizing darts.

The practice drills were intense. Brad and Meagan cruised around the marina inside Chomp and Tux. Ryan had to admit that the orca bots looked downright scary. If you were a pirate and you saw one of these things swimming at you, with its tall, black dorsal fin cutting through the water, like a hot knife through butter, you'd freak out. For hours and hours, the Seguin team attempted launches of the other animal bots from Chomp and Tux. All seemed to go well. Ryan was a bit disappointed that Townley favored deploying Scram by having him air lifted by Harris, Carmen's hawk bot, as opposed to being catapulted directly out of the mouth of one of the orcas, but Townley felt it was less risky.

"Scram can do things and go into places that other bots can't," Townley said. "We can't risk losing him if we bang him into the side of a yacht from a catapult."

One more significant development awaited the group at Creech. Freak and Zeek arrived the next day, along with Speakeasy. They were a little delayed getting to Creech, having been misunderstood by their taxi cab driver, who dropped them off at a casino just south of the Las Vegas Strip called Desert's Last Reach, as opposed to Creech, the air base.

"Well, we were doing fine at the blackjack table until Zeek got us kicked out for counting cards," Freak said.

"You were trying to come here to help plan an intricate rescue mission and you got caught up *playing blackjack?*" Mr. Sandhill asked in dismay.

"Well, uh, we were waiting for a cab," Freak explained.

"Waiting for a cab? In Las Vegas? You can't walk five feet there without running into one," Carlos Silva laughed.

"And you thought a *casino* would be a good place to catch a cab?" Mr. Sandhill asked in a tone of disbelief.

"Well, we were initially trying to wait *outside* the casino," Zeek said. "But then, Freak insisted that we just play one or two hands and it wasn't really me counting cards," he added. "It was Speakeasy."

"*You* were counting cards?" Rick Hutchins squawked at Speakeasy.

"Well, I only count cards when instructed," Speakeasy replied. He stared straight ahead, as if deliberately trying to avoid staring at Freak and Zeek.

Everyone's eyes turned suspiciously to Freak and Zeek. "What? What's everyone looking at?" Zeek said defensively.

15

STEALTH IN THE ROBOSPHERE

Townley and Mr. Sandhill had summoned Speakeasy to the mission for his speech recognition, mimicking, and translation capabilities. Mr. Sandhill informed everyone that during the previous few days, U.S. intelligence agents had learned the identity of the lead pirate involved in the hijacking. He was Korfa Raage, a well-known leader of a large terrorist pirate network in Somalia. Agents had, in turn, provided Freak and Zeek with video footage of Raage speaking Somali, his native tongue. Speakeasy knew Somali, as it was one of the over six thousand languages he spoke, and with a little work, Freak and Zeek enabled him to talk in the same accent as Raage.

"It took some effort, but not too much," Freak said.

"The recordings were a bit grainy, but Speakeasy got it after a little while," Zeek added, as if he had had nothing to do with Speakeasy's accomplishment.

"Too bad it didn't help us in the casino," Freak said.

"Yeah, being fluent in Somali doesn't help you much at a blackjack table in Vegas," Zeek admitted.

"Definitely not when you're being busted for counting cards," Freak noted.

"Okay gentlemen. Well, now that your little gambling diversion is behind you, let's focus on trying to win at this more serious game, shall we?" Mr. Sandhill urged. He led them into the large, open room with the workstations.

Freak and Zeek walked into the war room. They seemed unimpressed. Ryan figured these guys traveled all over the world and had probably seen the most cutting edge robotic science labs anywhere. Nonetheless, they did seem attracted to the wide array of screens on the computer workstations, as if they were kids on a playground looking for the play object they hadn't seen before.

"Ah, Freakster and Zeekster," Townley exclaimed when he saw them on the live video chat connection. "And Dr. Speakeasy! How are you doin', my man?"

"Let's just say I prefer being around students to gamblers, okay?" Speakeasy replied.

"What's that?" Townley replied. They related to him the story of Freak, Zeek, and Speakeasy getting kicked out of the Vegas casino for counting cards. Hearing it brought a big chuckle forth from Townley. "Always getting into trouble, aren't you, guys?"

"It's our job, isn't it?" Freak asked.

"Yes, yes it is," Townley nodded. "Speaking of which, what say we start talking about brewing up some trouble for a band of pirates who are holding our friends hostage, shall we?"

"Trouble's the middle name of you two," Speakeasy said to a stunned Freak and Zeek.

"Hey, who programmed him to say that?" Freak demanded.

Over the microphone, Brad and Meagan could be heard laughing.

"Hey! Have you been programming Speakeasy behind our backs? We're going to have a word with you two when you get back!" Zeek barked.

Everyone at Creech momentarily chuckled in laughter.

"*Everybody* programs Speakeasy behind your backs!" Jenny laughed.

"I know," Freak said.

"Yeah, because we're the ones who have to correct the code," Zeek added. By now it was pretty clear to Ryan that not much escaped the razor sharp minds of Freak and Zeek.

Since all of the bots had cameras and digital readers built into them, Ryan and his friends would be able to see, literally and virtually, everything that was happening through the eyes of their bots on the other side of the world. From the war room, several floors down at Creech, people were able to send their bots literally anywhere. In practice drills, they sent them from the ponds to the far ends of the air base and up into the nearby mountains. Ryan was amazed. They even practiced some ocean maneuvers in the Pacific Ocean with bot copies from a naval base in San Diego.

It took the defender nearly two days to return to the convoy from its base in the Seychelles, during which time the team at Creech continued to drill extensively. Townley was able to watch and direct from the defender. "Heck, I've got nothing better to do right now," he said from the defender. Brad and Meagan did likewise. The evening of the second day, as the defender grew closer to the hijacked convoy, Townley began to lay out the plan.

He walked everyone through the details of what was known about the kidnapped convoy at that point. It had started to chug towards Somalia under the power of the hijacked Dutch oil tanker. Its movement, however, had been relatively slow, and the pirates, evidently in no rush to get the kidnapped hostages to land, made a habit of stopping at night to sleep. The first target of the rescue team would be Yacht 4, the yacht on which they knew Carey was being held hostage.

"There are three cabins on Yacht 4," Townley said, reviewing a drill session they had gone over two days earlier. "This is the yacht of the Italian couple. The tangos have the husband and wife in separate cabins," he said. "They will likely have one cabin for their own personal use. They have Carey and the husband in the third cabin. It sounds like they're in the one up front. But, we need to confirm all that."

"How do you know all this?" Sammy asked.

"The microchip Carey's got on his fingernail," Townley said.

Everyone at Creech looked around the room at each other in stunned amazement. The whole operation was becoming more high tech by the minute.

As they had rehearsed over the past few days, the chosen bots for the Yacht 4 operation were Slidey and Skye. They had contemplated several possible ways to deliver the bots to the yacht. Now was the time to decide how they would do it.

They had debated whether to use Harris, Carmen's hawk bot, to fly in and deliver Slidey, James' snake bot, to the yacht, or whether to launch him with the help of Chomp or Tux. Townley said the winds were high enough and Slidey's weight sufficiently heavy that there was some risk that Harris could accidentally get blown into the ocean with the extra weight, or drop Slidey into the ocean, despite having excellent grip with his talons.

"We can't lose Slidey," Townley said. "We can't lose any of the bots. Everybody's coming home."

Ryan wondered if this were a statement of fact or more an aspirational hope on the part of Townley. He suspected the latter.

They ultimately decided to use one of the orca bots to launch Slidey. They would use the other to launch Skye who would fly under her own power, once launched. Brad, piloting Tux, would provide transport for Slidey. He had been sitting inside of Tux under water next to the defender for some time, awaiting his first mission. From a video camera mounted on the defender, the team at Creech watched. Ryan felt at once excited and terrified to watch Tux's dorsal fin pull away from the defender and gradually descend into the dark waters of the ocean. The scene was ominous, like something out of a horror movie.

"I sure wouldn't want to be the tangos," Sammy remarked. "They aren't going to know what hit 'em."

"I don't know," Carmen cautioned. "Based on what we heard about the first rescue attempt, they seem to shoot first and ask questions later."

"Bring it," Ellen said. "The orcas can handle it." Ryan hoped she was right.

Brad maneuvered Tux near to the midsection of the yacht. He guided Tux to the surface, and opened his mouth. Inside, curled in a tight, compact swirl was Slidey. Using the digital imaging camera mounted on Tux's forehead, they established the trajectory for launching Slidey up on deck. There was a catapult inside the mouth of Tux. Sammy pressed a button from Creech, and halfway around the world, Tux shot Slidey up onto the deck. Brad's hands were full steering Tux's fins to keep him as level as possible amid the rolling ocean waves, so it fell to James to perform the operation. Launching Slidey on the deck was a fairly risky move, since they didn't know immediately if someone, namely a pirate, was up on deck, even though they had examined the deck with Tux's night vision a few minutes earlier. Once on the deck, with the visual aid of Slidey's camera, James maneuvered Slidey to a corner of a deck bench where he slithered into a restful coil under a life preserver. No people were visible on deck.

"Gotta keep cool," James said, thumping his chest with his hand. His heart had been racing. For the moment, at least, Slidey was safe.

Meanwhile, Meagan had piloted Chomp toward the same yacht, but stayed about thirty yards off the stern. From here, she surfaced Chomp and then opened his mouth ever so slightly. Jenny's dragonfly bot, Skye, then flew out into the night air. Working the controls at her workstation on the other side of the world, Jenny sent Skye aloft, flying through the air. She made Skye gain altitude in a hurry to avoid getting swept into any surging ocean waves. It was a lot like a video game, she thought, but the consequences of screwing up were all too real.

In the air above the ocean, the breeze blew the lightweight Skye up and down. Jenny added torque to Skye's motor, increasing the speed of Skye's wings to help stabilize her. She brought Skye down on the deck of the yacht towards the stern, near the boat's steering wheel. The stern deck of the yacht was also unoccupied, which was not surprising, given the late night hour.

Jenny now walked Skye towards a wooden grate on the yacht deck that was positioned above what they knew was one of the bedroom cabins. Grates were often left unsealed on yachts, particularly in warmer weather, to allow a continuous stream of fresh air to enter the cabins. Once Skye reached the grate, Jenny walked her tentatively toward one of its square shaped holes. Here misfortune struck. The plan was for Skye to drop down through the hole of the grate above the chamber, but Skye could not fit. The holes were simply not large enough for Skye's wide wings to make it through. Worse than that, when Jenny tried to move Skye back out of the grate, she couldn't move.

"Great! I'm stuck," Jenny said tersely. She threw up her hands in frustration. "Even the monitor is telling me Skye can't fly." A button on Skye's digital monitor in front of Jenny was flashing red.

Jack Timlin from Creech quickly, but calmly approached her station. "Is the wing caught under the grating? Let's see here. Easy does it. Steady as she goes," Jack said. His unflappability in the face of the tension struck Ryan as remarkable.

He slowly and carefully maneuvered the wing through Skye's joystick at Jenny's workstation, and he could actually feel Skye being stuck.

"It's the left wing," he said. "So let's see if we can move the right legs a little bit here and…there we go, that should so it." The flight button on the digital pilot screen now flashed green, telling them Skye could fly.

"Wow, amazing! So what do we do now?" Jenny said, blowing at a wisp of a hair that had fallen in front of her eyes. Ryan had come to know that Jenny was highly frustrated when she did so. She was upset with herself for not being able to rescue Skye.

"Since we can't get through the grate with Skye, we'll have to go with something smaller," Townley said. His voice was tinged with the slightest bit of static as it came over the speaker. All in all, though, the sound quality was quite good, even better than a cell phone connection, which at a distance of over four thousand miles away was impressive, Ryan thought.

"So, you mean, like, a fly?" Jenny asked.

"That's what I mean," Townley replied. "Meagan, you're how far out with Chomp? About two hundred yards?"

"Yeah," Meagan replied. "Give or take." Meagan had pulled away from the yacht with Chomp once she had launched Skye.

"Okay," Townley said. "We need you to move in about a hundred yards or so to release a fly."

"Okay," Meagan replied. "Moving Chomp one hundred yards north-northwest." Ryan imagined the strong, stalwart tail of Chomp whipping through the ocean current as Meagan navigated him.

"In the meantime, James, can you pull up a file at your station for Skye? We're going to have you land Skye on Chomp once the fly launches. Jenny will have her hands full piloting the fly."

"You got it," James said. He proceeded to open up a file that showed him the view from Skye's camera and gave him the controls to fly the dragonfly bot.

Jenny had a hopeful expression on her face. She was glad to play a role even though Skye wouldn't be useful for this part of the mission.

On a large master screen at the center of the room that showed digital images of everything in the 'sphere, Ryan watched as an image of Chomp started to move in the direction of the yacht. Everything on this display was labeled. The yacht was labeled "Yacht 4" and Chomp was labeled, fittingly enough, "Chomp."

"The flies haven't been tested as much," Jenny cautioned.

"True, but it's dark. We know they can fly and we need to get a visual read of what's below that grate, Townley said.

"Right," Jenny said. She looked nervous.

"We can do this," Jack Timlin said, trying to put Jenny at ease.

A minute or two oozed past. "Chomp in position," Meagan said.

"Surface Chomp to launch fly," Townley said.

"Flick," Jenny said.

"What's that?" Townley asked.

"Flick—the name of the fly," Jenny said.

"Got it," said Townley. "Jenny, prepare to launch Flick."

"Done," Jenny said a minute later.

Flick flew up into the air. The flight path was turbulent. Down below Flick, Jenny could see specks of light dancing on the water, stippled reflections of the moon. She briefly caught a glimpse of Chomp's dorsal fin disappearing below the water's surface. She was momentarily awed by the notion that within the creature's belly, positioned somewhat awkwardly, sat Meagan. A brisk headwind buffeted Flick, causing the tiny bot to fly backwards despite Jenny's pushing the directional joystick all the way forward.

"Wow, stiff winds this evening!" Jenny exclaimed. She watched as ocean waves flew backwards past Flick down below, despite her efforts to fly forward.

"No question," Towney observed. He had the same night vision camera view aboard the defender as the team at Creech. "Just hold her steady, Jenny, you're doing fine. It'll pass."

"One of the challenges of a light weight bot," Mr. Sandhill observed. "She's handling it, though."

"Ah, here we go," said Jenny. The wind had now died down and Flick was now speeding ahead some twenty feet above the ocean waves.

"The ship is off to your right, Jenny, about twenty degrees," said Jack Timlin. He was watching the digital monitor that showed all the ships and bots in the 'sphere.

Amanda helped Jenny steer Flick in its general direction. She could see a digital image of the yacht on one of the screens out of the corner of her eye. Within about ten seconds they saw the image of the yacht, rolling easily in the waves. Soon, Flick was above the yacht's deck. Steering Flick through the grate was harrowing. Twice, a gusty wind swept Flick wide of the grate when Jenny was trying to steer and drop her through, and Flick flew against the adjacent paneling of the boat with a thud.

"Ouch! I hope this doesn't damage Flick," Jenny exclaimed.

"We'll find out," Mr. Sandhill said.

"She's tough, she can take it," Jack Timlin said. Everyone prayed he was right.

On the third attempt, Jenny got Flick through the grate.

"All right, let's see what we got down here," Townley said as he watched from the defender.

"Hopefully the camera hasn't been demolished," Jenny muttered. To the amazement of everyone, it wasn't.

Flick hovered in midair with her camera pointed down. Ryan and the others could make out the contours of a bed, a small nightstand to one side of it, and a small dresser against a wall on the opposite side.

"Woman's body, hands tied, hostage, sleeping," declared Townley in a low voice, almost as if concerned he might awaken the woman.

At first, Ryan could discern none of these things, but after staring at the screen for a few more seconds, he could see the figure was indeed that of a woman and he could discern a bulging mass about the woman's wrists—the rope that bound them.

"So what do we do now?" James asked.

"Land Flick on the dresser for the moment," Townley said. "Our next move is to locate the tangos. We know Carey's in the front cabin with the other hostage." Through the communication chip on his fingernail, Carey had communicated this information to Townley.

While Jenny had been maneuvering Flick, James watched the yacht's deck from Slidey's hidden place under a life jacket. Once it was clear there was no activity, Slidey proceeded towards the stairs that led below deck to the yacht's kitchen area.

Navigating the stairs proved challenging, though James had done it before. The snake had to brace itself down with the front of its body against a step to allow for its tail end to slither down to the same step. An added challenge was getting used to doing it with the night vision camera in near total darkness. It got easier with each stair step as James grew more comfortable with the controls.

At the bottom of the steps, there was a door, which was slightly ajar. Slidey eased through the crack in the door. He slowly slithered through the kitchen area and down a hallway toward what they knew from the yacht's plan was the main cabin bedroom. Slidey slid through the door slit beneath the cabin door, which was closed. In the darkness of the room, James elevated Slidey's head, to give a better scan of the room.

His camera revealed a bed. From slightly below the mattress of the bed, they could make out a figure sleeping on it. It appeared to be a thin man. An object with a long shaft stood on the floor and leaned against the bed frame at the head of the bed. Slidey had found a sleeping pirate.

"Tango, sleeping, with weapon at the head of the bed," Townley said in a now familiar hushed tone and sparse use of words. "Prepare darts," he continued.

Slidey's mouth opened up to unveil a pair of fangs. James used a dial at his control station that changed the angle of the fangs so that the tips extended out and up, such that they were nearly horizontal to the ground. Ryan could tell what was happening based on a digital silhouette of Slidey portrayed on a screen that showed his body in red and the fangs in neon green, all against a dark background.

"Are we shooting one fang or both?" James asked.

"Both," Townley said. "We've got extras."

"Wow, you don't leave much to chance, do you?" Ellen asked.

"We leave chance to the tables in Las Vegas," Townley replied.

"Right here is the button to fire," Debbie Tan said to James. "Ready?"

"Yes," James said.

"Three, two, one, fire!" Debbie said.

James pressed the button. A brief bleep could be heard from his work-station, signaling the event. Half a world away, the fangs, now darts, shot straight and fast out of Slidey's mouth, hitting the sleeping pirate in the neck. The man momentarily flinched, but remained asleep. He stirred and moved some, but did not roll over.

"Bingo. Sleep tight," Townley said over the line.

"How long will it keep him out for?" Ryan asked Carlos, referring to the tranquilizer that was now being injected into the bloodstream of the sleeping pirate.

"About twenty-four hours," Carlos replied.

"Wow," Ryan mused. "That's pretty effective for a couple of super lightweight darts."

"Yeah, he'll be wondering how he got the vampire bite," Debbie Tan said, "since the darts will have dissolved by the time he wakes up and he'll have two bite marks on his neck."

Ryan was becoming more impressed by the minute as he observed firsthand the so-called "enhancements" Amanda had casually mentioned a few days earlier that the Creech team had made to the bots.

"You guys don't fool around, do you?" Ellen said to Amanda.

"When it comes to saving lives, no," Amanda said. "Like Townley said, we try to leave chance to the blackjack tables in Vegas."

"Okay, now we're going to turn our attention to the mother ship," Townley said.

"So, we don't need to worry about Carey and the other hostages on Yacht 4?" Jenny asked.

"Not yet," Townley said. "We'll bust Carey out in a little while, but let's give him some rest. Also, we don't want to completely freak out the other hostage who's in the same cabin, although that may be inevitable."

Carmen, Ryan, Ellen and Carlos now looked on their screens at the image of the pirate mother ship. They sat across the room from each other, but could see from the images on their screens that their target on the other side of the world was far enough away that it was out of earshot of Yacht 4, the yacht on which James and Jenny had been operating. Not far to one side of it loomed the hulking mass of the Dutch oil tanker.

"Meagan, prepare to launch Harris," Townley said.

"Roger that," Meagan replied. "Chomp at surface. Loading Harris into Chomp's mouth... Harris in mouth... Mouth open... Open sesame."

Chomp had the same version of the catapult that had been installed in Tux, which Brad had used to launch Slidey. Meagan was preparing Chomp to launch Harris as well as something else—Ryan's lizard bot, Scram. Harris held Scram firmly locked in his talons. The team's earlier concerns about weight where Slidey had been concerned were a non-issue for Scram, who weighed significantly less.

"Let's go talk to Mama," Townley said, referring to the mother ship. "On my count... Three, two, one, launch!"

"Roger that," Meagan said. The group clustered around Ryan, Carmen, and Ellen heard a "beep" from the control room's computers. From an assortment of screens, they now saw a digital dot separating from Chomp, gaining altitude in the air. Harris was taking flight.

"Wow, it's breezy out here... I mean... there," Carmen observed as she worked Harris' controls.

"Here is there, isn't it?" Townley said. "Harris is there, so you are there. But, the breeze isn't too different from what you experienced in the mountains around Creech, is it?"

"Right. It *is* like the winds we had here in Nevada last August," Carmen agreed.

"You're all over it, Carmen," Townley said. "Okay. Let's air mail Harris right over to Mama." Once again, he was referring to the mother ship. Ryan knew Townley was continuing to speak in oblique terms so that in the unlikely event he was overheard by the enemy, they still might not understand what he was talking about.

After launching Harris, Meagan propelled Chomp towards the mother ship. As she did so, everyone got a better view of it. It was an old, rusty looking hulk of a boat that might have been a fishing trawler earlier in its life. At this stage, the ship showed stains, chipped paint, and corrosion on her hull that belied her age and lack of upkeep. Nonetheless, if anything, the ship appeared more ominous as a result. She was dark, and only occasional splotches of the light color of her sides revealed to Tux's night vision that she sat there, bobbing up and down on the waves. Ryan thought she looked ghostly.

"So we're going for the roof of the bridge, the upper deck, right?" Carmen asked, referring to the cockpit of the ship, the highest point on the boat.

"You got it. The bridge. Just like we practiced," Townley replied.

"Here we come," Carmen said. Harris was now about fifty feet above the water just then. "Lizard boy, you ready to roll?" she asked, smiling over at Ryan.

"Ready," Ryan said. He felt at once incredibly excited and terrified. Feeling anxious, he performed a check on Scram. He turned a dial that started Scram walking. He neither felt nor detected any movement at the control station, because Scram was still suspended in mid-air, held tightly by the talons of Harris. But, his control panel told him Scram's legs were moving. Satisfied, he turned them off.

From the camera located in Scram's eye, Ryan could see the desolate-looking mother ship getting closer. As Harris flew onward, Ryan watched the bridge of the ship grow nearer. Soon, its roof was nearly all he could see. Suddenly, the wind gusted up, causing Harris to veer sharply off to the side, and Ryan felt dizzy and disoriented with fear as Harris swerved over the side of the bridge, revealing a drop off of some forty feet to the black churning ocean below. For a moment, Ryan felt as if he were actually there, tossing in the wind off to the side of the ship. He heard Carmen loudly remarking in response, but in his concentration he didn't hear what she said. Harris soon swerved back over the deck rooftop. Ryan's heart was racing and beating like a drum in his chest. He wondered if this was what doing major surgery was like—where a sudden unforeseen turn of events could cause disaster.

"Whew!" Ryan exclaimed.

"Nothing we can't handle," Carmen remarked with determination from her workstation, some five yards away. Carmen and Ryan breathed a huge sigh of relief. For the time being, at least, it appeared the wind was not going to blow them to Antarctica.

"Okay," Townley said. "Let's drop down for a landing." That Townley did not make some more positive reinforcing comment just then made Ryan wonder if he, too, had perhaps experienced a split second of heart stoppage during the episode. If so, he didn't let on. That was Townley, cool under pressure, Ryan told himself. It seemed ice flowed through the man's veins.

Carmen changed the angle of Harris' wings so that he now hovered in place, directly above the bridge of the mother ship. The roof was now inches away. Ryan's workstation computer issued a beep that signaled Harris had landed. The hawk and lizard bots were now on the mother ship. Another beep told Ryan that Harris had let go of Scram. On one of the half dozen computer screens in front of him, Ryan watched as a digital image of Harris moved off to the side. Scram was now free to move about on his own.

"Okay Ryan, like we rehearsed," Townley said.

Ryan worked the controls and walked Scram to the edge of the bridge roof.

"His legs feel heavier," Ryan remarked, feeling more weight and slightly slower response to the control console that moved Scram's legs.

"Another enhancement," Amanda said. "With all that wind up there, we wanted to make sure Scram wouldn't get blown off the deck."

Ryan nodded. "Got it," he said.

He edged Scram over the side of the rooftop and eased him down the vertical wall of the bridge, steering clear of two large windows to one side. In their drills, Townley told everyone to assume that there would be a pirate in the bridge, occupying the captain's seat, who would likely be asleep at this hour. This hunch was confirmed moments later by Harris who peered down into the bridge and, using heat imaging, found that there was indeed a sleeping pirate on the bridge.

"Going below deck, right?" Ryan asked.

"Like we planned," Townley said.

Ryan guided Scram down to the deck of the ship. Little was visible on the deck, save for a few life jackets, oars and containers, and ropes in tangled piles here and there. There was no sign of people, which was not surprising given it was the middle of the night.

From the same digitized screen he had looked at before, Ryan saw a tiny, neon green image in the shape of Scram juxtaposed against a night vision view of the ship. He could see Scram's position exactly on the deck next to the bridge. Contours on the screen highlighted the stairways on the opposite side of the bridge that he would use to navigate Scram down into the ship's sleeping quarters.

Scram crossed to the other side of the bridge, climbed down a set of stairs to the ship's main deck, and then started down a second one. He was now immersed in what would have been total darkness without night vision. Slowly, but steadily, Scram crawled down the stairway, his toes holding him tightly to the vertical walls and horizontal surfaces of the staircase. At the bottom of the steps, Scram crept through an equipment room. It contained a bunch of life jackets, some clothes, a few shoes strewn about, weapons on one wall, and some trash. Evidently the pirates weren't neat freaks. At the far side of the equipment room stood a door that was very slightly cracked ajar, but otherwise closed.

Scram crawled through the cracked opening of the doorway. It soon became clear the room was a bedroom. Scram's night vision revealed a series of bed frames of metal tubing with flat stretched canvass wrapped around them. As Scram looked up, Ryan could see several sets of these stacked on top of each other in columns running from the floor to the ceiling. There appeared to be five in a column. In some of the beds Ryan could make out the shadowy outlines of sleeping bodies, arms, and legs. Tangos, in Townley parlance.

"Sleepy time," Townley said. "Ryan, climb the wall and scan the room, would you?"

Ryan guided Scram up one wall of the room, and then walked him over to another as the latter would give him a better vantage point from which to see most of the room and the beds within it. Ryan did a room scan with Scram's video camera, panning across the entire room. Then he focused in the middle of the room and scanned up and down, and again left to right. Everyone at Creech could see outlines of bodies on many of the beds, heads and torsos in some cases, legs and feet in others.

"I'd say we've got about twelve, no, about fourteen tangos on our hands," Townley said. "Creech, are you in agreement with that?"

"I counted thirteen," said Rick Hutchins.

"So did I," said Debbie Tan.

"Okay. Lucky thirteen," Townley said.

"What's our next move?" Ryan asked.

"Well, I don't think we should use darts, because we don't have enough," Townley said.

Ryan had suspected as much. He knew the Creech crew had found a way to put eight darts aboard Scram, but eight darts couldn't knock out thirteen tangos. They had discussed this scenario in their practice drills. "We could hit eight people with one dose, but it would only put them out for twelve hours and there would still be a number of tangos functioning," Townley had explained. "Not to mention, those still alert would wonder what the heck happened to their eight comrades."

"So, move to monitoring plan?" Ryan asked.

"Yeah, like we practiced. We need to monitor their communications. Let's get Scram to head upstairs. We can follow their communications in the morning."

"So why don't we just sink the mother ship right now?" Ellen asked Townley. "It's not like we don't have the firepower."

"True, but we'd awaken the tangos on the other boats, including the tanker," Townley responded. "They wouldn't be real happy if they saw their comrades turned into barbecue, would they? That would put all the hostages in even greater danger. So for now, we'll have to hold off on that, as much as I'd like to do otherwise."

"I get it," Ellen said.

"But, we may get that chance. Ryan, how're you doing? We've got a good amount of time to get Scram positioned up in the cockpit before they wake up."

"Climbing, Townley," Ryan responded. "Entering staircase… right… now."

Suddenly a shock hit on Ryan's computer screen. The floor about Scram shook mightily as his video camera was jostling around. Scram shook side to side as a result of something forceful, almost like an earthquake. In a millisecond they saw the boot of a person come down on the step directly next to Scram. Scram was jolted by this impact. Then, as quickly as they had seen it, the boot lifted up and trudged on, up the staircase. If the foot had landed another two inches to the right, Scram would have been squashed into a pile of computer chips, plastic, and metal. The entire mission could have been jeopardized.

"Wow, that was close," Townley exclaimed through the microphone. "Must be a shift change. So if someone's going up, that means someone else will be coming downstairs to sleep. Fortunately, that tango didn't see us in the dark. Ryan, get Scram to the side of the staircase and perch on a sidewall, if possible. ASAP."

"Roger," Ryan responded. He immediately steered Scram to the side of the staircase, saw the wall on his digital screen as well as with his night vision view, and climbed up the side of the wall. If a pirate was indeed headed downstairs, Scram would at least be out of the path of the pirate's feet.

Sure enough, about a minute after Ryan directed Scram's camera out from the wall, the staircase began to shake slightly. Scram's camera revealed a pair of legs and feet, presumably belonging to the pirate sentinel of the previous watch, trudging down the staircase.

"Okay, stay there a second," Townley urged. "Let's see if there's more than one."

They waited for a minute, then another. There was no sign of further activity. Ryan guided Scram up the sidewall to the top of the staircase. Just like a lizard could, Scram was clinging to the wall vertically all the while.

"Show off!" Townley mused. "Couldn't take the stairs, huh?" It continued to amaze everyone from Seguin how Townley could keep his composure and even make humor in such a tense situation.

"It's easier for Scram to just go up the wall," Ryan shrugged. "The stairs aren't built for his foot size, you know?"

"Roger that," Townley said.

Once Scram reached the deck at the top of the stairs, Ryan guided him to the door of the cabin he had climbed down earlier. The cabin door was closed, but the crack at the bottom of the door was high enough for Ryan to guide Scram through easily. From there, Ryan was able to navigate Scram across the floor, beneath the dangling legs of a sleeping pirate sitting in the tall captain's chair, fast asleep. While the pirate was supposedly on watch, the gentle rocking motion of the sea, combined with the absence of any other activity, had a lulling effect that made slumber simply too hard to resist.

Ryan guided Scram up a wall at the back of the captain's station, which was essentially a desk that abutted the cabin wall, with windows looking out in all directions. At the top of the captain's console, Ryan guided Scram to the back edge of the desktop. There was a stack of paper and booklets conveniently located there, and Scram hid beneath a miscellaneous stack of papers from the pile, so that Ryan could see the chest of the pirate in the chair, would be able to tell when he moved, and could pick up his voice.

"Yeah, that's a good spot," Townley said. "As good as we're gonna get."

At that point, Townley decided it was time to once again focus on Yacht 4 to free Carey and the other hostages while still under cover of darkness of night. At Creech, everyone shifted their computer screens, and attention, back to Yacht 4. They were alarmed to find that there was a second pirate on the bed in the middle cabin whom they had missed before on Slidey's first pass. He was sleeping on the other side of the snoozing pirate they had already tranquilized, which explained why they had missed him before. Fortunately, Slidey had more darts, and James guided Slidey over to the far side of the bed and hit the pirate with them. As with the first, he reacted to the impact, but only slightly, and then kept right on sleeping.

It took some time, but Slidey slithered back out of the main cabin, up the stairs to the front cabin and down through the grate of the front cabin, landing on the bed where Carey was sleeping. Slidey slid up to Carey and prodded him with his head, and he ultimately rolled over and awoke. As if it was the most normal thing in the world to wake up next to a snake, Carey held out his hands, and a very small circular saw came out of Slidey's mouth. Carey lowered his wrists so that the ropes that bound them rubbed against the blade, and in seconds Slidey had cut the rope.

"Nice job," Carey said, rubbing his wrists.

The husband of the couple taken hostage on Yacht 4 was also sleeping in the same cabin as Carey, on the far side of the bed. His hands were also bound. Carey pressed him on the shoulder a few times and he awakened slowly. His natural instinct was to rub his eyes with his hands, which he was soon reminded, were tied together. While disoriented and dazed, he seemed to know Carey was an ally and held out his hands when Carey gestured to him to do so. He momentarily freaked out when he realized Carey was holding a snake in his hands, but Carey calmed him down and assured him it was okay. Cary held Slidey's mouth close to the rope that bound the man's hands and his tiny saw cut promptly through it.

Carey then put his face close to that of Slidey so the snake bot's audio receiver would pick him up. In this way, Townley and the others listening could hear him. His own communications piece had been taken and smashed by the pirates when they captured him. "Carey from Yacht 4," he said. "This bird plus one has flown. On way to rear of the henhouse to spring another chicken."

"Roger that," Townley responded.

"You gonna come by and pick up some eggs?" Carey said.

"Roger that," Townley replied.

"Meet you at the back of the henhouse," Carey replied. "Over and out." At that point, he ushered the freed man, who was speaking indecipherable Italian, to the back of the boat. Carey couldn't completely understand the man, but he was pretty sure he was cursing profusely.

The defender approached the yacht. By the time it floated alongside, Carey and the man had awakened and unbound the hands of the man's wife in the rear cabin. They had all come up from the cabin below and Carey helped the man and his wife clamber off the yacht onto the defender. Several crew members from the defender assisted. The ocean wind lashed about the man and woman and they were acutely aware of bouncing up and down on the ocean waves as they leapt from one boat to the other. They were now quite awake despite the darkness and lateness of the hour.

Aboard the defender, the Italian man was saying something to Pascal.

"What's he saying?" asked Sammy aloud in the war room at Creech.

"He's asking where the bathroom is," Speakeasy said. "I think he wants to throw up."

16

ROUGH WATERS

Yacht 3 was the next target. Using another of the small motorized rafts from the defender, Carey had little difficulty boarding Yacht 3, anesthetizing the sleeping pirates, binding them, and getting to the husband and wife hostages on board. They were from China.

"Fortunately their English is a lot better than my Chinese," Carey said over the audio connection.

"Well, we have Speakeasy here if we need any translation," Zeek muttered to the room at Creech.

Ryan was beginning to think taking out the sleeping pirates on the remaining yachts was going to be a cakewalk, but soon discovered otherwise. A skiff launched from the mother ship and appeared headed towards Yacht 3.

"The pirates... I mean, tangos... must have tried to contact Yacht 3," Jenny announced to the war room at Creech.

"And didn't get a response," added Ellen

"Yep, here they come," Ryan observed. He could see the digital image of a skiff pulling away from the mother ship, and a night vision image from Harris' camera from atop the mother ship.

"Should I dive bomb them?" Carmen asked Townley.

"No, it's too risky," said Townley. "I think there are three pirates aboard the skiff. "If just one of them got a good punch or arm grab at Harris, they could take him out."

The bots were versatile and durable, but Harris was not built to withstand being smashed by direct, blunt force. His light weight, which enabled him to fly, meant he did not have the reinforcing armor that some of the other bots did, like the orcas, Leo, and Slidey.

The situation deteriorated as Carey tried to help the husband and wife board the defender, which had now pulled alongside Yacht 3. Members of Pascal's coast guard team were helping lift the couple off the yacht. Its deck sat a couple of feet below that of the defender, so a big step up was required to make the jump from the yacht. And that was in calm water. The waters were choppy, so the task became even more complicated. The boats bounced up and down next to each other in the rolling surf.

Just then gunshots rang out, piercing the peaceful sounds of the breeze and the glassy chimes of the ocean waves. Suddenly, a bullet ripped into Carey's left shoulder and pushed him back, away from the defender. Carey let out a cry of pain as he stumbled several steps backwards.

"Carey, come here! Get over here!" Townley shouted. "Pascal, someone needs to get over to help him!"

Incredibly, amid a hail of gunfire, Pascal and one of his crew leapt off the defender, jumped through the yawning stretch of air over the water, and landed in tumbling, quick rolls on the deck of the yacht. They immediately splayed out on the deck as bullets flew, whistling everywhere. Pascal quickly shuffled across the deck to the aid of the terrified man and woman. The other crewmember from the defender, a man named Luc, went to aid Carey. He stood low to the deck to avoid the whistling gunfire that continued apace.

From the night vision view at Ryan's workstation, it was difficult to make everything out, since the camera providing the view was mounted on the defender and was bobbing up and down with the rolling ocean waves. But, Ryan and the others could tell Carey was wounded seriously. Even as a shadowy figure in the night, his silhouetted image showed him clutching his shoulder in a pained clench. Luc was trying gently, but hastily to guide him to the yacht's edge so they could board the defender. Pascal was able to escort the man and woman hostages of the yacht onto the defender. He boarded the defender with them.

In the time it took to get the hostages off the yacht onto the defender, the approaching pirate skiff had now motored very close to the other boats, continuing to pepper the night air with gunfire. Townley and several others from the defender had started pumping machine gun fire at the skiff in return. Unfortunately, the skiff quickly edged behind the yacht, so the crew on the defender could no longer see it. Townley's furious shots streaked into the ocean and ricocheted off the front of the yacht into the sea.

By the time Ryan could see any more evidence of the skiff, he knew it was too late for Townley to do anything. He saw two shadowy figures of pirates mounting the yacht and aiming weapons at Luc and Carey. That was bad news. He could see one figure, presumably Luc, putting two hands in the air. Another, Carey, struggled to put just one hand in the air.

"Man, this is not Carey's week," James huffed.

"We're screwed," Sammy gasped.

"They're toast," Jenny groaned.

"Not yet, they're not," Jack Timlin said. "The pirates will want to keep the defender away from 'em, and to do that, they'll have to keep those two alive."

"Unless they want to invite a hailstorm of gunfire, that's exactly right," Debbie Tan said.

"Yeah, it's a bit of a stalemate," Brenda Gibbs observed. "They won't want the defender crew to board the yacht. They'll make it back away. And. the best way to do that is ensure that the hostages are alive."

"So now what?" asked Carmen. As Brenda had predicted, the defender had slowly started to back away from the yacht.

"Unfortunately, it looks like the next move belongs to the tangos," Sammy said. On one of his screens, he saw another skiff launch off from the mother ship. The skiff was probably a mile from the yacht.

"Not if we decide it doesn't," Ryan said. "Meagan and Brad, can you guys get to that skiff?"

"If we gun it, yeah," Brad called out.

"Gun it!" called Townley. He must have known what Ryan had in mind. "Prepare for dual chopsticks!" Townley barked.

"Dual chopsticks, what's that?" blurted James. "Oh, yeah, I think I get it."

"Bring it!" Ellen said.

Ryan and the others watched their monitors. They could see the digital images of the orcas moving at high speed towards the path of the skiff. Ryan saw their paths converging on a point. Under the ocean surface, the tails of the orcas were pumping up and down just like real killer whales, propelling them through the water with tremendous thrust. It was hugely nerve racking to watch.

"Make it!" Amanda Harte exhorted.

"Get there!" Carlos Silva urged.

In a few seconds, Ryan saw the skiff enter the point to which the orcas were swimming. Meagan was coming from the east in Chomp, Brad from the west in Tux. The skiff was now probably a hundred yards or so from

Yacht 3. The three digital images were just about on top of each other, which meant one thing.

"Chomp, time to grab some air," Brad said. "You ready? Initiate launch."

"Roger that," Meagan replied.

"On my countdown, Chomp. Three.. two... one!" Brad exclaimed.

Everyone at Creech watched on various screens as the orcas surged, incredibly, up out of the water with tremendous force, into the night air, where they hung for a full second. Then they plunged down towards the water, bearing the full weight of killer whales, Tux at the front and Chomp at the back, smashing into the hapless skiff. With hammer-like force the killer whales hit opposite ends of the skiff at the same time on their downward drop, and the skiff split like matchwood into two large pieces. Dozens of other shards of boat went sailing skyward in the night air, along with the three pirates who had been aboard. The skiff pieces twirled around several times in the air before falling back into the water. Even at Creech, people could hear the faint screams of the terrified pirates who had been launched tens of feet in the air, only to plunge black into the black ocean water down below.

"Yesss!" Townley exclaimed. "Nice job, Brad and Meagan! All right Pascal, let's go pick up some wet fish!" Townley was referring to the pirates who were now rendered impotent by the orca bots, having fallen into the water without any weapons, oars, or boat. But, they would become dangerous again if allowed to board Yacht 3.

"On the way, Monsieur Town," Pascal replied. Ryan realized "Town" was Pascal's nickname for Townley, having heard him use it several times.

"That's my man," said Townley.

Townley and Pascal sped off in an inflatable raft from the defender in search of the pirates. They trained a light on the ocean in front of them about thirty yards away. The defender hummed quietly behind. Townley and Pascal were an efficient team. They fished the pirates out the water one at a time, the imposing Townley binding their hands while Pascal trained a weapon on them that was amply convincing of the need for compliance. They shuttled the wet, sorry bunch of prisoners over to the defender and handed them up to the crew, where they were taken below deck into a small cabin.

"So, what do we do about the other ships and hostages, and Carey and Luc?" Ellen asked.

"Good question, Ellen," Townley responded. "Let's see..."

"Come on, what do we do?" Ellen pressed.

"I like your spunk," Jack Timlin remarked.

"Okay, alright already!" Townley responded. "I've got a plan for Yacht 3. We need a lift from the orcas to get there, though. Pascal, you with me?"

"Lead the way," Pascal said.

"After that, we'll tackle Yacht 2, like we planned," Townley said.

At Townley's request, Brad and Meagan guided their orca bots to the defender. After a quick status check, they determined the orcas were none the worse for the wear, having just chopped a skiff into firewood. Each orca picked up a rider, Townley and Pascal, who rode atop the orcas through the dark ocean waters, holding tightly onto their dorsal fins. The orcas cruised along at the water's surface. Dressed in black, Townley and Pascal were but obscure shadows against a dark sky in a pitch-black sea.

Chomp and Tux stalwartly hauled their riders through rough waters to Yacht 3. Townley and Pascal shifted their bodies to stay balanced on the orcas as they powered through the choppy ocean waves. Once they reached the yacht, Townley and Pascal clambered up onto it as if it were a jungle gym. Everyone at Creech was astounded by their adeptness and agility. Ryan thought if he had not actually known what was going on, he never would have believed it.

"That's why they get paid the big bucks," Jack Timlin said.

"Big bucks?" Townley whispered sarcastically.

"Well, compared to me you do," Jack said.

Townley and Pascal crept about the surface of the yacht. Soon they disappeared from view of the ocean level cameras mounted on the orca bots. Ryan knew full well they would have to tangle with armed pirates to free Carey and Luc. What felt like many nerve-wracking, painstaking minutes later, they emerged from below the ship's deck. Carey and Luc were in their company. Cheers went up from the team at Creech. The defender approached Yacht 3 and pulled up alongside her. It took long, painstaking minutes for the team to gingerly hoist Carey up onto the defender deck. Townley and Pascal supported him from below while defender crewmates helped lift him from above. At various points, Carey winced in pain. Once he was aboard, Townley, Pascal, and Luc boarded the defender as well.

"Breakin' you out is starting to become a habit, buddy," Townley said to Carey. He was trying to make humor and keep Carey's spirits up. Carey tried to smile, but he was hurt pretty badly.

Yacht 2 proved yet another challenge. The pirates aboard the remaining boats were now awake. Some had been alerted by the punctuations of gunfire. Others had been jolted out of their sleep by furious rants over their radio systems by Korfa Raage and his thugs aboard the mother ship. Yacht 2 was also critical to the Seguin students at Creech in another way. They all now knew it was the *Shakti,* the yacht of Catherine and Francois Bergeron and their film crew. But, on this mission, it was Yacht 2. Townley and Mr. Sandhill had warned the Creech and Seychelles teams in advance explicitly to avoid using the actual names of the yachts or people in case they were overheard or someone hacked their communications.

"Uh, I think we're going to need to get Harris and Scram off the mother ship," Townley said.

"Really?" Carmen asked, somewhat crestfallen. She was seriously stressed out by the acrobatic flying routine she had performed with Harris to land *on* the mother ship. Now, Townley was already talking about getting the bots *off.*

"We're going to need those two for the tanker," he replied, referring to Harris and Scram. "Ryan, can you maneuver Scram out of the bridge and up to the rooftop to arrange a rendezvous with Harris?"

"I think so," Ryan sighed. "He was staring straight ahead at a now very alert pirate on the mother ship and he would have to manipulate Scram past him without being seen. With all the recent noise coming out from the waters around the convoy—and a most unpleasant visit from Raage—the pirate had been roused from his sleep a little while ago. And he wasn't happy about it.

Ryan had to turn Scram around on the control desktop where he sat under the paper. There was a slit of space between the panel surface and the adjoining wall. It was just wide enough for Scram to shimmy through. Ryan had to get Scram to elongate his body to make it through. "Eesh," Ryan exhorted, as he felt the limited movements of Scram through his computer controls. "I don't like these tight fits."

"Tell me about it," Jenny said from across the room. "Now you know how I felt trying to get Skye through that cabin grate on Yacht 4."

Some minutes later, Ryan had walked Scram out of the bridge, out onto the bridge deck, and up the side to the bridge rooftop where Harris sat waiting.

"How much for the ride?" Carmen said with a wry grin.

"How much not to push you off the roof?" Ryan retorted.

"Hey, that's not nice," Carmen admonished.

"I guess I'm getting a little tired of the 'hitch a ride' thing," Ryan said.

"Fair enough," Mr. Sandhill interjected. "All right Ryan and Carmen, we need both of you to make it back to the defender." With that, Ryan edged Scram underneath Harris, who, at Carmen's command, gripped Scram in his talons and set off in flight.

Meanwhile, Chomp and Tux approached Yacht 2 and launched Trixie, Ellen's fox bot, and Skye without incident. From Creech, Carlos Silva and Debbie Tan had run some diagnostic tests and determined Skye had been unharmed despite her earlier run in with the cabin grating on Yacht 4.

Aboard Yacht 2, one of the pirates stood in a small cabin at the yacht's steering wheel, while the other was milling about on deck, brandishing a weapon. It was dark enough and the yachts were far enough away from each other that they were unaware of exactly what had transpired. But, they knew it wasn't good. As Trixie landed on the yacht's surface, this pirate heard a faint noise on the far side of the yacht from where he was standing and he strode over to investigate. By that time, Ellen had moved Trixie behind a container that held ship gear.

The pirate looked around. Through bleary eyes, he saw nothing on the deck. He then gazed out at the water, and thought perhaps he observed something that appeared to be sticking up out of it. Because he was tired and had been awakened suddenly from sleep, he wasn't entirely sure. But indeed there was something, some kind of thing—a fin, perhaps—about thirty yards off the starboard side of the boat. Just then he heard the report of a gun and a bullet whizzed past him about three inches from his face. He was now deeply alarmed, and much more awake. In a split second he looked back out at the ocean and saw the thing moving, whatever it was. He immediately raised his gun and started pumping metal furiously into in its general vicinity. Fire bursts rang out in the night air. A few more shots were fired back at him, but none as close as the first, which nearly took him out. Several of his bullets clanged off what looked like a dorsal fin. As they did so, sparks flew and there was a clanging sound. No dorsal fin made sounds like *that*.

The pirate, though now quite sure he was not hallucinating, was freaking out. There was something out there in the water that was impervious to machine gun fire and that had returned fire. Despite a creeping sense of fear, he continued firing his weapon until the bullet clip was empty. The bullets had landed harmlessly in the ocean and the thing he thought he had seen before—the fin, or perhaps a rudder— was now nowhere in sight.

The pirate started making his way towards the bridge of the yacht to talk to his comrade. But all of a sudden, he heard a low, ferocious growl coming from the shadows. It sounded like a wild cat, and it was terrifying. Instinctively, he raised his machine gun and pulled the trigger, but he was suddenly reminded to his horror that his clip was empty. The growl got louder and the creature took another couple of steps closer. He still couldn't see it, not that he wanted to.

He turned about, dropped the gun, and ran, up the side of the deck of the yacht. The growling followed him. It was maddening that he couldn't see the creature, but its furious, gnashing sounds could not be mistaken. He gained a pretty good head of speed as he neared the front of the yacht, panting and trying to catch his breath. There was no nowhere for him to go, except overboard. He ran to the tip of the bow of the yacht, hurdled the guardrail, and leapt out into the air, deciding to take his chances on the dark ocean rather than get ripped to shreds by a savage jungle cat.

Splashing down into the ocean, the pirate felt at once the relief of having escaped a fearsome beast on the yacht, but now wondered as he looked about how he would get himself out of the water. His question was soon answered, though not in the remotest way he could have expected. He was thrashing about in the water, swimming towards the rear of the yacht in hopes of shouting out to his comrade up on the bridge. It occurred to him his comrade might still be unaware of the wild beast stalking the deck, and thus might also be wondering why he had seen his comrade go running down the deck like a maniac and jump into the ocean.

At that moment, a dorsal fin rose up out of the water about ten yards from him, and what looked like a shark, arced its head out of the water. The man froze in utter terror. There was no escaping imminent doom. The creature approached, opened its mouth, and the man braced himself in terror for a painful, awful death. He had just a millisecond to process that the creature looked like something other than a shark. He didn't know what, but it was no less terrifying. Then something small hit him in the neck. He felt a brief, blossoming pang of pain and then knew no more.

Townley reached out from atop Chomp, and with a long, strong arm hauled the limp body of the pirate across Chomp's back, bracing the unconscious man between himself and the dorsal fin while ensuring the man could still breathe, and knocked on Chomp's back as a signal to Brad, piloting from down below, to get moving, back to the defender.

"How did Chomp take those shots and not get damaged?" Sammy asked in amazement.

"Chomp's dorsal fin has been protected by potent, light weight armor," Mr. Sandhill replied.

All of the Seguin kids looked on and gaped in astonishment.

"Let me guess, another 'enhancement' made by the engineering team here at Creech," Carmen said.

Rick Hutchins and several others from the Creech team had difficulty stifling a grin.

"Pretty darn good enhancement," Ellen mused.

From the bow of Yacht 2, Skye looked on as Chomp swam off with his passengers, staying at the ocean's dark surface while powering towards the defender. Half a world away, the team at Creech was abuzz with excitement. There, from a tiny, nondescript building among the mountains of Nevada, Speakeasy had produced the sounds of a leopard from the files that Ellen had used to create Leo, her leopard bot. Freak and Zeek had used Speakeasy to reproduce the leopard noises, with a few enhancements, of course, and broadcast them to dragonfly Skye. Despite her small size, Skye was able to amplify them over her audio system so that they sounded real—so real, in fact, that they terrified a pirate so badly, he jumped off his own boat.

On the yacht's bridge, in the captain's quarters, the other pirate on Yacht 2 had been awakened when he heard the gunshots from the yacht nearby. While he was on alert, he became restless upon hearing the gunfire exchange involving his comrade. He later saw his comrade go running down the yacht deck and disappear. Due to darkness, he hadn't seen where he had gone. The pirate had strict orders from Raage not to leave his post while sitting on the bridge, and he fretted about whether he should go investigate. He looked about nervously.

Just then the crackling sounds of a voice came over the receiver of his radio phone on the yacht's bridge. It was the voice of Raage.

"Roble and Labaan, you there?" Raage barked in Somali.

"Roble here," the man replied into his radio microphone.

"What the hell is going on over there?" Raage barked across the radio.

"Some kind of weapons fire exchange," Roble replied.

"Did you investigate?" Raage asked.

"I watched from the bridge, but did not leave," Roble responded, knowing Raage would have excoriated him if he had left the bridge. "Labaan fired some shots at something in the water. Then, he went running down the deck of the boat. I have not seen him since."

Raage cursed loudly. "What did the idiot do that for?" he spat.

"I don't know."

"Unbelievable," Raage barked.

"Do you want me to check it out? There's no one else here, so I will be leaving the cockpit," Roble said.

"No, wait a few minutes," Raage commanded. "I will radio back to you. If you haven't heard or seen anything by then, at that point we should probably investigate. But, hopefully the fool Labaan will reappear."

"Okay, I'll wait to hear back."

Roble lowered the radio mouthpiece and put it back into its bay on the dashboard in front of him. He paused for a few moments. He felt spooked. Suddenly, he heard a hiss off to his right. There was a flashlight sitting to his left on the dashboard in front of him. Alarmed, he grabbed it and pointed it in the direction of the hiss, which sounded like it had come from the same level as the dashboard. With his other hand, he wheeled his machine gun in the direction of the sound. The flashlight revealed a threatening, compact furry creature perched on the dashboard, coiled as if ready to spring. It stared at him with black eyes and bared menacing teeth. It was beyond terrifying to be standing eighteen inches from a beast in total darkness in the middle of the ocean. His light had hit it for a split second and he let out a shriek of utter fear. He had just moved to pull the trigger of his gun when he heard a faint "click" sound, and felt a brief, sharp pain in his neck. Clutching his throat, he slumped off his chair, unconscious. He was tranquilized, just as many of his unwitting his comrades had been.

"How's that for killing them softly?" Ellen asked her colleagues at Creech.

"Nice job!" Mr. Sandhill exclaimed.

Freak and Zeek gave each other a high-five. In reality, the pirate, Roble, had never actually spoken to Raage. Ellen had cut the yacht's radio cable with Trixie's micro-circular saw, and Speakeasy had mimicked Raage over the radio through Trixie's audio sound system. The pirate had no inkling he was talking to a robot.

"Great work!" Townley exclaimed. His communication was a little fuzzy, given that he was riding the back of a killer whale robot in the middle of a churning ocean while holding onto an unconscious prisoner.

"Okay, with Skye, let's confirm that there are only prisoners remaining on board. Jenny, you up for that?"

"Copy that," Jenny said. "Will start with the front of boat."

Everyone grew especially nervous then, since they knew in all probability the hostages on this boat were the Bergerons. Ryan considered how angry he would be if any harm had come to them at the hands of the pirates.

Turning to her array of computer screens, Jenny flew Skye up in the air and over the grate near the front of the boat, below which sat one of the bedroom cabins. In contrast to her earlier mishap that night, she did not try to send Skye through the grate. Rather, she had Skye hover in flight about eighteen inches above the grate. She pointed Skye's lightweight heat imaging camera down into the cabin. While the grate created some interference, several of the team members from Creech assessed the images on the camera shots taken from above and determined there was a person on a bed in the cabin—a woman. She sat in a semi-reclined position on the bed in the now familiar hands-tied position. Given all the noise that had been made earlier on the yacht, she was awake.

"Catherine," exclaimed Mr. Sandhill in a shrill whisper. He said what everyone had been thinking. Her silhouette was unmistakable.

There was a second figure on the heat image—another woman. She was a member of the film crew that was accompanying Catherine and Francois on their voyage.

"Okay, let's go to the back of the boat with Skye," Townley said. "Meanwhile, can we go down to the main central cabin with Trixie? There should be no one there."

"Roger that," Ellen replied.

"Yeah, uh, roger that," Jenny replied.

Yacht 2 was now as they expected it to be. There were no other pirates in the main central cabin and there were three hostages, all male, Francois Bergeron and two members of the film crew, in the rear. They, too, were awake. With the coast clear on Yacht 2, Townley and Pascal boarded from the orcas and freed up Catherine, Francois, and the members of the film crew. Catherine and Francois clung madly in an embrace when they first saw each other after having been imprisoned in separate cabins for the over a week. They and the film crew briefly embraced each other, a wild array of emotions washing over them.

"People, can we hold it 'til we get to a safer place?" Townley urged.

"We got more pirates out there, and they'll be coming this way soon. We've got to get you off this boat."

Catherine did not want to get off the boat. "All of my research, my computers," she pleaded.

"Hopefully it's all intact," Townley said. "I don't think the tangos were interested in studying marine biology," he added.

The defender approached Yacht 2 and Townley and Pascal helped the Bergerons and the film crew move from the *Shakti* onto the defender. Once again, it required a big step up and some help from the defender crew to hoist people up. They also collected Ellen's fox bot, Trixie.

"It's becoming a regular international dance party on the defender, I'd say," Townley guffawed over the audio. "We got people from Brazil, Italy, China, France, the Seychelles, and Africa on board. What kind of music are we gonna play?"

"What's going to happen to the yachts?" Ryan asked.

"Oh, there will be other boats coming from the Seychelles soon, I expect," Mr. Sandhill replied. "They'll wait to call them in until they have the pirates mostly contained."

Once aboard the defender, Townley told Catherine that the bot cohort students from Seguin Academy were helping the mission from Creech. She demanded to speak with them immediately over the video link.

"Well hello there students," Mrs. Bergeron said. She was beaming and seemed to be in great spirits, all things considered.

"Hi Mrs. Bergeron!" the Seguin students tooted back from Creech. They cheered, clapped, and whistled, and were gleeful to see her in relatively buoyant spirits.

"Is everyone okay?" they asked.

"We're fine. A bit tired, but otherwise fine. Now, have you started your Biology research term papers for this semester?"

"What? Seriously?" Sammy said.

"All in good time, Catherine, of that I can assure you," Mr. Sandhill interjected.

"If you say so, Thomas," she replied. "I will be expecting to see drafts of Biology term papers from these students within the next two weeks."

"Two weeks!" everyone moaned.

17

How to Empty a Boat in Five Seconds

Meanwhile, Yacht 1 had pulled in close to the mother ship after the pirates aboard her heard the distant battling on the other yachts. She was now tethered next to the mother ship, and it appeared that several pirates from the mother ship had boarded her.

Townley and Pascal disembarked once again from the defender riding atop the orca bots. Townley figured he could ride Chomp right up to Yacht 1, cut its tether to the mother ship, and set her loose on the sea. But, as he and Pascal approached, they were met with a hailstorm of machine gun fire. It sprayed across the ocean surface following the path of the orcas. Pirates from both the mother ship and Yacht 1 were furiously unleashing the barrage.

A bullet grazed Pascal's shoulder and he felt his uniform tear. He also felt a sting of pain as if from a burn, and he knew it could have been worse. Much worse. Townley and Pascal returned fire and momentarily threw the pirates on both boats into disarray, which gave them enough time to beat a hasty retreat.

"Brad, release Chinny 1," Townley called to Brad. "Make sure he's armed. Target—Mama."

"Huh?" Sammy asked. "I didn't know the orcas had Chinny units on board."

"You knew they might," Townley said. "When we talked about it the other day, I thought it sounded like a good idea. So, presto."

"Roger that," Brad said. "Let's see… Preparing Chinny 1, setting target to Mama. Chinny 1 is now armed." Moments later, a beep issued from everyone's work stations at Creech, and they saw a small digital ellipse pulling away from Tux, heading in the direction of the mother ship.

"So that's... Chinny 1, I guess," Jenny said.

"Roger that," Amanda Gibbs from the Creech team replied.

The Creech team followed Chinny 1 on the digital screen of their computer workstations. He took a curved route towards the mother ship, evidently lining up an approach so that he would impact the ship in its middle, on the side opposite from where Yacht 1 was tethered. That would hopefully leave Yacht 1 and its hostages on board relatively unscathed after a torpedo hit to the mother ship. Just then another skiff departed from the mother ship, heading in the direction of the defender.

"Sheesh. How many darn skiffs do the tangos have, anyway?" Carmen groaned. "This is ridiculous."

"Too many for our liking, that's for sure," Mr. Sandhill replied.

"Not as many as they used to," Townley said, although it was clear by now that he had miscounted the number of skiffs the mother ship had. Some of them had perhaps been kept on board and thus would not have been visible to be counted. "Somebody, what's the time to impact of Chinny 1?"

"T minus fifty seconds," Jenny replied.

"Dang! I was hoping for sooner," Townley said.

"Well, I took a wide arc to avoid Chinny being seen by the tangos," Sammy said.

"Sammy, think about it," Townley said. "It's a *pitch black* ocean. Do you really think the tangos would pick it up?"

"I guess not," Sammy replied sheepishly.

"But he does need to get up a head of steam—you know, speed—for when he hits the big one," Zeek observed.

"True," Townley agreed.

"T minus forty seconds," Jenny said, reading her screen.

"See? Chinny's closing fast," James said.

"Hopefully fast enough," Townley said. "We got company following us to the defender and a friendly visit is not what they have in mind."

"T minus thirty seconds," Mr. Sandhill called out.

Over the radio, the team at Creech could hear the staccato rat-ta-ta-ta-tat of machine gun fire, interspersed with the occasional metal ping of a bullet deflecting off the lightweight metal armor of an orca's dorsal fin. Now more gunfire rang out, issuing from the defender. The crew from the Seychelles was providing cover for Townley and Pascal.

"Hang it!" Townley shouted out of frustration with the hailstorm of gunfire that was besieging him. "I didn't want to do this, but Brad, lock and load Chinny 2," Townley urged. "This gunfire's too much."

"Roger that," Brad replied. "Activating Chinny 2... Now. Chinny 2 activated, ready to launch."

"Carmen, can you steer Chinny 2?" Townley asked.

"Roger that," Carmen replied. She pulled up a file at her workstation labeled "Chinny 2."

"Carmen, target skiff," Townley said.

"Targeting skiff," Carmen replied. A few moments passed. "Faint radar read, but I've got a lock on it. Target is set for skiff," she said.

"T minus five seconds—" Jenny said.

"Fire Chinny 2," Townley said.

"Firing Chinny 2," Brad said from Tux.

Just then a terrific explosion rang out as Chinny 1 hit the pirate mother ship.

"Direct hit!" shouted Pascal.

"Great shot!" Townley yelled.

The war room at Creech was abuzz with excitement as people watched their screens intently. Through the night vision view of the defender's camera, it was difficult to see much, as the mother ship was roughly the distance of a football field from the defender. However, they had seen a billow of grey smoke go up from the far side of the ship against the dark night sky after Chinny 1 hit it.

"I think Mama's taking on water," Luc said from aboard the defender. "It looks like she's started to list a little to the far side where she got hit. It will be a while before she sinks, and she may not sink. We'll have to wait and see. But, she's had her bell rung, no doubt about it."

"Carmen, where's Chinny 2?" Townley asked. Everyone had momentarily forgotten that Townley and Pascal were being assaulted by pirate gunfire from the skiff while riding atop the orca bots. Hopefully Chinny 2 would put an end to that.

"T minus fifteen seconds," Carmen replied.

"I'm out of ammo," Townley said. "Guys from the defender, can you keep up the pressure on them to divert them from me?"

"With pleasure," came the reply from a woman's voice. The voice belonged to Catherine Bergeron.

"Indeed," added a man. It was Francois Bergeron.

"Catherine, Francois, what are you doing on deck?" Townley asked. "You need to be in the bridge, ideally resting."

"Nonsense!" Mrs. Bergeron replied.

"I'll rest after we stick it to these idiots who took over our boat," Francois spat.

Just then the Creech team heard a furious, sustained fusillade of gunfire issuing from the defender. It lasted for about ten seconds.

"There's no deterring Catherine once she sets her mind on something," Mr. Sandhill mused.

"T minus three, two one," Carmen said. "Impact!"

To her horror, however, and that of the rest of the team, there was silence. Nothing happened.

"What's going on?" Mr. Sandhill asked urgently.

"I don't know," Carmen moaned.

"It didn't go off," Rick Hutchins said.

The pirates on the skiff didn't know that a robotic Chinook salmon torpedo capable of blowing them sky high had just contacted their boat underwater and failed to detonate. So, they simply kept motoring towards Townley and Chomp, who had now pulled up alongside the defender, firing their guns all the way.

"Should I bring Tux down on them?" Brad asked.

"I don't think you can get enough air in time," Townley said. "Uh oh. Here they come! I gotta hit the water. Luc, you and the defender team keep pounding 'em! Over and out!"

"Carmen, can you try to circle out with Chinny 2 and bring him back to the skiff?" Freak asked.

"Sure," Carmen said. "Do you think it'll work?"

"Arthur, that seems very dangerous," Mr. Sandhill remarked. Ryan knew Mr. Sandhill was serious because he called Freak by his actual first name. That almost never happened. "The skiff is practically sitting on top of the defender."

"I know," said Freak. "But we have to take out that skiff. The pirates—I mean, tangos—on board are going to try to take over the defender and there are still hostages on Yacht 1 and the tanker. They're totally nuts!"

"I guess that's why they're called that 'p' word," Ellen mused.

"Let's go for it," Luc said over the radio.

"Carmen, you have the ability to detonate Chinny from your computer upon impact," Mr. Sandhill said. We'll get Chinny 2 to detonate that way."

"I do?" Carmen said.

"Yeah," said Sammy. "There's a button you have to pull up." He came scurrying over to Carmen's workstation and grabbed her mouse and showed her the specific control on the screen. "It's right... Here."

"Are you sure you want to detonate weapon?" Carmen read on the screen. "Ah, I see you can set it to automatically detonate by synchronizing it with the time of impact. Wow. That's pretty smart."

"We think so," Brenda Gibbs said with a wry grin.

"Another 'enhancement,' clearly," Jenny mused.

"Okay. Chinny 2 starting an underwater loop from skiff with U-turn distance of fifty yards," Carmen said. If the real-life consequences of what was happening weren't so scary, Ryan would have been jealous of Carmen. She was playing an incredibly pivotal role in the mission at that moment. The digital screens showed a small dot arcing out from a mass of objects: the defender, the orcas, and the pirate skiff.

"Pascal, you and Townley must get aboard the defender now!" Mr. Sandhill urged

"Roger that," Pascal replied. He had ridden Tux to the far side of the defender. "These punks aren't getting their hands on my boat!"

"Meagan and Brad, once Townley and Pascal are off, you must clear the area with Chomp and Tux," Mr. Sandhill said. "Otherwise, you're going to get your ears boxed—in a major way."

"Roger," came the reply in unison.

"I'm on the defender now!" said Pascal. "Townley has now swum to the opposite side of the defender. We'll haul him out there."

"Chomp clearing the area," Meagan said.

"Tux clearing the area," Brad echoed.

On their workstation screens, the team at Creech saw two digital forms moving away quickly from the defender in opposite directions. They could also still hear sporadic gunfire through the communications transmission.

A few tense minutes later Pascal told everyone Townley was now aboard the defender. "Thanks for the lift!" Townley exclaimed in praise of the crew that had adroitly fished him out of the sea. He was now back online. "Everyone on the defender is behind the bridge on the side opposite the skiff," Townley said.

The crew and freed hostages had moved to the far side of the defender to avoid being made into Swiss cheese by the pirates' blizzard of machine gun fire. The pirates, emboldened by a sudden lull in activity aboard the defender, edged the skiff alongside her. One of the pirates was looking up from the skiff, contemplating how to board the defender from six feet below her deck. As if to assert his authority, he indiscriminately started spraying machine gun fire into the defender at the water line, presumably to try to blow holes in her hull.

"Idiot," muttered Pascal.

Amid the tension, Ryan and the others had forgotten something. All of a sudden, they were reminded of it. "T minus five, four, three, two, one... Impact!" Carmen said.

Her last word was lost in a crashing noise over the audio connection at Creech. Chinny 2 hit the skiff in its middle and it blew to pieces. The impact sent the pirates flailing and screaming up into the air, landing in impressive splashdowns in the churning seas. Cheers went up in the war room at Creech.

"Ka-pow!" shouted Townley, as if the explosion itself hadn't been loud enough. "We'll have to work on that detonator of Chinny," he remarked. "But, we'll save it for later. Great work, Carmen."

"Thanks," she said. "It's really Sammy to thank. He did all the work on the Chinook bot."

"No way. It's been a team effort," Sammy said.

"So what do we do about the other boats now?" Ellen asked.

"I'm thinking... You know, the Chinny 2 malfunction actually gives me an idea for Yacht 1," Townley said. "Let's see. Luc, what's the status of the mother ship?"

"She's definitely taking on water," Luc said gazing through night vision binoculars. "She's listing pretty badly. I think she's sinking. All the tangos seem to think so. They've all abandoned her and are now aboard Yacht 1."

"Okay," said Townley, who sounded deep in thought.

That the mother ship was sinking was definitely good news, but Ryan grew very concerned about Yacht 1. Sure, the team had been able to sneak aboard the other yachts in stealth and take out a couple of pirates and rescue the hostages, but a *whole yacht full* of pirates? That was a different thing entirely. Such a scenario would demand that they do things differently. But, how? Ryan wondered. Neither he nor the rest of the Creech team had any idea what to do about it.

The defender crew fished out still a few more hapless, waterlogged, and shell-shocked pirates from the water and added them to the cache of prisoners in the boat's lower cabin. Meanwhile, darkness remained in the 'sphere of operations in the Indian Ocean, though it had begun to grow ever so faintly lighter, as the sun would rise in less than a few hours.

"So, uh, Townley, what's the plan?" asked Zeek. He sounded like a professor asking a student for an assignment to be turned in. It occurred to Ryan that Townley probably *had* handed in a whole lot of assignments to Freak and Zeek back when he was a student at Seguin Academy.

"Yeah, how are we going to get like, fifteen pirates off Yacht 1?" Ellen said. "I'm guessing it's not with a couple of bots and you and Pascal," she added.

"Yacht 1 has untethered from the mother ship," James added, watching his screen. "I guess there's no point in being tethered to a ship that's going down."

"Okay, here's how it's going to work," Townley said. "Meagan, you have two Chinny units on board, correct?"

"Just one, remember?" said Meagan. "Chomp is carrying one Chinny units because we had to clear some room for additional payload."

"Right. Got it. And the beacons?" Townley asked.

"Roger that," Carlos Silva from Creech responded. "We've equipped the Chinny units with beacons."

"Huh?" several of the Seguin students said at once.

"Sounds like another potential 'enhancement.' Am I right?" asked Ellen.

"Something like that, yeah," Brenda Gibbs said.

"Okay, Meagan, what is your distance from Yacht 1?" Townley asked.

"About two hundred yards," Meagan replied.

"Okay. Ryan, let's prepare to launch Chinny 3. On my command, you are going to fire Chinny 3 at Yacht 1. Once Chinny launches, you will illuminate the beacon. Brenda, can you go to Ryan's station for a file assist?"

"Roger that," Brenda said. She strode over to Ryan's workstation and helped him pull up a "Chinny 3" file. There were several options displayed on a pop-up menu for what one could do with Chinny: speed up, slow down, fly, dive, surface, and so on. There was also an option entitled "beacon."

"Ryan, you with me?" Townley asked.

"Yeah," Ryan replied. He was stunned to have been spontaneously called on by Townley as if to answer a question in class, though this was anything but a classroom assignment.

"I know you can do this, because you have all practiced with everybody else's bots when you were at Creech in August. All you have to do is launch on my command. Set speed for fifteen knots. Also, Brenda, we're *not*, repeat, *not*, going to arm the torpedo."

"Fifteen knots?" Rick Hutchins called out. "But, the Chinnys can actually go forty-five or fifty."

"Correct," said Townley. "But, I want to make sure the tangos see it."

"And *not* arm the weapon?" Carlos Silva gaped.

At this point, Freak jumped into the fray. "Let me get this straight. You want to send a torpedo *at slow speed* at a boat loaded with enemies, *illuminated, so they can see it*, and then *not have it blow up?*"

"Right," said Townley. "Remember, there are hostages on that boat."

"I don't get it," said Zeek. "I mean, I don't want to blow up the hostages either, but, what's the deal?"

"Just trust me," Townley said. A depressing silence that couldn't have been that long, but felt like an eternity, hung in the room at Creech. "Okay Ryan, Brenda," Townley continued. "Load and prepare to launch Chinny on my count."

"Roger that," Brenda replied. Ryan was suddenly feeling like jelly. He was so nervous he thought he would slip off his chair and slide onto the floor. It was like standing in front of a class to give a speech and then completely forgetting what you were going to say, only a thousand times worse.

"Meagan, once Chinny 3 launches, you need to haul out of the 'sphere," Townley said. "Mainly so they don't see you and start shooting. We'll launch Chinny 3 out of the tube before, repeat, before we switch on the beacon. That way we won't give away your exact location."

"Roger that," said Meagan.

"Okay, prepare to launch Chinny 3."

Ryan clicked a button that said "Load for Launch." "Chinny 3 loaded and ready to launch," he said.

"On my three count, launch Chinny 3," Townley said. "Here we go. Three, two, one, launch."

Ryan clicked on the button that said "Launch." On the other side of the world, Chinny 3 launched out of a side tube from Chomp at a distance of roughly two hundred yards from Yacht 1. They waited a few seconds. Ryan could follow the digital dot of Chinny 3 on his screen moving away from the larger digital figure of Chomp. Meagan was now hauling away from the direction of the yacht in Chomp at a speed of roughly thirty knots.

"Beacon on," Townley said.

Brenda pointed Ryan to a button labeled "beacon" on his computer. She told him to click it. He clicked the "on" option. "Beacon on," he said.

"What is the depth of Chinny 3?" Townley asked.

"About three feet," Ryan replied.

"Let's make it one," Townley said.

"Elevating Chinny 3 to depth of one foot below surface," Brenda said, as she guided Ryan to a digital slider on his screen that could raise or decrease the bot's level in the water.

From aboard the defender, Townley, Pascal, Luc, and the others looked on. They could see the light of the Chinny 3 bot, and they were behind it. "That's a good sign," Townley said. "I can see it from here. Those lights are powerful. Thomas, I do believe you have outdone yourself once again."

"One tries," Mr. Sandhill said. Everyone in the room at Creech stared at Mr. Sandhill as the recognition slowly dawned on them that he had engineered the beacon that was positioned on the nose of Chinny 3.

From the deck of Yacht 1, it did not take long for the pirates to see an illuminated torpedo steaming its way across the ocean. Mayhem broke out, and they started screeching at each other in loud, crazed voices. Their colleagues soon alerted those not yet aware of the approaching torpedo and the entire group whipped itself into a teeth-gnashing, agitated frenzy.

A couple of skiffs were tethered next to the yacht, and some of the pirates started to climb down off the yacht into them to get away. It was a chaotic, hurried process. By the time one or two pirates had jumped into each, they selfishly started to pull away from the yacht, so that the next pirates trying to leap down off the yacht into a skiff found themselves where they least wanted to be—swimming in the ocean. One of those who made it into a skiff was Raage. He and another pirate sped off towards the oil tanker in their skiff, not looking behind for a moment. The other retreating skiffs made for the hijacked oil tanker as well.

The pirates who remained on board the yacht looked like caged beasts, pacing back and forth on the deck, feeling helpless. Close by, the mother ship was now listing heavily as more ocean water gushed through her pierced hull. She was indeed sinking. She would provide them no refuge.

True to form, several pirates pulled out their weapons and started shooting at the torpedo. Bullets whistled through the air and peppered the water around the beacon. "Ryan, lower Chinny 3 by one foot," Townley said. "It's getting a little busy near the water's surface."

With the torpedo at a distance of about fifty yards and closing fast, the remaining pirates on the yacht made the precipitous decision that a plunge in the ocean was better than being on a boat about to get obliterated by a torpedo. The torpedo was heading for dead center of the side of the yacht. So, to a man, the pirates all ran to the far ends of the boat, leapt across the railings, and jumped out into the sea, swimming away from the yacht as fast as they could, expecting to hear a terrific explosion at any second.

One pirate had the audacity to turn around just as the torpedo went into the yacht and immediately turned his head away in fear of an ear-splitting blast. It took a little longer than he expected for the explosion to happen. Then it took even longer. Then it became evident no explosion had occurred.

"You think the hostages are still on board?" Pascal asked Townley.

"Yeah," said Townley. "That's why we didn't detonate the torpedo. Now we need to go get 'em. Let's move!"

The defender raced through the water towards Yacht 1. The pirates, with their weapons either useless in the water or left aboard Yacht 1, were now completely de-fanged. They began shouting from the ocean.

"Oh yeah, we'll pick you up, don't worry about that," Townley laughed. "But, it'll cost you. Big time. This ride isn't free."

As the defender pulled alongside Yacht 1, Luc and Pascal boarded her and made for the cabins. There they found a terrified husband and wife, Canadians, who were now free from their harrowing ordeal. Townley led several others of the defender crew to pick up pirate prisoners out of the ocean. The pirates freaked out when approached by the killer whale bots, even more so to see humans riding atop them.

With so many additional passengers, including about twenty prisoners, the defender was now crowded and weighted down. The defender crew managed to get all the pirates, with hands tied, to fit into her lower cabin, but only by packing them in like a bunch of sardines. Pascal had radioed another Seychelles defender that he had summoned a day earlier with the mission of taking the liberated boaters out of the 'sphere and back to safety. That boat had pulled into the area within the past few hours.

"I don't think anyone expected we'd have so many people on one boat," Pascal mused. "We weren't planning on so many hostages."

"We got a bunch of hostages. I guess, two groups of hostages, eh?" Townley said. "One that's been freed, so they're *ex*-hostages. And the other, the tangos, that has been taken hostage. And in their case, '*prisoners*' is the more correct term."

Townley peered through a pair of binoculars watching the other defender approach from the distance. The sky was lightening up, and it would be daylight in little more than an hour.

"So how do we tackle the tanker? The same way we planned?" Ellen asked.

"Yeah. But we're going to have to be even more careful," Townley said. "There are a whole lot more tangos than we planned for, in addition to the hostages."

"Raage's now aboard the tanker with a couple more thugs, so it'll be more complicated for sure," Pascal said, nursing his wounded shoulder where the pirate's bullet had grazed it.

"Yeah, as if it weren't complicated enough already," Townley admitted. "That guy's a maniac."

18

THE HORNETS' NEST

"We are going to need to improvise a bit here to handle the larger number of tangos aboard the tanker," Townley replied. Ryan didn't like hearing Townley talk about improvisation in the middle of an armed conflict. As far as he was concerned, Townley was the master of advanced planning and practice. Then again, hostile circumstances probably required improvisation all the time in Townley's line of work.

"Well, you've got help," Catherine Bergeron said, through gritted teeth. Despite Townley's adamant protests, she and Francois had been unwilling to board the rescue defender with the other liberated hostages to be taken out of the area to safety. "Nobody messes with my boat unless it's me, or my students," she declared adamantly.

"Catherine, Francois. You do realize what it means to be staying on this boat, right? You're not going to be able to go anywhere else," Townley said. "It's dangerous enough as it is that you're still here. We will very likely get shot at. That's pretty much a guarantee. I could get my head handed to me for this."

"That may be, Jasper, but you'd have to pry Catherine and Francois off with a crowbar," Mr. Sandhill said from Creech. "I think Catherine is well enough aware that her students need her to grade their papers upon her return."

"Don't remind her," Ellen said.

"Or us," said Jenny.

"Has anyone even started their Bio term paper?" James asked.

"Ssshhh!" came a chorus of replies.

"I heard that," Mrs. Bergeron said. Ryan admired her effort to be funny despite the thick tension that hung in the air. A couple of the Seguin students tried to force a laugh, but they found the current situation anything but humorous.

"Be safe," Ellen blurted out. She looked desperately nervous at that moment.

"We will. I promise," Catherine replied.

"All right, let's get this party started," Townley said. "Brad and Meagan, I need you to get close enough to the tanker to start the orca-stra... I mean, the orchestra."

Orchestra, Ryan thought to himself. *Right. That was Townley's code word for what would come next.*

"Okay, we need Harris and Scram, Skye, Leo, Slidey, Flick, and the hornets," Townley continued. "Carmen, you will fly Harris with Scram to the front post like we practiced, right?"

"Roger that," Carmen said. "Yo Lizard Boy, what'll ya pay me for the lift?" Carmen said, smiling at Ryan.

"Very funny," Ryan retorted. "I won't have Scram puke on your bird. How's that?"

"You guys definitely have spunk," Debbie Tan said. "I like that."

At that moment, a pair of double doors leading into the war room opened. A guy from Creech rolled in a large table on wheels with foldout seats and a bunch of computer screens sitting on it. The computers were on. Debbie Tan and everyone else from Creech stood up and walked over to the table and folded out the seats, thereby creating a new bank of workstations. The Creech people sat down at the computer screens and started working the controls. Ryan and the Seguin group became nervous at this point. Each had come to rely on Creech team members hovering over their shoulders, providing crucial, reassuring guidance in what was a complex, intricate, and seriously dangerous operation. With no one there behind him, Ryan felt very much like he was flying solo.

Jack Hutchins picked up on the anxiety of the group. "We didn't go anywhere," he said. "We're right over here if you need us. We need the extra stations for the hornets."

Everyone at Creech watched on their screens as Chomp and Tux approached the oil tanker at a depth of about thirty feet. Meagan was piloting Chomp and had Slidey, James' snake bot, on board. Brad, piloting Tux, had Leo, Ellen's leopard bot, on board. Getting Leo and Slidey up onto the tanker would be one of the greatest logistical challenges they had yet faced.

Time was now more critical than ever. In addition to the sun's morning light just starting to peel over the horizon line, diminishing the cover of darkness, the tanker had started to move at high speed. Soon after the Chinny torpedo had hit the pirate mother ship, whereupon Raage and several of his pirate thugs had boarded the Dutch tanker, the tanker began to steam towards shore. She was heading east-southeast towards Somalia at about eighteen knots, or just under twenty miles per hour. No longer tethered to any of the yachts, she was now hauling as rapidly as she could on the open seas with a full load of oil.

The defender could more than keep pace with the tanker, as she was capable of doing over forty-five knots. Of far greater concern for Pascal and the defender crew, however, was running out of fuel in the middle of the ocean. They had brought several additional fuel tanks with them on board, and the excess weight meant the defender remained fairly over-loaded, even after unloading a bunch of people, and thus at greater risk for capsizing. She had to motor cautiously through the water, staying mostly behind the tanker to avoid getting caught up in her wake, which had the potential to swamp her. She also needed to keep her distance to avoid being fired upon.

Harris simply took flight off the roof of the bridge of the defender with Scram in his talons. He soared high in the air to avoid any close sighting by pirates who now occupied the bridge of the oil tanker. In the waning darkness that was giving way to morning light, it would be diffi-cult for unaided eyes aboard the tanker to discern what type of bird Har-ris was, but Townley didn't want to take any chances. If anyone got a close look at him, they would conclude he didn't look like a bird you would find hundreds of miles out in the Indian Ocean.

By now, Carmen was fairly comfortable piloting Harris, and she was also quite used to having Scram aboard, clenched in Harris' talons. The winds had died down and there was a gentle breeze that made flying Har-ris seem almost easy.

"This is a piece of cake," Carmen said as she landed Harris on the foremast, a high, thin tower that stood on the deck near the front of the tanker. It sat roughly a thousand feet away from the bridge, which, as Car-men knew from their exhaustive practice sessions, was at the back of the ship, also called the stern. Hopefully no one had taken notice of Harris gliding in and landing on the crossbar of the foremast. While he might appear slightly unusual, at a distance of a thousand feet, he wouldn't arouse too much attention, and might look like just another seagull in the waning darkness.

Launching Flick, Jenny's fly bot, was also fairly straight-forward, as

Flick was aboard the defender. Jenny had flown him back to the defender after he helped rescue Yacht 4. Flick lofted up, high into the air, and flew several thousand yards to the tanker, perching beneath a railing by the door to the ship's bridge tower. The plan called for Scram to meet up with him there shortly.

To get Leo and Slidey aboard the tanker, Brad and Meagan had to bring the orcas to surface, and pull them up under the overhanging eave of tanker's stern, right in her powerful back thrust, to avoid being seen from anyone on the deck. Propelled water from the tanker's engines was now hitting them full on. In a risky operation, they had to launch the snake and leopard bots from compartments just behind the dorsal fins of Chomp and Tux. Installed in each of the bots was a fine steel cable with a grappling hook that they would shoot up at the bars of the railing on the ship's stern, some sixty feet above the water.

"Man, the tanker's thrust is powerful stuff," Brad said. "We gotta move fast, 'cause I'm not sure how long I can hold Tux here."

"Ditto, Chomp," Meagan said. "I don't think these bots were made to withstand this type of force."

"They can take it," Sammy said, self-assured. Ryan and the others hoped he was right.

"Okay, let's move. Load bots to dorsal compartments," Townley ordered. He was getting nervous. There was a brief interlude of silence as Brad and Meagan worked the controls to move their bot payloads to the dorsal launching compartment of the orca bots, all while being jolted by the thrusting surge jetting at them from behind the huge tanker.

"Done," Meagan and Brad answered in unison.

"Okay, Ellen and James, on my count, fire grappling hooks at right and left stern railings on the elephant. You got that?"

"Copy that," Ellen and James replied. "Elephant" was the team's agreed upon name for the tanker. Meagan and Brad were to the left and right sides of the stern of the tanker inside the orcas, perilously close to the tanker's churning propeller.

"Ellen and James, confirm read on deck railing," Townley commanded.

"Confirmed," Ellen and James said.

From his seat, Ryan could see Ellen and James had digital reads on the railings, a digital circle that looked like a bull's eye pointing at something dark and obscure. The position from which the bull's eye was captured was constantly changing, caused by the huge, powerful stream from the tanker's water propulsion that the orcas were swimming in. You could tell it was a rough ride.

"Let's move it, quick!" Meagan said.

"Okay, fire grappling hooks on one," Townley ordered. "Three, two, one!"

In the war room at Creech, simultaneous beeps could be heard from everyone's computers.

"Leo grappling hook secure," Ellen called out.

"Slidey grappling hook secure," James called out.

"Reel 'em in," Townley said. "Just like we practiced."

"Bots away from the orcas," Ellen called out. "Reeling in cable and approaching tanker deck."

"Dorsal compartment closed," said Brad and Meagan in unison.

"Well done, Chomp and Tux," Townley said. "Now dive away from the elephant and get yourselves out of that churn."

With a powerful headwind coming off the tanker, the bots were now flying out like kites on their tethers behind her. Each bot was now reeling in cable and thus getting closer to the railing on the deck of the tanker.

Ryan had had precious little time to follow the action of the orcas after Harris landed on the foremast. Scram had to climb down the mast and traverse nearly one thousand feet to the tanker's control tower at the stern end of the ship where he would rendezvous with Flick. Walking Scram wasn't difficult, but the passage was scary nonetheless. Knowing a pirate could take out Scram with one shot or a well-placed boot could mean endangering the lives of his colleagues, and the entire mission. So Ryan kept Scram as far underneath the surface pipes as he could to keep Scram from being detected.

Ryan felt at once anxious and excited while piloting Scram on the seemingly treacherous passage. Townley had told them during their practice sessions that the surface pipes running the length of the ship were distantly connected into the ship's oil storage containers, so an errant shot from a weapon into one of them could send the tanker, and everyone on it, sky high in a massive, fiery explosion.

"Prepare hornets," Townley commanded. Aboard the defender, the hornets were stored in long, thin, black cylindrical cases that looked like they contained fishing poles. Luc from the Seychelles team opened up the two cases; inside of each were four hornets. He and another Seychelles crewmember positioned the cases on the deck of the defender, holding onto them so they would not topple off the boat's edge into the sea.

"Hornets ready," Luc said.

"Launch hornets," Townley said.

At Creech, Ryan and his Seguin colleagues heard beeps cross the room at the computer consoles on the other table. "Hornets away," came a chorus of voices from the other table in the Creech war room.

All six of the Creech team, plus Freak and Zeek, were piloting a hornet. Though Ryan had seen a little of the hornets in action in the practice drills in the Seychelles, there sure was a lot of brainpower behind them. Freak and Zeek hadn't been part of the Seychelle practice drills, but they had been working with Jenny on the hornet bot designs in Robotics at school. Ryan figured they knew more about how to operate the hornet bots than anyone else.

The hornet bots flew up in the air from the deck of the defender. Given the backdrop of a dark ocean and a hazy horizon line, the small cloud of insects, which would have been difficult to see in broad daylight, were invisible to the naked eye from the tanker. The defender was holding steady behind the tanker, traveling at her speed at a distance of about three quarters of a mile.

Everyone had a digital architectural plan of the Dutch oil tanker on their computer, courtesy of the Dutch oil company that owned the tanker. According to the ship's plan, there was an airshaft on each side of the tanker near the stern. As the team had practiced, half of the hornets broke to the left and flew into the shaft on that side, and half diverted to the right and did the same thing on that side. As the hornets entered the shafts, Ryan could see on the computer screen digitally enhanced images of the shaft's contours, so the hornets knew where to fly. They were now effectively flying down large metal tubes.

They all knew the tanker would be the most challenging and dangerous operation of all. Townley and the Creech team estimated that there had been a total of roughly twenty-five pirates in all involved in the hijacking of the six boats. At that point, the rescue team had captured sixteen, two from each of the yachts and two sets of three whose skiffs they had "incapacitated," to use Townley's word. Thus, they believed there were nine pirates on the Dutch fuel tanker, including the ringleader, Korfa Raage. So once the hornets descended into the bowels of the tanker, they were stunned to count seventeen pirates aboard the Dutch tanker.

At the base of the airshafts, some forty feet below the surface of the tanker, were vent slits just large enough to permit the passage of a hornet bot. Only one, Debbie Tan's hornet bot, went through a slit initially to get a visual read on the surroundings. Once her bot crawled through, she trained its camera down on the large common room beneath the ship's control tower.

The hornet bot revealed all eighteen of the Dutch prisoners and twelve pirates in this room. The pirates all wielded weapons. Several held pistols and others held what looked like machine guns. The Dutch crewmembers were all seated at tables and their hands were bound in front of them on the tabletops. Everyone looked groggy, but was awake. It appeared they had been forcibly assembled in the common room at this early morning hour by the pirates.

Jenny had sent Flick up to the bridge of the tanker, where his camera revealed another five pirates, including Raage. The men were alternately looking at the sea ahead of them and behind them at the defender. At Townley's command, Jenny then sent Flick down the stairwell and into the common room for surveillance.

"Seventeen tangos," muttered Freak under his breath. "That's more than you expected, Towns."

"Yeah, I know," Townley replied.

"But it makes sense," interjected Mr. Sandhill. "They brought out some reinforcements. Intelligence agents must have missed the additional ones. But, if you're trying to capture a hundred million dollars worth of oil on a tanker, you'd want some backup support, too, if you could get it."

"I guess that also explains why there were more skiffs than we expected," Carmen said.

"Yes," Mr. Sandhill agreed. "It's a pretty long distance for skiffs to travel, but once they arrived, they had plenty of fuel."

"Perhaps the skiffs were dropped off by another pirate… I mean, tango… support boat," Catherine Bergeron suggested.

At Creech, Freak and Zeek had been working intently at their computer stations in the war room. They somehow figured out how to access a computer on board the Dutch tanker and access its radar monitoring system, from which they were able to discern that a ship was now approaching the tanker from the east, and was currently positioned about thirty nautical miles away.

"Uh, speaking of additional tangos, it looks like we're going to have some company," Freak announced to the group.

"What do you mean?" Amanda Harte asked.

"Ship approaching from the east at nine o'clock, and I'm pretty sure

Townley didn't send for it. It looks like the size of the mother ship we just sent to Davy Jones' Locker."

"Another tango ship," Mr. Sandhill said.

"What do we do?" Ellen said.

"We're out of Chinny class torpedoes," Pascal said.

"I say we send one of the orcas at it with an active payload. Tux is up for the job," Brad said from within the belly of Tux.

"Wow, losing an orca, I hadn't thought of that," Townley said.

"If we don't lose an orca, we may lose the tanker," Brad responded. "There's no way you can take them with the defender, and we have to stop any more tangoes from reaching the tanker."

Townley thought for a second. "Yep, you're right," he said.

"Uh-oh, now you're really feeding his ego," Meagan said.

"Hey!" Brad said in a mocked offended tone.

Townley laughed briefly, and then got serious again. "Okay, so Brad, you'll need support from Meagan, since she's going to be your taxi ride back from the dance once you put Tux on auto pilot."

"Roger that," Brad and Meagan replied in unison.

"Sammy, can you help monitor Brad as he prepares to arm Tux for the dance?" Townley said.

"Roger that," Sammy replied. "The dance" was clearly Townley's term for confrontation, and in this case, it was likely to be an explosive one.

A few tense minutes later, there was movement happening just outside the common room on the tanker. Light and shadows could be seen. A figure entered the common room. It was Raage. He barked something out to the room in Somali.

"Translator on," Freak said to Zeek. Speakeasy sat between Freak and Zeek at the second bank of workstations. From the tip of one of Speakeasy's fingers a cable ran into the computer Zeek was working at.

Now a streaming line of translation ran across the bottom of everyone's computer screens. They could understand with a split second's delay what was being said over audio. Raage continued to bark at the room in Somali, which, presumably, no one other than his fellow pirates could understand.

"We are taking you ashore." He paused and repeated the occasional word—like "shore"—in rough English, hoping the Dutch crew might understand. But, most of his banter was in Somali. Ryan watched the translation run across the screen. "There is nothing you can do to stop us. We will hold you hostage there until your ransom is paid or we kill you.

And, even if the ransom is paid, we still might kill you," Raage spat in an evil, cynical tone with an equally acerbic laugh. Ryan figured it was probably best that the Dutch crew understood very little, if any, of what was being said just then. But, by interpreting Raage's body language and gestures, you knew he wasn't saying anything good.

"It's too bad no one can hear you," Raage continued to bark at the Dutch crew. "Don't you wish you were a fly on the wall right about now?" The Dutch crewmembers stared back at him blankly.

"But I *am* the fly on the wall," Jenny hissed under her breath from Creech. A critical role for Flick on this part of the mission was to get close to the operatives, including Raage, so the team could pick up what he was saying, thus making it possible for Speakeasy to translate.

It was risky, but Townley wanted to get all the hornets into the common room, so he ordered their pilots at Creech to send them through the vents one at a time from each side. Their movement proved to be too much, too fast. Just as the third hornet on each side was flying through the grate, Raage and others looked up. Seeing the group of hornets, Raage cursed aloud. He grabbed the machine gun slung over his shoulder and started firing in their direction. Bullets whizzed around the hold, clanging and bouncing off the reinforced metal walls. Sparks flew everywhere. Hostages from the tanker and pirates alike shouted in alarm and dove under the tables in fear, holding their arms over their heads, desperately hoping to avoid an errant ricocheting bullet.

A thin, gaunt pirate was not so lucky. A ricocheting bullet clanging about the steel hold hit him in the side and he crumpled to the ground. A fellow pirate turned to him and began tearing strips of cloth from his shirt to aid the injured man. His wound was not life threatening, but it was severe enough to disable him.

"Fool!" yelled one of Raage's Somali henchmen. "Do you not see that you will blow this entire ship apart?" While most of the pirates had cowered in fear of Raage, when faced with their own destruction at his hands, they were showing themselves quite capable of lashing out in rage.

"Back off!" Raage barked. "Somebody else help Nadif," he said, referring to the man he had just injured with his errant bullet. "Take him to the restroom and clean him up." He paused and looked up to see if the hornets were still by the air vents. They had dispersed. Raage then ordered most of the pirates to take a prisoner to a series of small bedroom cabins off the hallways that ran down each side of the ship from the common room and to await further orders. He told a small group of pirates to remain in the common room with a small number of the Dutch prisoners.

This was a moment of opportunity for the Creech team. "Okay," Townley said. "Hornets, proceed down hallways from the common room and in sequence, one through four and five through eight—one hornet enter each cabin. When you get inside the cabin, incapacitate tangos."

"Roger that," came a series of replies from the second war room table at Creech.

The pirates each escorted a prisoner down one of the two hallways. Unbeknownst to them, up above and ahead of them, the hornet bots flew down the dimly lit corridor. Once each hornet was in a cabin, they perched in the corner of the room nearest the door, upside down, with their eyes and minute, embedded cameras trained on the doorway. As the prisoners entered the rooms followed by their pirate escorts, Townley spoke. "Arm hornets," he said.

Each hornet was armed with an anesthetizing dart, the same as had been used on earlier operations. Ryan knew that with so many of the pirates now isolated, the team was being presented with a golden opportunity to anesthetize a bunch of them all at one time. *Improvisation*, he thought to himself.

"Hornets armed," called out Debbie Tan from the second war room table.

"Fire when you have a clear shot," Townley commanded.

A series of staggered beeps erupted throughout the room as those piloting hornets fired their darts at pirates. From different computer screens, you could see pirates reacting to a sudden pain in their necks or shoulders, and then crumpling to the ground unconscious.

"So, aren't the Dutch sailors going to freak out at their captors just dropping like a bunch of flies?" Zeek said.

"Yeah. They will wonder what the heck happened," Townley acknowledged. "Jenny, can you send Flick into one of the rooms? We'll use Speakeasy to communicate to a freed prisoner about what is happening."

Flick flew down the hallway on the left side and into the first bedroom cabin he came to. A bewildered Dutch crewman stared down at the pirate who only moments before brandished a gun at him and had ushered him into the room. That man now lay crumpled on the floor. Flick landed on a small desk sitting next to the bed in the room.

"Okay Dr. S., do your thing—Dutch style," Freak said.

Out of a speaker implanted in Flick, a voice started speaking Dutch to the crewman. At first he looked around the room, trying to determine where the sound was coming from. "I'm down here!" called out Flick in Dutch. "Yes, I know it's strange." The crewman, who was somewhat worse for the wear having been held hostage by pirates for the past two weeks, squinted, and leaned over the desk where Flick sat. He now stared at the fly on the desk.

"I am a robot, part of a team that is aboard the ship to rescue you and your fellow crew members," said Flick.

"You are? Okay," said the Dutch man, still perhaps not completely convinced sleep deprivation hadn't gotten the better of him. "What do you want me to do?"

"I want you to tell the others," said Speakeasy through Flick.

"We will cut you loose soon," Flick said. He went on to explain the types of bots that the crewman might expect to see, including a snake, a lizard, and a leopard.

The man gave a look of disbelief, but after all he had been through, he would have believed just about anything at that moment. At Flick's instruction, the man proceeded quietly to the cabins down the corridor to inform his colleagues what was happening. They were equally bewildered that their captors had spontaneously keeled over.

With eight pirates "incapacitated," to use Townley's phrase, that left nine aboard the tanker that had to be dealt with. Three were in the restroom, the injured man and two colleagues tending to him. Two were in the common room watching other Dutch crew hostages and four, including Raage, were up on the bridge.

Townley directed James to send Slidey down the stairs to the common room area. Slidey had slithered to a junction of wall of the ship's bridge tower and the deck near the doorway to the stairway. The stairs of the tanker proved tricky. They were fairly steep, and had diamond plate texturing to prevent slipping. Unfortunately, the texturing was not super helpful if, like Slidey, you didn't have feet to slip with in the first place. But Slidey was able to slither down the steps, despite their slick metal and texturing. Once down, he slithered into the common room and in very rapid succession took out the two pirates there with a dart to each of them. The hostage Dutch crewmembers sat, looking stunned as a black snake slithered out from beneath the table at which they sat, and spoke to them. "I am a robot," Slidey said to them in Dutch, thanks to Speakeasy. "I am here to help you. Come over here and I will cut the ropes around your hands." The crewmembers looked at each other, dumbfounded.

Their fellow crewmembers then emerged from the corridors. "Can you believe it?" one of them said to his colleagues. "We got freed by a snake."

"Well, for us, it was a hornet," another replied.

The Dutch crew then took the weapons of their former captors and stormed the bathroom, where one of the hornets had informed them they would find three pirates, one of whom was injured. The crew took the weary, frightened pirates into custody, who were in no frame of mind to argue. The injured man was simply happy to have his wound dressed.

Flick had flown up to the bridge, through a slit opening in the doorway and landed on the ceiling, and the Creech team now had a bird's eye view. From it, looking out at the ocean, one could see a dorsal fin poking up out of the water, cutting though it at about twenty knots, and one could see a wake trailing behind, as Tux's powerful tail powered him through the water.

"Sammy, you are on the controls from here on out," Brad said.

While Tux was swimming at a clip of twenty knots, Brad flipped the hatch of the orca bot, stood up, and poked his head and upper body up and through the opening. Tux didn't miss a beat. Meagan had pulled Chomp up alongside Tux and was swimming at the same speed through the choppy ocean. Brad stood up, and with a moment's hesitation to maintain his balance, leapt off Chomp across the water to Tux, landing on Tux's back. He clung tightly to the dorsal fin.

The pirates on the approaching boat were no doubt mystified by what they were seeing, and at a distance of several hundred yards, it was still not entirely clear to them *what* that was, even while observing with binoculars. But, after seeing Brad make his incredible leap, they knew the approaching animals or torpedoes or submarines—or whatever they were—were not allied to them. So, they brandished their weapons and started firing on Brad. Meagan had deftly steered Brad off to the left side of the ship once he was aboard Chomp. The approaching pirate ship was still a hundred yards away, and now Chomp was swimming away from it at a slightly faster speed than the ship itself was moving. Bullets pierced the water around Brad, clanged off Chomp's dorsal fin, and whistled through the air around him.

From the tanker's bridge, Raage looked on in stunned amazement. He wondered if perhaps exhaustion and sleep deprivation were catching up to him and he was seeing things. Of all the strange things he had seen recently, he simply could not comprehend how a man could be climbing out of the body of a killer whale.

"What is this?" Raage asked in his awkward English, pointing out at the water.

"The future," said the Dutch captain, who had been looking on, equally amazed.

Meanwhile, Chomp continued to swim towards the approaching pirate ship. Once the pirates realized that hitting Brad was an increasingly futile endeavor, they trained their guns on Chomp, who, with his hatch closed up and now being piloted by Sammy, dived. The pirates briefly saw the hulking black creature submerge under the water, still swimming directly towards their ship. They looked about anxiously, peppering the water with machine gun fire, but without a specific target to aim at since the orca was now too deep to see.

Chomp soon made his whereabouts known, however, as a terrific explosion rocked the pirate ship at the back of the boat. Chomp had surfaced underneath the ship and, with a charge activated by Sammy at Creech, had become a smart torpedo that went off right as Chomp contacted the ship's propeller. The terrifically loud explosion blew a hole in the ship, and simultaneously eliminated its ability to move by taking out its source of propulsion. The ship quickly began to list toward its stern as it rapidly took on water.

The ship sank so fast that there was no time for the stunned pirate crew to unclasp the skiffs on her deck. The pirates aboard soon found themselves in the ocean, staring up at the crew of the defender, as Pascal headed for the sinking ship once the explosion occurred. The Seychelles crew aboard the defender now held the pirates at bay in the water.

Meanwhile, Townley, Luc, and another member of the Seychelles crew had taken an inflatable raft from the defender and used it to chase after the tanker, a bold and dangerous undertaking. Townley and Luc used grappling hooks, which they fired up and latched on to the side of the tanker to hoist themselves up, in a way similar to what Leo and Slidey had done.

Once they reeled up to the tanker's deck, Townley and Luc clambered aboard and had raced up to the bridge. They had gone unnoticed largely because the attention of everyone on the bridge was turned off the port side, where the approaching pirate ship had just been hit and was now sinking. Raage had watched and paced the captain's bridge anxiously. His plan was falling apart.

Townley and Luc raced into the bridge and, with weapons pointed, forced the pirates to drop theirs and put their hands in the air.

Raage initially put his hands up, but then became desperate. "Well, it looks like we'll all die together, then," he said in Somali. The maleficence in his tone was deadly earnest. Townley looked at him through frightened eyes. At that moment, Raage slung the machine gun around that had been hanging on his shoulder. He had not dropped it before when putting his hands in the air. He pointed it towards an array of pipes that ran up the wall at the far side of the room.

"Uh-oh," went up a number of gasps at Creech, as people read the translation of what Raage was saying. They knew the havoc that was possible by shooting up certain pipes aboard the vessel.

Just then, Leo, who had been perched just outside the door to the bridge, darted in and leaped at Raage. Raage, stunned, wheeled around and fired on the leopard. Metallic screams were heard as bullets from his weapon pierced the body of Leo. One of the bullets hit circuitry that connected Leo's central control function panel to the extremities of his body. The leopard bot fell, but not before Ellen was able to fire a dart out of Leo's mouth at Raage. Ragge grabbed his shoulder where he was hit by the dart. He was at first stunned, then quickly became disoriented, and a second later, he crumpled to the ground unconscious.

19

BACK AT SCHOOL

From that point, the mission at Creech wrapped up quickly. For Townley, Brad, Meagan, Carey, and the crew from the Seychelles, there was more work to be done. They had to secure all of the pirates onboard the defender and take them to the Seychelles. There proceedings would commence for trying them under international law. "There are far worse places to be held prisoner, that's for sure," Townley noted.

"So what's next for us?" Jenny asked, as the operation in the Indian Ocean wound up. She was thinking about the bots as much as about herself and her friends from Seguin.

"I think everyone has earned a nice meal out on the strip somewhere, don't you think?" Freak said. "Maybe we can even persuade those in command here at Creech to give our Creech friends the night off to go hit the town?" He meant Las Vegas. A number of enthusiastic cheers went up from the group.

It was late at night, but given what they had been through, everyone's energy levels were running high, and they were all wide awake. "Besides," said Zeek, "Ten o'clock at night in Las Vegas could just as easily be mid-morning, mid-afternoon, whatever. The city just doesn't sleep."

"Spoken like a guy who's hearing the call of the blackjack tables," Freak mused.

"Well, we can't legally gamble, so that could put a cramp in your style," Ellen said.

"It's probably just as well," Zeek said, "given what happened the last time we were in the casino."

"A tasty meal certainly sounds good right about now," Mr. Sandhill acknowledged.

"Yeah, it sure does," Speakeasy said. Everyone looked at him quizzically. "What?" he said, looking around. "Just because I don't eat doesn't mean a tasty meal doesn't sound good. Besides, it'll allow me to avoid having to play babysitter with those two," he pointed with his eyes at Freak and Zeek.

"We really are going to have to stop allowing Brad and Meagan to program Speakeasy when we're not around," Freak said. Everyone laughed.

Back at Seguin Academy, Ryan and his friends endured the clutches of winter for a few more weeks. It was surprisingly easy, as they had so much homework they barely noticed the cold air and snow outside. They completed their Biology term papers in rapid fashion, as Mrs. Bergeron gave them only few days' extra time to turn their papers in.

"Look at it this way, she's interested in reading our papers," Carmen said amid the groans of everyone over the challenges of completing their papers.

"Yeah, and she has plenty of extra reading time on her hands because her research trip got interrupted," Sammy mused.

A few days later, after the conclusion of the mission, Townley stopped in Boston on his way back to Creech from Djibouti, where he had returned after stopping off with the defender team at the Seychelles. "You know, I had to stretch my legs after the ten hour flight from Djibouti. And get a cup of coffee, and of course, visit you guys," Townley laughed. They went out for pizza near the campus of Weatherall University on the evening of his stopover. Everyone in the restaurant was staring at the Seguin group, along with Meagan, Brad, Carey, Mr. Sandhill, Mrs. Bergeron, and Townley, who were laughing uproariously as they recounted different parts of the mission and their experience together, talking in oblique terms all the while. All of the other restaurant patrons must have felt like they were missing out on some serious fun. Carey's arm was in a sling, but he was recovering nicely. Ryan hadn't had this much fun in a long time.

Townley departed the next morning. As always, the man had such a big personality that you literally felt a void when he departed, Ryan observed. Others were sad to see him go.

"Oh, you'll see me again, soon enough, I expect," Townley told them at breakfast.

"When?" Jenny asked. Everyone wanted to know.

"Soon, as I'm sure Mr. Sandhill will plan some other activities for us, right Thomas?"

"We'll definitely look into it," Mr. Sandhill smiled. "Although hopefully the circumstances will be considerably less… consequential."

"And complicated," Mrs. Bergeron chimed in.

"And dangerous," Ellen offered.

"I know what you mean," Townley smiled. "Well, we've got to keep working on those bots. They're incredible."

Most Seguin students looked at the bot cohort members suspiciously when given their explanation of "field project" as the reason for their absence from school for a week.

"They may not be buying the field trip story, but there's no way they'd buy the truth," James said of their Seguin classmates. Everyone agreed.

The rescue of the convoy of ships in the Indian Ocean had made the news around the world. Little mention was made about the rescue team, other than to say that forces from several different countries participated and conducted an intensive, stealthy operation to free the hostages. The hostage-taking pirates, led by Korfa Raage, were now in custody and awaited trial in an international court. Raage was wanted in connection with a number of hijackings and his capture was considered highly significant.

After the Indian Ocean mission, school almost seemed dull by comparison, though it kept everyone plenty busy. Ryan played baseball in the spring and, incredibly, managed to find a way to keep up with, or at least not fall completely behind, his studies. Ryan and his friends found that the classes with teachers who had shared the rescue mission with them—Mr. Sandhill, Mrs. Bergeron, Freak and Zeek—were particularly interesting, since they had now seen their teachers in action, in settings that were completely different from school. They had established a strong bond that felt it would endure for some time to come.

There were two other memorable surprises for Ryan and his friends that spring. Hae Jung Park, the violinist they had met two summers ago at Tanglewood, stopped off in Boston to play with the Boston Symphony Orchestra. The bot cohort from Seguin went into Symphony Hall in Boston to hear the performance. Even more surprising was that the band members of Voltaic were in the audience, and at one point, Vape got invited up on stage to sing a piece with Hae Jung. Hae Jung's sequin-studded outfit looked right at home next to Vape's trademark flowing coat tails.

"You know, this is something you definitely don't see every day," Mr. Sandhill said with a smile.

As if that weren't enough, Voltaic played the spring dance at Seguin Academy. There had been no forewarning. It just happened. Actually, there had been bogus advertisements with a fake named band that no one had heard of posted around campus. For that reason, a lot of people had considered not going. But, at a school meeting leading up to the dance, Mrs. Bergeron suggested that people would really regret missing it if they didn't go, and, since her word carried a ton of weight, pretty much everyone from Seguin went.

Ellen asked Ryan, Sammy, and James as a group if they were planning to go to the dance. "We can all go as a group," she said to them. They acknowledged that after hearing Mrs. Bergeron's strong recommendation, they were going. "I'm glad you're going," she said to Ryan as he held a door for her on the way between buildings.

"She likes you," Carmen teased a few seconds later as she caught up with him while they traipsed across campus.

"No, she doesn't," Ryan said.

"Does too," Carmen teased.

Ryan shrugged. He wasn't sure what else to say.

Everyone was stunned at the dance to see Vape, prancing around on the stage, rollicking and dancing about with guitarist Chet Harmon. Wearing his trademark coat with billowing coattails, he was in his element strutting and prancing around the stage.

"And to think he learned at least some of that at this school," Mr. Sandhill whispered into Mrs. Bergeron's ear.

"Only the good parts," Mrs. Bergeron replied.

Rook was mastering the sound mix at the back of the room, sitting behind an unbelievably cool-looking mixing board that had so many digital lights and screens it looked like the cockpit of an airplane. He had a couple of people assisting him. He looked like a crazy cook run amok in a kitchen.

After the dance, the bot cohort had a reunion with the band backstage. Ryan and his friends couldn't believe it. Mr. Sandhill and Mrs. Bergeron joined them as well. "We should take you guys on tour with us!" Vape exclaimed.

"Maybe that would keep us from running into real trouble!" Mrs. Bergeron remarked, reflecting on her experience being taken hostage aboard the *Shakti*.

"*Voltaic* played your spring school dance? That's a joke, right?" one of Ryan's friends from home asked him when told of the event.

"No, it totally happened!" Ryan exclaimed.

Ryan felt like he did okay—not great—on his final exams. If he aced anything it was Robotics, largely because the mission at Creech essentially packed several semesters' worth of material into a one-week time frame. But, in some of his other classes, his teachers were not overly sympathetic to the absence of the bot cohort, despite the fact that Mr. Sandhill had assured Ryan and his friends that the "field project" had been explained to them. The "field project" certainly had not excused them from roughly a thousand pages of reading that they had missed in their absence.

With the gauntlet of exams behind him, Ryan was looking forward with great excitement to seeing friends and family back in Texas. On the other hand, he would miss his bot cohort friends quite dearly. He knew they would stay in touch, but he really enjoyed the camaraderie of everyone working together on their bots, pushing their limits, and discovering new things to do with them.

"You won't be gone for long," Mr. Sandhill said one sunny June day at the airport. "The summer will fly past, and you'll be back here before you know it."

"Is that a promise or a threat?" Jenny asked. She was joking, and her smile let everyone know it.

"What do you think?" Mrs. Bergeron asked.

CPSIA information can be obtained at www.ICGtesting.com
Printed in the USA
BVOW04s1540150614

356266BV00004B/8/P

9 781939 166456